Gray Visions

Book III
of
The Alternative History Trilogy

by

R. W. Richards

Also by R. W. Richards:
A Southern Yarn   ISBN 0-9625502-0-5
                LC   89-092811

Brothers in Gray   ISBN 0-9625502-1-3

Survival, Book I: The Story of the New Southland
                ISBN 0-9625502-4-8

Library of Congress Cataloging - in - Publication Data

Richards, Ronald: 1947
Gray Visions, by R. W. Richards
ISBN 0-9625502-2-1

Gray Visions is published in the United States by
RoKarn Publications
P.O. Box 195
Nokesville, Virginia   22123

First Printing, December 1995
Printed in the United States of America

The War for Southern Independence was finally over. The brilliant tactics employed by General Robert E. Lee along the North Anna River resulted in a devastating Union defeat, leading in turn to the surrender of Ulysses S. Grant and the capture of Washington, D. C. Negotiations between Jefferson Davis and Abraham Lincoln, himself a prisoner, result in an independent Confederacy and the abolition of slavery. By the Winter of 1865, all of the Union troops have been withdrawn from the now independent Southern States, and the citizens of these Confederate States are enjoying the first fruits of their sovereignty. Yet dark clouds have gathered on the horizon. The land has been ravaged and the challenges posed by reconstruction seem overwhelming. Moreover, millions of newly freed slaves are finding themselves with no means of support, frequently facing hunger, with no alternative but crime to avoid starvation. Civil unrest begins to grow, and reports of clashes between blacks and whites are heard more often. A solution must be found and found quickly, lest the newly independent country flounder and collapse from within.

Once more I find myself most grateful to a number of people whose time and energy made the completion of this Trilogy possible.

For the production of the manuscript , my thanks to Winnie and Stuart Bowcock, as well as my daughter, Tara Lee Richards.

Thanks also to Jeffry R. Bogart, my editor, and to my wife, Lacey, for their time, skill, and patience.

Special thanks are due to John f. Cummings III, of Fairfax, Va., not only for the cover, but also for the marvelous ideas which became part of this story.

I am honored to dedicate this book to the many people who have devoted their lives and energy to the preservation of Southern heritage, a rich heritage, one most worthy of their efforts.

For my brother, **William R. Richards, Jr.**; from him came the title, **Gray Visions**. Thanks, **Bro**!

~Chapter One~
1865

Peace had come at last. To war-weary Southerners of all races, the agreement negotiated between Jefferson Davis and Abraham Lincoln in the Autumn of 1864 could not have come too soon. The conflict between the North and South had raged for over three years and left Southerners facing devastation the likes of which no modern people had ever faced. From Virginia to Texas, from Florida to Kentucky, farms, plantations, towns and cities lay in ruins. With the arrival of peace and the abolition of slavery the Southern people, blacks as well as whites, turned their eyes toward an uncertain future.

True, the Confederate States had won their independence. Lee's victory over Grant on the North Anna River in May of 1864 triggered a chain of events which led ultimately to negotiations and an end not only of the war, but of slavery as well. Lincoln had agreed to pay reparations to the newly independent Confederacy and the last of the Union troops were withdrawn from Southern soil. The first few weeks following the agreement were filled with joy. Euphoria swept across the land like a brush fire over the prairie, but as the weeks slipped by and winter approached this elation faded quickly. A stark reality loomed before the citizens of the Confederate States.

Problems abounded but solutions seemed few and far between. The agricultural base of the South had been ravaged. Southern railroads had been left largely in tangled ruins. Only the fractured remains of a transportation system were available for use.

GRAY VISIONS

What had once been the proud city of Atlanta was nothing but piles of smoldering ashes. One thing was painfully obvious as the people surveyed the scene of destruction which covered the South: reconstruction would prove far more a challenge than the war just concluded.

Compounding the crisis posed by rebuilding was a factor even more complex. Well over three million of the South's people were experiencing freedom for the first time. Slavery was finished in North America. Most of the former slaves were illiterate. Would they be capable of handling the responsibilities which came hand in hand with freedom? Would the abolition of slavery trigger chaos in a land already drained by war? An answer to these questions was of necessity the first objective of the Confederate government as it entered the post-war period. Moreover, time would simply not allow the luxury of extended debate and hand-wringing over the problem; something would have to be done quickly.

No few of the large slave owners balked at the idea of granting freedom to their slaves. They knew resistance within the Confederacy itself would be useless as Lee had already committed the support of the army to the emancipation. Therefore, many chose to leave. Taking as many of their slaves as possible, these people put their land and homes up for sale and opted to migrate to Brazil. By the beginning of 1865, the bulk of those who had chosen to leave were gone. Those who stayed were turning their attention to finding a resolution to the crisis posed by slavery's abolition.

With regard to a program of action, the Confederate government found itself in a situation which may accurately be described as fortunate. Elsewhere in the world there was one other example of a country dealing with a similar situa-

tion on a far bigger scale. This country was Russia. Feudal-
ism had developed in Russia at about the same time it was
winding down in Western Europe. By the early nineteenth
century most of the Russian people were serfs, peasants who
were bound to the soil. These people had never known freedom. Their lives and fortunes were completely controlled by
the Russian aristocracy. Serfs had no rights. Their feudal
masters could buy and sell them at will. Their status was
virtually the same as slaves.

All through the first half of the nineteenth century,
pressure had been building in Russia to improve the lot of the
serfs. By 1860 this pressure was proving difficult to resist,
and it would no longer be satisfied with a better life for the
serfs. The movement had as its goal the abolition of serfdom
and nothing less. In 1861 Czar Alexander II signed and issued
the Emancipation Edict, granting freedom to the Russian serfs
and ending the institution of serfdom forever. Alexander and
his advisers realized the potential for chaos in Russia if these
people were left landless and without a source of income. A
plan was devised which insured land for all the former serfs
but it was not without its drawbacks. The plan left these same
people with a mountain of debt which many found difficult to
service.

It wasn't necessary to look all the way to Russia to seek
solutions. Prior to the war there were over 150,000 free blacks in
the South. Prosperous communities of free blacks could be found
throughout Northern Virginia. Charleston, South Carolina and New
Orleans, Louisiana also boasted of large communities of free blacks
who appeared to be doing quite well for themselves. In all these
situations one item seemed the deciding factor between success and
failure: land. Land would be the key in administering a

program of emancipation in the Confederacy, and land was something the South had in abundance.

The citizens of the Confederate States weren't the only ones whose attention was riveted on the challenges posed by emancipation. Much concern had arisen in the United States as well. Maryland and Delaware were the last two states of the Union to abolish slavery, but it wasn't the former slaves of loyalist states which concerned most Northerners. Fear was fast growing throughout much of the United States, a fear of a mass migration of newly freed Blacks from the Confederacy to the United States. Many people who toiled for a wage in northern factories expressed alarm at the prospect of Southern blacks migrating north. They were afraid these former slaves would take their jobs at lower wages. As a result of these fears a number of northern states, particularly those bordering the Confederacy, passed laws prohibiting free blacks from entering their domain.

It was against this background that the Confederate Congress convened in early February of 1865. As agreed to by President Lincoln, monetary reparations from the United States had already begun to trickle into the Confederate treasury. The problem facing the Confederate Congress as it gathered in Richmond was how best to use this money to stabilize the economy, reimburse the former slave owners for the slaves who were now free, and to prevent social chaos. No easy task to be sure.

A major priority would be placing the government itself on solid financial ground. During the war every department of the Confederate government operated at a deficit. Every department save one that is. The Postal Service of the Confederate States managed to outshine the rest of the government by emerging from the war debt free, a rather fine example of efficiency in austere circumstances.

Fortunately, the victorious conclusion of the war provided a ready-made solution to these financial difficulties. Federal war reparations would quickly erase the various deficits run up by the Confederate government. Thus were the Southern legislators freed to turn their attention to more pressing problems. Among these was runaway inflation which had ruined their currency. However, the infusion of Federal gold promised to bring this raging beast under control with very little pain involved. The most pressing crisis was that posed by the newly freed slaves. Their plight would have to be addressed first, lest chaos rear its ugly head and rip the new country apart. To this end, public hearings were scheduled in the Confederate House of Representatives to debate the merits of a bill coming from the hands of Jefferson Davis himself. The bill would essentially allow black men, who could establish a need, to apply to the government for a grant for the specific purpose of acquiring land and securing a home. Controversy was fast on the heels of this bill as it entered the halls of Congress. Many of the die-hard slave-holders of old were determined to see it defeated. They preferred to see a program which would leave the blacks free but penniless and with no means to support themselves. In this fashion they hoped to insure themselves a bountiful supply of cheap labor. All eyes were on Richmond in those stark, cold, dreary days of February. Much depended on the outcome of this debate.

* * * * * * * * * *

A bitterly cold winter wind whipped across the gently

rolling hills of the Covington Farm. Wil Covington paused in his labors to pulled his ragged scarf more tightly about his neck. His ears were freezing and he lacked gloves, which left his hands red and raw. For several moments he stood motion- less with his head bowed and his back to the wind. At last it died down and he raised his head. He'd been working most of the day and had managed to split nearly half a cord of oak, maple, and locust. Ideally, he would have been working with well seasoned wood but these were not ideal times. He and Levi Henry had been away fighting the war for more than two years before their return in late 1864. Much had changed.

In the summer of 1862 the two boys marched off to join the Confederate army. They left behind two prosperous farms. During their prolonged absence only their fathers remained to work the land, and both of these men were reaching advanced years. Tom Covington was nearing sixty and had nearly four hundred acres to toil. Moses Henry had only forty acres to work, but he was almost seventy years old and no longer had the physical strength to keep pace with the demands of the land itself. In addition, the war did not pass them over as they had vainly prayed back in 1861. The Shenandoah Valley had been ravaged by the fighting, particularly the lower end from Staunton through Winchester and on to the Potomac itself. Farms along with their crops and cattle were fair game to the Union army. Few were spared.

The Henry farm and that of the Covingtons managed to remain intact for two years until the summer of 1863. Not long after Gettysburg and Lee's retreat into Virginia, a company of Union cavalry descended upon these two farms with a vengeance. All of their crops and livestock were seized or destroyed. The barns and other out buildings were put to the torch. Not a single rail of fencing remained when these raiders in blue finished their grisly work.

Unlike many of the Valley's people, the Henrys and Tom Covington considered themselves fortunate. The Union captain in charge of the raid experienced a moment of sympathy for the aging black couple and their white neighbor. He did not burn their homes nor did he allow his soldiers to wreck their furniture or rifle through their personal possessions. This was a rare act of compassion when contrasted with the experiences of most the Shenandoah's people.

Both Tom Covington and Moses Henry sank into despair as they watched their lives' work go up in flames. Trying to rebuild was out of the question. There were no materials, no one to help them, no animals to be had. Besides, the Yankees would only tear it all apart again. Were it not for Sarah Henry they all might have starved. She had the foresight to keep a supply of seeds hidden. As her husband and Covington sat staring at the devastation through tear-filled eyes, Sarah went to work. Using her sewing scissors as a digging implement she began turning the earth and planting vegetables.

It was to a scene of devastation that Levi Henry and Wil Covington returned in the late Autumn of 1864. There was no thought of attempting to rebuild right away. Winter was fast approaching and at this point survival was the only priority.

Wil raised the axe high overhead and split another log cleanly in two. Each piece he cut in half before stopping again as a spasm of grinding pain ripped through his right hip. The old wound he'd sustained in September of 1862 at South Mountain still haunted him, especially when winter was at its worst. He placed the head of his axe on the frozen ground and leaned on the handle. With an audible groan, he pressed his right fist tightly against his hip and clenched his teeth waiting for the pain to pass.

Slowly, it eased and he allowed himself to breath again.

GRAY VISIONS

The gray sky overhead was heavy with the promise of new snow and he knew the ground would be thickly covered by the next morning. His intention that day had been to split enough wood to keep the stoves going for two or three days in case the weather interfered with his daily routine. Plus, he planned to leave for Richmond within a week. He was familiar with the Negro Resettlement Bill which President Davis had submitted to Congress. He planned to express his opinion in support of the bill during the public hearings currently underway. His intention was to insure his father wouldn't lack for the necessities during his absence, but the pending snow and the nagging, painful reminders of his damaged hip worked against his designs.

"Reckon this'll just have to do," he muttered to himself as he surveyed the results of his day-long efforts. "Time to get this stuff inside." With a weary sigh he glanced over at the house. Thin columns of bluish-gray smoke snaked skyward from both chimneys. Shifting his gaze his eyes found the Henry's home well north of his own and very near the ice-covered Shenandoah River. The impending storm severely limited visibility so he could barely make out the house itself, but he knew Levi was engaged in similar chores down there someplace. He let go of his axe and began to pile wood onto his left arm.

Moments later Wil's arms were full and he began to trudge slowly toward the house, limping noticeably with each step. His thoughts wandered northward toward a small farm not too distant from Thurmont, Maryland. Emily was there. When he and Levi were discharged from the army they returned home from Richmond with the intention of staying but a few days before making a trip to Maryland. Both young men were eagerly anticipating a reunion with the two young women who had stolen their hearts. Unfortunately, the trip had to be postponed. Neither Wil nor Levi fully realized the extent of the damage done to their farms until they returned and saw it with their own eyes. Emily and Naomi would have to wait.

A smile appeared on Wil's face as the image of Emily Havelin filled his mind. Since the end of the war they had been able to correspond on a regular basis and had decided upon the middle of June as the best time to have their wedding. Wil frequently found himself counting the days until June, but this often created pressure he didn't really need to feel. The thought of marriage was not the source of this pressure. He rather looked forward to being married. It was the work which weighed so heavily on his mind. There was just so much of it to be done....so much destruction....so much mayhem....so much to put back together. He wanted so badly to have a perfect home for his bride to be, but June was only months away and much remained to be done. Sometimes it seemed impossible, and he sat slumped in despair staring at the barren brown hills nestled against the Shenandoah River.

As he neared the house, Wil's eyes drifted to the left and fell upon the tombstone which marked his mother's grave. The name of Mary Ann Covington was still readily visible but the stone itself had been weathered by the passage of time. His thoughts began to wander and he thought of his mother. What had she looked like? If she hadn't died giving him birth what would she look like today? Would she approve of Emily? Wil felt certain she would have. He stopped and allowed his eyes to linger on the tombstone. "I wish you were here to see the woman who will bear your grandchildren," he said softly and resumed his trek, mouthing a silent prayer of thanks that this grave had not been desecrated by the Yankees, as so many others had. Federal troops in their zeal to loot real or imagined wealth had vandalized thousands of graves across the South, but not this one. He reached the side door of the house and opened it with his free hand. His nose was greeted at once by the delicious aroma of soup simmering atop the stove. His father stood nearby peeling onions and adding them to the broth. "Smells good," remarked Wil. "Is it chicken?"

"Not a lot of chicken in it," replied the elder Covington. "Just what I was able to boil off the bones."

"How long till it's ready?"

"Another hour...no more."

"Good. I worked up an appetite."

"I shouldn't wonder. You didn't have to cut up the whole forest."

"Just wanted to make sure you'll have enough while I'm gone in Richmond."

"You worry too much. I'll manage fine. I'm old, true, but I'm not feeble...at least not yet. How's the hip?"

"Hurts, but not quite as bad as yesterday"

"I figured you might could use a hot brick. There's one on top of the stove in the other room."

"Thanks, Pa. I appreciate that," Wil deposited his armload of wood next to the stove in the kitchen and proceeded into the next room. Using the small towel his father had left hanging on the back of a chair he grabbed the brick from the top of the woodstove, wrapped it inside a double fold of the towel and pressed it directly against his hip. Relief was instant.

He sat down in an armchair and kept the brick against his hip. Heat radiated out through the hipbone and its adjoining muscles. Wil sighed out loud and rested his head against the crown of the chair. As the pain eased and his mind cleared he began to focus on his upcoming trip. For several weeks he had been aware of the public hearings scheduled to debate the merits of the Freedman's Bill. He had written Richmond requesting an opportunity to speak and within two weeks he received the official approval of this request. As he sat there recovering from the rigors of the day's work, Wil contemplated what he would say when the time came.

"Feelin' better?"

Wil opened his eyes and looked up as his father entered the room. "Much better, thanks."

"You still plannin' on taking the stage next week?"

"Most likely. The train takes a long roundabout route."

"True, but it would probably cause you a bit less pain."

"I'll be fine, Pa. No need for you to be worried. I spoke with Levi this mornin'. He told me Sarah was bakin' bread and she said she'd send us a couple of loaves this evenin'."

"Bakin'? Where'd she get the flour?"

"Bought it over in Staunton."

"Yeah, but where did it come from?"

"Don't know."

"Yankee bread," Tom Covington seemed to spit out those words. "Sure as shootin'."

"Would you rather do without?"

"Don't get uppity with me, boy. It just don't seem proper that's all. After everything they've done to us over the years it just don't seem fittin' for us to be buyin' their flour."

"Better to have Yankee bread than none at all."

"Just ain't fittin'. Seems like they're all the time makin' money off of the South. War...Peace...don't make no difference, they find a way to make a profit."

"Probably true, Pa, but we have to face reality. There's no wheat from the valley this year. It won't hurt us that much to swallow a little pride to avoid goin' hungry."

"Humph," grunted the old man.

"What else you puttin' in the soup?"

"Rice...and it's Confederate rice at that. Come up from Louisiana."

Just then there came a knock upon the door. "You stay put," said Wil's father. "Let that heat work on your hip. I'll see who it is."

"Most likely Levi," observed Wil from his seat.

His prediction turned out to be correct. Tom Covington opened the door and shivered in the face of a blast of cold air rushing in through the opening. "Levi!" he greeted as he spied the only son of the slave couple he'd freed so long ago. "Come on in here, boy! You look half froze to death! Hurry now, feels like the Yukon out there!"

Levi fairly jumped through the open doorway and Tom Covington quickly pushed the door closed behind him. "God, it's cold!" stammered the young black veteran whose teeth were clattering loud enough to be heard by anyone standing close by.

"Go stand by the stove," suggested Tom, "It'll thaw you out right quick."

"I'll do that. Where do you want the bread?" Levi held two deep pans up for inspection. "Mama's been bakin'. She sent these up to you."

"You tell your Mama we're much obliged," said the older man as he took the cloth-covered pans from Levi. "Even if she did use Yankee wheat."

"Ain't no other wheat to be found, suh. You know that."

"So they tell me. Go on over there and warm yourself up, hear? Go ahead."

Levi stepped quickly over to the wood stove and rubbed his hands together close to the red-hot flue. "Howdy, Wil, the hip painin' ya?"

"Some. It's startin' to feel better now."

"You still plannin' on goin' to Richmond?"

"Day after tomorrow."

"Wanna know what I heard when I was over to Staunton the other day?"

Wil turned his head and glanced curiously at his life-long friend. "Go ahead," he urged.

"Heard Mrs. Andrews was makin' the trip to Richmond as well."

"Really?" The image of Lonnie Andrews' mother came to Wil's mind. That family had suffered dearly during the war. Lonnie was killed at Second Manassas. In fact, he had died in the arms of Ivory, a slave from South Carolina, who had served in the army of Northern Virginia as both a teamster and a cook. A frown crossed Wil's face as the memory of that day welled up inside him. The loss of their only son was tragic enough but the travails of the Andrews family didn't stop there. The same raid which devastated the Henry and Covington farms dealt an irrevocable blow to the Andrews. Their farm was utterly destroyed and Lonnie's father was killed in a vain attempt to defend it. Not a single building was left standing. All of the furniture was dragged from the house and smashed to pieces and the home itself was put to the torch. Widowed and homeless with two young daughters to care for, Mrs. Andrews had little choice but to seek shelter and help from friends and neighbors. "Is she goin' to testify in front of Congress?"

"That's what I heard."

"I wonder what she can say that'll help the Freedman's Bill?"

"You're assumin' she's for it. Maybe she's gonna argue against it."

"Maybe, but I don't think so. She's not like that."

"Reckon we'll know soon enough. Tell me when you get back, okay?"

"No problem," nodded Wil.

*   *   *   *   *   *   *   *   *   *   *

Less than a hundred miles from the Covington Farm, three men had gathered under decidedly different circumstances. Robert E. Lee, wearing civilian clothes, had arrived at the home of Jefferson Davis mere minutes ahead of Judah Benjamin, the Secretary of State. As the three of them gathered in the sitting room each recalled a similar meeting held as autumn was just getting underway. Conditions in the Confederacy at the time was desperate. There was little to eat or drink as these three men met to work out a formula which might lead to a negotiated peace with the United States. Fortunately for the people of both countries the efforts of these three individuals bore fruit and the long agonizing war was brought to an end.

As part of the final agreement, the government of the United States agreed to pay war reparations to the now independent Confederacy. Said reparations were to be triple the value of each slave in the Confederate States. In a sense the United States was buying the freedom of these people. On this winter night in February of 1865, Jefferson Davis had summoned the other two men to discuss the prospects of his freedman's bill and to assess the condition of his country in the first few months of its independence.

For people of substance and position, much had changed since the war's end. The extremely effective Federal blockade of the southern coastlines was gone, as were the tens of thousands of blue-coated soldiers who had done so much damage in the South.

Ships laden with foodstuffs and medicines plied the waters of the James nearly every day. As a result the pantries of the Davis home were quite full and Mr. Davis himself was able to offer his guests an ample selection of cheeses, breads and meats, not to mention the best examples of European wines.

It was Lee who was escorted first into the President's sitting room. Servants appeared quickly bearing trays of exotically prepared foods from which to select. Within minutes the Secretary of State was ushered in to complete the trio. General Lee had filled a small plate and was nibbling a piece of cheddar cheese as Judah Benjamin sat down and began to eye the tables' fare.

"General," said the President, "May I offer you a glass of wine?"

"No, thank you," replied Lee, "to be truthful I think I'd prefer buttermilk."

"I should have known," smiled Davis. "Fortunately that's a request we can fill rather quickly."

Lee merely nodded his thanks.

"Well," declared Benjamin, "if the general chooses to abstain that leaves more for me. It's been a long time since last I tasted a good wine. I believe I'll have to indulge. By chance do you have a Bordeaux in stock?"

"No problem," replied Davis, nodding toward one of the servants who in turn departed to seek the Secretary's choice among the president's wines. "I suppose you might be wondering why I've asked the two of you to come here tonight," added Davis.

"The question did occur to me," replied Lee.

"To myself as well," observed Benjamin as he bit into a piece of German sausage.

"My reasons aren't too different from the last time the three of us sat down for an evening in this same room," said Davis, "I seek your help."

"Well," noted Benjamin, "our last meeting was followed by a rather marvelous sequence of events. I don't think
we can hope to match its results."

"I think we have to," countered the President. "Not
only match, we should exceed the results of our last meeting.
Otherwise we might live to see the whole thing crumble around our
ears."

"Rather a somber outlook," mused Lee.

Just then the servant returned bearing a freshly opened
bottle of fine red wine and a glass into which he poured a
small quantity for the Secretary to sample. Benjamin took a
sip which he swished around inside of his mouth for several
seconds savoring every moment of the tasting. "Nectar of the
gods," he smiled after swilling the sample. The glass was then
filled to the brim by the servant who retired quietly from the
room. "By the way," said Benjamin, "I think I agree with
General Lee. Your prognosis of our future does seem a bit
severe."

"Perhaps," nodded Davis, "but I believe my concerns
are justified. I recall something you said, Judah, when last we
met like this. You mentioned something about us not being
engineers of society, that instead we were merely politicians."

"Hoping to be remembered as statesmen," continued
Benjamin correctly recalling the statement to which his
president was referring.

"Exactly," said Davis, "but I'm afraid the time has
come for us to take a crack at engineering our society. If we
don't we may end up facing some rather dire circumstances."

"Explain," said Lee as he reached for another piece of
cheese. "Are there slaves who haven't been freed yet?"

"No, they've all been freed, all save those whose masters emigrated to Brazil."

"Have the Federals reneged on their promise to pay us reparations?"

"No, money continues to come in and we've been able to reimburse most of the slave owners. The others are bearing with us."

"What is it you find to be so critical?"

"Many of the former slaves have been free for several months. They are experiencing a condition they've never known before. Some are equating freedom with liberation from a life of hard work. Others want to work but can find no gainful employment. With no source of income their situation is becoming desperate. Is it surprising to hear that many are stepping outside the law to supply their basic needs?"

"No," said Lee, "not in the least."

"Reports of violence in various places are reaching this city nearly every day. If they continue I can easily envision a day when whites and blacks in the country will no longer look upon one another with friendly eyes."

"A development which threatens to crumble us from within," noted Lee.

"Exactly," affirmed Davis.

"This problem is made worse by our former enemies in the North," Benjamin joined the conversation. "Several of the northern states closest to us have passed laws which explicitly deny free blacks admission to their territory."

"They have indeed," said the President. "These laws you speak of are inspired by fear - the fear of a massive migration of blacks to the North. Northern whites fear for their jobs."

"So it seems," agreed Benjamin. "It makes me curious as to their intentions toward us had we lost the war."

"Interesting that you should bring that up," said Davis. "I've been curious about that myself. In fact I've had some of our secret service people working in Washington to see what they could learn."

"Spies?" asked Lee with something of a surprised expression on his face.

"I suppose they could be called that. They've been able to glean quite a bit of information."

"Do go on," urged Benjamin, "I'd like to know what they've found out."

"So would I," added Lee.

"We'd have been treated as conquered provinces," explained Davis. "My sources have focused their efforts on the most radical of the republicans... Stevens, Sumner, that crowd."

"I know which ones you're referring to," nodded Benjamin. "They're certainly no friends of Lincoln."

"Agreed. Some of my people think they would have found a way to rid themselves of Lincoln had the Union prevailed in the war. They thought his post-war designs to have been too lenient."

"What were they planning?" asked Lee.

"A long occupation for one thing. Aside from that they planned to seize our most valuable resources and turn them over to their industrialists. Coal, for example. The theft of land to satisfy the captains of northern industry would have been enormous."

"It's what they were after all along," said Lee.

"And the trap you set at Ox Ford foiled every one of

their designs. As for the negroes their plans were just as insidious. The biggest fear of northerners has been of a massive migration of former slaves into the north. Lincoln spoke often and fondly for his plans to colonize the liberated slaves outside of this country, primarily in Africa...places like Liberia."

"I'm familiar with his plans," noted Benjamin.

"The radicals had other ideas," continued Davis. "They planned to create a political paradise for the Negro in the South...one of them described the South as the ideal tropical habitat for Negroes."

"How would they have created this political paradise you spoke of?" asked Lee.

"By denying the vote to all whites who were in any way connected to the Confederacy, then giving the vote to the blacks."

"Disenfranchise the whites, give the franchise to the blacks," mused Benjamin.

"That would have been a recipe for disaster," argued Lee. "It would have poisoned relations between our races for at least the next century."

"Our friends in the North would have been able to use the former slaves as pawns so they could loot our state treasuries with no one the wiser."

"Exactly," affirmed Lee with a nod.

"Meanwhile several of the states in the Union have been passing laws forbidding free blacks from even stepping across their borders," added Davis.

"Ingenious," sighed Benjamin sitting back from the table running his hands across his suddenly full stomach.

"Not exactly the word I had in mind," countered Lee. "I was thinking more in terms of the whole thing being rather sinister."

"That too," concurred Benjamin with a grunt.

"No matter," gestured Davis, "in the final analysis all of their plans have gone for naught. The challenge which confronts us today comes largely from within, though I would not discount the possibility of foreign interference. If I remember my history correctly both the Spanish and British hovered over the United States in the late 1780's like a pair of jackals waiting for the new country to fall apart. I have no doubt the United States will be looming over us with the same intentions even while sending war reparations every month."

"Mr. President," ventured Benjamin, "are you straying from your point? I believe you were about to voice your concerns about internal threats.

"I was," nodded Davis, "and the threats are quite real. Hundreds of thousands of former slaves all across the Confederacy now find themselves destitute. They have left the plantations which were once their homes. They are experiencing freedom for the first time and have no desire to work, at least not on a white man's plantation. These people have no land nor any means to support themselves. Yet still they must eat. As a result lawlessness is on the rise throughout the country. If not dealt with promptly this situation threatens to explode in violence. The reports I spoke of earlier concern both rioting and vigilantism in both Louisiana and Arkansas. All of this must be nipped in the bud, which requires that we move swiftly."

"Do you plan to send the army?" asked Lee, who was wondering why he had been summoned.

"No," demurred Davis, "A move of that sort would provide a temporary solution at best. Do you remember Thomas Jefferson's vision for what America could be?"

"Of course," affirmed Lee. "He envisioned a nation where the political and economic power would be spread out among small farmers as opposed to the concentration of such power in the hands of the bankers and industrialists favored by Alexander Hamilton."

"Exactly," nodded Davis.

"Interesting," said Benjamin."In the words just uttered by the general I see the seeds which grew into the war we've just concluded."

"Agreed," continued Davis, "and here we are with the opportunity to see the dreams of Jefferson come to fruition. Plantations not withstanding, the Confederate States are populated primarily by small farmers, people with the ability to sustain themselves indefinitely from the land itself. Is this not true?"

The other two men both nodded in agreement.

"Except the slaves," said Davis.

"Former slaves," corrected Benjamin.

"You both know what I'm trying to say," returned Davis. "We're talking about a large number of landless, jobless people. Unless we resolve their dilemma they could prove the undoing of us all."

"Is this not the purpose of the bill you've already presented to Congress?" asked Lee.

"Indeed it is and that is precisely why I asked you here this evening, General."

"I'm not sure I understand," said Lee.

"Allow me to explain..."

Just then a servant entered the room with an armful of logs which had been neatly quartered. Outside the wind was howling through the streets of Richmond, rattling the shutters and windows of the Confederate White House penetrating even the tiniest of cracks. The servant opened the wood stove and piled several pieces inside. The wood was well-seasoned oak which burst into flame almost as soon as it came into contact with the bed of red-hot coals which covered the floor of the stove. Within seconds warmth began to radiate from the stove and the flue. The servant adjusted the damper slightly then turned to leave.

"Thank you, Thomas," said Davis.

"You're welcome, Mr. President," returned Thomas with a smile. "Is there anything I can get for you gentlemen?"

"Not right now. I believe we have everything we need."

"Very well, suh," Thomas turned and quietly left the room.

"Where were we?" asked Davis, scratching his head.

"I was inquiring as to why you summoned me," said the General.

"Ah, yes! The Bill...the Freedman's Bill... it faces a tough road in Congress. I'm not at all confident that it will pass. The opposition is formidable."

"What do you want me to do?"

"Testify on its behalf. Public hearings have already begun. No doubt they'll continue for several weeks. At the earliest possible moment I'd like to see you in Congress lending your knowledge and prestige to this effort."

"As you wish, Mr. President. I will do whatever I can."

"Thank you, General. I confess to feeling better already. You're very much the hero of the moment. Your word carries a great deal of weight within this government. I'd wager you're the odds on favorite to replace me when my term of office expires."

"I don't know about that," chuckled Lee, "but I will certainly lend my efforts to the passage of this bill."

"Thank you," sighed Davis. "Much will be riding on your testimony."

"Am I to testify as well?" asked Benjamin. "I don't know that the opinions of a cabinet member would be of much use in this regard, particularly since my field of expertise centers on foreign relations."

"No," Davis shook his head, "your testimony is not what I require. I need your help in another regard."

"Explain."

"Should the bill pass, we will have achieved only part of what I have in mind. Black people will be able to support themselves on their own land. More will need to be done, not only for blacks but whites as well. Before I leave office I'd like to set this country on a firm course toward achieving the ideals of Thomas Jefferson."

"No small challenge," mused Lee.

"Agreed, but if the reparations from the United States continue on schedule we will have the financial capability to do it."

"To do what?" pressed Benjamin.

"Schools," replied Davis. "Thomas Jefferson believed that Democracy could only flourish if the citizens were well-educated."

"You're talking about schools for blacks?"

"Whites as well."

"Thomas Jefferson did not free his slaves," argued Benjamin, "and I seriously doubt if he ever envisioned a time when slavery would cease to exist."

"He did not free them because he felt a responsibility toward them," countered Davis. "Many times he said he could not grant them freedom for fear of they're becoming destitute.

In reference to the doubt you just expressed, I believe you're mistaken. He wrote and spoke frequently of the need to abolish slavery, but he also advocated the same sort of colonization program recently espoused by Lincoln."

"I see," nodded Benjamin. "I'm simply trying to point out that he never dreamed of a situation such as confronts us today."

"True, but if the Freedman's Bill passes we'll be able to prevent the type of destitution Jefferson feared. Thus will we have the ability to take yet another step."

"I'm not so sure," Benjamin continued to play devil's advocate. "There are many whites who abhor the thought of blacks being educated."

"It's not just the blacks I have in mind, but we'll talk about them first. What were some of the rationales behind slavery?"

"Cheap labor," returned Benjamin.

"Besides that."

"There were many slave owners who justified the institution on humanitarian grounds," noted Lee. "In their minds they were doing God's work, at least in a sense. They saw it as their duty to uplift and civilize the Africans - to teach them our way of life."

"Precisely!" Davis nodded enthusiastically. "Perhaps I view myself in that light. I never degraded my slaves with slang names. I made sure they had full names. I tried to teach them our ways of doing things. I allowed them to resolve their own disputes with their own version of our judicial system. Those who strayed beyond the rules were put on trial by their fellow slaves, their fate to be decided by a jury of their peers."

"Your approach was well known," said Benjamin. "As to whether it was widely emulated, I think that might be an arguable proposition."

"I wasn't trying to elicit admiration from anybody. You

know as well as I that one of the basic arguments for slavery rested on the theory that whites had some sort of responsibility to uplift the blacks, to teach them our way of life."

"I'm aware of the argument."

"Then I suggest it would be logical for us to pursue the whole concept to its conclusion. "The days of slavery are behind us. If we have been teaching blacks our way of life then perhaps it's time for our pupils to graduate. In point of fact they already have. Emancipation has seen to that, yet my instincts tell me that most of the former slaves are not the least bit ready for the freedom they are now experiencing."

"I'd say your instincts are fairly close to the reality of the current situation." Benjamin took a sip of wine, clearly relishing the fine vintage.

"If we are ever to attain the ideals left to us by Thomas Jefferson we must see to the education of our citizens... all of them, black, white, or whatever."

"Where do I fit into this?" Quizzed Benjamin.

"I'm asking you to create and chair a committee composed of other members of the cabinet as well as select members of Congress, preferably from both chambers."

"Our task?"

"Devise a program which will use some of the money from Federal reparations to build, equip and staff a system of public schools throughout the Confederacy...separate of course...one system for blacks another for whites."

"This idea will also come under fire," said Benjamin.

"No doubt, but if we persevere we should be able to prevail."

"Time will tell," sighed the Secretary of State.

"It surely will," concurred the General, whose efforts against

Ulysses Grant along the North Anna River had made it possible for the discussion just concluded to take place.

*   *   *   *   *   *   *   *   *

"The stage leaves in thirty minutes," explained Wil as he handed a cup of hot tea to Amanda Andrews, a woman younger than his father by several years.

"Thank you, Wil," she nodded as she took the cup and saucer with one hand while tightening her shawl around her throat with the other.

"There's no sugar," he continued, "but the innkeeper sweetened your tea with some honey."

"That'll be fine," she smiled.

"Can I get you anythin' else?"

"No...the tea's enough. You don't have to concern yourself with me, Wil Covington. I'm quite all right."

"I'm sure you are, Mrs. Andrews, but a trip across the mountains by stagecoach in the dead of winter isn't as easy as you might think, especially for a..." he paused, unable to choose the right word.

"An old woman?" she cast him a sideways glance with one eyebrow arched so sharply it reminded Wil of a church steeple.

"I wasn't goin' to say that."

"But you were thinking it, weren't you?"

"Well..." again he hesitated, "I guess I was. The trip won't be easy, Mam, are you sure you want to go?"

"Have you ever given birth to a child, Wil?"

The question caught him completely off guard. "Pardon me?" he stammered. "Mrs. Andrews...that's not even a fair question!"

"I know," she offered him her most matronly smile. "When you can say you honestly understand what a woman experiences in childbirth, then - and only then - can you assume to lecture me about the rigors of a coach-ride to Richmond. In the meantime you needn't be so worried about my well-being. After what I've gone through over the last three years, I think I can adjust to the hardships of a trip to Richmond winter or not."

"Yes, mam," he returned, "I imagine you can but I am curious. Why are you goin'?"

"I'll wager my reasons are quite similar to yours. I'm going to express my thoughts on the Freedman's bill."

"For or against?"

"For it, of course, and I think you understand why."

"Does it have to do with Lonnie?"

"It does."

"I understand," he turned and glanced out at the gray, heavy winter sky.

"Look there," she pointed down the dirt covered street. "I think that's our stage coming up the road."

A combination of forces combined to forestall their arrival in Richmond. The weather certainly did its part to slow them down. Through most of the journey they had to put up with snow and freezing rain. This in turn made the roads quite difficult to traverse... roads which were never anything to brag about even in the best of weather. The animals were also a factor. At the war's, end good strong horses were a rarity in the South, especially in Virginia. Grain to keep them fit was also difficult to obtain and good grass for forage was virtually impossible to come by in the dead of winter. A team of six horses was harnessed to the stage but these animals had all the shortcomings just described and required frequent rest. As a result they could only make Charlottesville the first night out from home.

The next day's journey was decidedly easier. There were no more mountains to cross, and the storm which had made life so unpleasant the day before had finally blown itself out during the night. The air was dry as they moved steadily toward Richmond beneath bright blue skies through which drifted a parade of fluffy white clouds. Much of the previous day's snow had melted, so the roads themselves had been reduced to a muddy morass. Within an hour after nightfall they reached Richmond, exhausted by the two-day sojourn, a trip which required but half that time under normal conditions. The two travellers checked in to an aging hotel, not far from the Capitol itself, and retired quietly to their respective rooms.

Early the next morning, Wil dressed and prepared for the short trip over to the Confederate Congress. As they had previously arranged, he first called upon Mrs. Andrews so the two citizens from outside of Waynesboro could make the trip together. After a breakfast which gave no indication of the shortages being experienced elsewhere in the state Wil Covington and Amanda Andrews hailed a carriage and soon found themselves staring awestruck at the Confederate Capitol, a building which had been patterned after the Roman . Senate. To describe it as rich in history would surely be an understatement. Both Wil and Mrs. Andrews found themselves feeling awkward as they sought their place in the halls of power. Unlike many of the well-dressed politicians, who seemed always to be dashing purposefully from one place to another, these Valley citizens were attired in old homespun clothes, and appeared more lost than anything else.

On this particular day a joint session was scheduled. All of the members of the Senate were crowded in the House chamber along with a crowd of spectators and witnesses which filled the hall beyond its capacity. There wasn't even standing room as every spot along the walls was occupied.

"This reminds me of St. Paul's," Wil turned to speak to Mrs. Andrews who was seated next to him."

"St. Paul's?" She looked at him curiously.

"That church here in Richmond where me and Levi bumped into Marse Robert before we came home."

"Oh, yes," she nodded, "I remember hearing about that. Perhaps this crowd is here for the same reason. I've heard rumors that General Lee might testify in behalf of the Freedman's Bill. Those rumors might be true and maybe today's the day."

"That would be somethin'," smiled Wil. "It kinda makes me feel like we're about to witness history...maybe even be part of it."

"We're all part of history, Wil. Each of us has played a part in the creation of this nation. All of us made history during the war. We continue to make it every day that we remain an independent country."

"I understand all that," said Wil. "Still the same, it'll be special if we can be here when General Lee speaks. It'll be somethin' else I can tell my grandkids about someday."

"You're right," she smiled. "Speaking of grandchildren, when do you plan to marry that girl up in Maryland? What was her name?"

"Emily," he replied. "We're hoping to be married by early summer. I've got a lot of work to get the farm functionin' again before I fetch her down here. To tell you the truth I'm not so sure I'll ever get it all done. Get's frustratin' sometimes."

"I know," she sighed. "All of us face the same challenge. We need to stand together and help one another get through this. It'll all pass someday. Everything does."

GRAY VISIONS

Just then a hush fell over the entire chamber as General Robert E. Lee entered and was escorted to a seat of honor next to the podium where witnesses would soon be expressing themselves as to the merits of the Freedman's Bill. The talking started again but was quickly stifled by the Speaker's gavel as the entire chamber was called to order. That day's proceedings were underway.

As so many witnesses had done during the days preceding the arrival of Covington and Andrews, those who were scheduled to testify sat quietly awaiting their turns as the minutes and hours slipped slowly past. A wide range of testimony was presented to the legislature of the Confederacy. The range varied from those who mouthed the most racist invective and called for a revival of slavery to those who occupied the extreme opposite position. Some in this latter category thought the Freedman's Bill inadequate. They argued in favor of granting full rights of citizenship to the newly emancipated blacks, including the right to vote. Sentiment of this nature was difficult to find no matter which side of the Mason-Dixon one happened to reside. As a result those who called for citizenship for the Negroes were frequently shouted down. Fortunately, those who merely voiced support for the Davis program had a better go of it. Sentiment over this bill seemed fairly evenly divided.

"It's almost eleven o'clock," Wil leaned over and whispered to Mrs. Andrews as another witness finished speaking and sat down. "I hope they call us soon."

"So do I," she nodded without noticeably changing her erect formal posture. She sat her seat seemingly the embodiment of stoicism as she patiently awaited her turn at the podium.

Another thirty minutes passed before her patience was

finally rewarded. The speaker of the House rose to announce the next witness. "Augusta County sent us two witnesses this morning," he declared. "I understand one of 'em is a veteran from General Lee's army, and the other is a widow who lost her only son at Second Manassas. I think we should hear from her first. Amanda Andrews, are you here?"

"Yes, Mr. Speaker," Mrs. Andrews rose to her feet.

"Would you come forward please?" he beckoned to her.

She nodded and started making her way to the podium. Quickly, she became the focus of attention as it was a rarity to see a woman in a congress which was very much dominated by men. Prior to the war she had been a portly woman, but three years of shortages left her but a shadow of her former self. Save for the ill-fitting clothes on her back all of her belongings were destroyed by the Federal troopers who laid waste to the Andrews Farms in the summer of '63. Aside from her pride and her two daughters Amanda Andrews had been left with nothing.

The dress she wore that day came to her by way of the charity of her neighbors in Augusta County. It was old and worn and didn't fit her very well at all, but she used her skill with a sewing needle to make the necessary repairs and adjustments. She did not appear as an example of high fashion that morning but she certainly looked presentable.

She reached the podium and stepped up to face the assemblage of Senators, Congressmen and concerned citizens. They in turn gazed quietly at the face of the woman who was about to speak. She wore no bonnet. Her long hair was gathered behind her neck in an old tattered snood. Her hair had gone to gray for the most part but those closest to her could discern hints of the blondish red locks which had once bounced freely about youthful shoulders. The expression on her face was calm and resolute, but grief and fatigue could be easily read in the deep lines which creased her forehead and chin. She had the appearance of someone who had suffered but had emerged from the pain as a stronger person. Hers was a demeanor which generated respect and so it was that this crowded chamber became silent as those assembled waited for her to speak.

"The speaker was kind enough to introduce me," she began in a voice suprisingly strong for a woman who had endured so much, "so you already know who I am and where I'm from. Getting here from the valley this time of year wasn't easy, but I felt I had to come and say my piece about the bill Mr. Davis has presented to you. I've been listening to other folks, all morning and I have to say it hurts to hear some of the remarks I've heard today about the negroes. I believe such commentary arises from ignorance more than anything else. To those of you who argue for a restoration of slavery. I ask this. Where would we be today were it not for the blacks who stood by us through the last three years? Would our farms and plantations have continued to operate had these people not remained loyal? Could we have sustained our armies in the field without the support of the black people? Could the Tredegar Arms works have produced so much weaponry without the skill and loyalty of black artisans? These Confederate States of America owe their very existence to the strength, endurance and courage of their people and that statement most definitely includes their black people." Here she paused and sipped from a glass of water which had been provided for her. She coughed quietly and cleared her throat before resuming her discourse.

"I have deeply held personal reasons to explain why I chose to stand before you today. I lost my only son, Lonnie, at the Second Battle of Manassas. I do not tell you this to elicit your sympathy. I am but one of tens of thousands of mothers across this land who have been dealt such a loss. I am not alone in my grief, and I take solace in knowing that he died doing the duty he believed he was called to, and that he performed that duty well.

"Lonnie was a wonderful boy. He was full of curiosity and he always had a boundless enthusiasm for life. You'll soon be hearing from one of my neighbors, Wil Covington, a veteran of the same fighting which claimed my son. It was Wil who told me how Lonnie died. He was hit in the stomach by a yankee's bullet on the first evening of the battle." Here again she paused. A noticeable quiver had shaken her voice as she relayed the story of her son's mortal wounding. Tears came to her eyes and it was obvious to all present that she was struggling to control her emotions. Aside from an occasional cough there was no other noise in that chamber as the assemblage respectfully waited for her to continue.

"Wil," her voice broke again and she had to dab at the corner of her eyes with the hankie she clenched tightly in her left hand. "Wil carried him back to the surgeons but every step they took brought my son closer to death."

Wil could see her chin quivering with every word she spoke.

"He never made it to the surgeon's table. There was a slave outside the tents helping with the wounded. His name was Ivory. Wil told me all about him. He came up here from South Carolina. His master hired him out to the army. He was a teamster and a cook, but to me he'll always be much more than that. He took Lonnie from Wil and laid him on the ground. He must've known at once that Lonnie was..." her voice failed her again. "That Lonnie was dying. Wil told me every detail of what happened. Lonnie called out to me...he kept calling for me, just as thousands of our sons called out for their mothers in their last moments of life." Again, she paused to wipe away a single tear which had been falling slowly down her right cheek. "I wasn't there for him, I...I couldn't be there. Ivory was there. He took my place. He helped my son make peace with God. He offered him comfort. He told him how much I loved him.

"I cannot imagine what Lonnie was going through in those last moments. I don't think any of us can. To this day I shudder when I think of all the pain he must've been in. I go cold inside when I try to imagine the fear he felt as his life was ebbing away. I know my son, I know he would have been desperately trying to hold on...clinging to every moment of life." She paused a few seconds and drew in a long deep breath of air to calm herself.

"This man, Ivory, did what I could not do. He eased the passage of my only son to the next world. I thank God every day that Ivory was there at that particular moment in time, and that he had enough love in his heart that he would give of himself like he did. The last face my son saw before he died was the face of a black man. He died in the arms of that same black man. How many of our sons died the same way in the surgeon's tents all across the Confederacy in every battle? I think all of you know that number is not small. I thank God every day that Ivory was there for my son. It means more to me than I could ever put into words." Here she stopped and took her eyes from those who had listened intently to her every word. Some among these people thought she had said her piece and would now stand down. Such was not the case.

"I have other reasons for favoring the Freedman's Bill," she proclaimed as she raised her eyes once more to the chamber. "The Yankees burned us out during the summer of '63. My husband tried to save our house. They killed him.

They left nothing. The livestock was all killed, the fencing destroyed, the crops burned. When they pulled out I was left a homeless widow with two daughters. We had nothing but the clothes on our backs. Again I feel obliged to say I'm not telling you this to elicit your sympathy. Countless thousands of us have gone through this, especially in the Shenandoah Valley. My purpose in telling you this is quite simple. I had no one to turn to but neighbors and that includes black neighbors. Sarah Henry comes to mind. She's a free woman, has been for over twenty years, she and her husband both. Her son, Levi, marched off to war with the same regiment as my own boy. She took care of me and my girls. She brought us food and made us clothing with her own hands. In the moments of my darkest despair she would be there...always with words of encouragement. She helped to bring strength to our spirits. She guided us away from despair and helped us find hope again." She paused and sighed loudly enough to be heard through most of the hall.

"Most of the negroes stood by us throughout the war," she continued. "Whether they were slaves or free it doesn't matter. Without their support would it have been possible for us to be here today arguing about a bill? I think not. It would be very small of us to turn our backs on them now, especially in light of what we all went through together. That's all I have to say. I'm not a politician. I can't even vote. I suppose it could be said that I'm nothing but an old woman, a homeless woman at that. But I am a citizen of this country and the freedom of expression is supposed to be one of our fundamental rights. I've expressed my thoughts and I do want to thank all of you for allowing me to speak and for taking the time to listen." With that she stepped down from the podium and started for her seat.

The man seated next to Wil leaned over and whispered, "An old woman she may be, but she has a certain eloquence about her. No one can deny that."

Wil could only nod in reply.

Most of those present were moved by her words but the reaction could not be gauged by any audience response. Touched they may have been but an applause of ovation of any sort seemed inappropriate, given the nature of the proceeding. The entire chamber sat in respectful silence as she moved through the aisle to her place.

After she resumed her seat Wil leaned over. "You were wonderful," he said softly.

"Your turn," she replied with a smile.

"We've one more witness from Augusta County, Virginia." The voice of the Speaker sang out across the hall. "Is Wil Covington here?"

"Yes, suh!" Wil stood at once, feeling somewhat awkward as so many pairs of eyes shifted in his direction.

"Well, come on up, boy!" called the Speaker. "We're waitin' to hear from ya."

Wil made his way out into the aisle and walked quickly to the podium.

"She's all yours, son," said the Speaker as he stepped aside.

Wil stepped up to the podium and stared out at the sizeable crowd of people which filled every nook and cranny of that chamber. Butterflies had been fluttering through his stomach all morning as he waited his turn. Speaking before a large group wasn't something Wil had ever done before and as he looked out over that hall a feeling of dread began to overwhelm him. His stomach muscles were doing a dance of their own making and Wil was now thinking he'd probably prefer a trip to the dentist to the challenge he was about to undertake.

"Go ahead, boy!" huffed the Speaker. "There's a lot of folks still waitin' their turn!"

"Yessuh," Wil nodded nervously. "Good mornin'," he raised his voice several levels so that he could be heard throughout the hall. Taking a deep breath to calm his nerves he continued. "As this gentleman said, my name is Wil Covington. I was a private in the Army of Northern Virginia. I joined back in the summer of '62 right after General Lee took command. I served through the rest of the war with the 5th Virginia infantry. Like Mrs. Andrews over there I too have strong personal feelin's about the Freedman's Bill. I didn't join up by myself. My oldest friend joined with me. His name is Levi Henry and he's a negro. In the early 1840's his father and mother were slaves. They belonged to my father and mother. My Pa freed them in 1842, only a few months before Levi and I were born. He also deeded part of our farm over to them, just over forty acres I think, and helped the Henrys build their home and barn.

"Our families have always been close but even more so since the Henrys became free people. My mother died while giving me birth. It was Sarah Henry, the same black woman Mrs. Andrews told you about, who nursed me as an infant and helped to raise me. She's the only real mother I ever knew. When Levi and I marched off to war, she was the one said the good byes and made a fuss over us....Y'all know how the women can be sometimes. She didn't want us to go and shed a whole lot of tears tryin' to change our minds" He took a break for water and suddenly realized he'd been talking for several minutes and that his belly was no longer fluttering.

GRAY VISIONS

Confidence began to grow within his breast and when he turned to face the crowd in that chamber his face held an entirely different expression.

"The Henry's were free for almost twenty years before the war started. Theirs' is a success story and the key to their success was land, the land my father gave them. Before the war they were prosperous folks. So were we for that matter. Then came the war. The Henrys are Virginians. That's how they've always thought of themselves and that's how they responded when the war started...like Virginians. Their taxes helped support this government. Their crops help feed our armies. When I decided to join up with the 5th Virginia, Levi insisted he was goin' as well.

"There was no shortage of black soldiers in our army; I can tell you that for a fact. I marched with Robert E. Lee for more than two years and I saw thousands of black men in our ranks. Far and away most of 'em were slaves but the point is they were with us. Their loyalty for the most part was above reproach. I don't mean to sound disrespectful, but while you politicians were wringing your hands over whether or not to bring blacks into the army the blacks were already there and they were distinguishing themselves time and again.

"Mrs. Andrews told you about Ivory. He's one of the bravest most selfless men I've ever known. I watched how he took care of her son as he died that evenin' outside Manassas. Levi was there as well. He was helpin' in the surgeon's tents, as were scores of negroes. Levi was part of the team that took General Ewell's leg and saved his life. I ask you this: how many of us are still alive today due to the efforts of black men in the surgeon's tents? A lot...I'll warrant ya that.

"The Second Battle of Manassas saw heroism on a huge scale particularly by the men in Stonewall Jackson's corps, and not just the white men. Mrs. Andrews told you about Ivory and what he did for her son. Let me tell you another story about him. On the third day of fighting the Yankees were stormin' our position on the unfinished railroad embankment. We were badly outnumbered but we were used to that. The problem was ammunition. There wasn't enough. We were runnin' out of bullets all up and down the line. Some of us threw rocks at the Federals. Some waited with bayonets fixed. Things were lookin' pretty bleak along our sector of the line and all of a sudden Ivory shows up. He'd driven a wagon full of ammo as close to the line as the trees would allow and then he came forward on foot with a box of bullets under each arm. He saved our skins no question about it, and got himself shot in the process. Lucky for us it was just a flesh wound.

"Ivory wasn't the only black hero. There was another slave from South Carolina, his name was Wade Childs. His master, I think he was a captain in Orr's rifles, name of Cothran if memory serves me, was wounded by the Federals and Wade Childs rushed right out into the field of fire to save him, heedless of any danger to his own person. And then there's Levi, the black boy I grew up with. He's the closest thing to a brother I've ever had. At one point the Yanks pushed us off the line. I didn't see what happened 'cause I took a rifle butt in the face....lost a couple of teeth and ended up unconscious on the ground. Levi didn't retreat with the others 'cause he wouldn't leave me to be finished off or taken prisoner. He ended up savin' one stand of colors, killin' a Yankee officer and capturin' two of their soldiers. Levi and the other negroes were just as much heroes as any of our white soldiers... every bit as much." Here he paused to sip water and organize his thoughts. He noticed at once how quiet the chamber had become. The murmuring which had been going on as he began his discourse had been stilled.

"Levi and I stayed together and fought side by side through the rest of the war. At South Mountain he saved my life. I took a ball in the hip. I would've ended up a prisoner or dead if it weren't for Levi Henry. He and another man carried me out of harm's way. Levi managed to get me to a farmhouse in Maryland up near Pennsylvania. Now we're both home on our farms and facin' the challenge of rebuildin' what the Yanks burned or vandalized. We've got a handful of problems facin' us but I didn't come here to complain or seek sympathy. We've got a future, me and Levi, we've both got land. That's the key to the future...land. It's somethin' this Confederacy has plenty of. There's millions of black people out there who are experiencing freedom for the first time. Most of them have nothing but the clothes on their backs. We as a people cannot allow this situation to continue. If we do I think I can safely say the future of our country will be bleak beyond our wildest imagination.

"I reckon that's about all I have to say and I honestly don't know whether the opinions of someone like myself matter much to you folks. I'm just a soldier and a farmer, but I know what I've seen, and I've seen thousands of black Confederate soldiers taking the same risks as white soldiers like myself. They deserve better than to be abandoned now that the war's over. My thanks to you for lettin' me say my piece."

With that he turned away and stepped down from the podium. The building itself was cold and damp that day and Wil had been very tense all morning as he waited his turn to speak. These factors probably accounted for the sharp pain which shot through his hip causing him to limp noticeably as he made his way slowly back to his seat. He made it a point to look at the faces of those he passed, trying to gauge their reaction by the expressions he saw. Some appeared quite receptive to his arguments. Others had obviously not been moved.

Three more witnesses followed before the break for a midday meal. One of these, an accomplished speaker by all accounts, voiced a vehement argument against the bill. An hour after adjourning, the members of Congress reconvened for the afternoon session. As the day waned the sky grew thick with dark rolling clouds heavy with the threat of more snow. Against this backdrop Robert E. Lee was announced as a witness in the matter of the Freedman's Bill. To those present, he appeared larger than life. His victories over Grant and his capture of Washington, D.C. had astounded most people and in the minds of these people he seemed somewhat like a God. Senators and Congressmen held him in awe. Governors and bureaucrats were often tongue-tied in his presence. Up until now he had been silent about the Freedman's legislation. Whatever opinion he held was kept to himself. Today would see the end of his silence.

With bearing worthy of a king, the General took his place behind the podium. As those gathered waited for him to commence his address it would have been quite easy to hear a pin drop anywhere within the Capitol. Among those who counted themselves supporters of the Freedman's Bill hearts were beating just a little faster. All of them knew this would be the pivotal moment of the entire process. Many uttered softly spoken prayers, entreaties to God that the General would not disappoint them, that his impact would be just as potent as they had hoped from the outset. A moment of truth was arriving for the Congress of the Confederacy.

"Good afternoon," announced Lee as he began his discourse. "As those who have preceded me, I too would like to thank you for giving me this opportunity to speak. It has been with no little interest that I've listened to the testimony all of you have heard throughout this day's session. I've been impressed, often moved, by the passionate arguments I've heard today on both sides of the issue. It's my understanding that rumors as to my intentions regarding the Freedman's Bill have circulated rather liberally through the city these last several weeks. I must accept responsibility for those rumors and the gossip which accompanies them. It was my silence which spawned these rumors in the first place. I should have made my feelings known earlier but that is all hindsight. I cannot change what has already transpired, but I can at least put an end to all the idle speculation. You need wonder no more, my friends. I am throwing all my support behind the Freedman's Bill."

Reaction was instant. Suddenly the entire chamber was abuzz as men and women alike gasped in surprise and, as if by instinct, shouted out their feelings either in support of or opposition to the General. The ruckus continued for a couple of minutes until the Speaker was finally forced to call out for order as he slammed his gavel resoundingly upon his desktop. Quickly the crowd grew quiet and after taking a sip of water the General continued.

"My reasons for doing so are many. Time would not allow me to explore each in detail in a forum such as this, but I will endeavor to explain those I deem most important. Let me tell you at the outset how much I love this country, and in particular this state, more deeply than most of you could possibly imagine. When Virginia left the Union I resigned my commission in the United States Army. Some of you may recall that I said I would not draw my sword again save in defense of my native state. Obviously I, like tens of thousands of my fellow Virginians, was called upon to do just that. We answered your call just as hundreds of thousands of our compatriots across the South. What exactly were we fighting for?" He paused to reflect upon his next words and to sip from the glass of water sitting to his right.

"Were we fighting to preserve slavery? Some would say so. No doubt there are some among us who were. The largest slave owners certainly come to mind. Our enemies certainly spared no effort nor expense to convince the entire world that the war was about slavery. The propaganda barrage was fierce and if we had lost the war that same propaganda would no doubt have been recorded in the textbooks of the future as history.

"Fortunately we did not lose the war. By the blessing of Providence we emerged with our independence...our freedom from the clutches of the oligarchy which came to power in the United States in the election of 1860. Moreover we made the decision to abolish the institution of slavery so that all of our people can now claim to be free.

"I did not take up arms to preserve slavery. I can honestly say that I know very few men under my command who were there to make sure negroes remained slaves. I fought to defend my home against a foreign invasion. The vast majority of the men who wore the butternut and gray of this Confederacy did so for the same reason and no other. The war was not about slavery. Our two countries separated over a deep division of economic and political philosophy. The roots of this schism go all the way back to the ratification debates which started in 1787. Each of you in your hearts know this to be true. Radically divergent views on the nature of government were argued between 1787 and 1789, and those arguments didn't cease miraculously when George Washington took the oath of office as the first president."

GRAY VISIONS

Pausing to take a breath Lee let his eyes scan the assemblage slowly from left to right as he resumed his speech. "All of us know who Alexander Hamilton was. He can surely be described as one of the most powerful of the Federalists. He had little use for the common man. To him the yeoman farmers who make up the majority of our population were little more than a dirty mob. He said that bankers should run the government...they and the largest merchants and industrialists. He wanted to see the economic and political power concentrated in the hands of these people. To him a Federal union was the best mechanism to accomplish this aim, but behind this facade of Federalism stood an oligarchy.

"Compare his views with those espoused by Virginia's Thomas Jefferson. Are they not completely opposite? Jefferson valued the small farmers above all others. To him they would be the backbone of the nation. In his mind, the power would best be spread out among a population of small farmers. Moreover he saw the dangers inherent in the concentration of political and economic power. In discussing the need for a bill of rights, for instance, he specifically detailed the necessity for protecting the people against the power of monopoly. This is not ancient history. It seems like only yesterday that this conflict between Hamilton and Jefferson spawned two political parties, the Federalists and the Democrat-Republicans. There you see the planting of the seeds which grew into the war we've just fought, not in the argument over slavery." Again he paused momentarily to quench his thirst and organize his thoughts.

"No doubt many of you are wondering why I'm talking about any of this. All of us have our opinions about why we left the Union, and I'm sure you're curious about what this issue has to do with the Freedman's Bill. Please bear with me.

I'm not wandering aimlessly, though perhaps, it may seem so. Let me ask you this. If we were fighting merely for the right to own slaves would the slaves themselves have remained loyal to our cause? True, many did not remain with us. Tens of thousands joined ranks with the Federals. Just as true, however, is this. The vast majority of this nation's black population remained loyal to the South and the Confederacy. Do you recall the furor raised by Lincoln's Emancipation Proclamation? Do you remember the clause which certainly seemed to invite insurrection by the slaves themselves? Did not the slave population have it within their power to wreck our war effort? They could have...and easily. Did we have enough troops to fight the Federals on the battlefields and control rebellious slaves simultaneously? I believe you all know the answer to that question. Yet the mass insurrection never materialized. If anything the opposite is the case. On the plantations and farms, in the towns and cities, in the mills and foundries, and within our armed services the negroes played roles which were crucial to the success of our cause. Now they are free, all of them.

"The war has been over for several months and with the ending of the war slavery too saw its final days within this Confederacy. What has freedom brought thus far? To many of the former slaves freedom has meant nothing but disaster. Overnight they found themselves homeless, landless and with no source of income. They quickly found they were not welcome in the North but here at home their situation rapidly deteriorated into desperation. They've had little recourse but to steal in order to stay alive. Therein lies a prescription for disaster. Violence has already broken out in several places. Militia have been called to arms and in some cases we have had to send troops from the regular army to restore order. This is not a situation which can be allowed to continue for much longer. It threatens to unravel everything we fought so long to build. Now is the time for all of us to join together. We can prevent any further fragmentation and turn back the forces which otherwise will lead to our ruin. The solution is land and this body...this Congress...holds the key to that solution.

"Earlier today you heard from a young man named Wil Covington, a private in the army I commanded. I knew he looked familiar to me but I didn't remember him until he spoke of his black companion. That's when I knew I had met him before. It was at St. Paul's Episcopal Church here in Richmond several weeks after the war ended. Wil's friend, Levi Henry if memory serves me, a young black soldier in our army, defied tradition and stepped to the communion rail while whites were being served communion. I'm sure you know the incident I'm referring to; it was mentioned in several of the newspapers. I'll speak more about Private Henry later. Right now I'd like to focus on certain facts earlier relayed to you by young Covington.

"This soldier told you that he marched with me for over two years and in that time he saw thousands of blacks in our ranks. He neither lied nor exaggerated. I am in a position to know perhaps better than anybody. Most of our musicians were negroes, and the same could be said of our teamsters, blacksmiths, and cooks as well as the men who toiled at the sides of our surgeons. These are non-combat roles to be true, but the military contributions of blacks to our cause go well beyond the tasks I've just described. Free black men fought along side their white compatriots from the very beginning of the war. This is a fact all of us know to be true. I can testify to you in all honesty that many of our deadliest snipers were black men. I can also say that it wasn't at all unusual to see negroes servicing our guns in the heat of battle. During battles there were frequent occasions when a slave would pick up the weapon of his fallen master and continue in the dead man's place.

"Acts of heroism as a rule tend to fill our hearts with pride and admiration, do they not? Stories of heroism on the part of slaves are too numerous to recount. Such bravery was demonstrated frequently by negroes on the battlefield, but these acts were not by any means confined to the area of combat. Many of you are familiar with the courage of slaves on plantations seized by Union forces. Many were tortured to force them into revealing the hiding places of a family's silver or jewelry, yet most of those unfortunate souls endured the pain and would not break down.

"Slavery is now behind us all, and in truth I believe it's abolition has freed the white population as well. All of us were chained to that institution in one fashion or another. Are we indebted to our former slaves? Without question. I honestly don't believe we could have emerged from that war with our independence without the support of our black population. The question remains. What do we do?" Letting this question hang answerless for the moment he paused and took several deep gulps of water. Turning back to face the crowd he resumed his oration.

"Earlier I spoke to you of an encounter I had with one of our black soldiers at St. Paul's Episcopal church. His name is Levi Henry. He and Private Covington joined the army together back in '62, as the young man told you a little while ago. The two of them grew up together over near Waynesboro and both could be called heroes many times over. I remember that day in the church. Levi Henry made it a point to defy tradition and walk to the communion rail before the whites had been served. In his own way young Henry was making a statement. He had many times risked his life for these Confederate states and I think he felt he had earned the right to be treated as an equal. He decided to make a statement and he did so by defying tradition. I too thought it appropriate to make some sort of statement, and I did so by kneeling next to him at the communion rail. My feeling is this: separate races we may be, but we are all people of the South. This is the bond which we share no matter our race. It was as one people that we faced the Federal invasion and as one people we have emerged triumphant. Upon leaving the service at St. Paul's that day I was set upon by a horde of newspaper reporters but I managed to break free of them when Levi Henry left the church. He said something to me that I haven't been able to put out of my mind. Part of what he said was predicated upon my having political ambitions, and to be honest with you, I have none. Nevertheless, Private Henry spoke to me as someone who might make a difference in the future of black people within this Confederacy. He reminded me that negroes stood by the Confederacy throughout the ordeal of this war. They were killed and wounded as we were. They endured the same sufferings and deprivations. He asked me not to forget them. I haven't forgotten, nor will I." Again he paused. To him it seemed as though he had been talking for hours and his throat was parched to the point where it hurt to raise his voice.

"Comes now the solution," he declared boldly after taking a long drink of water. "It has come to you in the form of the Freedman's Bill from the desk of President Davis. I believe it is common knowledge that we are receiving war reparations from the Federal government of the United States. This money has helped stabilize our currency, and we have used it to compensate the owners of slaves for their property loss linked to the abolition of slavery. I think it is proper that we do so. I also think it proper to use at least some of this money to ease the passage of former slaves into freedom. This is our challenge and to delay would be criminal.

As several previous witnesses have testified, *land* is the key to the resolution of this crisis. The Freedman's Bill will use a portion of the Federal reparations to provide land for every free black family. Our goal is to set up each family with at least forty acres. This is certainly commensurate with the loyalty shown by most black people throughout the Confederacy, and for the sacrifices so many of them made.

"Can a program of this design and purpose actually work? In other words can we stop the social dissolution already upon us by helping negroes purchase land? I believe that we can. More-over, it is incumbent on us to at least try. To do otherwise is to invite disaster. Land is indeed the key to this whole dilemma and land is something this Confederacy has plenty of.

"Can this idea succeed? Absolutely. Here in Virginia it isn't necessary to look very far to find examples of such success. When the war broke out there were over 60,000 free black people in this state, more, I believe than in any other state of the Confederacy. Many of these men served in the army I commanded during the war. No few of them gave their lives for our independence. Who are these people...people like Levi Henry and his family? How have they lived? How have they supported themselves? For the most part land has been the key to their deliverance. Many, like the Henrys, were given land by their former masters. Others earned and saved money with which they purchased homes. Theirs is a success story few have bothered to notice, but it has been there under our noses all along. Several counties in northern Virginia offer proof to what I'm saying here. Prince William County comes quickly to mind, as does Loudoun, Fairfax and Fauquier. Hundreds of free black families have lived in those locales in peace and prosperity for many years. This example can be duplicated throughout the Confederacy.

GRAY VISIONS

"In offering this example it wasn't my intention to neglect other regions of our country. Charleston, South Carolina boasts of a large and for the most part prosperous population of free negroes, as does New Orleans, Louisiana. I'm merely pointing out conditions are key to true independence. We have an opportunity to adopt a program which will work. It's called the Freedman's Bill. It deserves your vote. More importantly, the people it is designed to benefit deserve your vote."

The General stopped speaking took a quick sip of water and gazed silently at the crowd of people gathered within the Confederate Capitol. He had said most of what he had to say, and now he pondered his closing words. "I am a soldier," he declared calmly. "Much of my experience...the foundation of my philosophy toward life...has revolved around the military. There are certain maxims I know to be true. One of these revolves around the idea of conquest. As it is stated it seems quite simple: divide and conquer. Was not the Emancipation Proclamation of Abraham Lincoln an attempt to divide us by race to facilitate our conquest? The northern invasions were designed to separate our western states from the East, the upper South from the lower. All of their efforts ultimately failed, yet the theory holds. If we fail to act now we risk dividing ourselves according to race. Blacks will turn on whites and vice versa. There are certain places where this is already happening, but it isn't too late to undo the damage and to prevent any further deterioration. The means are available to us. We need only manifest the will. No one can do it for us. The program must begin soon and it must start here from within this institution. To do otherwise is to invite calamity and I, for one, love this country far too much to stand idly by while everything we fought and suffered for is lost. My friends, I thank you from the bottom of my heart for allowing me to address you this afternoon. I believe I speak for the president as well as myself in urging you to vote for the Freedman's Bill. It offers us the best opportunity to resolve this crisis before it tears our country apart. Good afternoon to each of you."

*　*　*　*　*　*　*　*　*

"You haven't told me much about what happened in Richmond," said Levi as he and Wil made their way down the mountain on a narrow foot path. Several days had passed since Wil along with Amanda Andrews had returned from their mission to the Capitol. Little had changed. The weather was still bitterly cold. Food remained scarce. There was always wood to be cut and split. Earlier that morning Wil and Levi had taken their muskets and hiked well up into the Blue Ridge in search of game. All through the day they maintained the hunt but there was little to show for their efforts. They had seen one deer, a doe, but the elusive animal bolted swiftly out of sight before either man could get a shot off. By day's end they had managed but two kills, an underweight rabbit which made the mistake of tarrying too long atop a fallen tree and a squirrel with some decent weight to it. With a dead animal hanging from each of their belts the two veterans headed for home, hoping to make it back before sunset.

"I enjoyed the experience," replied Wil, "especially seein' Marse Robert again."

"I know that. You done told me that a couple of times. I want to know what you think! Did it do any good? Are they gonna pass that bill or what?"

"Don't know."

"Okay, so you don't know, but you must at least be thinkin' somethin'!"

"I think we did all that could be done. Mrs. Andrews was great. She talked a lot about Ivory. Talked about your mother and

GRAY VISIONS

how much she was indebted to you folks. I told 'em all about you, how you saved my life and such. I thought Marse Robert did the best of all of us. He spoke about that day you turned the church upside down...acted like he was right proud of you."

"I'm proud of him. Always have been."

"Me too. He talked about all the free Blacks that have been in Virginia for years, used them as an example of how this whole thing could work. I think he impressed some folks. Last I heard they were supposed to be votin' on it this week. Reckon we'll know soon enough...one way or the other."

"I suppose," sighed Levi. "Anyway, I think we stayed out here too long. My ears are frozen. Same with my fingers. If I had to load this musket right now I'd be in a world of trouble."

"Me too. Hang in there, we ought to be home in an hour."

"It'll be dark."

"No problem. We'll be home."

The sun had just set when they topped a rise from which they could easily see both farms. The Western sky was ablaze in color. To the eyes of humans it looked as though someone high in the heavens had tossed huge boulders into a sea of orange creating colorful tendrils which leapt skyward. There was still a great deal of daylight remaining, enough that Levi and Wil could easily see their homes. "Look there," gestured Wil pointing toward the Covington house, "looks like your folks are headin' for my place."

"I see 'em. Wonder what's up."

"We'll know soon enough. Let's see if we can pick up the pace some."

"No problem by me. You're the one with the bad hip. I could've been home an hour ago."

"You had to remind me, didn't you?"

"Hey, you brought up the idea of walkin' faster! Not me!"

By dark they were home, and both trudged wearily through the front door of Wil's house. Once inside they spied the Henrys gathered around a table in the kitchen with Tom Covington.

"What's goin' on?" asked Wil as he tossed the rabbit onto a counter and moved quickly to the side of the woodstove to warm his hands and face. His chin was so cold it was difficult to open his mouth and the words didn't come out quite right.

"What'd you say?" his father glanced over at Wil.

"I said, what's goin' on?" Wil made an extra effort to enunciate each word.

"Big news from Richmond," replied Moses Henry.

At once both of the young men forgot about being cold and joined their elders at the table noticing for the first time the newspapers which were opened in front of their parents.

"Did they vote?" pressed Levi.

"They sho' did," replied his father.

"What's the verdict?" followed Wil.

"They passed it," replied the older Covington, "barely, but they passed it."

"How barely?"

"Three votes in the House, one in the Senate."

"Thank God!" breathed Wil with an audible sigh.

"Yes, indeed!" beamed Moses Henry. "It's a great day...a great day for us all!"

"How did you find out?" asked Levi.

"Mama caught a ride into Staunton with Mrs. Epps this mornin'. She picked up these papers from Richmond. Has the whole story! They say General Lee was the reason it passed. Without his support the bill would've failed."

"I don't doubt it," nodded Wil. "I was thinkin' that when the General was talkin'. I knew he'd make a difference. Those fellas in Congress are a lot more inclined to listen to Marse Robert than to the likes of me or Mrs. Andrews."

"I don't know if that's entirely true," argued Tom Covington. "I'll agree that Marse Robert was vital to this vote, but there was a place for us little folks as well. Why else would they have allowed you to speak if they didn't care what you had to say?"

"That's true, Pa, but General Lee was the one who made the biggest impact."

"Maybe. The point is, it worked. Everything you, Mrs. Andrews, the General and all the others did and said was effective. The Bill passed. The former slaves will have access to land. We'll be able to step back from the brink of certain disaster."

Later that night, in the living room of the Henry house, Levi was packing the woodstove with logs and adjusting the damper to assure they would burn slowly till the wee hours of morning. Sarah Henry had already retired for the night and Moses was preparing to join her.

"You've been awful quiet this last hour," said Moses as his son closed and latched the door of the stove."

"Been thinkin'," replied Levi.

"Kinda figured that. What about?"

"The future I reckon. This law that Congress just passed will make a difference...a huge difference. It'll go a long way toward savin' the country, a long way toward makin' sure whites and blacks don't turn on one another, but it's just a step, Pa, a first step in a long journey,"

"Well now, a step it may be, but at least it's that much. Think what it would be like if they hadn't said yes to the Freedman's Bill."

"I have and I know it wouldn't make for a pretty picture, but I still see it as just a first step."

"Toward?" pressed Moses, who was both fearful and eager to hear what his son might say.

"Toward equality."

"I thought you might say somethin' like that." Moses had climbed several stairs but turned and descended toward Levi. "You'd best be careful what you're sayin', boy, and who you say it to."

"I'm careful," came the reply. "But that don't change my mind. I fought in the war same as any of the white men. I killed Yankees. I got shot a couple of times. Seems to me I should have the same rights as a white man."

"What mo' rights do you want, son? You own a farm, at least you will when me and yo' Mama pass on. Yo' money spends same as a white man's."

"White men can vote."

Moses took another step down the stairway. "You'll be treadin' on awful thin ice if you start makin' noise like that!" His voice had risen a decibel or two.

"You don't agree with me?"

"I didn't say that. I'm an old man, Levi. I've been free a good many years, but I was a slave for a lot longer, me and yo Mama both. We remember what it was like. It ain't somethin' we ever want to live through again. We appreciate what we have."

"We're not even citizens, Pa. Not like the whites."

"True, son," Moses nodded, "but we're free. More free now than ever we've been. Slavery's gone. That's a start ain't it? Our people will all have land, ain't that true? They'll have a future beyond the hangman's rope and the prison cell. Don't that mean somethin' to ya?"

"You know it does."

"Then you got to be patient, son. You got to be. Change comes slow in this world. That's just the way it is. We've seen big changes lately, big ones...for all our people. Now is the time to be patient. Mo' change'll come...in its own time. You say you want to vote? That ain't an idea that's gonna please too many white folks and you know it."

"That don't mean we shouldn't have that right."

"No it don't, but you got to play the hand you was dealt. You know what pleased me most when Marse Covington gave us our freedom?"

"Your freedom...the farm?"

"Neither. Yo' freedom, son, and you wasn't even born yet. When I knew you was gonna be born free I cried mah heart out, and them was tears of joy I can tell you that. You understand what I'm trying to say?"

"Maybe," the stern expression on Levi's face relaxed for the first time and the hint of a smile appeared. "I think maybe you're sayin' that I may never have the right to vote, but maybe my sons will."

"At least yer learnin' how to listen." Moses smiled broadly as he crossed his arms over his chest. "There's hope fo' you yet!"

"If you say so Pa."

"I do. And I got one mo' piece of advice for ya. You get yoself on up to Maryland and fetch that girl, Naomi, on down here. How are yer sons gonna ever be able to vote if you ain't got no sons?"

"Damn if you ain't full of good ideas tonight!" laughed Levi.

"You just remember that, boy, and remember what I been sayin' to ya."

~Chapter Two~
The Reunion

A soft early morning breeze wafted through the open bedroom window, gently billowing the lace curtains Emily had hung so many years ago. The sun had been up for perhaps a half hour but had yet to melt the moist dew which covered the rolling hills of the Covington Farm. Outside, an energetic bobwhite had awakened to the new day and was gleefully announcing the arrival of dawn to all who cared to listen. It was early May in the Shenandoah Valley. Everywhere the land was abloom. The bright pastel colors of spring decorated every corner of the landscape. Dogwood blossoms both pink and white were especially abundant as were those of apple and cherry trees. Far and away the most dominant color was green - not the deep heavy green of mid-summer mind you. It was a pale delicate shade of the color... Spring green if you will. To an outside observer it must have seemed as though a massive carpet had been laid across the land...a beautiful green carpet at that. The starkness and long stillness of winter had passed. Everywhere the earth rejoiced in the warmth of new life.

Wil Covington awoke to the song of the bobwhite. His eyes opened but his body refused to stir. At once he became aware of the soft womanly presence nestled at his side. Emily was still asleep. She lay on her side, her head resting on her husband's upper arm, her own arm lying across his chest. Her long honey blond hair, streaked now by more than a little gray, was in a single braid, part of which covered Wil's hand. He moved slightly and took the braid in his hand all the while relishing the delightful scent of her hair. She sighed and snuggled closer causing him to smile as his eyes gazed out through the window at the surrounding hills. Waking up next to Emily filled him with contentment as it had every morning for the last nineteen years. Wil Covington was a happy man.

As he breathed in the warm spring air he began to reflect over the life he and Emily shared. He wasn't entirely sure of why his mind was drifting back in time. Perhaps it had something to do with the reunion he and Levi were anticipating later in the month. All the surviving veterans of the Army of North Virginia had been notified, at least all those who could still be found. Soon they would be gathering on the North Anna River over in Hanover County. The Twentieth anniversary of the Battle of Ox Ford was approaching and a massive celebration was in the works. Rightfully so, since Ox Ford proved to be the turning point of the War. Here it was that Lee destroyed roughly half of the Army of the Potomac, a victory which ultimately allowed Lee to trap Grant against the Rappahannock River and force his surrender. Having removed Lincoln's best army from the playing board, Lee moved swiftly to capture the city of Washington and its most important resident. All of this led to the negotiated peace which saw the abolition of slavery in the South and the recognition of an independent Confederacy. There was talk of creating a national park along the North Anna, a suggestion which Wil found entirely appropriate. He remembered the tenth year anniversary reunion which had been held back in 1874. Tens of thousands of Lee's veterans were present and no few of the Federal troops who had been captured there as well. Wil wondered if as many people would make it the second time around.

As for Robert E. Lee, he would only be present in spirit and in the memories of the soldiers who had so fondly dubbed him, "Marse Robert." In 1866 he had bowed to popular demand and made himself available for the presidency. The result was a foregone conclusion and the General succeeded Jefferson Davis as the second president of the Confederate States of America. Alexander Stephens, who had already served once as vice-present found himself in the same role for the second time. As president, Lee worked tirelessly to insure a rapid and equitable reconstruction of the war-ravaged regions of the Confederacy. He also made it a priority to facilitate a peaceful transition for the black population from slavery to freedom and to maintain a climate wherein relations between the races would continue to be peaceful and mutually beneficial. Sad to say, however, the health of this indomitable man did not hold up for long. In 1870 with two years remaining in his term of office, Lee's heart failed him. Surrounded by the people who loved him the most the General in his final moments seemed to be recollecting his years of campaigning with the Army of Northern Virginia. His last words were, "Strike the tent," and with those words his spirit passed to the next world. Southerners of all races mourned this loss but didn't lose their faith in the future their beloved president had been working to create.

By this time, Wil was hopelessly awake and decided it was time to get out of bed. "Darlin'," he said softly.

"Hmm?" came an even softer reply.

"I think I'm gonna go ahead and get up."

"Okay," she said as she rolled over and snuggled up to one of the fluffy down pillows.

Wil got out of bed, shed his night clothes, pulled on his overalls and a blue checkered flannel shirt. He reached for his cane and with the additional support it provided he made his way to the broad windowsill and sat down to enjoy the warmth of the early morning sun. The two decades which had passed since the war's end had been kind to the Confederacy and to the Covingtons, with one reservation: Wil's injured hip, the one which had been shattered by a Federal bullet at South Mountain. With the passage of time the bone had deteriorated to the point where he required the assistance of a cane to walk - especially over long distances. Wil had no choice but to develop a high pain threshold particularly during the cold wet days of winter. Many a hot brick had been applied to that hip during the winter months, another reason Wil so enjoyed the advent of warm weather.

"Twenty years," he mused as he gazed out at the beautiful hills and mountains which surrounded their farm.

So much had changed. The war damage had long since been repaired. Within three years of the war's end all of the outbuildings had been rebuilt as well as the fences. Livestock was plentiful again and each successive harvest seemed more bountiful than the last. A program started during the Davis administration produced a dual system of public schools in which white children and black children received at least a reasonable education. The resulting decrease in illiteracy on the part of both races was significant and a huge step toward realizing the dreams of Thomas Jefferson had been taken.

Moreover, the Confederacy itself was on the verge of growing. The people in the Indian territory, or Oklahoma territory as it was called, had taken a vote and had chosen to affiliate themselves with the Confederate States, a choice which the United States did not challenge. Emboldened by this development two other territories, Arizona and New Mexico, made the same choice. Although relations between the United States and the

Confederate States remained somewhat strained, outright hostility was in the past and the economic relationship between the two countries was growing year by year.

Wil let his eyes wander over the grounds closest to the house. They came to rest on three tombstones in the family cemetery. His mother's was the oldest and the passage of time had taken its toll on the inscription which had been engraved over forty years ago. Next to this one stood that of his father, Tom Covington, who had fallen victim to pneumonia in 1869. A much smaller stone had been placed adjacent to the elder Covington's. It marked the grave of Wil's fourth child, a little boy whom they named Albert. As soon as he was born they knew at once he lacked the vitality to live and their suspicions were confirmed within three days. With a silent prayer for the souls of his parents and little Albert, Wil turned his eyes away and continued scanning the grounds till he spied the wooden swing suspended from a heavy branch of a billowing oak tree some twenty yards from the barn. Here he paused to reflect.

This reflection in turn brought a smile to his face. He could picture every one of his five surviving children using that swing. This might he trivial to some, a child's toy, a play thing for a toddler to pass idle time. Not so in Wil's mind. His father had hung that swing back in 1867, two years before his death. "This is for my grandchildren," he had instructed Wil, "every one of 'em." The old man had used a heavy five inch plank for the swing itself and thick steel bolts to secure the ropes. As for the ropes themselves, it was his wish that they last forever, or at least through the childhood of each of his grandchildren. He had chosen the finest hemp available and wove the strands by hand into ropes every bit as thick as a man's forearm. That swing was more than a mere distraction for a restless child. It was a testament to a man's love for his grandchildren, even those who had yet to be born. It was a link between two generations of Covingtons and as such it was precious to Wil and Emily.

The smile on Wil's face seems to broaden as he thought of his children. "What a crew!" he thought. His oldest was a girl, Sarah Ann, named for Levi Henry's mother. She was born back in '67. In fact it was her birth which inspired her grandfather to put the aforementioned swing together. Now seventeen, she was the apple of her father's eye, as well as a much sought after Belle among the young men in the area.

Next was David, a young lad of fifteen. Standing close to six feet in height he was already taller than his father but he was skinny as a rail. His friends at the school liked to call him "Beanpole," but this didn't bother him. He knew he'd fill out in time.

Edward, at thirteen, was the third of the five. Typical of his age group he was as rambunctious as the day was long. The school marm was often heard blaming "that Eddie Covington" for the many gray hairs on her head. In truth, she may have been at least partially correct.

Victor has just turned twelve and was the third boy of the lot. The ever present adolescent gleam in his bright blue eyes suggested his parents would have their hands full as he entered his teens.

Five years passed before the arrival of his last child. It was during this long interval that Albert had been born and passed away. The youngest of Wil and Emily's five children was their second daughter, Danielle, who, at seven years of age, showed the promise of being every bit as lovely as her older sister.

Wil was thinking how blessed he and Emily had been over the years when suddenly the delicious aroma of bacon drifted past his nostrils. Sarah was up early and was already busy in the kitchen. "God's been good to us," he thought as he rose from the sill and started toward the bedroom door, "good to us all." Looking back on his life with Emily he could think of only one thing which inspired any sense of regret. His youthful desire to attend college had never been realized. Following the war there was simply too much rebuilding to be done and as the farm became operable again the demands on his time and person would simply not allow the luxury of being able to leave for several years. Add to this the responsibility which came with wife and children and one can readily understand how the goal of a higher education receded further with each passing year. Wil left the room closing the door behind him. The sound of his cane on the hardwood floor could be heard throughout the house as he moved toward the stairway.

"Good mornin', Father," greeted Sarah as Wil entered the kitchen.

"Good mornin'," he returned. "Bacon smells mighty good."

"Thank you," she smiled. "It's almost ready, coffee too."

"You're my girl!" chuckled Wil as he eased himself into a chair at the table.

"Is mother coming?"

"In a little while. She's sleepin' in late this mornin'. Where's everyone else?"

"I sent David out to chop firewood. Eddie and Victor are still asleep." She paused to crack two eggs into a mixing bowl, "so's Danielle."

"What are you puttin' together there?"

~ 63 ~

GRAY VISIONS

"Grannie Sarah taught me a new way to mix up batter for hot cakes. I thought I'd try it out on y'all this mornin'."

"Gonna experiment on us, eh?" chided Wil.

"Well...maybe you could say that. Anyway you're not takin' too much of a chance. Grannie Sarah says I've turned into a right good cook!"

"And you have!" agreed Wil. "Coffee smells like it's about ready, would you pour your old man a cup?"

"My pleasure, suh," she curtsied and reached toward the cabinet for a cup and saucer.

* * * * * * * * *

At the Henry house that same morning a similar scene was playing out. Naomi was in the kitchen scrambling a mess of eggs to go along with the two pounds of bacon which had already been fried. Sarah Henry, known to her seven grandchildren as "Grannie," and to the five Covington children as "Grannie Sarah," was seated at the table sipping a cup of tea - a special blend of tea which she had created herself many years ago. She was one of the oldest women in that region of the Shenandoah Valley, but still quite spry for someone of her age. Her mind was still as sharp as ever, which she always attributed to the special tea she sipped morning and night. With her snow white hair pulled tight behind her head and a shawl draped over her frail shoulders she sat upright and allowed her eyes to drink in the beauty of the surrounding hills blossoming with the splendor of spring.

Across from his aged mother sat Levi Henry. There was quite a bit of gray scattered across his head giving his hair the appearance of a mixture of salt and pepper. The day before had been a busy one. He, Wil, and all of their sons had worked till nearly dark planting ten acres of corn where the two farms joined. As a result he never had time to look through the mail before collapsing exhausted into bed. As he chewed on a strip of bacon he looked through the stack of letters and bills which had piled up in the kitchen.

"Levi," said Naomi.

Her husband turned to face her.

"That pitchfork's broken again. Ain't no fixin' it this time. We're gonna need a new one."

"I'll make a trip into Waynesboro monday mornin'." he pledged. "Either that or I'll send Jefferson." he added, referring to the oldest of his seven children, a young man who had just past his eighteenth birthday.

"See that you do," she feigned a scolding tone as she stirred the eggs in the skillet. "Don't want no problems when you two go runnin' off to Hanover County."

"Now, Angel," he smiled, using his favorite nickname for his bride of nineteen years, "we'll only be gone for a few days at most."

"Don't you Angel me!" she continued to feign irritation. "You got no call to be runnin' off to no reunion when there's work to be done around here!"

"Crops are planted, love. Mother nature'll take care of the rest. Besides, it's just me and Jefferson goin'. Ely and little Moses will be home, and they're both old enough to take care of things around here. We'll be back befo' you know it."

She pulled the skillet from the fire and wiped her hands on her apron. Stepping softly she came up behind Levi and put her arms around him.

"I know it's important to you, darlin'." she said in a

soothing tone. "I was just funnin' ya."

He reached up with one hand to caress her cheek. "I knew it all along," he declared, then braced himself for the jab in the ribs he knew would follow.

They were interrupted by the arrival in the kitchen of two young girls, Mary Ann, aged nine, who went by the nickname of May, and Elizabeth, a precocious six year old everyone called "Sparkie."

"Breakfast ready?" asked the older of the two.

"Sure is!" declared Naomi, "You just sit your little behinds down at the table and behave yourselves, and be careful you don't spill Grannie's tea, you hear?"

"Yes, Mama."

Twelve year old Robert was next to arrive. He walked slowly into the kitchen still rubbing the sleep from his eyes.

"G'mornin', Bobbie," smiled Naomi.

"Mornin' Mama."

"How you doin', son?" asked Levi.

"Sleepy."

"You got homework from school?"

"Pa, it's Saturday mornin'".

"Don't make no never mind. You got homework?"

"Some."

"Eat your breakfast first, then get it done 'fore you start your chores."

"Yessuh," Robert reached his chair and sat down wearily.

"Where's Alicia?" wondered Levi, returning to his sixteen year old daughter.

"She's still in bed," said Robert.

"Let her sleep awhile longer," Sarah spoke for the first time with a voice not the least bit indicative of her advanced years.

"She's got work to do," objected Levi.

"Let the girl sleep," insisted Sarah. "Lord, son, it's Saturday!"

"Listen to your Mama," instructed Naomi as she moved past Levi with a plate of scrambled eggs, pausing to playfully box her husband's ear before serving breakfast to her children.

"I suppose Ely and Moses are sleepin' in as well," huffed Levi.

"They worked hard yesterday, Levi," declared Sarah. "They deserve a little rest. Don't you begrudge it to 'em."

Levi sat back and looked over at his mother with a broad grin on his face. "Papa would be proud," he observed. "After all those years you're still gettin' the final word in this house."

"The way it oughta be," nodded Sarah as she lifted her teacup to her lips.

"No argument from me," chuckled Levi. "I know better," He turned his attention back to the mail as he picked up a forkful of scrambled eggs. "Well lookee here!" he announced moments later.

"What's that?" Naomi had seated herself opposite her husband and was munching on a freshly baked cinnamon bun still warm from the oven.

"Letter from South Carolina! Bet you can't guess who it came from!"

"That's a bet I'll take," smiled Naomi. "You don't know but two people down there. It's either Ivory or that fellow Miles. I'll guess Ivory."

"You nailed it," returned Levi. "Ivory Lee Davis to be exact." He tore open the envelope and carefully removed the letter it contained. He unfolded it shook his head and laughed. "Look at this handwritin'! Any of the kids could write better

~ 67 ~

than this! I'll bet Sparkie could do better!"

"Levi," Sarah sent a cold stare in the direction of her only child. "You should be ashamed of yourself fo laughin' like that. Ivory was a slave most of his life! No one ever taught him to read or write! He didn't learn till well after the war!"

"I'm sorry, Mama," there was genuine contrition in Levi's voice. "It just looks awful funny, that's all."

"What's he say?" asked Naomi.

"Says he's comin' up for the reunion at Ox Ford, him and Miles Turner both. They may not make it on the first day, but he says to look for 'em on the second."

"That's wonderful!" exclaimed Naomi. "You've been talkin' 'bout those two for the last twenty years!"

"So I have," mused Levi. "It's been a long time. Ivory must be close to seventy by now. I wonder what those two look like." Quickly he finished his breakfast then rose to leave.

"Where you goin'?"

"Got to show this to Wil. Can you believe it. We're gonna see Ivory! Jefferson'll get to meet him. Never thought I'd see the day! Twenty years! Listen when Eddie and little Mo' get up tell 'em to draw water from the well and sprinkle those potatoes and onions we planted last week. Okay?"

"I'll take care of it," nodded Naomi.

"Send Jefferson out to the barn. All of our tack needs to be cleaned and oiled. There's one bridle out there that needs a new bit."

"Go on ahead, Levi," she gestured with a shooing motion "we'll take care of things here."

*　　*　　*　　*　　*　　*　　*　　*　　*

THE REUNION

The train's whistle competed with the loud squeaking of its brakes as it pulled slowly to a stop amid clouds of billowing steam at the depot in Hanover Junction. Jefferson Henry and David Covington had their faces pressed against the window pane as the train drew to a halt. Their eyes were wide open in fascination as they took in every detail of the depot, its surroundings and the thousands of middle aged men who milled about. They were the veterans of the Army of Northern Virginia, "Lee's Miserables," as they had laughingly styled themselves so many years ago. Most were dressed in their old uniforms or bits and pieces thereof. Some even carried the Enfields they had wielded so effectively over these same hills back in '64'

"I've never seen anythin' like this in my life," said David in a voice of sheer wonder.

"Ain't seen nothin' yet," returned his father with a smile. "Wait'll we get to the battlefield. Your eyes are gonna pop."

With their bags in hand the four of them detrained with the other passengers and called for one of the dozens of carriages waiting to transport the many veterans to the North Anna. The driver of the carriage they chose charged twenty-five cents a head to ferry the four of them up to Ox Ford. They rode in a four-seat open carriage which allowed them to enjoy the warm air of late May and the bright colors of spring which decorated the hillsides. After a trip of some forty minutes they arrived at a staging area just south of the battlefield itself. Both Jefferson and David gasped in surprise and delight as they surveyed the scene before them.

A large field of several hundred acres normally used as pasture for cattle had been made available by its owner for the reunion. Here the visitors from the Valley found a city of white canvas tents stretching as far as the eye could see. On its perimeter sat two rows of vendors catering to the veterans every need or whim. It was truly a sight to behold, not only for the youngsters but the old-timers as well.

"Looks like the whole army showed up," noted Levi.

"Does at that," agreed Wil. "I wonder if all these guys were with us at this battle."

"Probably not," mused Levi, "but this is supposed to be the biggest reunion since the war. I'll bet there's a bunch of people from the Army of Tennessee out there. What do you think?"

"Most likely. One thing for sure, we didn't have accommodations like this twenty years ago."

"You got that right," chuckled Levi, "reckon that's a sign of how far we've come, eh?"

"Amazin' what a few years of peace will do," nodded Wil.

They reported to the Reunion headquarters where they checked in and were assigned a tent. With a map of the facility in hand they shouldered their bags and started walking. Before long they were settled in and socializing with old acquaintances. The organizers of this affair had done an admirable job in that they assigned the veterans of each regiment to the same cluster of tents and the maps they provided depicted the position of each unit within the reunion camp. There were lots of familiar faces to be found, though in truth twenty years had taken their toll on those same faces. The veterans weren't the only ones there by any means. Some of the men brought their wives. Many, like Wil and Levi, brought their sons to see the place where Lee sprang the trap which turned the tide of history.

Thus the first day of the gathering could best be described as one huge party. Tears and laughter abounded as old acquaintances were renewed and new friendships were forged among the younger generation. The older men were quick to notice the most obvious difference between the reunion camp and the deployment which took place back in '64. In a word it was food. In those desperate days in the spring of 1864 food was scarce to say the least. It was a miracle any man survived at all with the pitiful rations they were allotted back then.

Not so today. The Reunion camp was alive with aromas from scores of cook fires and sutter's grills. It was almost impossible to walk through the camp without salivating. There was no shortage of beef. Quite to the contrary, it seemed to be cooking over every fire, available to anybody who could afford it. Thousands of chickens were roasting over these same fires as well, along with pork, rabbit, venison and at least one selection of rattlesnake meat. Suffice it to say no one was allowed to go hungry as the day passed.

Early in the afternoon the Covingtons and Henrys left their camp and hired a carriage to tour the main points of interest along the North Anna. Their first stop found them standing on the front porch of Ellington, a lovely home just south of the river itself. The family who owned the home had graciously allowed veterans to come and visit the porch. Unfortunately, they were unaware of how many men would take advantage of their hospitality. Wil counted no fewer than seven carriages parked in front of the house when they arrived. Dozens of middle-aged veterans and no few of their children were crowded on and around the front porch. Most of them were gawking at the Union artillery shell which still protruded from the door frame. The story behind this shell fragment made Ellington a must see attraction of this twentieth anniversary gathering.

A quick review of the home's not so distant past is sufficient to explain why this was the case. As the Army of the Potomac took up positions on the north bank of the North

GRAY VISIONS

Anna back in May of 1864, R.E. Lee was conducting a personal reconnaissance of his own positions on the southern side of the river. The owner of Ellington, who did not live long enough to take part in the festivities of 1884, invited General Lee to partake in refreshment on the front porch of the home. While Lee was sipping buttermilk and eating a piece of bread, Union gunners on the far side of the river spotted his gray uniform and opened fire. The shell slammed into the door frame but did not explode, leaving it imbedded there for posterity. Consistent with his steel-like demeanor under fire, Lee did not react at all except to glance casually at the still-smoldering projectile after finishing his buttermilk.

For awhile the crowd on the porch threatened to grow beyond anyone's ability to control it and the family who resided within those walls began to fear for the security of their home as souvenir hunters scoured every inch of the grounds and began casting covetous eyes toward the house itself. Fortunately most of those present weren't looking for souvenirs and harbored no malicious intention toward the house or its contents. Most were content to merely stand on the same spot where their hallowed commander had once stood. Many was the hand which touched the imbedded shell but not one attempted to remove it. It seemed like every man there wanted to hear the story told by one of the family members. Why did the crowd keep growing? No one wanted to leave. It was as if these veterans were able to establish a link with their lost General by lingering on or near the porch. In the hearts and minds of these aging soldiers this ground had become sacred.

Luckily for those who still resided at Ellington the house came through the day unscathed. This proved to be a marked difference when compared to the vandalism sustained

twenty years beforehand. Lee had departed the porch quickly
in order to spare the house any more attention from the gunners across the river. This attempt on his part was only partially successful. The Union gunners shifted their attention
elsewhere but the infantry which followed were quick to take
their frustrations out on the house and its contents. Fox, the
owner of Ellington, was a pharmacist by trade and his home
was also his laboratory, workshop and storage facility. By the
time Grant's men were finished with his belongings he had
precious little he could still call his own. It had all been
broken or stolen. This was one experience which was not
repeated in the reunion of 1884.

For their next stop, the Henrys and Covingtons journeyed
by carriage to the opposite side of the battlefield to walk the
grounds near Jericho Mill where A.P. Hill had launched a half-
hearted attempt to push the Federal troops back into the river. It
was this action which opened the fighting on the North Anna and
the failure by Hill resulted in a rare show of temper on the part of
Robert E. Lee. Enroute the topic of conversation centered on the
illness which befell General Lee not long after he departed from the
porch of Ellington. "I think it was the buttermilk," insisted Levi's
son, Jefferson, "There was somethin' in that milk that made the
General sick."

"May well have been," nodded Wil with a reflective smile.
"Out in the trenches rumors were flyin'. Nobody knew for sure
why the General was keepin' to his tent. We figured somethin' was
wrong but we had other things to worry about at the time."

"Yankees to be exact," said Levi.

"Did they attack you?" asked David.

"Nope," replied Wil. "Me and Levi was dug in back that
way," he gestured in the direction from which they had come,

"Hancock's corps of Federals were entrenched opposite us.
They had tried us before on the last day of fighting at
Spotsylvania and we punished 'em right proper. We fully
expected them to come at us again here on the North Anna and
holding our line was the foremost thing on our minds. We
didn't know nothin' 'bout Marse Robert's health. We heard
the rumors of course, but our officers would neither confirm
nor deny them. To be honest with you, I don't think they
really knew either."

"Can we go back there?" asked Jefferson, "and see where
y'all were dug in?"

"Sure," said Levi, "We'll head that way after we see Jericho
Mill."

Not long after that they were heading downriver again. This
time the topic of their conversation was A.P. Hill's aborted attempt
to throw the Federals back after they had crossed the North Anna.
The two boys found themselves agreeing with General Lee that Hill
was at fault for deploying his forces piecemeal rather than attacking
with all his strength as the legendary Stonewall would have done.
Their fathers both pleaded Hill's case noting that he had also been
quite ill and had still not entirely recovered as the fighting on the
North Anna got underway. They also maintained that the failure at
Jericho Mill actually worked out for the best because it was this
action which led General Lee to construct his lines like one might
close an umbrella, thus creating the inverted V anchored at Ox
Ford, a tactical move which ultimately proved disastrous to the
Army of the Potomac.

The four of them spent more than two hours along the
trench line which had been home to General Ewell's corps during
the deployment and the battle which followed. Here they
encountered hundreds of their former comrades and their

families. Together they browsed in and around the trenches and shared memories of these three fateful days in May of 1864. The trenches themselves were remarkably preserved. One man remarked that it seemed as though the veterans had only left yesterday because so little had changed. In many places the headlogs were still in position atop the trenches Mother Nature herself accounted for the changes which were taking place through most of the line. Saplings had spouted in many of the trenches and had been growing unperturbed for years.

"We were right here," declared Levi as he moved along the base of the trench.

"Are you sure?" asked Wil, "I thought we were dug in another twenty yards down the line."

"Nope, right here," insisted Levi. "I remember this view. This is where we were. This is kind of a weird feelin, Wil, don't you think? We're standin' exactly where we were twenty years ago. Seems eerie don't it?"

"Yeah, it does," agreed Wil. He moved to the front wall of the trench and dropped to one knee as he gazed out over the open field which was rapidly filling with the growth of new timber. Turning to his left he pointed at the ground perhaps five feet away. "Fella by the name of Thomson was right there when Hancock charged us," he said. "We didn't sustain too many casualties from that assault but he was one of them. Hell of a lucky shot I'd say. The bullet went through these few inches of space between the dirt and the head log. Hit Thomson in the forehead right between the eyes. He was dead before he knew what hit 'im".

"I remember that," nodded Levi. "He was older than us by a good ten years. Had a wife and a couple of kids I think."

All of them fell silent at that point, content to listen to

the sounds of spring mixing with the many conversations going on all around them.

"David," Wil addressed himself to his son several moments later, "in your school do they tell you how we dug these trenches?"

"How you dug 'em?" A perplexed expression appeared on the young boy's face. "No, suh, they don't say much about that. No one's ever gone into that much detail," he glanced over at Jefferson. "How about your school?" he asked.

"Nope," Jefferson shook his head. "Reckon y'all used shovels and picks and such."

"Not hardly!" laughed Levi. "Oh there was some that had shovels but not too many."

"How'd you do it then?" asked David.

"On our hands and knees," replied his father, "Using anything available, bayonets, cups, saucers, spoons and forks, whatever we could scrape dirt with."

"Are you serious?" Jefferson found it hard to believe.

"Yep. And we did it fast."

David climbed out of the trench and began to survey the line. What he saw was that much more impressive considering what he had just heard. As far as he could see in both directions lay a complex system of trenches, traverses designed to contain any breech of the line, gun pits, pits for medical personnel and pits for regimental commanders. "You did all this with your mess kits?" he asked.

"And our bayonets," came the reply from Levi.

"This is amazing."

"I think that's what the Yanks thought when they first laid eyes on it." agreed Wil.

"Lookee here!" called Jefferson who had been scraping

his boot along the floor of the trench.

"What is it?" David jumped back in.

Jefferson bent low and scraped some more earth away. "Looks like a bullet!" he exclaimed. He picked it up and examined it closely. "Do you think it's one of yours?" he asked glancing at Levi.

"Not likely," replied the older black man. "It probably came from the other side."

"I wonder what else is buried here," mused David as he began to dig with the heel of his boot. Before long a number of relics began to turn up. Used percussion caps were the most numerous items. Bullets were plentiful. Here and there a belt buckle would turn up on a badly weathered piece of leather. It was Jefferson who turned up the piece which would be most prized of all.

"I got me a coat button!" he cried as he quickly began scaraping the dirt from it. I'll be darned," he smiled. "It's from the 5th Virginia."

"Really?" gasped David. "I'll trade three of these bullets for it."

"No way!" the black boy shook his head, "Keep your Yankee bullets! This one's all mine!"

"You see," said Levi, speaking to Wil, "I told you this is where we stood."

"You were right," grinned Wil.

"Again," added Levi as he gently jabbed an elbow into his best friend's ribs.

"No need to gloat," smiled the white man.

"Pa, you think this button was yours?" Jefferson looked over at his father.

"Don't know. I lost a few buttons through the course

of the war. I don't remember if I lost any here or not. Might have."

"Do you want it?"

"Nope. You dug it, it's yours."

The idea of digging along the floor of the trenches was quickly spreading until the booming voice of an elderly man brought it all to a halt. "Stop this!" he cried. "All of you! Have you no shame?" Instantly he had everyone's attention. Those who were kneeling in the dirt rose quickly to their feet as they brushed the dirt from their trousers and wiped their hands on the seats of their pants. Here and there the sounds of relics finding their way back to the earth could be heard. "This is sacred ground!" The old man's voice had risen to a shout and his face had turned beet red, so vivid was his anger. "Here it was we turned the tide!" he continued, "On this ground we won our freedom! Would you defile this place like a pack of scavengers? Twenty years those trenches have lain undisturbed! Do you not feel a responsibility to those unborn? Would you deny future generations a portion of their heritage? If you continue this behavior like a pack of raven-ous dogs that's exactly what you'll accomplish! You'll de-stroy these trenches along with their history. I say to you again, stop all of this! Don't pull another relic from the ground! These are the earth-works you yourselves built twenty years ago! They survived the battle, did they not? They've survived all that the weather could throw at them through two decades! Will they survive this reunion?" Slowly his gaze shifted from left to right, meeting the eyes of each individual along the way. Then without another word he turned and walked away.

"Who was he?" whispered David.

"Don't know," replied his father, "I think he was an officer,

~ 78 ~

a colonel maybe. I don't think I ever knew his name.

"He's sure mad," observed Jefferson.

"Makes me feel like a school boy caught with my hand in the cookie jar," nodded Wil.

"Yeah, but I think he's got a point," said Levi, "This place deserves to be preserved for the future. We ought to leave it be."

"Agreed."

"I'm keepin' the button," insisted Jefferson.

"That's fine," said Levi, "but no more. Let's move on."

Both boys quickly left the trench followed by Levi who turned to see Wil dropping something into one of the shallow holes they'd dug on the floor of the trench. With his boot he pushed loose dirt over the hole and stamped it down. With the support of his cane Wil then started out of the trench but found the effort more taxing than he anticipated. Fortunately Levi was there waiting with an arm extended to help his friend as he had done so many times over the years.

"What did you just bury?" asked Levi after Wil was safely out of the trench.

"You might say I'm playin' a practical joke on all those unborn generations that old colonel spoke of."

"What do you mean?"

"Human nature is human nature. People will come here long after we're gone and they'll dig for stuff same as us."

"And what exactly did Wil Covington leave for them to find?"

"Not much," he smiled in reply, "Just a penny."

"How's that gonna be a joke?"

"It's dated 1880."

"Ah, nodded Levi. "Too bad we won't be around to see their faces, eh?"

"Fur sure,"

The four of them started walking up the trench line toward its apex at Ox Ford. Their going was necessarily slow as Wil was simply not able to move with any speed worth noting. They hadn't gone far when Levi stopped and pointed, "That could only be one person," he declared.

Wil stopped and glanced in the direction Levi was pointing. "Yep," he nodded. "Ox. It's gotta be him."

"You think Reilly's with him?"

"I'll bet he is. C'mon, let's find out."

Moments later they reached the big man known as Ox and were delighted to find some of the others from the famed Stonewall Brigade. Jonas Willem was among them as was Whitt Simmons. Sure enough, there too stood Seth Reilly. Every hair on his head had gone to gray along with his beard. The scar from a Union officer's saber at Second Manassas had faded somewhat with the passage of twenty-two years but was still the most prominent feature on his face.

"Lieutenant Reilly!" called Wil as they approached.

Reilly glanced up at Covington and recognized him at once. "Wil," he grinned, "Levi! I was hoping the two of you would make this one!" He stepped forward to meet them, shaking each man's hand in turn. "What have we here?" He asked as his eyes appraised the two boys who trailed their fathers.

"My oldest son," Wil was first to reply. "Not my oldest child mind you, but my oldest son. David, this is Lieutenant Seth Reilly. We always called him Professor."

"How do you do, suh?" David stepped up and shook hands with Reilly.

"I'm doing fine thanks," came the reply. "I'll have to

say you remind me a lot of your father when I first met him. Of course that was a long time ago." He shifted his attention to Jefferson. "And who might you be?"

"My oldest," proclaimed Levi.

"Name's Jefferson Henry." said the younger black man as he stood forward and offered his hand.

"My pleasure," nodded Reilly as he took that hand and shook it.

A half-hour was quick to pass as this little group of veterans shared memories and swapped yarns among themselves. It was Reilly who brought up a subject Wil knew was bound to surface. Addressing himself to David he said, "Your father saved my life, did you know that?"

"Yessuh, I've heard the story."

"Happened at Second Manassas," continued Reilly. "The Yankee who did this," he laid a finger along the long purplish scar, "Was about to finish me off. Your old man stopped him."

David glanced over at his father with eyes which glowed with pride.

"Which I would not have been able to do had not Levi saved my life only moments before you went down," interposed Wil.

"Yep," Jefferson said with satisfaction and thrust his chest out a little further as he stared at his father with adoring eyes.

The conversation continued to bounce from one topic to the next until Reilly brought up a subject which had been on the back of his mind since the Covingtons and Henrys had joined their little group. "Wil, do you remember the day we all said our good-byes outside of Culpeper?"

"Sure do, like it was yesterday."

"I recall you're saying something about how you wanted to

attend college, and whether or not I'd have wanted to see you come to William and Mary as a student."

"I remember."

"After I resumed teaching at the college I used to check the admissions office each year to see if you were coming our way. Your name never appeared."

"I know."

"Did you attend a different college?"

"Nope," sighed Wil. "I never did. It wasn't a lack of desire on my part. I can assure you of that. In fact me and Levi made a deal with each other a couple of weeks after that day in Culpeper. He was gonna help work my farm so I could head off to school and I promised to do the same for him. I guess we were both kind of naive in those days. Neither of us were takin' into consideration the amount of work waitin' for us at home."

"I know exactly what you mean," said Ox with a sympathetic nod as he opened a bar of chocolate he'd just pulled from a pocket.

"Me too," agreed Whitt Simmons, "My place was a mess."

"That's what we found when we got back to the Valley," said Levi. "Both our farms were in ruins. The houses were still standin' but that was about all."

"My father's health was failin'," continued Wil, "and that left all the rebuildin' to me. Then I married Emily - smartest thing I ever did, mind you, and the kids started to come and...well, I think you get the picture. The opportunity to go to school just never materialized."

"I understand," said Reilly with a nod.

"On the brighter side," noted Wil, "Levi and I are both figurin' our kids will have the opportunity we never had. So instead of teachin' me, maybe you'll get David here."

"That would be fine," smiled Reilly who then turned to Jefferson. "There are several good colleges starting up for negroes. Will you attend one?"

"I hope to," he replied, "and I will if the Lord so wills it."

The conversation drifted subsequently back to those three days in May, twenty years past. Ox and Whitt teased Reilly about the amount of effort on his part required to persuade Cody Wilder to start digging the trench. "That was one of your longer-winded moments," chuckled Ox.

"True," admitted Reilly with a sheepish smile, "He was one head-strong kid, I'll sure give him that much. He sure didn't cotton much to the idea of digging."

"And he was one of the lucky ones," laughed Ox, "The boy had a shovel to use. All I had was my bayonet and a coffee mug."

"Cody was somethin' to behold," mused Whitt with a nod.

They fell silent for a moment, each of them focusing on his own respective memories of Cody Wilder, the young boy who had joined their ranks during the battle of Spotsylvania and served with distinction until his tragic death as he carried the battle flag over the last Federal barricade in the battle to capture Washington, D.C.

Sensing this as a good moment to change the subject Jefferson spoke up, "Were any of you here when the Yankees charged this line?"

"None of us," replied Reilly. "We were part of the assault force Marse Robert put together to make the charge against the opposite end of the Union position. I think your father and Wil were still here when Hancock charged. Am I right?" he asked as he glanced at Levi.

GRAY VISIONS

"Yep," nodded the black man. "We received that charge. Grant was desperate by then. He knew he had to act fast and whatever he did had to stop or retard the attack on his right, otherwise the game was up. He knew it, so did we. I think most everybody knew what was shapin' up. Grant figured that Lee must've stripped this line of its defenders in order to mount the charge takin' place on the opposite side over there. He was wrong. Marse Robert pulled ten thousand men off the lines to make that charge, but that left plenty to hold this position. Lookin' back on it now I remember feelin' sorry for 'em. They didn't have a prayer of knockin' us out of these trenches and I'll bet every one of 'em knew it before he took his first step."

"He's right," said Wil with a nod. "They tried to soften us up with a pretty intense barrage of artillery but we were dug in pretty tight. The effects of their guns were negligible at best. I remember thinkin' the same thing as Levi. Seems like Grant was wastin' a lot of good lives when he gave Hancock the order to make that charge. 'Course at the time I guess his decision was fine with me. We were lookin' to decimate the Army of the Potomac. By the time the last shot was fired we had done just that. I remember walkin' out there between the lines after Hancock pulled back across the river. Their attack on our line only lasted ten or fifteen minutes before we broke it up. We tore 'em up right proper ... artillery mostly, but enfields took their toll, you can believe that. A lot of the dead Yankees out there had pieces of cloth or paper pinned to their backs. They had written their names, units, and the fact that they had been killed on May 25, 1864 at the North Anna. Weird how so many of 'em knew they were gonna die."

Again there were several moments of silence as each of

those present contemplated the magnitude of what had taken place on those grounds two decades past. It was Jefferson who broke this silence addressing himself toward Reilly he asked, "What were y'all doin' while they were holdin' the Yankees off on this side?"

"Us?" Reilly appeared startled for just an instant as though he had been deep in thought when the question arrived at his ears. "Those of us who were left from the Stonewall Brigade, and there wasn't but a handful of us, got orders to report to a position midway between our two trench lines. All in all there was maybe ten thousand of us. General Gordon was in command."

"We learned that in our history classes," interrupted David.

"Did you now?" Reilly arched one of his trick gray eyebrows in David's direction.

"Yessuh," stammered the boy a little nervously.

"Kinda makes you feel like a fossil don't it?" chuckled Whitt, who had served as a corporal with Reilly during the war.

"Kinda," mused Reilly, "Time does march on...not a whole lot anyone can do about that.

"Anyway we were out there with he assault force Marse Robert had put together. Night had fallen and most of us had bedded down on the ground content to see what the morrow might bring. While we were tryin' to sleep General Hampton had scouts out searchin' for a way to get around Grant's far right."

"We learned that too," offered Jefferson a little sheepishly.

"Don't seem like there's much you can tell these boys, Professor," chided Jonas.

"Does seem that way," sighed the lieutenant. "I'll tell you what, instead of me tellin' you things you seem to already know, why don't we go on over there? It's too late this evenin' we can head that way in the mornin'. We'll take y'all to our jump-off spot and we'll walk the course of the battle from there. We can show you things and tell you things your history teachers never dreamed of. You game?"

"You bet!" nodded David with an excited grin.

"Absolutely!" concurred Jefferson.

"What about your hip?" Reilly directed his concern toward Wil. "Can it stand a walk of that length?"

"Don't let me hold you back!" came the reply. "I'll manage just fine. Besides, I might learn a few things myself."

"Then it's settled" said Reilly, "We'll move out at first light."

"Yessuh!" affirmed David making no attempt to hide his excitement.

The sun was edging toward the western horizon as the group made their way back to the main reunion camp. Once again the veterans and their guests were treated to copious meals featuring a wide variety of meats, cheeses, breads, vegetables and desserts. Long into the night they indulged their appetites almost as if they were there to celebrate the surplus of food rather than reliving the Battle of Ox Ford. This was understandable. We must remember how little was available for these same men to eat when they were facing the Federal juggernaut back in '64.

At first light the Covingtons and Henrys were dressed, out of their tent, and ready to travel.

They joined Seth Reilly and his men, whereupon they journeyed together in two carriages to the jump-off point where General John B. Gordon and his men launched themselves upon the unsuspecting defenders of Grant's far right flank. Since all of these veterans had aged considerably and Wil's hip definitely limited his mobility, they did not trace the actual route which Gordon had followed to get into position. To do so would have required a somewhat tortuous march well around the extreme flank of the Union position. They would have had to walk through thick brush some swampy ground, and then ford the little River. From there they would have been forced to hike along a narrow animal trail through a thickly grown copse of woods briars and vines. Wil Covington would simply not have been able to do this, relying heavily as he did, on his cane for support.

Instead, they rode the carriages around the trench line and passed the little knoll where Lee had watched the battle unfold almost from the outset. They crossed the ground between the Confederate and Union lines and brought the carriages to a halt just shy of the wood line where Gordon's men had waited for the first appearance of the sun twenty years ago. They dismissed the carriage driver and made their way by foot into the woods.

It didn't take long to find the position where 10,000 Rebel soldiers hid from hostile eyes as they waited for the dawn. Jefferson and David couldn't resist the temptation to search for relics. They rearranged a considerable quantity of leaves and mulch but found little to justify their efforts.

"I think I was layin' down right about here," announced Ox as he stopped just shy of a large tulip poplar. "I remember this tree. I remember the Professor tellin' me to watch out for the kid."

"What kid?" asked Jefferson.

"Cody Wilder. You heard us talkin' 'bout him yesterday. He was just a wee thing. I don't think he was much more than twelve or thirteen. He joined up with us at Spotsylvania."

"What happened to him?"

Ox paused for a moment and a shadow seemed to come over the big man's face. "We lost him. It happened while we were takin' Washington. He carried the battle flag over the last Federal defenses inside the city. That's where they got him. I think he was one of the last to fall. It was sad...real sad. We were all kinda partial to that boy."

"Ahem," interrupted Reilly. The expression on his face had also changed noticeably while Ox was relaying the story of Cody's untimely death. "If memory serves me I think we're supposed to be explaining to these boys what happened out here twenty years ago."

"Sure, Professor," nodded Ox, "ain't nobody better'n you for that. Go on ahead."

Reilly glanced over at Whitt Simmons as though to seek the approval of his corporal.

"You're the one with a mind for details, Professor," said Whitt. "Go on and tell 'em."

"All right," Reilly ran one hand through his thinning gray hair then began tugging at the chin whiskers of his beard as his eyes shifted to study the remains of the Union earthworks across the way. "We waited here on our bellies till first light," he began. "I imagine Marse Robert must've been feeling pretty confident as dawn approached. He had managed to get 10,000 of us into the Federal rear without anybody finding out. I'm sure he knew what kind of damage we could do and how the day might turn out. Anyway, there wasn't any artillery barrage to precede our attack. Wasn't a need for one. Most of the Yankees were asleep and those who were awake had their eyes riveted on A.P. Hill's boys to their front. As soon as the first hints of the sun edged up over that horizon General Gordon rose to his feet. Our hearts were pounding and our throats were all going dry -- fear'll do that to a man -- as we watched for Gordon's signal. Then he took off his hat and that's all we had been waiting to see.

"What a sight it was!" He flashed an excited grin at the two boys whose attention he had firmly captured. "We rose to our feet like we were one organism. We poured out of these woods at a fast trot. Not a sound did we make. No Rebel yells. No guns fired. We knew we had the advantage of surprise and we wanted to hold it for every precious second. Our battle flags were flying high and seemed to glow with the first rays of the morning sun. Some of the boys charged that way," he pointed toward his right where a couple of Union regiments had been dug in close to the Little River, "The rest of us headed for the tail end of their main line. We covered maybe fifty or sixty yards before they spotted us. Someone shouted a warning and they began to scramble, but it was way too late. We picked it up to a dead run and the Rebels yells rang out loud and clear. With one good yell I think we scared half of 'em into surrendering!"

"Aw, now, Professor, don't you think you're stretchin' the point a tad?" chided Whitt with a chuckle.

"Well maybe a little," admitted Reilly. "The point is we were on 'em before they even realized what was happening. We captured two or three batteries of guns straight away and within a few seconds more that end of their line was ours. We took three or four thousand prisoners within a couple of minutes. Paid 'em back right proper for what they did to the Stonewall Brigade at the Mule Shoe. We were whooping it up and having ourselves a good ol' time but Gordon...Gordon was all business. He knew what was at stake, that we weren't there just to pinch off an isolated piece of Grant's army. Our job was to roll 'em off that line and drive 'em toward the North Anna. He wouldn't let us celebrate, nor would he allow us to disintegrate into a mob. He held us to the purpose Marse Robert intended." He paused and turned to Wil, "Are you ready for a little walk?"

"Let's do it," came the reply.

Leaving the woods they moved at Wil's pace until they reached the remains of the Union trenches. Twenty years had erased much of the evidence that a fierce battle had been fought there. As they gathered along the rim of the trench Reilly continued his explanation: "Gordon detached some of our boys to herd the prisoners off in that direction." He pointed toward the Confederate earthworks across the way. "The rest of us began to sweep through this trench. We moved fast and the Yankees had no time to organize into a proper line of defense. Under Gordon's direction we formed a line which ran at an oblique angle from this trench. That way we overlapped the Union position all along the way. It was a smart move on Gordon's part because it kept the Federals pinned more or less against their own trenches, thwarting any possibility of escape in the direction of Quarles Mill upriver. C'mon, we'll keep moving up the line."

As they walked Reilly continued pointing out where certain events had taken place, noting that the assault force actually grew in size as it progressed toward the river. A. P. Hill had accounted for this by sending his own troops across from their earthworks as each section of the Union line was emptied.

Upon reaching a slight depression in the ground some thirty yards behind the Union lines Ox paused and began to study his surroundings looking for familiar signs.

"Watchya doin'?" asked Jonas.

"I think it was here," replied Ox.

"What was here?"

Ox looked at Jonas then realized that the younger man had no idea what had happened there. He had been wounded at Spotsylvania and was still recovering in Richmond when the

Battle of Ox Ford took place. "You remember Cody don't ya?"

"Ox, don't be ridiculous," huffed Jonas, "Of course I remember him. I met him when I rejoined the unit in Fredericksburg just before we trapped Grant against the Rappahannock."

"That's right," nodded Ox. "Anyway, I think it was right in here someplace that I saved Cody's life. He took on a Yank closer to my size and came out on the losin' end real quick. That Federal was gettin' ready to finish the boy off when I stepped in with my bayonet. The Yankee fell dead on top of Cody, almost suffocated the kid with his weight before I rolled him off," he paused and let his eyes drift in a half-circle to study the surrounding terrain. "This was one hell of a battle," he offered.

"Sure was," agreed Reilly who was standing nearby. He turned and directed his next words toward Jefferson and David. "Have you boys been taught anything of Cannae."

"Yessuh, " replied Jefferson, "learned about it in my Western Civilization class."

"We've talked about it in my Latin class," added David.

"That's heartening," said Reilly with a smile, "Our schools are actually doing what they're supposed to be doing teaching the next generation. Maybe there's hope for us yet. Now what can the two of you tell me about Cannae? Talk to me while we're walking."

"Well," David spoke first, "It was one of the biggest battles of ancient times..."

"Antiquity," interrupted Reilly.

"Suh?"

"Antiquity...it's just another way of saying ancient times. Anyway, don't mind me; go on with what you were saying."

"It all happened in one afternoon," continued the boy. "The Romans had a huge army somethin' like 80,000 men I think. The Carthagenians were led by a man named Hannibal who had never lost to the Romans. My teacher said he was a military genius. His was a much smaller army but he was able to trap the Romans in a double envelopment. Very few of them escaped. It was the worse defeat the Romans ever suffered up to that point in their history."

"It was indeed," nodded Reilly who found himself quite impressed with the lad's knowledge. "A battle along the lines of Cannae was Marse Robert's goal from the moment he took command. It was here along the North Anna that he finally achieved something of that scale." He paused for several moments as they continued following the path of Gordon's momentous charge at Ox Ford. "Tell me something, he said at last unable to contain the teacher within himself, "What differences can you detect between Hannibal's victory at Cannae and Lee's victory here on the North Anna?"

"I can think of a few," volunteered Jefferson quickly.

"Go ahead," urged Reilly.

"There was no envelopment here," said the boy, "not like there was at Cannae."

"You're right," agreed Reilly.

"Hannibal was in Italy...enemy territory," added David, "whereas, General Lee was defending his home ground."

"True again," said the Professor.

"Grant wasn't destroyed here on the North Anna," continued David. "At least half of his army escaped and they were subsequently reinforced from the Bermuda Hundred by way of Port Royal. It wasn't until Lee trapped him against the Rappahannock that Grant finally chose to surrender."

"Also true, but would that chain of events have occurred if we hadn't devastated the Army of the Potomac here on the North Anna?"

"Nope," admitted the boy.

"There's one more difference between the two battles," said Jefferson "Hannibal's victory at Cannae was largely fruitless. Despite wipin' out that Roman army he was not able to even contemplate a move on Rome itself. It's like he won the battle but lost the war. Cannae allowed him to wander at will throughout Italy but he could never bring the war to an end on terms favorable to Carthage. Eventually the Romans landed an army in Northern Africa to threaten Carthage itself. Hannibal had no choice but to abandon Italy and confront the Romans on his home soil."

"Leading to which battle?" pressed Reilly.

"Zama," replied the black boy, "and the end of Carthage as a power capable of threatenin' Rome."

"Very good!" smiled Reilly, who found himself quite impressed with the quality of the education these boys were receiving.

"The same could not be said of Ox Ford," continued Jefferson. "Lee's victory over Grant here led directly to Grant's final surrender followed quickly by the capture of Washington City and the conclusion of the war on terms favorable to the Confederate States."

"You're a perceptive young man," said the Professor. "Both of you are."

"Thank you, suh," Jefferson beamed with pride.

By this time, they had reached a position on the field which marked another critical juncture of the battle of Ox Ford.

"This is where Sheridan hit us," explained Reilly. "We were quite fortunate in that Wade Hampton's cavalry had been tracing their approach and gave us ample warning. It was a desperate move on Grant's part. We were rolling up two Corps of his infantry, nearly half of his Army. Grant ordered Sheridan to attack us with all of his cavalry for the same reason he ordered Hancock to make that fruitless charge against your father's position on the opposite side of our position, which is to say he was trying to force General Lee to abort the attack which was shattering both Wright and Warren."

"We were lucky in a couple of ways," added Whitt. "Hampton's warning certainly helped, but Gordon's leadership was critical to our success against Sheridan. He kept extending our line at an angle from the Federal earthworks. As A. P. Hill's men continued to join with the attack Gordon was able to extend our line to a point where we completely overlapped the Federals. There were three or four thousand of us in this sector with no enemy to our front. When word of Sheridan's impending charge reached us all we had to do was turn around. We formed by ranks and prepared to receive the Yankee horsemen."

"We were supposed to wait for orders to fire," said Ox, "But Cody was a little anxious to get things started. He couldn't wait."

"He had a Whitworth," continued Simmons, "You boys familiar with that weapon?"

"No suh," Jefferson shook his head.

"It's a sniper's dream," said Whitt, "has a scope and a range of about a half-mile."

"Cody fired the first shot," noted Ox, "and I'm sure that's the one that felled Sheridan. I can't prove it of course, but I'm convinced of it, have been from the instant I heard that shot go off."

"Then what happened?" pressed David.

"What happened?" repeated Whitt, "Well, we gave 'em what for, that's what happened. We cut 'em down by the hundreds. Some of 'em managed to reach, even break, our lines but they were all shot or captured in short order. We forced the main body to break it off but as they were tryin' to retreat Hampton's boys pitched into 'em from over there," he pointed toward the wooded hills where Hampton had hidden from view the bulk of his cavalry, "and chased 'em pell mell across the river."

"That was Grant's last move," said Reilly. "He had no more reserves. Using first Hancock, then Sheridan, he had thrown two punches at us. We deflected both of them and continued driving Wright and Warren toward the North Anna."

"Let's shift direction and head up to the bluff overlooking Ox Ford. From there you can get a better sense of how the battle ended."

The walk to Ox Ford itself consumed the better part of a half-hour the last few minutes of which were spent on an increasingly steep grade. By the time they reached the crest of the ridge the soreness in Wil's hip was approaching a point where it would be difficult to bear. Here it was that Seth Reilly finished his explanation of this the most critical of battles. "Once he knew victory was ours, Gordon acted quickly to insure it by dispatching a sizeable force of infantry upriver a piece to cut off any of the Yanks trying to escape in that direction. Once we had sealed off that escape route the survivors of Wrights corps and those of Warren found themselves being herded straight into the river beneath the guns Marse Robert had up here on the bluff. It was pretty much a slaughter by that time. Wasn't pretty to look at, even from our perspective. The Federals knew they were beaten and they began surrendering not by the hundreds mind you, but by the thousands."

After he had finished speaking there was silence for

several minutes save for the birds in the trees and the soft rippling of water over rocks near the ford below. Beams of sunlight filtered through the newly budding foliage coming to rest on the gentle waters of the North Anna, creating the illusions of sparkles across the surface of the river. Jefferson and David were both fascinated by the things they had seen and heard. As they stood high atop the bluff overlooking the North Anna River at Ox Ford, each of them was able to appreciate the tactical genius of the man known to his soldiers as "Marse Robert." The bluff itself was the apex of the entire Confederate position on the North Anna. It stood at least fifty feet above the river and the slope down to the water was perilously close to being vertical. As the older men drifted through their memories the two boys tried to imagine what it must have been like standing on that same bluff twenty years ago. As the battle was reaching its zenith the river was choked with fleeing Northern soldiers many screaming in panic as shells and bullets made their passage all but impossible.

"It seems so peaceful now," remarked David as he stared down at the softly flowing waters of the North Anna.

"I was just thinkin' the same thing," agreed Jefferson. "I can't even imagine what this must've been like for the people who took part in it."

"Me neither."

The group stayed there on the bluff for nearly an hour sharing memories and questions before retiring in the direction of their camp. Leaving the trenches behind them, they soon reached Ox Ford Road, a narrow, seldom used dirt lane which traversed much of the Confederate position south of the river. They hadn't gone far when they spied a rather impressive carriage approaching them pulled by a team of four immaculately groomed horses.

Two men were up on the driver's seat, one of them white the other black. No other passengers were visible. The black man seemed to be of substantial build. His shiny black head was completely bald but on his face grew a silvery-white beard and above his eyes grew two bushy, snow-white eyebrows. Reilly stopped, as did the others, all of them peering curiously at the carriage as it drew closer. "Is that who I think it might be?" asked the Professor.

"I think it is," replied Levi.

"Ivory," whispered Wil.

"I think you may be right," said Reilly.

As the carriage drew closer the first impression of these men were confirmed rather quickly. They had found Ivory. More to the point, he had found them.

GRAY VISIONS

~Chapter Three~
The Telling of Chancellorsville

"Ivory!" called Levi, "That you old man?"

The carriage halted at once and the heavy-set black man rose from his seat and peered curiously at the small band of veterans and youngsters arrayed on the road before him.

"That's a voice what sounds familiar to me!" cried Ivory. "You wouldn't be Levi Henry, would you?"

"Sho' am!" grinned Levi, pleased that Ivory had recognized him.

"Well I'll be!" returned Ivory. "We been lookin' for you boys all afternoon! Where you been?" He stood with one hand holding the reins and the other on his hip. The expression on his face was much like a parent scolding a child who was late for supper.

"Been diggin' up old memories," replied Reilly.

"Professor? Is that really you?"

"Sure is, I wouldn't have missed this for the world."

"And Ox ... that's got to be Ox, ain't nobody I know could be that big!"

"It's me," admitted Ox a little sheepishly.

"What about Miles?" Wil Covington threw this question up for grabs.

The white man seated next to Ivory rose to his feet and removed the fine felt derby from his head. His hair, what was left of it, now matched the color of the uniform he'd worn twenty years ago, but the mischievous glint in his eyes was still very much visible. "What about me?" His reply came out as something of a challenge.

GRAY VISIONS

"Well," said Wil, "I was just wonderin' if that was you. Ain't heard from ya in a couple of months of Sundays!"

"Sorry," the affable grin which had always been a trademark of Miles Turner made its first appearance of the day and at once he was recognized by all those present, save for the two lads who had never met him. "I was never much for writin' letters, you boys know that."

Without another word, Ivory set the brake on the carriage and tied off the reins. As he climbed down to the ground the others were able to see how good the last twenty years had been to him. He'd put on more than a little bit of weight. In truth he wasn't that much smaller than Ox, but it wasn't his size that impressed his fellow veterans; it was his clothing. As Wil was later to explain to Emily, "He had on a suit that put my best Sunday-go-to-meetin' clothes to shame." He wore tails, perfectly tailored of course, and a shirt of silk which would be the envy of the richest New York bankers. Turner also left the carriage. He too was dressed in the finest styles available. One thing was apparent to the others as they watched Ivory and Miles approach on foot. Whatever business the two of them had started at war's end certainly didn't fail. Both appeared prosperous, although prosperous may be too mild of a word to properly describe them. They walked to within a few paces of the others then stopped. Several moments passed as this gathering of veterans paused to appraise one another. Wil could scarcely believe these were he same two men he and Levi had said goodbye to on that field outside of Culpeper so many years ago. Truly, much had changed.

"Sakes alive, boy!" Ivory held his arms open wide and looked straight at Wil. "Are you gonna stand here lookin' half-moonstruck or are you gonna c'mere and give ol' Ivory a hug?"

The ice was broken. Limping noticeably and leaning heavily on his cane, Wil stepped into the welcoming embrace of the black man from South Carolina. Levi was right on his heels and Ivory responded by taking one man in each arm and squeezing the two of them in a suffocating bear hug. The others came forward as well, and this particular moment in time could only be described as joyous. David and Jefferson held back, not so much out of shyness as the fact that they had never met Ivory or Miles. They only knew these men from the stories their fathers had told over the years. Out of respect for their elders they held back and remained quiet, watching curiously as a small crowd of aging veterans mobbed around Ivory and Miles. David was sure he could see Ivory blinking back tears as he held Wil and Levi in his arms. Others wanted their turns as well, and it seemed a quarter hour of chattering and laughing past before Ivory caught the eyes of the two boys who stood out on the periphery of the circle. Clearing his throat he loosed his hold on Whitt and Jonas and addressed himself to these boys. "Tell me now," he smiled, "who belongs to these two yearlings?"

"That's my boy, David," said Wil in reply.

"The other one's Jefferson," declared Levi, "He's my oldest."

"Well c'mon over here, young-uns! I got a hug or two left in me!"

The two lads drew cautiously near, and in a matter of seconds both were enveloped within Ivory's burly arms. "Lawd have mercy!" cried Ivory. "These are two fine young men you boys have here!" This time he made no attempt to hide his tears as his mind drifted back in time, and he recalled the two young boys from the Shenandoah Valley who joined up with the army just after Cedar Mountain. "Tell me somethin' young-uns, do y'all know how long ah been knowin' yo' daddies?"

"Twenty years," mumbled David in reply.

"More'n that," said Ivory shaking his head so that his jowls seemed to quiver beneath the fleecy whiteness of his beard. "Seems like it might be twenty-two."

"Will be this summer," said Wil.

"I knew it," nodded Ivory. "Seems like you two weren't much older than these boys when I first met ya."

"We were older," said Levi, "but not by much."

"Thought so," grunted Ivory.

Here the excitement of acquaintances renewed finally subsided and something resembling normal conversation took its place.

"Hey, Ivory," Levi spoke up, "I remember back in Culpeper when we were sayin' goodbye, we said you were gonna have to pick yourself a last name. Did you?"

Ivory released his hold on the two boys then meticulously smoothed the wrinkles from the sleeves and body of his top coat. "Well now I reckon I did," he replied.

"Well tell us!" demanded Jonas, perhaps with a little too much impatience in his voice.

"Okay I will. From now on you boys can address me as Mr. Davis...Mr. Ivory Lee Davis to be exact." He seemed to stand a little straighter as he said this and his chest seemed to puff out more than usual.

"Not a bad choice," smiled Reilly.

"I thought so," said Ivory, "named myself after the two men I admire most!"

"The way I see it," declared Levi, "You've made a bunch of

good choices since the war ended. If you can afford to wear clothes like that and if you can rent a rig like this, you must be doin' okay for yourself."

"Rent?" Miles chipped in with a one word question. "Did he say rent?"

"I did," nodded Levi. "Y'all rented that carriage didn't ya? Or did somebody loan it to ya?"

"Neither," said Miles.

"It's mine," added Ivory.

"What did you say?" This from Ox.

"I said the carriage is mine. So are the horses."

"You own that carriage?" Jefferson acted as if he were stunned.

"Sho' do."

"Y'all drove it all the way up here from South Carolina?"

"Nope. Shipped it up by train."

By this time, every man there appeared to be in a state of shock. The Ivory they had known had been a slave. He had served with them all through the war and had been paid a salary equal to theirs, but certainly not enough to make a man wealthy.

"You came here on a train and you shipped the rig and the horses?"

"And a steer."

"A steer?"

"You don't think I'd see you boys again after twenty years and not cook you a meal do you?"

"A steer?" Ox was beginning to salivate.

"Yep. Ain't makin' no makeshift stews and you boys won't be eatin' no hardtack tonight! No, suh! We're gonna eat fine tonight!"

"No doubt," muttered Levi as he scratched his head in puzzlement.

"Ivory," posed Reilly, "You've aroused our curiosity, not to mention our appetites, at least some peoples," he paused and playfully poked Ox in the ribs. "Anyway, don't you think you owe us an explanation? You and Miles have obviously done well for yourselves. Would you share your secret?"

"Weren't no secret to it, Professor, all comes down to hard work and the Lawd's blessin'."

"We'd still like to hear."

"And I'll be happy to tell it. Miles too for that matter, right Miles?"

"Sho'nuff," said Turner, "On the way back to camp."

"Right," nodded Ivory, "We can all pile into the carriage and head back. We'll explain along the way."

The open cab of the carriage was designed to hold six average size people. It filled rather quickly not only the seats but the floor and running boards as well. In deference to the others, Ox rode on the driver's seat next to Ivory.

The veteran teamster quickly turned his team around and started the trip back to the reunion camp. As they proceeded at a slow pace down the narrow lane, Miles and Ivory relayed to the others the details of their successful business venture. After saying goodbye at war's end they had journeyed to the plantation of Ivory's former master near Greenville, South Carolina. Here Ivory bade farewell to those for whom he had long toiled, gathered his life savings, nearly $500.00 in gold and silver coins, which he added to the $200.00 he'd managed to save during the war. After leaving the plantation, they journeyed east, then south to the bustling harbor city of Charleston to begin their new lives. The idea for a business came from Miles. He was well acquainted with Ivory's culinary skills, and he also realized how good the newly liberated slave was with horses. He thought it might be a good idea for he and Ivory to start a taxi service. They purchased two old buggies and two strong draft horses and into business they went. In time, hard work and patience began to pay off, and both men displayed a fairly decent aptitude for making a company work. They added more supplies and animals, so they hired more drivers. Gradually they accumulated a substantial reserve of capital.

Their next step turned out to be their ultimate goal. In the mind of Miles Turner the taxi service was merely a means to an end, no matter how successful it might become. The end he had in mind was an Inn or Tavern, someplace where Ivory's skill with food could be readily brought to bear. Midway through 1876 their opportunity arrived. They purchased and renovated an old home on the outskirts of town, named it Westside Inn, and launched their next venture into the business world.

It was an instant success. Serving three meals a day and renting out the four guest rooms on an overnight basis to travellers they quickly found themselves with more business than they could handle. Ivory's reputation as a chef spread rapidly through the entire region. By 1879 they were opening a second restaurant called Battery Watch near the waterfront of Charleston. Two years later they were both wealthy men.

Time and experience in the business world had done much to change Miles Turner. He no longer gambled, at least not the kind of gambling one normally associates with cards and gaming tables. If he could be called a gambler at all it would apply only to his business decisions, but these he made in conjunction with Ivory's common sense and practical experience. Inevitably these decisions resulted in an increase in the duo's fortunes.

Prior to opening of Battery Watch, Ivory found himself a wife. He was almost sixty years old when he finally married - late in life by anyone's standards -- but he wasn't the least bit deterred by his advanced years. His bride, Dierdre, was twenty-five years his junior and was thoroughly captivated by the man she affectionately called "the master chef." Theirs proved to be a fruitful match and when Ivory journeyed north for the reunion he left four young children behind. As for Miles, he had been enjoying a rather active life as a bachelor for many years and preferred to keep it that way. Marriage wasn't something he ever seriously contemplated.

As Ivory pulled the luxury carriage into the camp and the story of his and Miles' success concluded, the other veterans found themselves somewhat speechless. If they weren't seeing evidence of their wealth for themselves they probably would never have believed that Miles and Ivory were capable of such achievements. As the saying goes, seeing is believing.

As soon as the carriage stopped, everybody piled out. It was early in the evening and all of them were hungry. They scattered to their own tents with the intention of regathering around Ivory's cook fire after dark. Ivory disappeared inside of his tent only to emerge within fifteen minutes entirely changed. Gone was the expensive suit of clothes with its finely tailored top coat and felt hat. The Ivory of old was the man who stepped from that tent. He was wearing the same bits and pieces of a uniform he had worn all through the war. To see him was to step twenty years into the past.

"Ivory," said Wil as the black man approached. "You've gained some weight over these last two decades. How is it you can still fit in those old clothes?"

"Had 'em altered," came the reply. "Cost me four

dollars but ah reckon it's worth it. Ah just thought ah'd like to really get into the spirit of this reunion. You know what ah mean?"

"Yep," nodded Wil. "I know exactly what you mean."

Ivory grunted something in Wil's direction and turned his attention to the younger Covington and Henry. "You boys see that fire, yonder?" he asked.

"Yessuh," nodded Jefferson quickly.

It ain't big enough," announced Ivory. "Ah need me a real fire ... gotta have one three times the size of that one. I got me a couple of hundred pounds of free beef supposed to be here any minute. Need me a big fire, you know what I'm sayin?"

"You're sayin' you want us to gather firewood," said David with a grin.

"Lots of it. And be quick. It'll take awhile to cook all this food, and ah got hungry people waitin' for it. You catch my meanin'?"

"We're on our way!" Both boys darted toward the woods at once.

Within the hour the boys had gathered more than several armloads of wood and had stacked it all just beyond the fire pit. Minutes later, a wagon arrived at the campsite and the driver began asking for the location of Ivory Lee Davis. Upon meeting him, they immediately set about unloading the beef -- nearly 250 steaks in all.

"Yessuh!" Beamed Ivory as box after box of steak came off of the rig and circled the camp fire. "We're gonna eat fine tonight!" He curled a thumb under each of his suspenders and peered happily at the collection of faces, old and young, which had gathered around the tent he shared with Miles. "Gonna be like old times!" he declared with a broad grin. "It sho' is!"

"Does have that feel about it," agreed Wil with a nod. "I'll tell ya somethin', Ivory, "I can't tell you how many times I've thought about you over the years. No way to count 'em all."

Ivory glanced away for a moment, perhaps feeling a little self-conscious at Wil's expression of affection. Then he turned to meet the eyes of the white man he'd been so close to during the war. "Me too," he said simply. Changing the subject quickly, he addressed himself to Jefferson and David who were standing just a few paces away. "You boys look like you both got a healthy set of arms hangin' from yer shoulders. Can either of you swing an axe?"

"You'd best believe it!" replied Jefferson with a smile.

"Good!" nodded Ivory. "Cause I need me a heap of firewood, this ain't enough. Y'all understand what ah'm sayin'? Lots of it, and it's got to be dry. They's a couple of axes in the tent. Do you think yer fathers would mind if I put y'all to work?"

"I don't think we'd mind a bit," said Levi quickly.

"Reckon us old fellers could use a break," agreed Wil.

"It's a done deal," smiled Ivory. "You boys fetch them axes and have at it."

Jefferson scanned the perimeter of the camp and turned his eyes to meet Ivory's smiling face. "Looks like the nearest woods are a good hundred yards away," he said.

"Yep," nodded Ivory.

"What if we cut more than we can carry?" probed David.

"Then ah reckon we'll send some help to haul it in," replied the veteran teamster. "In the meantime you'd best be movin' along. Y'all ain't got but two hours of daylight left and it'll go quick."

"We're halfway there!" laughed Jefferson as he reached into the tent, grabbed an axe and started away followed quickly by David.

By sunset, a rather substantial stack of wood stood but a

few paces from the fire itself. The western horizon was ablaze in orange as the sun disappeared from view. As darkness approached dozens of veterans, white and black alike, began gathering in the general vicinity of Ivory's campfire anticipating not only the meal it would soon produce but also the stories they knew were bound to follow.

Of stories there seemed to be no end. There were thousands of men in the camp that evening most of whom had not seen one another for a decade or more. So many years to catch up on. So many tales to tell. The noise level was at times deafening. Here and there could be heard the catchy tunes of a banjo player, the foot-stomping tunes of a skilled fiddler or the soulful melodies of a fine harmonica.

In the middle of it all stood Ivory, sometimes telling yarns other times listening to those of the men with whom he had once served. All the while his swift hands were cutting and slicing vegetables for the feast to come. Onions there were aplenty, along with peppers and piles of mushrooms. Ivory Lee Davis had spared no expense.

Miles Turner was enjoying himself to no end. He and Ivory had been partners for so long he had long since grown accustomed to the speed and skill with which the black man could create not just a meal but a feast. As the sky grew steadily darker he drew much in the way of contentment by watching the wonderment reflected in the eyes of the younger boys as they listened open mouthed to the yarns the older men spun; an emotion which deepened each time he looked over at Ivory and saw the absolute joy in the black man's eyes.

Night came but the camp itself was well illuminated in the glow of dozens of bonfires and thousands of lanterns. Over the heads of the revelers and all through the fields and trees which surrounded them, countless thousands of fireflies danced to the music provided by equal numbers of cicadas. Oh, what a sight it must have been from the air and oh what a night it was!

Among those gathered around Ivory's fire, appetites were reaching a fever pitch. Two kettles full of water had already been put to boil. Into one he poured a sackful of freshly peeled potatoes, in the other rice -- not just any rice as Ivory quickly pointed out, but South Carolina rice. A small oven was in place from which would soon emerge fresh mouth-watering biscuits. Then came the beef, skewer after skewer laid across the fire just beyond the reach of the crackling flames. Ivory produced a huge skillet into which he plopped gobs of butter, waiting until most of it had melted before he introduced his copious mixture of peppers, onions and mushrooms. "It won't be long, boys," he beamed as he stood back hands on hips to admire his handiwork, "won't be long a'tall!"

The others stood by waiting with varying degrees of patience unable to control their salivating glands as the aroma of beef drifted past their nostrils.

Ever the patient one, Ivory moved casually from one pot to another, then to the skillet, then a turning of the beef, now and then adding his own special mixture of spices where he thought it would do the most good.

"God that smells good!" chortled David who had worked up a tremendous appetite while cutting the wood which was now cooking his supper.

"Sho' do" agreed Jefferson with a nod.

Ivory glanced over at them with an expression which suddenly seemed quite serious. "You boys ever been hungry?" he asked.

"I'm starvin' right now!" gasped David. "If it ain't ready soon I think I'll die straight away!"

"No, no, boy. Ah ain't talkin' 'bout wantin' to eat. I'm talkin' 'bout hunger. Have you ever known hunger?"

"You mean like never havin' anythin' to eat?"

"Or too damn little," nodded Ivory. "Have you ever known that?"

"No, suh,"

"Pray you never do. You see these men around you? Your fathers? Me? All those old fellers with their hair gone gray or white? We've known hunger. Durin' the war the Yankees used to call us scarecrows, and I reckon that's what we musta looked like. We was one lean bunch I'll tell you true! Did your daddies ever tell you what their daily rations was?"

"They said it wasn't much," replied Jefferson softly.

"Not much?" Ivory took in a deep breath of warm spring air and loosed an audible sigh. "Well I guess they was right about that. Durin' the winter that your fathers rejoined us outside of Fredericksburg things was pretty bad so far as food was concerned. The basic ration for each man for any given day went somethin' like this: for meat he'd have to make due with 'bout a quarter pound of bacon and all too often it was rancid...foul to the taste. Along with this he'd get eighteen ounces of cornmeal, but a lot of this was the cob itself, all ground up. Every third day or so we'd get 'bout ten pounds of rice to divide among a hundred men. Now and then there'd be a few black-eyed peas and some dried fruit, but it weren't much." He paused and stirred the mushrooms while sprinkling in a handful of ground black pepper. "That's the first time in mah life I ever saw scurvy," he explained. "It scared me but I'll tell ya true, it worried Marse Robert a lot more. He knew we needed fresh vegetables so he started sendin' the boys out to gather sassafras buds, wild onions and such. It helped some but not near enough. That's when some of the boys began takin' matters into their own hands, 'specially them Texans," he stopped speaking for a moment and glanced over at Wil with an anticipatory smile.

"You always said them Texans was a wild bunch!" laughed the elder Covington as he recalled those days long past.

"I sho' did!" Ivory shared Wil's laugh.

"Amen, Ivory!" cried one of those same Texans who had journeyed all the way from El Paso to take part in the reunion on the North Anna.

"Yes, suh!" nodded Ivory. "General Hood was the head Texan in this army and I remember hearin' Marse Robert sayin' somethin' to him one afternoon." he paused and thoughtfully scratched the kinky white hair of his beard, then turned to his longtime business partner. "Miles, do you remember what he said?"

"Sorry, old friend," chuckled Miles, "You never told me that one."

"Lemme see now," muttered Ivory, "If I recall rightly some of the local folks was complainin' 'bout their chickens disappearin' ... Oh, yeah! Now I remember! Marse Robertsaid to Hood, "When you Texans come about, the chickens have to roost mighty high!"

"They shore did!" laughed the fellow from El Paso. "I done plucked a few of them birds myself!"

"I'll bet you did!" Ivory gestured toward the man and laughed heartily.

"Lemme tell y'all somethin'," interjected Levi as he shared in their mirth, "Ivory's right 'bout how little the army gave us to eat, but what he ain't tellin' ya is how far he could stretch it and how good he could make it taste!"

"Well," said Ivory, "Modesty aside ah reckon ah did have my ways."

"Amen to that!" agreed Miles. "Now when you gonna quit jawin' and serve up some of this food you got goin' here?"

"Well now, Miles, y'all got to be patient, you hear? Food ain't done till it's done, you know that!"

"Miles?" a new yet familiar voice sounded out from the darkness. "When'd you start callin' him Miles? Last time I saw you boys you were callin' him Massa Turner." A tall lean man stepped out of the shadows. His was a distinguished almost aristocratic demeanor as he moved into the light. The gray hair on his head had thinned considerably. His face was dark, and clean-shaven save for the closely cropped mustache atop his upper lip. He was wearing an old Confederate uniform, grown tattered by the years, which bore the buttons of the 10th Louisiana infantry.

"I'll be damned," whispered Miles as he recognized the newcomer.

"Armelin," said Wil as he too recognized the Cajun who became his friend during the second battle of Manassas.

"In the flesh," said the man from Louisiana.

"David," Wil turned to his son, "this is the man we called Tiger."

"Really?" the boy glanced up at the new arrival. "My Pa's right fond of you."

Miles rose quickly to his feet as did Wil, Levi and Reilly. At once they moved to greet the man with whom they had shared many a campfire.

"I've been searchin' for you boys all the day long!" declared Armelin as he reached to clasp the many hands ex-

~ 113 ~

tended in his direction. "Good thing I heard Ivory talkin' 'bout those Texans or I might never have found you. Actually that's a lie," he flashed a happy grin. "All I had to do was follow my nose. There ain't a fire in this whole camp that can boast of the aromas this one has! You think you can spare a little for a Cajun far from home?"

"Lawd Almighty!" replied Ivory with a smile, "the day'll never come when me and Miles don't have enough food for you! Sit yo'self on down here! Join the party!"

Only too happy to comply, Armelin found himself an open spot of ground and sat down Indian-style to await the meal which would soon be forthcoming. "You still haven't answered my original question," he said as he glanced up at Ivory, "when did Massa Turner become Miles?"

"Oh that," Ivory ran a hand across his bald head and let its fingers wander down to scratch through the hairs of his beard as he pondered his answer. "To be honest, Armelin, I don't rightly remember. I know I was still callin' him Massa Turner for some time after the war ended."

"Three years," Miles supplied the missing answer.

"Really? That long?"

"Well now y'all know how hard it is to break old habits. Lawd knows I was a slave for nigh on forty years! Anyway it ain't all that important how I talk to him. His name's Miles and he's my business partna. That's all anyone needs to know."

"Fair enough," nodded Armelin as he turned his attention to Turner, "and you my friend, might I persuade you to join me in a friendly game of poker at supper's end?"

"Nope," came the quick reply from Miles, "I done gave it up. Knowin' you was good for me, Armelin. Taught me a lesson it did. Ain't picked up a deck of cards in close to twenty years! The only gamblin' I do anymore is with the decisions me and Ivory make about our businesses and most of them have paid off."

"Rather handsomely if you'll allow me to say so."

"I'll allow it," said Miles with a grin. "What's more I'll agree with ya a hundred percent. Me and Ivory...well, we've done all right for ourselves."

"Sure does look that way," nodded Linscombe.

"What about you?" asked Miles. "Somethin' tells me you can afford clothes a whole lot nicer than that ol' uniform."

"Well," Armelin hesitated a moment, not wanting to appear boastful, "I suppose it could be said I've been fortunate. A couple of years after the war I was able to buy a small shrimp boat and I went into business down in Calcasieu Parish. Today my wife and I own a pretty decent seafood business. We've got five boats now...maybe twenty employees. We harvest and sell all kinds of stuff, shrimp, crabs, fish...even crayfish. We've done well."

"It appears most of us have little cause to complain," Reilly joined the conversation. "We've all much to be thankful for."

"I should say so!" Agreed Whitt, "and if we wanted to pick one place...one event...the one thing most responsible for our good fortune, it would have to be this battle...this ground."

Most of the men there were in agreement on that point. It was the North Anna which launched the final offensive and the negotiated peace which brought independence to the South and freedom to her slaves.

"Y'all ready to eat?" Ivory's booming voice caught the attention of all present.

"Long past ready, Ivory," replied Levi with an eager expression on his face.

"Then I reckon it's time we have at it."

"I'll fetch the plates," said Miles as he rose to his feet and disappeared into the tent.

"Plates?" asked Wil.

"Gonna do this thing right," grinned the black man.

"Me and Miles brought some of our supplies from Battery Watch; not the good stuff, mind you, old plates and silver we don't hardly use no mo'."

"Yes, indeedee!" agreed Miles as he re-emerged from the tent with a substantial stack of plates in his arms, "Gonna do it right! David, Jefferson, how about grabbin' some more of these plates inside, and a bunch of that silverware too!"

Both boys leapt to their feet, eager to be on with the feast.

Ivory prepared each plate himself, several at a time, skillfully he would remove a skewer full of beef from the fire and with swift moving hands he cut each chunk into smaller pieces. Each plate received two pieces of meat which Ivory smothered with the mixture of mushrooms, peppers and onions. To all this was added a helping of potatoes or rice depending on the preference of the man or boy on the receiving end.

"This was cooked perfectly," noted Wil in a highly satisfied tone, "pink in the middle...just the way I like It!"

Armelin was next in line. As Ivory handed the Cajun his plate he smiled and said, "Bon Appetit"

"Thanks," grinned Armelin. "I never knew you spoke French."

"I don't" chuckled Ivory, "but I know what those two words are all about."

Armelin picked up one of the hunks of beef from his plate and took a hearty bite. An expression bordering on ecstacy passed across his face as he chewed with deliberate slowness. "You do at that," he admitted with a nod.

A quarter hour passed before everyone who desired a plate had been served. Some were already coming back for seconds but Ivory had settled down comfortably with his own plate. "You boys go on ahead and serve yourselves," he instructed. "You know where everythin' is. Eat to your heart's content! We got plenty of food!"

There must have been three or four dozen people partaking of Ivory's fare that night and once the food was on their plates little conversation could be heard anywhere. This is not to say there was no noise mind you. There was a lot of loud chewing going on and a seemingly endless chorus of contented sighs and moans as this gathering of veterans proceeded to gorge itself courtesy of Ivory Lee Davis and Miles Turner.

An hour later, coffee was ready, fresh and hot off the fire. It was a far cry from the coffee imitations these same men had to drink twenty years prior. This coffee was one of the best blends to come from Brazil and had been ground that very morning. Miles and Ivory had imported a substantial quantity for their restaurants and brought some to Virginia to share with their old comrades.

An hour after the last of the food had disappeared most of those present were lying prone with their stomachs stuffed beyond normal capacity. Conversations began popping up again as the collection of veterans resumed the swapping of tales to relieve past glories. David and Jefferson had both attached themselves to Ivory, hanging on his every word as they helped clean the mess created by their feast. Ivory thrilled them with his stories of battles and camp life, of the famous and the unknown. It was David who brought up a subject which caused the old black man to pause in his labors and reflect upon his answer. "Ivory, did you know Stonewall Jackson."

"Know him? I reckon you could say I knew him. Cooked a few meals for him I did. Some good ones too."

"Were you there when he died? Could you tell us how it happened?"

Here the old man paused a moment or two before making his reply. "I reckon I can tell y'all how it happened. Won't be easy though. It'll bring up some sad memories fo' me. I loved Stonewall. Hell, we all did."

"Ivory," Levi joined in, "ain't no way you can tell these boys 'bout Stonewall dyin' without tellin' 'em 'bout Chancellorsville."

Ivory glanced over at Levi and nodded his agreement. "Reckon you're right." he said. "Course...that might take a spell."

"None of us are goin' anywhere...least not till the mornin'."

Ivory looked back at David and Jefferson. The eyes of both boys were wide with anticipation. They were eager to hear every detail. "You boys make yourselves comfortable, hear? Throw some mo' wood atop the fire! Build it up the way it oughta be! May be Spring but this night air's awful cool, you know what I'm sayin'? We should do this down in Charleston. We'd be in short sleeves and wouldn't need no fire. Not in May, no, suh!'" He disappeared into his tent and re-emerged quickly with a three-legged stool on which to seat himself close to the fire.

"Hey, boys!" Levi called out loudly to those who were still trying to recover from their meal. "Spread the word and gather around! Ivory's gonna tell Chancellorsville!"

Word quickly spread and before long a crowd of two or three hundred people were pressing close to Ivory's campfire, straining to get as near as possible that they might not miss a single word.

"Looks like you're gonna have to raise your voice a bit, Ivory," said Wil with an understanding smile. "It appears you've attracted somethin' of an audience here."

"Sho' does seem that way," agreed Ivory with an appreciative grin. "Haven't told this story in a long while. Reckon I can do it one mo' time."

"I don't doubt it fo' a minute," returned Levi. "I gotta admit I was hopin' you'd go through one of the battles. Chancellorsville is one I'd like to hear."

"Hear it you will!" nodded Ivory. "Sit on down and make yo'self comfo'table 'cause it's comin' yer way."

"Not yet!" The cry came from one of the veterans well back in the crowd. "Hold on a minute, Ivory!"

"I'm holdin'," nodded Ivory, though he had no idea who he was talking to.

Moments later several men who were probably in their fifties made their way through the crowd carrying heavy wooden crates. Reaching Ivory's side they proceeded to build him a makeshift stage with the crates. With two layers of these boxes they arranged it so Ivory would be perched on his stool atop the crates perhaps four feet off of the ground. "This way we can see ya and hear ya better," explained one as they started back toward the perimeter of the circle.

"Thank ya kindly," grinned Ivory as he shifted the stool up to its new home and climbed up after it. After testing the stability of this arrangement, he seated himself with feet planted widely apart and one burly hand on each knee.

"All right," he mused in a deep booming voice that all could hear, "Chancellorsville...where's a good place to start...?"

"You could tell 'bout when

GRAY VISIONS

Hooker crossed the Rappahannock and positioned himself squarely in Lee's rear," suggested David.

"You've obviously never heard Ivory tell a battle," chided Jonas Willem.

"Just met him today," explained David a little defensively.

"You can't start a tellin' in the middle," continued Jonas, "Least ways Ivory don't tell 'em that way. Ain't that right, Ivory?"

"You know it," declared the aging black man. "Y'all got to have the background first if you wants to really understand how it all happened. Sit on back now and let me tell ya how this thing shaped up.

"The winter of '63 was a rough one. I'm not talkin' so much 'bout the weather although that was bad 'nough. The main problem was food. There just wasn't enough. I already told you young boys how puny our rations was...just barely enough to sustain a man. You remember how I told y'all 'bout the scurvy what was poppin' up here and there. It had Marse Robert plenty worried, but long 'bout mid-February he done figured out a way to solve that problem."

"It was the 18th of February if memory serves me." The voice came from somewhere in the darkness but something about it sounded familiar to Ivory, almost like a ghost from the past.

Ivory scanned the crowd of faces illuminated by the glow of the fire searching for the source of that voice. From the shadows stepped a tall, burly man with a heavy beard. He was dressed in an old dress uniform with the stars of a major-general. "Lawd have mercy!" whispered Ivory, "Are you who I think you are?"

"I remember that day in 1862 at Sharpsburg," replied the

~ 120 ~

newcomer, "the day you helped me and my staff serve a battery of guns."

"General Longstreet," an expression of surprise and delight appeared on Ivory's face, "Come on in, suh, join us...have you had supper?"

"I'm afraid so," answered the general, the man whom Lee had dubbed "my old warhorse," "but judging by the faces of these men I think I should've waited. Apparently you haven't lost your touch with food."

"Would you join us anyway?"

"I'd be honored...I heard through the grapevine that you were tellin' Chancellorsville."

"Word does travel fast," remarked Wil.

Time had been kind to Peter Longstreet. His was still an impressive build and his skin showed few signs of his age, although his hair and beard had long since gone to gray. Someone rolled a stump in close to the fire and the general proceeded to seat himself. He was the last of the men often referred to as "Lee's Lieutenants," and as such he held a position of respect bordering on awe among the veterans and the younger folks who had gathered for the reunion.

"General," said Ivory, "I was just fixin' to tell these boys how Marse Robert solved the food problem back in the winter of '63. Since you was the solution, maybe you should be the one tellin' that part of the story."

"Ivory," Longstreet smiled warmly, "I'd be delighted to share in this story with the likes of you."

"Well go on ahead, suh," gestured Ivory as he returned the smile, "I'll just sit back and listen a spell. If you get hungry while yer talkin' you just let me know, hear? I'll fix you up right proper."

"Of that I have no doubt," Longstreet flashed a quick grin

as he shifted on the stump to face the gathering of aging soldiers. "Were any of you with me that year when we marched into the southside of this fair state?"

Several hands shot into the air and quite a few of those present affirmed their participation in that mission vocally.

"Well now if there's something I can't remember I trust you boys 'll set me straight. In any event, it was my first independent command of the war. It arose as a result of several factors not the least of which was the critical problem of food, as Ivory has already pointed out.

"But food was only part of the problem. The Federals had occupied much of southeastern Virginia since the outbreak of the war, not to mention much of the coastal regions in the northeastern areas of North Carolina. By the beginning of 1863, Union troops were moving toward Richmond, getting perilously close to Petersburg. Essentially our mission was three-fold: We were to thwart the Federal attempt to capture Richmond with a combination of their southside forces; we were to conduct foraging expeditions throughout the region and ship the fruits of our efforts north by rail to our comrades camped south of Fredericksburg; finally, we had to keep ourselves in a position to return to Lee's side on very short notice should the Army of the Potomac move against him. My men and I were also asked to drive the Federals from Suffolk, a request which presented quite a challenge since there were substantially more Federals within its fortifications than we could bring to bear against it. Do any of you remember conditions in Richmond when we marched through?"

"We was knee-deep in snow if I recall," returned an old man off to the left.

"Yep," nodded Longstreet, "at least the shorter men were. The taller men only had to plow through calf-deep snow, the result of a heavy storm which struck the city the night prior to our arrival. Two divisions of my corps were in that column. General Hood's and General Pickett's, all of them veterans. According to Seddon, Secretary of War at the time, our presence had a most positive impact on the morale of Richmond's citizens.

"First and foremost was the matter of foraging for provisions. The region in question was, and still is, an agricultural paradise, rich in livestock and produce. Unfortunately it was also under Union occupation for more than a year. To accomplish this facet of our mission we had to convince the Federals to withdraw to their fortified positions and remain there long enough for our foragers to ply their trade." Here Longstreet paused for a moment. It was obvious to himself and to those listening that he lacked the flair for spinning yarns that was to be found in one Ivory Lee Davis. As a soldier and tactician he had proved himself brilliant on countless occasions, but as a teller of stories he left something to be desired. He thought of explaining the many decisions made during his brief independent command, but it wasn't strategy this group had gathered to hear...at least not his. He decided at once to shift directions.

"Some strange things happened during those weeks. I recall one rather macabre incident which demonstrated the difference between General Hood's Texans and some of our other boys. If memory serves me it deprived us of the services of four very good men."

"I think I know which one yer talkin' 'bout" called out an old bald-headed man with a deeply wrinkled face. "Did those four boys belong to Jenkins South Carolina Brigade?"

"They did. Would you like to tell how it happened?"

"No suh. You go ahead."

"All right," nodded Longstreet. "As the gentleman just said

these fellows were in the South Carolina Brigade of Hood's division. Jenkin's boys."

"My boys!" chimed Ivory.

"They were Hood's largest brigade and they had themselves something of a reputation. They prided themselves on their uniforms and their superb discipline. General Jenkins drilled them thoroughly in every detail of military bearing. When they marched they did so in perfect unison, a marvel to watch no question, but on this day their precision did not work to the advantage of those four men.

"Our route of march brought us relatively close to a river, the name of which escapes me I'm afraid. Jenkin's brigade was marching in formation, moving past a brigade of Texans who had fallen out to rest. Unfortunately a federal gunboat was out on the river within our range. Jenkins' men were marching four abreast when that boat began lobbing shells in our general direction. Their aim wasn't particularly good and we gave them scant attention. The shell which did the damage seemed a stray more than an intentional shot. These four unfortunate fellows were each about to plant their right feet in unison upon the ground when the shell burst and severed the right foot of all four men, tumbling them into a heap upon the ground."

"I knew one of those men," said the old man who had spoken previously. It was a tragic thing what happened to him...I'll give you that."

"Sad," muttered Ivory, "Ah'll tell ya true."

"So said the Texans who were watching from the side of the road," continued Longstreet. "but some among them saw it as vindication for their own ...shall we say less than precise habits? One of them cried out to the four victims, "There! You see! That's what you get for keeping step!"

Here the old general paused to allow this story to rest upon the ears of his listeners. As he scanned the expressions upon their faces he quickly sensed a down swing in their mood, not the effect he had intended. Searching through his memory of those days long past he came upon another story and shifted direction again. "Do any of you recall the story of Julius Caesar?"

"Caesar?" David's voice had an incredulous tone to it as he recalled his lessons in classical civilization. "What could Julius Caesar have to do with our War for Independence?"

Hearing no other reply to his query, and sensing the curiosity he had aroused among his listeners, General Longstreet moved quickly to elevate their mood. "Listen well, young man," he said to David, "and I'll be quick to explain. The incident in question happened as the Federals were falling back to the security of their fortifications in Suffolk. Moving into their old positions our troops were quite taken with a tall pine tree which the Federals had been using as a signal station. They had trimmed off most of the branches from the top and had constructed an observation platform in their place. One of our fellows found his curiosity too much to resist. Up the tree he scampered, all the way to the platform where he proceeded to make himself quite comfortable, enjoying a fine view of the Federal troops inside their earthworks. One of their artillerists allowed him a few minutes to satisfy his curiosity then fired a rifle shot from one of their pieces. The shell screamed toward its target and burst in the air treacherously close to our man in the tree. He in turn did not want to appear unduly perturbed so he chose to remain atop the platform for just awhile longer. Then a second shell burst perilously close to his platform convincing him to make haste down the tree hence to safety as fast as his legs could carry him, Union shells bursting closer to his heels all the while. Needless to say, this affair was the source of much amusement for the men of both sides, and of no little embarrassment to the fellow who was on the receiving end of their taunts.

"Night came and our man resolved to have the last laugh. He set about constructing and equipping a full-size man and dressed it in a brand new uniform, our best shade of butternut. Operating with the cover of darkness he carried his new recruit up the tree to the platform, but not before he christened his creation Julius Caesar. Anyway, he put Julius Caesar in a soldierly position on the platform and bound him securely to the platform with sturdy cords. Satisfied with his work our fellow hastened back to his comrades leaving Julius Caesar to face the dawn, and the enemy alone.

"Come the dawn and with the light of the new day the Federal gunners were quick to spot the new rebel who so boldly challenged their abilities with their guns. Shells began to whistle past the platform. Shell bursts showered Julius Caesar with fragments but he seemed oblivious to it all, much to the chagrin of the Federal gunners. Undeterred, they kept up their barrage and increased its intensity, yet Caesar budged not the slightest. More perplexed than ever the Federals loaded their pieces for another round, when suddenly a cry rang out from our lines. Three cheers for Julius Caesar! And the response from hundreds of throats, hip hip, hoorah!

"At this point the Yankees knew they'd been had, but they didn't brood over it, in fact they joined in the merriment, adding their own voices to the chorus for our dear Julius!" Then, turning to address himself to young David Covington, he said, "and that my young friend is how Julius Caesar entered our War for Independence."

"It sure was!" cried another of the older veterans out in the crowd. "I remembered it after you started tellin' the story! Ol'

Julius was one helluva good lookin' soldier!"

"Sure was," agreed Longstreet, satisfied with himself as he surveyed the smiles on the faces in the crowd. With the mood of the gathering sufficiently uplifted, he decided the time had come to yield the floor, or the stump as the case might be, to the superior story telling talents of Ivory Lee Davis.

"Let me conclude by saying this," he said. "We were successful with our most important mission, relieving pressure on Richmond. We were also very good at gleaning the countryside for provisions. We purchased thousands of hogs and cattle and shipped them by rail to our comrades below Fredericksburg. We filled their bellies which gave them the physical strength they would soon need when the Army of the Potomac made its move. As for the Battle of Chancellorsville itself, I'm afraid I missed it along with my two divisions in the Southside.

"To set the stage for Ivory let me add this. On the last day of April in '63 I received an urgent telegram from Adjutant General Cooper in Richmond. He told me of a dispatch just received from General Lee saying that Hooker was across the Rappahannock in great strength above and below Fredericksburg. I was instructed to rejoin General Lee without delay. At the time all of our wagons were still out in the countryside gathering provisions and I inquired by cable whether they were to be abandoned in the face of the enemy, and if he thought it wise for me to disengage so quickly in the face of a numerically superior foe. On the first of May I was instructed to conduct the operation without bringing undue risk to the wagons and my troops. By the second of May our wagons were in and I ordered the men to withdraw from their fortifications and head for Petersburg. To retard any possible pursuit we burned all the bridges behind us and littered the roads with fallen trees. We were north of the Blackwater by the fourth and reached Petersburg on the fifth. By noon of the sixth I was in Richmond making arrangements to send Hood and Pickett north by rail to join in the battle but by then our presence was no longer needed. As to how this came about, you have only to listen to my friend Ivory. He will explain all as no other can."

Turning to face the former slave Longstreet raised his right hand in a beckoning gesture. "Ivory?"

"Mah pleasure, General," grinned the black man. "It sho'nuff is!"

Longstreet shifted on his stump as Ivory collected his thoughts for the story to come. Before long, the old black man lifted his eyes to scan the faces of those gathered by the fire. "You boys 'll have to understand somethin'," he said in the deep, clear voice for which he had always been known, "I'm an old man now. Don't have the memory ah used to have. Might need some help from time to time, 'specially with the names of them towns up there along the Rappahannock River. Been gone from Virginia a long time....can't remember everythin' any mo'."

Here he paused for a moment and ran his aged fingers through the snow white kinky curls of his beard. "I recall a day in the Spring of 1863," he said softly and thus began the telling of Chancellorsville. "It was somewhere around the middle of April ah think. Weather was just startin' to get warm. We all knew somethin' was brewin' on the other side of that river. The quiet days of winter was over and a lot of the boys was itchin' to come to grips with the Yankees again. I'd just cooked up a mess of bacon from one of those hogs General Longstreet's boys sent up to us. My fire weren't but ten to fifteen paces from Stonewall's tent. He stepped out with another man, a staff officer ah think. They was walkin' mah way and ah heard General Jackson say, `We must make this campaign an exceedingly active one. Only thus can a weaker country cope with a stronger. It must make up in activity what it lacks in strength.' Ah suppose in a nutshell that describes what we was all about in those days.

"Later that afternoon Stonewall was by hisself in his tent. I was walkin' past with a new set of harnesses for mah mules when I hears him say, `My trust is in God.' I stopped and looked inside, not sure exactly what to say just then, or whether ah should say anythin' at all. Then all of a sudden-like he comes a boltin' outta that chair like he just got stung by a hornet or somethin'! His eyes was all a glow and ah thought it best for me to just stand still and hold mah tongue. Stonewall looked north toward the river and shouted out. `I wish they would come!' and ah thought to mahself, they be comin' soon enough and when they do...well suh there is a feelin' in mah bones like nothin' ah'd ever felt befo'. There was sho'nuff a battle comin' and ah felt it would be like nuthin' we'd ever been in ."

He stopped speaking for a moment and poured himself another cup of coffee, sipping from it twice before he continued. "Reckon that brings me to Hooker," he continued. "Had himself a nickname he did, earned it out West. They called him Fightin' Joe Hooker. Marse Robert used to call him Mr. F.J. Hooker, and ah didn't think he was payin' him no compliment, ah 'll tell ya true! Anyhow, Hooker was the man what President Lincoln picked to take Burnside's place in charge of the Army of the Potomac. Ah 'll tell you boys somethin'. In those days it seemed like the Yankee generals liked to bluster a lot. You know what I'm sayin? Hooker weren't no exception. President Lincoln told him to go forward and win victories and when he came at us he expected not just victories, no suh! He figured to bag us all. He said the

GRAY VISIONS

Army of the Potomac was the finest body of soldiers the sun ever shone on, and then he said, `My plans are perfect and when I start to carry them out, may God have mercy on Bobby Lee, for I shall have none.' Y'all see what ah mean? He was talkin' one tough line, but when push came to shove it turned out to be so much bluster, not much else."

After a brief pause to catch his breath he continued. "Now I suppose y'all are wonderin' just what these perfect plans of Mr. F.J. Hooker's was. Basically his idea was the same one that inspired Burnside's mud march - you boys remember that one, don't ya? 'Cept Hooker was smart enough to wait for warm weather and dry ground. He planned to cross the Rappahannock well above Fredericksburg where the river was nice and narrow and there were several good fords. He tried it first with cavalry, and I'm afraid my memory ain't so good here...anyone know who their cavalry commander was in those days?"

"Stoneman!" someone called out from the crowd.

"Stoneman!" echoed Ivory as he jabbed an arm in the direction of the faceless voice. "Yessuh! That's him! Long about the middle of April, Hooker ordered Stoneman to cross the river some thirty miles upstream from Fredericksburg. Had himself 10,000 sabers behind him and a mess of guns! Hooker figured that a move like this around our flank would force us out of our trenches and make us retreat toward Richmond. Stoneman had instructions to take big and little slices out of us all along the way...figured he could too, cause his cavalry outnumbered Stuart's boys betterin' three to one! And you know what happened?"

"No suh," replied Jefferson, his eyes opened wide as he listened to the man who had become a living legend in the lives of the Henrys and Covingtons, to name but two.

"Not a thing," declared Ivory with a huff.

"How's that?" demanded David.

"Well, I suppose you might say mother nature intervened in our behalf. The weather turned wet all of a sudden like, and when I say wet I don't mean damp! No suh! I mean to tell you it rained like there was no tomorrow! The Rappahannock went over its banks! So did the Rapidan and all them little creeks and streams what feed both rivers! What a mess it was! Ah'll tell ya true, it only took that Stoneman fella a few days to forget the whole operation, lock, stock and barrel!"

The younger generation continued to watch and listen in captivation. Those who were a little older, like David and Jefferson, had already taken history classes and knew what they had just heard was merely the preliminary. Younger boys who knew nothing of the battles glanced at one another with perplexed expressions on their faces as if to say, "Is that all there is?"

"All right now," continued Ivory, "let's get down to some serious business! Mr. F. J. Hooker was powerful disappointed 'cause General Stoneman couldn't get across the river, but he didn't change his basic ideas, and he sho' didn't give up! No suh! In fact, he decided to go himself one better. Instead of cavalry he'd go with infantry, lots of 'em. Ah 'll tell ya why he was so bold. Had himself some real good spies he did...and balloons! Y'all knew 'bout them balloons didn't ya? Big ol' yella things! They used to fly 'em over Fredericksburg and watch us from the air! Can y'all imagine that? This world sure is a changin'! Anyway, Hooker probably knew more 'bout us than we knew 'bout our selves. He had us outnumbered by way mo' than two to one and figured to divide his army in two, knowin' good and well that each wing would outnumber us.

GRAY VISIONS

"The only question left for him to answer was where to make the crossin'. This is where I'm gonna need some help from some of you Virginia boys. Ah can't fo' the life of me remember the names of those fords on the Rappahannock, but ah do remember there was three of 'em".

"Banks Ford, Kelly's Ford and U.S. Ford!" cried out an old soldier from the crowd.

"Which one was farthest upstream?" asked Ivory.

"Kelly's," came the reply.

"That's the one!" Ivory snapped his fingers as he recognized the name. "The other two was right close to our left flank and we had them fortified, but Kelly's...horse of a different color that one! If memory serves me that ford was some fifteen miles upriver from where the Rapidan joined the Rappahannock. It's up near a place called Morrisville, is that right?"

"Sho'nuff." nodded Wil.

"Hooker figured he'd get three corps of infantry over the Rappahannock way out on our left, then over the Rapidan and then into the wilderness, which would put them square in our rear! He sent his orders and put his boys in motion. Three corps headed for Morrisville on Monday, the 27th of April. Lemme see now...Meade led one of 'em...Howard another..."

"I believe the third was Slocum's," Longstreet added the missing name.

"Thank you, suh." Ivory nodded in the general's direction. "Now I'll tell you boys somethin' else. Them Yankee soldiers never had to deal with the shortages we had to put up with, ah 'll tell ya true! Every one of them federals was carryin' fifty to sixty pounds on his back. They had blankets, overcoats, rations, ammo...it adds up! A lot of them boys got tired of carryin' that stuff long befo' they reached Morrisville. They was tossin'em aside all over the road and the local folks were quick to snatch em up."

"Can I ask you somethin'?" posed Jefferson.

"Sho'nuff," nodded Ivory, "that's why ah'm sittin' here."

"How is it you know so much? Particularly about what the Yankees were doin'?"

"Son," Levi thought to hush the boy lest Ivory take offense.

"No, no," Ivory gestured toward Levi, "The boy asked a good question." Then addressing himself to the younger Henry he offered this reply. "Ah talk a lot, son. Must be my nature. Ah talked to a bunch of Yankee prisoners after the battle, talked to local folks when I was out foragin' for provisions. And ah listened too. Listened to a mess of our own soldiers and officers. On top of that a lot of what ah'm gonna be tellin ya ah saw fo' mahself when the battle got goin'. The good Lawd blessed me with a stone cold memory, 'cept I gotta admit its startin' to fade a bit. Reckon ah must be gettin' old. Anyhow, that's how ah learned all the stuff you're hearin'... you understand?"

Jefferson made no verbal reply but quickly nodded his head.

"Now where was I?" Ivory scratched his bald head and smiled.

"Three corps of Yankees headin' up toward Morrisville," returned someone from the crowd.

"Sho'nuff!" grinned Ivory, "And the next day Hooker himself is ridin' after em, just to make sure they stayed on schedule...checkin' up on 'em, you know what ah 'm sayin'. Anyhow by day's end his boys were approachin' Kelly's Ford and ol' Hooker, he was feelin' right pleased with the way the whole thing was goin'.

"By dawn of the next day all three of those Federal corps

was across the Rappahannock along with most of Stoneman's cavalry. They didn't waste no time, not a minute, off they marched for the Rapidan and by day's end they had captured and crossed both fords on that river..." he paused searching his memory for the names of the fords.

"Germanna," said someone.

"And Ely's!" grinned Ivory as the second name came to him. "Didn't take much to capture either one 'cause we only had a handful of boys watchin' em. Anyhow, by dawn of the next day they was on the move again and long 'bout noon they started filin' into an eerie lookin' region called the Wilderness. Now you old fellers know good and well what place ah 'm talkin' 'bout, but you young-uns listen good and ah'll describe this place for ya.

"The Wilderness ain't no virgin forest, that's for sho'! Secondary growth all through there...scrub stuff... oak, pine mostly; all of it covered with vines and brambles so thick it choked out the sun most days! A man couldn't walk through there without havin' his clothes torn by all them thorns and such. A long time back some folks used to live in there, not many, but a few. Here and there the Yankees would come upon an old abandoned cabin or a barn all broken down. They say General Meade was awful nervous 'bout bein' in that maze of undergrowth and he pushed his boys hard to get 'em through as quick as they could.

"'Nuff of them for the moment," Ivory smoothly shifted direction, "Let's get back to Fredericksburg. Remember what ah said earlier, General Hooker done left three corps of Infantry to stay in front of us. The man in charge here was..."Again the name eluded him. "Oh what's the matter with me?" he complained with a smile, "Ah can almost picture the man! He's the one that one of our snipers killed a year later at Spotsylvania..."

"Sedgwick," said Longstreet, "It was General Sedgwick."

THE TELLING OF CHANCELLORSVILLE

"Yessuh, it sho' was," nodded Ivory. "General Sedgwick did exactly what he'd been told to do. He threw pontoon bridges across the river well below Fredericksburg out of the range of our guns, and then he set up a strong bridgehead on the south bank where he could hit the right side of our line. So now the Army of the Potomac was divided in two, half of 'em facing our right, the other half closin' in on our rear.

"Now let's get back to that other group. Havin' crossed both rivers, the Federals easily swept our boys off of U.S. Ford, which sent Hooker's mood just-a-soarin'! Now he could move troops quickly at will back and forth across the river...whatever the situation called for, and just to drive that point home he shifts one corps of infantry from Sedgwick's bunch on down into the Wilderness, plus another one that was upriver from Fredericksburg. All in all, by the last day of April he had himself five corps of infantry behind us in the Wilderness, plus all his cavalry. You boys know how many men we're talkin' 'bout here? Close to 80,000, ah'll tell ya true! That's more' n twice the size of the army we faced at First Manassas! 80,000 of 'em and they was settin' square in our rear!"

"Sounds like they was tryin' to do to us what Marse Robert done to Pope at Second Manasses," observed a middle-aged veteran somewhere in the crowd.

"Close," agreed Ivory. "Cept they didn't quite pull it off, but let's give them boys credit where credit's due. They pulled a march on us and got themselves behind us without us knowin'. I heard General Alexander talkin' 'bout it some time later," he paused and glanced at General Longstreet. "You remember him suh? He was your chief of artillery."

"I remember him well," smiled Longstreet. "I imagine there's a lot of Union generals who remember him even better,

~ 135 ~

though not as fondly as I."

"Ah'll bet they do!" Ivory flashed a hearty grin. "Anyhow, I remember hearin' General Alexander describe this move of Hookers as the most brilliantly executed maneuver ever attempted against us. Ah reckon it may've been. The Yankees sho' did think so. In any event it didnt turn out quite the way Hooker figured on."

"He was hopin' General Lee would fall back, right?" The question came from young David, his wide-open eyes riveted on Ivory Lee Davis.

"Pretty much," nodded Ivory. "The whole thing was designed to get us out of our trenches. He figured we'd either retreat in a hurry toward Richmond or turn to face him on open ground. Either way it was supposed to be the end of the Army of Northern Virginia, but ah'm tellin' ya true, Mr. F. J. Hooker sho' wasn't plannin' on what happened next."

"What did happen?" One of the other youngsters in the gathering was growing impatient.

"Gimme time, son, gimme time," Ivory raised an open hand palm outward in the direction of the boy's voice. "Ah'm gettin' there.

"By this time Hooker was settlin' in to his headquarters in Chancellorsville, which may sound like a town to some of you boys but in those days it weren't no such thing. It was just an intersection of two dirt roads what ran through the Wilderness only a couple miles or so from the eastern edge of that region. One home was all that was there, a big ol' place built out of brick and logs with a two-story veranda out front, a few outbuildin's scattered 'round and 'bout a hundred acres of cleared fields. There was some ladies at home when the Yankees came marchin' in, and ah can tell you they was none too pleased at havin to entertain all those northern generals, but they sho' wasn't in much of a position to argue 'bout it. Ah think this is where Hooker made his first mistake. He stopped there. I guess he wanted to wait and see what Marse Robert was gonna do in response to all this. Right then he gave up the initiative and passed it on over to General Lee, and y'all remember Marse Robert, he wasn't 'bout to give Mr. F. J. Hooker a second chance."

"Amen!" Someone shouted.

"Yessuh!" Ivory nodded. "If ol' Hooker had kept goin' they'd of probably dragged us back into the United States, but he hesitated...and y'all know what they say 'bout folks what hesitate!"

"So what did our army do?" The question came from a boy whose years could scarcely have numbered twelve.

"Patience," counseled Ivory with a smile, "You'll soon know." Then he raised his voice so all could again hear him. "So far ah 've been tellin' y'all what Hooker was up to and how he done crossed the river and got behind us. I ain't said nothin' 'bout what we was doin' so ah reckon the time's come to tell that part of the story.

"Seems like I got started cause these boys here asked me 'bout Stonewall Jackson. So if you older fellers don't mind too much, ah'll tell the young-uns a little bit of Stonewall durin' the winter and spring of '63. The Fredericksburg line was quiet for the most part from January through April. I guess you could say it was kind of a stalemate. He had his headquarters in an office cottage on a plantation in the Moss Neck area. The folks what owned this place was well-to-do and this cottage ah'm talkin' 'bout was furnished real nice...almost too nice from Stonewall's way of lookin' at things. You older men know how he was. He looked at the world through the eyes of a Presbyterian deacon...didn't much care for creature comforts...preferred a simple strict regimen, and here he found himself in the midst of splendor!" he paused and chuckled to himself, "And ol' Jeb...Jeb Stuart couldn't resist chidin' Stonewall from time to time, actin' all horrified at his supposed fall from spirituality. Even Marse Robert had a few words to say, all in humor of course. Ah heard this from one of the servants of that plantation. Stonewall had a supper one night...all the brass was there, Marse Robert included. A fine meal it was! They was dinin' on stuff simple soldiers like us could only dream of!" He stopped for a second and glanced at General Longstreet. "Ah hope you didn't take offense at that suh. Just tellin' like ah heard it."

"Of course not," Longstreet eased his concerns with a smile. "I'd be a liar if I didn't admit that rank does have its privileges from time to time. Go ahead with your story."

"Sho' 'nuff" continued Ivory. "The meal...well let's just say it was one Helluva supper! Roast turkey was the main course but on the side they had several different preparations of oysters. Makes mah mouth water just thinkin' 'bout it! Near the end of the meal General Lee says to all of 'em that they was only playin' at bein' soldiers, that if they wanted to see how real soldiers lived they should come dine with him sometime. Stonewall didn't quite know what to make of all this.

"By April he had moved his headquarters back to his tent near a place called Hamilton's Crossing and Ah remember hearin' him say what a relief it was to be someplace less comfortable. Made him feel better 'bout himself.

"Ah want to tell you the part what touches mah heart most deeply. On the 20th of April - and y'all keep in mind how close that was to the day we lost him fo'ever - Mrs. Jackson arrived to visit with her husband. Not just her; she brought their baby girl, five months old and just the sweetest li'l' ol' baby you ever set eyes on! Keep somethin' in mind here. Over a year had passed since Stonewall had seen his wife; and the baby he'd never seen at all, not the first glimpse. Her name was Julia and her Papa got to hold her in his arms for the first time that day. She weren't but five months old...just a little bundle...can y'all imagine ol' Blue Light holdin' that li'l' baby girl?

"Now a soldier's tent ain't exactly the ideal place for a family reunion...especially a general's. And since his family was gonna be stayin' awhile, mo' suitable accommodations had to be found. There was a family by the name of Yerby what had a right big house nearby and they offered the Jackson's one room -- which Stonewall was quick to accept. Those few days in April were a precious time for all three of them. Ah ain't never seen Stonewall so happy in all the days ah served with the man. Sometimes he and the Mrs. would go walkin' outside together and ah'd see 'em a lot cause ah was usually drivin' mah wagon, fetchin' supplies from one section of the line to another. The thing was...the war...you know it just wouldn't go away. The Yankee guns was right across that ol' river, always visible. And them big ol' yella balloons was up in there in the sky, every day lookin' down on us. One day ah happened to pass by General and Mrs. Jackskon when they was standin' close to the road. Ah looked over and tipped mah hat to her, but she weren't lookin' at me. Had her eyes fixed on one of them balloons. There was a strange expression in her eyes, ah can't quite describe it, but ah 've always wondered what was goin' on in her mind. Never got the chance to ask her. Maybe someday our paths 'll cross again and ah'll think to ask.

"We knew trouble was comin' on the mornin' of the 29th. The Yankees was working like a hive of bees throwin' their pontoon bridges across the river long about a mile below the town of Fredericksburg. Someone went to tell Stonewall and I don't think he had a whole lot of time to say farewell to his wife and daughter.

GRAY VISIONS

If ah remember correctly the General's staff chaplain helped her pack and escorted her and the baby on down to a Richmond-bound train with gunfire breakin' out all around."

He stopped speaking for a moment and stood, pressing his hands into the small of his back and stretching up on his toes with a loud groan. "Gettin' old," he chuckled with a shake of his head as he stepped over to the woodpile. He motioned for several of the boys near the fire to build it back up, a request which was quickly taken care of. Flames were soon licking hungrily at the new arrivals and quickly shot higher into the night air. "Seems like it's a bit mo' chilly than awhile ago," he said as he climbed back onto the crates and seated himself again.

"Yer just gettin' soft in your old age, Ivory," joked Turner.

"You go on now, Miles," returned Ivory with a jovial expression on his face and the light of the fire dancing in his eyes. "Where was I?" He suddenly looked perplexed as he scratched his bearded face and tried to remember exactly where he'd left off.

"You just told us how General and Mrs. Jackson parted company on the mornin' of the 29th," explained Armelin.

"Ah sho' did! Thank you," Ivory nodded at the Cajun. "I was awake befo' sunup that mornin,'" he continued, "gettin' a breakfast fire started fo' the boys. Ah was comin' back with an armful of wood and movin' past Marse Robert's tent when one of Stonewall's staff officers showed up to give General Lee the news. Marse Robert must've been in a good mood that mornin' cause he teased the fellow, actin' like he was upset. He said...and I still remember these words...don't know why, they just stuck with me... He said, `Captain, what do you young men mean by waking a man out of his sleep?' That Captain was quick to explain that the Federals was comin' across the river on pontoon bridges, and Marse Robert says to him, `Well, I thought I heard firing and I was beginning to think it was time some of you young fellows were coming to tell me what it was all about. You want me to send a message to your good General, Captain? Tell him that I am sure he knows what to do. I will meet him at the front very soon.' Lemme ask y'all if that sounds like he was ruffled? Anyone think so? Well, y'all can take it from me that he wasn't the least bit riled. Ah'll tell you true, Marse Robert had nerves like cold steel, yessuh, just like steel.

"Wasn't long after that General Lee was up on the line seein' fo' himself what was happenin'. The whole camp had come to arms by that time and we was tradin' lead with the Federals, but neither side was doin' too much damage. Bluecoats was down by the river just as thick at flies, but they didn't seem to be in no hurry to come our way. For awhile it seemed like Marse Robert might order an attack, but he thought better of it. The Federals was pretty safe down there 'cause they was under the cover of long-range guns from up on the heights across the river. General Lee decided we'd make our stand right there on the same ridge where Jackson's corps had fought back in December and he ordered Stonewall to bring up all his reserves, artillery and infantry, and put 'em into the line. That's 'bout the same time he sent that message on down to Richmond what General Longstreet told y'all 'bout earlier. The battle was on or so we thought."

After taking a few sips from a freshly poured cup of coffee Ivory collected his thoughts for the next stage of the story and resumed his tale. "Let's get on back to Hooker and his boys over in the Wilderness," he declared with a broad sweep of his right arm. "Remember how happy ah said the Federals was 'cause they stole a march on us and got in behind us. And remember what ah said 'bout the mistake Hooker made when he ordered his boys to stop in them woods. General Lee found out 'bout them bein' there long 'bout noon if ah recall rightly. It seems ol' Jeb Stuart had his troopers nippin' here and there at Hooker's infantry as they was passin' through the woods. He wasn't tryin' to stop 'em,- - Lawd knows he didn't have the numbers to even think along those lines. Instead he'd nab a few prisoners from different points along their line of march. That way he could find out what units had crossed the river and was comin' our way. Stuart's first report said there was 'bout 14,000 men comin' our way. By late afternoon he had prisoners from three Union corps and said they was all movin' toward the Rapidan. Marse Robert couldn't ignore that information, and he sho' couldn't leave ol Jeb out there where he might get cut off from the rest of us, 'cause cavalry...well...that's the eyes and ears of the army. Without them we'd been fumblin' round like a bunch of blind men. So he sent word for Stuart to clear out of that region quick-like and get back to the army. Jeb did like he was told but not befo' he did a little mo' lookin' 'round, and what he saw he didn't like. He sent the General one mo' courier who reached us long 'bout dusk; said there was two long columns of bluecoats and they was across both Rapidan fords movin' toward the Wilderness. By the time it got dark on the 29th General Lee knew Hooker had got in behind us in strength. With Stuart comin' back in, the Federal cavalry, more than 10,000 of 'em, was free to tear up our line of supply. Their infantry was in two places ready to snap us up like the powerful jowls of a wild animal! Yessuh! The Army of Northern Virginia was all of a sudden in deep trouble, but Hell, it ain't like we was never in trouble befo'!"

"Tell 'em, Ivory!" came a voice from the crowd.

"You know ah will!" returned the old black man with a hearty smile. "After that last courier came in General Lee knew he couldn't afford to wait another minute, no suh! No, suh! Not one!

THE TELLING OF CHANCELLORSVILLE

He sent word to General Anderson to pull in his two brigades what was guardin' U.S. Ford and to take them, along with his other two brigades and to march west toward Chancellorsville. General Anderson was one of Longstreet's, so was McLaw's They was the two General Longstreet didn't take with him to Southside. Marse Robert told McLaws he'd best be ready to move out at the tap of a drum just in case. It rained like the dickens that night, but General Anderson got his boys on the march 'bout nine o'clock."

"I was one of 'em!" shouted an old man who had joined the swelling crowd of people gathered to hear Ivory tell Chancellorsville.

"Me too!" cried another.

"And bless the both of ya!" grinned Ivory. "For the next three hours them boys marched through the rainy night. By midnight they was diggin' in just shy of Chancellorsville, one division, mind you, and they was facin' more than 60,000 Yankees with mo' on the way!

"Mornin' came soon enough and Marse Robert kept his attention fixed on them Federals on our side of the river. There was a lot of 'em down there but it didn't look like they was in any hurry to come at us. In fact they was diggin' in all along their perimeter lookin' mo' like they was gonna receive an attack rather than deliver one. Stonewall and General Lee disagreed 'bout whether to oblige the Yankees or not. Ol' Blue Light...he was all for pitchin' straight into 'em, but Marse Robert was too worried 'bout them big Federal guns up on the heights 'cross the river. The mornin' dragged on and finally General Lee says he'll allow an attack if Stonewall could make himself certain that it would accomplish somethin' worthwhile. Stonewall left right 'bout then to scout the terrain out fo' himself. While he was gone mo' riders started comin' from the

GRAY VISIONS

Wilderness. They reported huge columns of infantry comin' east from Germanna Ford and Ely's too! Long 'bout mid-day word comes in from General Anderson. He said he was diggin' in just east of the Wilderness and that all he'd seen of the Yankees so far was a handful of cavalry. Lee sent word back for him to redouble his efforts to set all his shovels to workin' as vigorously as possible. That's exactly what he said...Ah remember every word. He was startin' to worry 'bout that side of our line...that much was plain. He even scraped up another battalion of artillery and sent it that way along with a passel of engineers to design their lines.

"Meanwhile Jackson comes back lookin' all sad and forlorn cause, try as he might he just couldn't find a weak spot in the Federal bridgehead down by the river. Marse Robert pulled out his binoculars to study a bit mo' on his own. An argument got started among his officers right then. Ah don't mean to say that like they was mad and ready to come to blows, but they was havin' themselves a right spirited discussion about where they thought Hooker was plannin' to land his heaviest punch, upriver or downriver. Marse Robert settled the whole thing real quick-like when he put his binoculars back in their case and announces that the main blow was aimed at our rear. Then he had to make himself some quick decisions 'cause Hooker's boys was gettin' closer to General Anderson's by the minute.

"What to do? Ah'll tell ya one thing true, there sho' wasn't a lotta time fo' thinkin' 'bout it! Course that was one of Marse Robert's strong points. He never did need much time to make a decision. The enormity of what Hooker had already done was makin' itself pretty damn obvious. The force comin' at us through the Wilderness, however big it was, was in a position to put itself between us and Richmond. The General couldn't let that happen. By the same token there was a whole lot of bluecoats starin' at us from that bridgehead and mo' comin across on those pontoon bridges. We could hardly afford to ignore 'em, now could we?"

He paused and ran the fingers of his right hand over the top of his head as he stared intently at the fire while organizing his thoughts. "It was some time after dark befo' Marse Robert wrote out his orders for the next day, and what he decided didn't come as no surprise to any of us. Since the main threat was rollin' in behind us he chose to take the bulk of the army off the Fredericksburg line and head down toward Chancellorsville to meet it. Jackson's corps got the call. Wil, you and Levi remember that don't ya?"

"Sho' nuff," nodded Wil.

"One of his divisions was ordered to stay put and keep tabs on them Yankees in the bridgehead...was it Early's?"

"It was," affirmed Levi.

"Wasn't just him," mused Ivory his brow furrowed as he tried to recall the missing details.

"One of Mclaw's brigades was ordered to stay with him," recalled Miles.

"That's right," nodded Ivory, "altogether there was maybe 10,000 of 'em left up on the Rappahannock. That's all, just 10,000. And with them General Early had to contain any attempt by that General Sedgwick to break away from the riverbank. The rest was to march fo' the Wilderness come mornin'. If ya throw in ol' Jeb's cavalry we had maybe 48,000 to face what Mr. F. J. Hooker was puttin' together out there near Chancellorsville. The odds was long, sho' nuff, but they was destined to get a whole lot longer fo' the smoke cleared."

He paused a moment and shook his head as the memories of that time suddenly flooded back into his mind. Quickly he resumed the story. "The 1st of May dawned just like a beautiful spring mornin' oughta. The air was warm with just a little mist huggin' the ground. Flowers was openin' up their petals to the sun. All the trees was in full foliage with that light green color you see 'round us now. 'Cept the dogwoods; you could pick them out right easy, all white or pink against the green. Sho' didn't seem like no day for warrin' on each other, but that's exactly what was 'bout to happen'.

"Y'all remember what ah said earlier 'bout Hooker? How he used U.S. Ford to move another Corps 'cross the river on the last night of April? He sho'nuff did and that gave him nearly 80,000 muskets to throw at Jackson when the time came. Keep that in mind hear?

"Back up on the Fredericksburg line General Early was sayin' every prayer he knew. He had his one division along with that extra brigade from McLaws. Ah remember now...it was Barksdale's boys from Mississippi, and y'all know what that bunch did to the Yankees in the battle of Fredericksburg! Anyhow General Early had his boys stretched out over five miles of entrenchments, all the way from Marye's Heights on down to Hamilton Crossin'. That's why he was prayin' so hard! His was the thinnest of thin lines, ah'll tell ya true! Marse Robert told him to make his few look like many. They had to move 'round a lot, and make it appear like they was gonna charge any minute! It was kinda like a poker game when you ain't holdin' nothin' but a pair of deuces, but you're bluffin' up a storm like you was holdin' all four Aces! You know what ah'm sayin?"

Here he paused again and rose from his seat. He stepped down from the crate and snatched up the metal rod he'd been using earlier to shift logs in the fire. Stepping over close to David and Jefferson he glanced up into the crowd. "Ah just want to draw this in the dirt for these young boys," he explained. "You old fellas 'll know what ah'm talkin' 'bout." He proceeded to jab a hole into the ground and announced, "Chancellorsville." Then he pulled back nearly two feet and slightly to the left, drilling another hole which he proclaimed to be Tabernacle Church. Whereupon he reached to his right perhaps fourteen or fifteen inches and forced a third hole into the ground. "This was a mill up near Banks Ford," he said, "but ah'll be hanged if ah can remember the name of the place."

"Overson's," called one of the middle-aged men in the crowd.

"If you say so!" Ivory grinned in the direction of that voice. Then he turned his attention back to the collection of youthful faces whose attention was thoroughly fixed on his story. "This here mill, Oversons, was the extreme right of the new line our boys was erectin' opposite Chancellorsville. General Mclaws held that part of the line. Down here," he pointed toward the hole in the ground which he had designated Tabernacle Church. "This was the far left held by Anderson's boys. By sunrise on the 1st, spades were flyin' up and down this line, diggin' trenches to receive an attack everybody figured was comin'.

"Lo and behold," he proclaimed as his eyes scanned the assembled faces, "here comes Stonewall Jackson ridin' at the head of his three divisions! He sees Anderson and Mclaws diggin' in to defend, but ah'm tellin ya true that just wasn't Jackson's way! He wanted to go after 'em! Now Marse Robert...his orders to Jackson the night befo' left a good bit of room for interpretation. That's kinda the way he liked to operate. Anyhow, he done told Stonewall to make arrangements to repulse the enemy. To some generals that meant trenches and head logs, but that's not how Stonewall Jackson saw it. In his mind the best way to repulse the enemy was to find him and drive him from the field! He told Generals' Anderson and Mclaws to put those shovels down and pick up their muskets. Chancellorsville was four miles from this line. That's where the Yankees was and that's where Stonewall chose to go! Two roads ran that way, the Orange Turnpike and the Plank road. Mclaws took the first one, Anderson the second. Stonewall was close on their heels. They was on the march a good hour befo' noon and within twenty minutes we could hear muskets firin' off in the distance. Stonewall had said to keep movin' till we hit somethin' solid. Our boys did just that. Word soon came in from Stuart sayin' he was close on Stonewall's flank and would do everythin' he could when the ball opened...that's just the way he put it too...when the ball opened. Ol' Jeb closed that message with a prayer that God would grant us a victory. Ah was close by when Stonewall wrote his reply and he kinda talked it while he wrote it. Ah remember his expressin' his trust that God would grant us a great victory, but at the same time he didn't forget to remind Stuart to keep hisself closed on Chancellorsville.

Here he paused to catch his breath and partake of a glass of water. Turning to face Miles he chuckled and shook his head, "Ah must be gettin' old, Miles. Tellin' these stories never used to tire me so."

"Take your time, old friend." continued Miles with a look of concern on his face. "It ain't like we're in hurry to go no place."

"Sho'nuff," smiled Ivory as he drained the glass, took a deep breath, and continued. Using the poker he drew the roads in the dirt so his listeners could see how they converged at Tabernacle Church, then separated as they moved through the Wilderness only to converge again at Chancellorsville. "We were marchin' this way," he explained. "Hooker had his boys on the march from Chancellorsville 'bout the same time. Meade was up on the Turnpike and Slocum was comin' along down here on the

Plank road. They had three more corps comin' along behind 'em. Now y'all picture that for a second. Hooker had five corps of infantry to face only five divisions under Jackson. Think 'bout that.

"Anyhow, Federals was on the move comin' toward us. They was told that the new headquarters was gonna be Tabernacle Church. Of course to get there they had to push Stonewall Jackson out of the way. No easy job that one! This is where the terrain of the Wlilderness worked to our advantage. Once these two roads separated, Meade and Slocum lost contact with one another. In a sense, each one was isolated from the rest of their army. It was Sykes division of Meade's corps what made the first real contact with us. You older fellas'll remember them boys. They included those Zouaves from New York what slowed us down at Henry Hill durin' Second Manassas. They ran into Mclaws' skirmishers on the face of a long rise at the eastern fringe of the Wilderness. Drove 'em back too, till they saw Mclaws whole division arrayed in battle formation up on the crest. Then we stopped 'em cold and real quick-like started pushin' 'em back. That fella Sykes started callin' for help in no time flat, ah'll tell ya true!

"Help was quick in comin'. Another corps of Federals under General Couch was close at hand. He sent Hancock's division to support Sykes and that was enough to stabilize their line. Y'all remember Hancock don't ya? He was a corps commander by the time we fought him at Spotsylvania. If memory serves me he was the one we roughed up right badly in the muleshoe and again on the last day. He was the one dug in out there in these woods here on the North Anna opposite the right wing of our line. Anyway, with Hancock's help, Sykes got himself reorganized and the two of them was preparin' to go back on the offense against Mclaws when the strangest thing happened! Orders comes to 'em from Mr. F. J. Hooker himself, and those orders says to disengage and retire at once to Chancellorsville! Neither one of them generals could believe their eyes when they read that order! They knew how badly they had us outnumbered and they were sho' they could sweep the field!

"Down on the Plank Road the same thing happened. General Anderson fought General Slocum to a standstill, but then the weight of numbers began to tell...and whoa! Slocum gets the same order from Hooker, greets it with the same disbelief, but obeys it.

"Way up in our right General Meade had overlapped our line -- not hard to do when you think how short that line had to be! He'd made virtually no contact with us and was within sight of that mill - Overson's. When he got the order to withdraw he almost fell into a state of shock! All them corps commanders were beside themselves with disbelief! What happened to Fightin' Joe? What happened to the idea of a new headquarters at Tabernacle Church. Ah think it was General Meade what asked this question: `If Hooker didn't think he could hold the top of a hill, how did he expect to hold the bottom of it?'" Here he paused and addressed himself specifically to his younger listeners. "Might one of y'all venture an explanation?" he asked.

"Explanation?" David glanced around nervously like a pupil in a classroom who'd just been asked a question the answer to which was quite beyond him.

"Uh-huh," nodded Ivory. "Can any of y'all tell me why Mr. F. J. Hooker pulled back after makin' contact with our boys in those woods?"

"I'm not sure," stammered David.

"Maybe he just lost his nerve," offered Jefferson.

"I've heard that," agreed Ivory, "some of his own

officers said they thought he lost faith in himself at the last minute, but what ah want you to tell me is why? What caused him to go timid all of a sudden like that?"

A young boy sitting behind Jefferson and off to the right a piece decided to take a chance. "Maybe he realized who was in front of him."

"Maybe he did!" Ivory emphasized the point with a slap of his knee. "And just who was in front of him?" he pressed.

"Stonewall Jackson!" grinned the youth.

"Who else?"

"Robert E. Lee," declared another.

"That's it!" smiled Ivory. "You got to remember the reputation that our generals had in those days. General Lee and General Jackson...General Longstreet sittin' here with us today...Jeb Stuart...all these men had acquired quite a name with the Yankees. Some of the Federal officers held them in awe, and ah think Hooker was one of those. All that braggin' and blusterin' he done was a smoke screen. Deep down he must not have believed he could face Robert E. Lee and Stonewall Jackson, and ah think. when he found out these two were in front of him he flat out lost faith in himself.

"Still the same," he continued, "It wasn't just his awareness of Lee and Jackson what made him turn so cautious when he may have been on the verge of a tremendous victory. There was other reasons."

"Well, you'd best be tellin us," insisted David.

"Ah was just fixin' to do that," grinned Ivory. "The whole thing was like a chess game," he declared. "All the while there was a game of wits goin' on between Mr. F. J. Hooker and Marse Robert. Lots of factors was playin' in to it, not just the fightin' along them two roads. Now ah honestly can't say whether Marse Robert did this on purpose or whether the deserter was for real."

"Deserter? What deserter?"

"The night befo' the battle started the Yankees captured themselves a deserter, or so they thought, and took him to their headquarters outside of Fredericksburg. He was real cooperative. Ah'm tellin' ya true! Told 'em that Longstreet's whole corps had left Suffolk by rail and was already in Culpeper, directly behind Hooker and his boys in the Wilderness!"

"Rest assured," added Longstreet, "we were still down in the Southside at that point."

"Sho' was!" chuckled Ivory, "Another deserter said that Hood's Texans was already with Lee, which contradicted the first one who put Hood with Longstreet in Culpeper. You wanna know what ah think? Ah don't think either one of them boys was deserters. Ah'll betcha both of 'em was plants put out there by General Lee to raise questions and doubts in ol' Hooker's mind, and ah'm inclined to think the ruse did just what it was supposed to do.

"Now remember what ah told ya earlier 'bout Hooker's intentions when he chose to flank us in such strength. He figured a move like that would force us to either retreat toward Richmond or turn to attack him at Chancellorsville, but it wasn't the second option he was countin' on. He really wanted to see us strung out on the roads toward Richmond where he could tear us up piecemeal. At the outset, befo' he heard that stuff from the deserters he knew how badly we was outnumbered, and Ah think he believed in his heart that the logical thing for us to do was pull back toward Richmond. The problem for him was this. General Lee didn't do what Hooker thought was the logical thing. In fact, Marse Robert wasn't behavin' at all like a badly outnumbered opponent who'd just been completely outmaneuvered, and that put even more questions into the mind of Fightin' Joe Hooker.

"Here comes another twist. You remember them balloons ah told ya 'bout? Well that big ol' yella balloon was up in the sky just like it was every day, and it had a telegraph wire runnin' back to the ground. By late mornin' the sun had burned all the mist away so that fella up in the balloon had himself a bird's eye view of the whole region. He could see Anderson and Mclaw's diggin' in along the new line and he watched Jackson's boys marchin' in behind him. What he saw he relayed to Hooker on the wire. Told him 'bout heavy concentrations of troops movin' toward Chancellorsville, but he also let him know how thin Early's line was up there on the Rappahannock. All this new information did nothin' but pile mo' questions into Hooker's mind. Ah think he began to believe what one of them deserters ah spoke of said the night befo', namely that General Lee had announced that this would be the first time he'd get to fight an opponent with equal numbers. That's why ah think he lost his nerve.

"There's one mo' mistake Hooker made at Chancellorsville. Y'all know how impo'tant cavalry is to the army."

"Eyes and ears," observed Armelin.

"Exactly," nodded Ivory, "and Hooker sent all of his cavalry off to the south to do whatever damage they could. In a sense he poked out his eyes and cut off his ears. Marse Robert had no such problem. Ol' Jeb, he was on hand both to scout and to fight from the time the first musket sounded."

Here he interrupted the story for the moment and glanced curiously at Miles Turner, who had just placed a skewer of fresh beef over the fire. "What are you up to?" he asked.

"Figured you must be workin' up a powerful appetite,"

came the reply. "Don't you mind me. Go on 'bout your story. I'll take care of this."

"Well thank you, Miles. You're lookin' after this old man, eh?"

"Somebody has to," chuckled Miles as he brushed a generous quantity of tangy sauce across the meat. "Now get back into the story! I'm startin' to get intrigued... and I was there for Lord's sake!"

"Okay," nodded Ivory, but then a puzzled expression passed across his face. "Where was I?"

"You just told us how General Hooker deprived himself of his own cavalry," replied Longstreet.

"Ah sho' did!" grinned the aging black man. "Now y'all think 'bout all the different factors ah've told ya 'bout over the last few minutes, all of 'em buildin' doubts in the mind of Mr. F. J. Hooker. Then comes the clincher. He didn't expect to be attacked when his two columns started east from Chancellorsville on them roads that mornin'! Stonewall's decision to attack the Federals along with the initial success of those attacks just compounded the doubts naggin' away at Mr. F. J. Hooker's backbone. He started to fall victim to them same bugaboos what used to plague George McClellan. Remember him? Remember how he always used to assume we had 'bout twice as many men as we really had? I think Hooker musta succumbed to a touch of whatever illness that was.

"What did it do to him?" he gestured with one hand overhead in a circular motion to draw the attention of every eye present. "Done robbed him of his nerve that's what. Done robbed him clean. The caution bug bit him. He pulled his loins in and decided to go on the defense. Oh, he didn't go completely timid. He figured he was facin' the bulk of our army - which he was 'cept it just wasn't as big as he was thinkin' - so it made sense to use the other wing of his own army, Sedgwick's troops dug in nice 'n snug in that bridgehead up on the river. So he sent word for them to attack as soon as an openin' presented itself, and then he sat back to defend Chancellorsville. It was like he was invitin' Marse Robert and Stonewall to come get him. Lawd knows neither one of them was ever the kind to turn down an invitation like that! Ah'm tellin ya true!

"Course ah'm gettin' ahead mahself. Ah done already told ya how angry Meade, Covel and Slocum was. Hooker musta sensed it...how could he help it? He knew he had to put the best possible face on all this or he'd have trouble on the home front as well. He done took over the Chancellor house for his headquarters and to him came the corps commanders wantin' to know what happened. Y'all won't believe what he had to say! Ah found out later from one of the prisoners we took . Made me laugh...sho' did! He talked to Covel first and told him that he had Lee just where he wanted him! Said he had now forced us to fight him on his own ground. 'Magine that? Ah don't know if any of y'all have read what General Covel had to say 'bout that meetin' long after the war ended. 'Parently he wasn't too impressed by all that bluster. Said he walked away from Hooker convinced that his commander was a whipped man.

"Later that afternoon Hooker was meetin' with a bunch of his officers on the veranda of the Chancellor house. The sun was shinin' and the sky was just as blue as it could be! And here was Mr. F. J. Hooker actin' like everythin' was goin' his way. He wasn't the least bit bashful 'bout declarin' that the rebel army was now the legitimate property of the Army of the Potomac. Ah'm tellin' ya true! He called Marse Robert a desperate man...said he had no choice but to attack the Federals on their own ground. Claimed that his army stood as a shinin' example for all the other

GRAY VISIONS

Union armies to follow. Meanwhile, his soldiers was diggin' trenches all along a six mile front. From the Rappahannock river all the way down to a mile or so west of Wilderness Church. Every mother's son of them was waitin' to see what Robert E. Lee was gonna pull out of his sleeve."

After a silent yawn and a stretch of his arms, Ivory continued his tale: "That evenin' ah spent some time early on with General Alexander. He and his guns had been on the forefront of the action along the Plank Road all afternoon. They used up a lot of powder and shot and so ah was called on to carry a wagon load on over to him. Shared his cook fire fo' 'bout an hour and helped him put together some rations for some of the boys in his batteries. He done told me a few stories ah still remember. Said he got to within sight of the Chancellor House at one point and saw thousands of Yankees diggin' in. Told me how proud he was earlier that day when Lee and Jackson rode up together. Said it gave him chills to hear the men singin' out and cheerin' their commanders, and how he knew we'd prevail befo' the day was out. Still the same, he was seemin' kinda blue if ya know what ah'm sayin'. Even mah cookin' didn't seem to cheer him up too God-awful much, so ah sorta intruded on his thoughts. Said he was feelin' bad for a couple of reasons, both of 'em had to do with gunners. Earlier that day one of his pieces was bein' loaded in an apple orchard off to the side of the Plank Road. The charge blew up befo' it was s'posed to and took both hands off the man who was doin' the rammin'. General Alexander was still feelin' bad 'bout that. Later in the day after the Yanks pulled back and the fightin' stopped he and his battery was comin' back to the rear. They came upon a whole line of Yankee knapsacks that some regiment had thrown down on the side of the road as they ran. You young boys listen up now, hear? This'll give you an idea how close Ol' Stonewall stuck by the book. He was a soldier down to the marrow of his bones! As General Alexander and his gunners was passin' them knapsacks one of his sergeants stopped fo' a minute and got himself a brand new rubber overcoat. Them Federals always seemed to have the best stuff money could buy, ah'm tellin' ya true! A little while later General Alexander came upon Stonewall Jackson and rode over to report what he'd seen by the Chancellor house. Ol' Blue Light spotted that sergeant with the new coat and asked Alexander how he got it. When he heard the answer Stonewall ordered that the man be put immediately under close arrest for stopping to plunder on the battlefield. Alexander did like he was told but he felt awful bad cause he'd watched the sergeant stop to pick up the coat and hadn't objected. He sorta felt like an accomplice but hadn't seen no harm in it cause the fightin' had long since stopped and they wasn't in any particular hurry to get no place."

"What happened to that man?" pressed David.

"He was back in action the next day. Alexander said he was too good a gunner to keep out of the battle. He took personal responsibility fo' releasin' him from arrest."

"What about that man who lost his hands?" wondered Jefferson.

"Don't know," Ivory shook his head. "Fo' all Ah know he's sittin' 'round one of these fires tonite," he gestured with one arm in a sweeping motion. "There was one mo' thing naggin' at General Alexander that night," he continued. "One of his officers had given him a cup of coffee a few minutes befo' ah left. Turned out to be real coffee, not that awful-tastin' fake stuff we used to put together. Where do you suppose it came from?"

"The Yankees," replied a young boy several faces back in the crowd.

"Sho' did!" nodded Ivory. "They got 'em off of some dead

Federals. There was a bunch of these little buckskin bags with the coffee already ground up and sugar mixed into it!"

"They didn't lack for much, those bluecoats," commented Wil.

"Just like ah said earlier," agreed Ivory. "The best stuff money could buy. Anyhow, when Alexander realized he was drinkin' battlefield plunder he started feelin' mo' guilty than ever and ah figured it was time fo' me to fetch mah wagon and be on mah way," he grinned.

"Now let's get back to the situation after that first day's fight. We'd stopped the Federals along both roads, and with Hooker losin' his nerve they all pulled back into a defensive posture. Hooker was convinced we had a whole lot mo' men than we really had, so he sent fo' another corps from the northside of the river. They came over U.S. Ford durin' the night and they brought his strength up to 105,000 men...six corps in all! They was in front of us. Sedgwick was still in the beachhead on our side of the river below Fredericksburg with 25,000 mo'! Front and rear we had lots of bluecoats to deal with. Against all this we had maybe 48,000, but we were already splintered up! Barksdale was up across from Fredericksburg with 2,000. Early had 'bout 10,000 spread real thin to keep Sedgwick in check. Marse Robert with Stonewall had but 36,000 there at Chancellorsville to facin' odds that was better than 3-1. Course y'all know we faced long odds befo'. Sharpsburg comes to mind real quick when you start talkin' 'bout desperate fights with long odds! The thing was, Marse Robert didn't think we could just sit and wait for Hooker to come our way. Too many of them...too few of us. Hooker had passed the initiative on to us and Marse Robert sho' didn't relish the thought of givin' it up. So a plan had to be found." He paused here and glanced over at Turner who had just placed the now cooked beef on a plate.

"There ya go," announced Miles as he handed the plate to the black man who had been his partner for nearly two decades.

Ivory took the plate and feigned disbelief. "That's it?" he demanded in an incredulous tone. "You ain't gonna smother it with any of them mushrooms and onions and such?"

Miles glanced into the pot in which that mixture had been prepared. "Scraped clean," he returned. "Looks like we ate every damn bit of it."

"Yer' kiddin!"

"Ivory when do I ever kid 'bout food?"

Ivory, eyed the meat carefully as if trying to decide whether or not to eat it.

"Look" said Miles, "I might could find a piece of bread or somethin' 'round here to slop the juices with."

"Ah'd be obliged to ya," Ivory nodded toward Turner and accepted the offering. He placed the plate on his broad lap and sliced off a small chunk of beef which he chewed slowly, savoring every moment. "Yer' learnin'," he pointed the business end of his fork at Miles. "Reckon ah'll be makin a cook out of you yet."

The only reply from Miles was a smile and a shrug of his shoulders.

"Where was I?" Ivory glanced back at his listeners with a puzzled expression on his face.

"General Lee and General Jackson had to find themselves a plan to deal with Hooker when the sun came up," volunteered Jefferson.

"So they did!" nodded Ivory, "and what a plan it was! Lemme tell y'all how it all fell into place. The two of them came together out on the Plank Road maybe a mile southeast of the Chancellor's house. The sun had set but there was still a good bit of light remainin'. They started talkin' 'right there on the road but a Federal sniper up in a tree spotted 'em real quick and started shootin'. They got the hint pretty quick and skeedadled off into a thicket of pines to continue their conversation. Even there it wasn't too peaceful 'cause the pickets on both sides had found each other's range, and was pepperin' back and forth with muskets. With all that goin on behind them Marse Robert and Stonewall dismounted and found themselves a big ol' log lyin there on the ground to sit on. Side by side they sat...probably the two most important men in the Confederacy at that time. Marse Robert told Stonewall he'd already been upon the right to scout the Federal lines...lookin' for any weak spot he could find. He said it didn't look good up there. The terrain wasn't right. The Rappahannock looped south there so there wasn't a lot of open ground to move around on. Worse still he found the Federals to be dug in thick as flies in strongly fortified entrenchments. The way Marse Robert put it to attack there would be to invite certain destruction."

"How'd Stonewall feel 'bout all that?" asked David.

"He didn't think the two armies would come to blows again," replied Ivory. "It's not like he wasn't itchin' to pitch in to 'em again. He'd done like Marse Robert did out on the right. He personally scouted Hooker's center and found it too strong to assail. The Yankees was deployed three deep hard at work makin' their trenches stronger by the hour. Behind those lines they had dozens of guns set hub to hub ready to tear our boys up as soon as we made a move in their direction. He didn't figure it made sense to try it, but like ah said a few minutes ago he didn't think it would be necessary. The way he saw it, the ease with which we'd stopped Hooker on the opening day was proof enough that the

Federal commander didn't really want to come to grips with 'em. He told Marse Robert that by mornin' there wouldn't be any of the Federals on our side of the river."

"Really? He thought that?"

"Sho'nuff," offered the black man.

"What did General Lee say to that?" wondered Jefferson.

"Didn't see it the same way. Oh, he was curious same as Stonewall 'bout how come Mr. F. J. Hooker pulled back at the first contact, but Marse Robert knew that 100,000 Yankees weren't just gonna disappear by mornin'. He was sure Hooker was up to somethin', and he really wanted to find a way to keep one step ahead of him. Since they only had those few hours of darkness to think it through, he wanted to keep workin' on it till they came up with somethin'."

"Did Stonewall argue the point?" the question came from David.

"Nope. Remember what ah said befo'; Stonewall was a soldier. His General wanted him to help find a way to get at Hooker, so he put his mind to doin' just that. The two of them kept talkin' for a spell, tossin' 'round possibilities. They decided the center of Hooker's line maybe deserved a second look, so they each sent one of their engineerin' officers to scout that section of the line one mo' time. While they was talkin', guess who rode up?"

"Stuart?" ventured one of the younger boys.

"You'd best believe it!" grinned Ivory. "How'd you know that?"

"My history teacher told us last year," replied the lad who was rapidly blushing blood-red.

"Well he done told ya true!" chuckled Ivory. "He came ridin' in just a shakin' with excitement! The moon was good and bright that evenin' and it's light brought out the crimson in his beard and the scarlet linin' of his cloak. His report came out of his mouth as quick as water dashes over a falls! He'd come in from Catherine Furnace, the mid-point of Stonewall's position. He'd just received a report from Fitzhugh Lee who'd ridden west to scout the Federal position. He went all the way out across the Plank Road several miles west of Chancellorsville, then across the Germanna Ford Road and on up beyond the Orange Turnpike. They turned east here and moved real easy-like through them woods till they located the far right flank of Hooker's whole line. Guess what Fitz found there!"

"Tell us!" someone cried.

"The Yankees done left their flank in the air that's what!"

"In the air?" asked a young freckle-faced boy of about ten.

"That's soldier talk," explained David. "Means the end of their line wasn't anchored against anythin' and they didn't build no trenches perpendicular to their line."

"Perpin...?"

"Perpendicular," smiled David. "It means like this," he held his hands out together in the shape of a "T" indicating his top hand as the one which represented the missing entrenchments.

"Oh," said the boy, but his expression still revealed a bit of confusion on his part.

"Ah wasn't close 'nuff to see fo' mahself," explained Ivory. "but ah'm willin' to bet Marse Robert's heart started beatin' just a little quicker when he heard those words, but he held his composure. What he wanted to know straight away was info'mation 'bout roads. The question was this: could a large body of troops be moved to that point without being detected by the enemy? Stuart had no answer to this, but he remounted and took off straight away to find out.

"Meanwhile General Lee and Stonewall was still sittin' on that log. Both of 'em were starin' at a map spread out on Marse Robert's lap. The two officers who they sent out to scout the center came back with the news that it was too heavily fortified to attack, but neither general paid 'em much mind. General Lee was starin' so hard at that map his eyes mighta' burrowed two holes through it. He wondered aloud how we could get at those people . And Jackson says to him, `You know best. Show me what to do, and we will do it.'" Here Ivory paused and stepped down from his crates once again so he could draw more diagrams on the ground. "Remember," he cautioned, "Chancellorsville was here." He jabbed the poker into the same hole he had drilled earlier. "With one finger the General traced a course on the map somethin' like this," with the stick he charted a course which led west and south of Chancellorsville until it was well past the Federal entrenchments, then north a bit, then east to fall directly upon the exposed Union flank. "Then Marse Robert looked up and told Stonewall this would be his movement. Jackson stood up with a big ol' smile on his face and saluted, then he said his troops would be ready to move at 4:00 a.m."

He stopped his discourse for the moment to collect his thoughts but he was quick to resume. "Ah was fo'tunate to be close by that night. Reckon too many years have gone by 'cause ah can't recall exactly why ah was close by but ah had mah bedroll no more'n fifty feet away from 'em. No sooner had the decision to flank Hooker been made than both generals decided to turn in right there in the woods. Each of 'em took his saddle blankets and laid 'em out on the ground for a bed. Seems like they was both asleep pretty quick. They was both pretty well worn out. Ah woke up 'bout two hours later cause ah heard voices. It was Marse Robert. He was soundin' kinda' sleepy but it seemed like he was talkin with a chuckle in his voice. You know what ah'm sayin? Like he was wakin' up light-hearted. He'd been nudged from his sleep by one of Jackson's officers, a captain who'd been sent to scout the Union right. The General greeted him to make his report. When he was finished the General started teasin' him 'bout the young men not bein' up to the challenge like the older generation. He wasn't serious, you understand, he was funnin' with that Captain...wanted to know why the young men couldn't find a lonesome Federal battery what held up Jackskon's advance the previous day. That po' captain didn't know what to say. Ah think bein' in the General's presence musta' flustered him up some 'cause he just stood up, saluted, and stumbled off into the woods. Marse Robert had himself a good laugh over that, not mean but light-hearted...you know what ah'm sayin'? It was good to hear him laugh like that considerin' the circumstances we was in. It told me he was feelin' confident about the next day. It made me believe he'd find a way to get us out of that mess in one piece. The General lay back down to sleep and ah reckon ah wasn't to far behind him." He paused to chew a couple of forkfuls of beef.

"Stonewall was up first," he explained several minutes later. "He had a little fire goin' and was settin' on an empty hardtack box the Yankees left behind. He was just starin' at the fire, warmin' his hands, Marse Robert woke up befo' too much longer and joined Jackson by the side of that little fire. General Lee pointed out that it was already past 4:00 am and Stonewall didn't seem to be marchin' anywhere like he said he would. Stonewall explained to him that his staff chaplain had once been a minister to a church nearby, and he knew the roads. He sent him along with that mapmaker of his..." He tried to recall the name, snapping his fingers in frustration.

"Major Hotchkiss," said Longstreet, "Jebediah Hotchkiss."

"Sho' was!" gasped Ivory. "Now how come ah couldn't remember that?"

"A lot of years have passed."

" Reckon so," nodded Ivory. "Anyhow, the Chaplain and Major Hotchkiss was out scoutin' them roads through most of the night. They was lookin' for a way to move a lot of men without the Yankees noticin'."

"Kinda' like what Wade Hampton did here at Ox Ford," observed Seth Reilly.

"Yessuh," agreed Ivory, "you could sho' make that comparison. Anyways, long 'bout first light the two of them managed to get back to make their report. The major got off his horse and stepped straight over to the fire where Marse Robert and Stonewall was warmin' their hands. He fetched another one of them hardtack boxes -- the Yanks left plenty of 'em lyin' around -- and set it on the ground right in front of the generals. Then he pulled out a map he'd been drawin' himself and spread it out on the box. Ah was watchin' the two generals while they were lookin' up at him. Their faces were lit up by the glow of the fire, and ah can tell y'all one thing, whatever they saw in the major's face they mus've liked, 'cause ah could sure see it in their faces!"

"What was it they liked so much?" demanded one of the younger boys.

"Watch careful-like and ah'll show ya," said Ivory in reply. Using the poker again he drew several lines in the dirt to represent the roads and trails which Jackson used to flank Hooker at Chancellorsville. "This here is Catherine Furnace," he said as he poked a hole in the dirt. "It was the mid-point of Jackson's line. There was a trail what led from here south aways till it curved west like this and met another road right about here. Notice how they'd be marchin' away from the enemy. Now once they got to this road..." he paused and glanced in Longstreet's direction with a question in his eyes.

"The Brock Road," smiled Old Pete.

"Brock Road," repeated Ivory. "Once they reached it they'd be shiftin' to a northwest direction like this," he drew a long straight line in the dirt. "Now listen careful," he raised one finger to capture the attention of his audience, "they couldn't use this Brock Road straight away cause it woulda' brought 'em within sight of a federal signal station. That wouldn't do a'tall, so they moved on to a dirt trail just past the Brock Road where they could stay out of sight till they got past the signal station," he drew a line parallel to the one which represented the Brock Road. "They'd keep movin' this way till they'd cross the Plank Road up here then the Orange Turnpike up here. Once there they'd turn east and bump right into Hooker's right flank. According to Major Hotchkiss the whole march was 'bout ten miles, every bit of it shielded from unfriendly eyes. He said the ground was solid on all the roads and trails he'd charted. It could support wagons and guns along with the infantry. That's all he had to say. He just stood there waitin' fo' a response. From where ah was sittin' ah could almost see his eyes shiftin' from Lee to Jackson and back again, waitin' fo' one of 'em to speak. The generals just kept starin' at that map for the longest time. It was Marse Robert who finally broke the silence. He looked up from the map, and glanced over at Stonewall and said, `General Jackson, what do you propose to do?' With one hand Jackson traced the route Major Hotchkiss had drawn and said, `Go around here.' General Lee kept his eyes on him and asked him what troops he planned to take on this march, and ol' Stonewall straightaway told him he was gonna take his whole corps." He paused here to let the full impact of those words sink in.

Several of his younger listeners were quick to grasp the significance of Jackson's decision. "Wait a minute," said David, "Did you say he planned to take the whole corps?"

"Ah did."

"But what about General Lee? What was left for him to hold off Hooker?"

"Marse Robert must've been wonderin' 'bout that himself. He looked over at Stonewall and asked him the same question. 'Course it was probably a useless question to ask. There was nothin' left 'cept Anderson's division and McLaw's. That's what Stonewall told him, and then he held his tongue waitin' to see what the General was gonna do. The final decision had to be General Lee's. If he took the gamble he'd be left with maybe 15,000 men to hold off the five corps of infantry Hooker had at Chancellorsville. Ah think ah know what mighta been goin' through his mind right 'bout then. Ah'll bet he was thinkin' how would he hold off close to 90,000 with a mere 15,000. Then again he saw how easily Hooker recoiled at the first contact the day befo'. The real gamble came down to this: was Hooker plannin' to attack or stay put? Marse Robert could see that all of the Federal preparations had been defensive...lots of trenches...earthworks everywhere. That by itself sent a message, namely that Hooker was mo' interested in receiving an attack than deliverin' one. With that in mind General Lee made his choice. With the sun peepin' up over the trees to our east, Marse Robert looked over at Stonewall and said, `Well, go on,' and with those three words the die was cast."

Having finished with his diagram in the dirt, Ivory placed the poker against one of the rocks ringing the campfire and climbed back up on the crates where he could perch himself and be visible to all those present. With his feet planted wide apart and a hand gripping each knee he leaned forward slightly and resumed his tale. "Stonewall was already four hours behind his own schedule when he rode back among his troops. There was a bunch of 'em what rose to their feet to cheer him but when they saw him comin' closer they held their tongues. They could tell by the way he carried himself and by the expression on his face that there was battle in those blue eyes of his and these boys just stood by waitin' to see what he was gonna order them to do. The first regiment got underway long 'bout 8:00 a.m. headin' south away from Catherine Furnace. One regiment after another fell into the column along with caissons and guns. Stonewall took all of his own artillery along with some of Anderson's guns under General Alexander. General Lee met with Stonewall one mo' time as the troops filed away south. Both of 'em was mounted. Ah'm 'fraid ah can't tell y'all exactly what words passed between 'em, but ah can wager a guess or two. Ah 'magine Marse Robert was remindin' him of how dangerous our situation was gonna be, what with the whole army divided in three pieces, spread out all over the landscape, and Hooker sittin' there with all that power at his disposal. Ah think maybe the General was remindin' Stonewall to hit Hooker real hard and not let up for a minute cause if the Federals were able to absorb that punch without retreatin' we'd be in desperate straits. Hooker might realize how small the force in front of 'em really was, and then there'd be hell to pay. Ah'm tellin ya true, Marse Robert, he took his fair share of gambles in those days, but this one, Chancellorsville, that was the longest shot of all. Anyways, they said farewell to one another right there. Ah 'magine they wished each other well. Stonewall raised his arm and pointed west. General Lee just nodded at him then watched silently as Stonewall Jackson disappeared down the trail.

THE TELLING OF CHANCELLORSVILLE

"A lot of folks have talked 'bout this battle through the years," he continued, "some to praise others to criticize. A lot's been said 'bout the amount of time it took us to cover that ten miles around to the Union right. Folks claim we took too long, didn't leave ourselves 'nuff daylight to do the job proper. Maybe so, but ah gotta throw in mah two cents here. People say we shoulda left earlier but that would've been a foolish move. Stonewall's decision to have Major Hotchkiss map a route fo' us was the right one. Otherwise we'd have been stumblin' 'round in the dark and may never have reached our destination a'tall.

"As fo' roads, some of 'em weren't really roads like we think roads oughta be. Some were just trails which could support no mo' than three or fo' men abreast. That was the main problem, the roads was too narrow. If we coulda moved that column eight men abreast we'd have cut the time in half, but that was impossible. We're talkin 'bout a column what stretched out fo' miles. Not only infantry but guns and caissons were in that column and ambulances and ordnance wagons, like the one ah was drivin'. Out on our flank Stuart and his cavalry was screenin' our march. In a situation like that, the head of the column can make good time. No one's in front of 'em and the dirt under their feet is still pretty solid. But as each unit passes the ground gets chewed up a little mo'. Wagons and guns make it even worse. So the middle of the column will slow the pace some and that in turn holds up the rest. If a wagon throws a wheel or breaks an axle, or if a mule goes lame the whole march feels it. That's pretty much why it took us so long.

"General Jackson took every precaution to make sure we'd reach their flank without bein' detected. There couldn't be any extra noise. There weren't no cheerin' of the officers or anybody else. By and large those who was ridin' and those walkin' did so in silence. Stonewall himself didn't have all that much to say. From time to time he'd urge the infantry to press forward but that was about all. Ah do remember hearin' him say somethin' though. He'd come on back in the column with some of his officers, checkin' on things...y'all know what ah'm sayin'? He was settin' his horse off to the side of the trail watchin' us as we passed. Right 'bout the time mah lead mule came abreast of his horse Stonewall turned to one of his staff officers and said, `I hear it said that General Hooker has more men than he can handle. I should like to have half as many more as I have today and I should hurl him into the river!' Ah'll tell ya true, if Stonewall had those extra men he was wishin' fo', and a couple more hours of daylight he'dve done it!" He paused here and let his eyes drift skyward as if in search of a missing detail.

"Two o'clock!" he exclaimed at last. "Long 'bout two o'clock Fitz Lee comes gallopin' down the column and presents himself to Stonewall. He was awful excited. You could tell by his voice and the expression on his face. He asked Stonewall to ride off with him to view the enemy's right flank. They rode off quick like, just the two of them along with one courier. Ah talked to this courier the next day and he told me what happened. They rode through the intersection of the Plank Road and swung east into the trees. Fitz led him to the top of a little hill where they could see straight down to the Federal line. They stayed back from the crest and the leaves did a good job of hidin' their presence. The sight what met their eyes sent Stonewall's mood just a soarin'! The Federals was only a few hundred yards away. They was dug in solid. They had abatis in the ground all along their front, but the thing what looked most promisin' was this: Their weapons were stacked behind the trenches, long lines of 'em far as the eye could see. Their boys was relaxin'! They had no idea we was comin', not the first hint! Most of the troops in view were behind the lines loungin' 'round playin' cards and such, laughin' and smokin'...pretty much the same as we did when there weren't no battle pendin'. A ways behind them they could see mounted Yankees drivin' up cattle to slaughter for the evenin' supper. Whenever ah think 'bout these days ah gots to chuckle. We hadn't had nothin' to eat since breakfast and our bellies was growlin' at us. Them Yankees was gettin' ready to eat steak! Can y'all 'magine?

"Now ah got to tell y'all Stonewall Jackson was feelin' right pleased with himself cause we pulled that march off without bein' seen by the wrong eyes, or so he thought. But there was a problem. At first he'd planned to attack straight up the Plank Road, but when he rode off with Fitz he changed his mind. The Federal line crossed that and kept goin' on passed the Orange Turnpike. We didn't march that far just to hit 'em straight on. What Stonewall wanted was for us to hit 'em where their flank was in the air. That meant a couple mo' miles of hoofin' it. He told the courier to ride to General Rodes, who commanded the forward division, to keep movin' across the Plank Road then on up to the turnpike where he was to stop and wait for Jackson. Stonewall himself stayed on a while longer studyin' the Federals, then he turned and galloped down that hill so fast that Fitz Lee thought sure he'd fly straight over Little Sorrel's head!

"When he got back to the column he pulled one brigade from General Colston's division and sent 'em up the Plank Road a piece, but still out of sight of the enemy."

"That was us," interrupted Reilly.

"I remember," nodded Whitt Simmons.

"Sho' was," grinned Ivory. "Their job was to screen our own right when the fireworks started. By this time it was close to three o'clock. The afternoon was passin' awful quick. This is when Stonewall took a few minutes to jot a note to Marse

Robert to fill him in on what we'd done so far and to let him know
we'd soon attack."

"That's why Hooker should've held on to his cavalry," observed Jefferson.

"Yer right," nodded Ivory. "Like ah said befo' cavalry is
the eyes and ears of any army. If Hooker had kept his troopers
close by and they was doin' what they was supposed to be doin,
we'd've never made that march. Anyhow, after Stonewall sent that
note off to Marse Robert he caught up with Rodes and gave orders
to deploy for the attack. General Rodes had five brigades. Four of
'em went into the first line on a low-lyin' ridge perpendicular to the
Union flank. Two were to the left of the Orange Turnpike and two
to the right. They stretched for a mile on either side of that road,"
he stretched both arms out as far as he could to emphasize this
point. "The fifth brigade backed up the far right of this line and
General Colston's remainin' three brigades joined them to extend a
second line northward some two hundred yards behind the first.
A.P. Hill's boys would come in behind General Colston to form a
third line. It was like Stonewall formed his whole corps into a single
fist," Ivory formed a fist with his right hand and held it up for all to
see, "to deliver one solid knock-out blow."

He paused and sat straight up , his arms folded across his
chest, shaking his bald head with a hint of sadness in his eyes.
"Problem was, it was takin' an awful lot of time to get that last
division into formation, especially the last two brigades, not because they was slow marchers up from Harpers Ferry to bail us out
at Sharpsburg! They could move, ah'm tellin' ya true! Marchin'
wasn't the problem. Fightin' was the problem. They had to
conduct a rear-guard action earlier that afternoon, but ah'll explain
that one in a minute or two. It was pushin' five o'clock and Stonewall was gettin' mighty antsy and still we waited fo' them last two

brigades."

Again he stopped, cupping his thickly bearded chin with one hand as deep furrows appeared across his brow. "Reckon this is a good point to shift directions and let y.'all know what was happenin' on the other side of the lines," he said, "and in so doin' ah'll have to admit our march wasn't as well hidden as we thought, although them Federals sho' didn't do much of a job gettin' ready fo' us. Anyway, when dawn broke Mr. F. J. Hooker was in fine spirits and with good reason." He paused a moment and leaned forward slightly to direct his comments toward his younger listeners. "The night befo' while Marse Robert and Stonewall was makin' their plans Hooker was gettin' messages from spies he had down in Richmond. He found out that we was only receivin' 'bout 59,000 rations each day. He also got word from down in Suffolk what told him that Hood and Pickett was still down there. So he knew them stories the deserters told was just that...stories. And he knew we couldn't come close to matchin' his numbers. He expected us to attack. In fact he was hopin' we would. He'd already send for another corps of infantry and that gave him ninety thousand men to face us. He figured his army would maul us like we mauled it at Fredericksburg, and that he'd have an easy time roundin' up the survivors. Y'all might say he was salivatin' at the prospect. He spent the mornin' ridin' 'round with a whole column of staff officers to inspect his defenses. Had himself a beautiful horse, a proud high-steppin' steed just as white as the driven snow. Everywhere he went he was cheered by his soldiers and everythin' he saw looked to be impregnable. Yes suh, ol' Hooker was feelin' right good 'bout himself while Jackson was sneakin' away.

"Hooker was back at his headquarters at the Chancellor house by mid-mornin' and he got news that convinced him that his original strategy was bearin' fruit. One of his corps commanders, ah think it was General Sickles, had sent a single division to take over some high ground in front of the center of the Union position, place called Hazel Grove if ah remember right."

"You do," nodded Levi.

"Thanks," Ivory glanced at Levi with a smile, then he quickly returned to his story. "This Hazel Grove place was only a mile north of Catherine Furnace, the jump-off point fo' our flankin' march. The Yanks up there had a clear view of what we was doin', but remember what ah told ya earlier, we didn't head west straight away, we marched south first, and those Yankees saw every step we took! They sent a courier back to Hooker and told him there was a long column of our boys movin' south and disappearin' into the trees. They said our column seemed to go on fo'ever, and included lots of wagons, ambulances, and artillery. Hooker checked his maps and he found the road we was on, and he saw that it veered off to the west, but that didn't seem to concern him at first. He figured Marse Robert was givin' up any thoughts of an attack and that we was in full retreat toward Gordonsville. This was an assumption on his part which in turn was based on another assumption, namely that his cavalry had struck Gordonsville and had severed one of our two main supply lines. Still it wasn't Hooker's nature not to be cautious and he usually paid attention to even the smallest details. It was General Howard's corps out there on the right flank and Hooker figured it would be a good idea to let Howard know somethin' was afoot. He sent word that a large body of Rebels had been seen movin' west through the woods and that vigilance on Howard's part might be a good idea. Now the thing is, Howard spotted us too and sent a message to his commander befo' he received any instructions from Hooker. This message said that he was takin' measures to resist an attack from the west. To Hooker it appeared as if Howard was on top of things and there was no need to worry 'bout the western end of his line.

"Now he was free to focus his attention on what he believed our movement meant. Remember what ah said 'bout Hooker's original purpose in crossin' the Rappahannock up there at Kelly's Ford. He figured this would force General Lee to abandon our lines at Fredericksburg and retreat toward Richmond. What he most wanted was to catch us strung out on the road where he could chew us up piecemeal, and this is what he started to plan for. Through his scouts he found out that General Early's division was all we had on the Fredericksburg line. He knew that General Sedgwick had 'bout 30,000 troops at his disposal so he sent word for him to attack if he had a reasonable expectation of success. By mid-afternoon he was sendin' out orders to all his corps commanders to get themselves ready to chase after us the next mornin'. Then he started gettin' messages back from General Sickles. Ah guess it was 'bout noon when Sickles pitched into us at Catherine Furnace. By that time, most of our column had passed, but he captured some wagons and men and he forced those last two brigades of A. P. Hill to go into a rear-guard action. Sickles told Hooker that most of our column had already passed well beyond his reach and this news was music to Hooker's ears. There was no question in his mind now but that we was in full retreat and would soon meet our demise Lawd knows he couldn't have been mo' wrong if he tried!

"Prisoners ah talked to after the battle told me that long 'bout 4:30 that afternoon, while Stonewall was concentratin' his boys on Howard's flank, Mr. F. J. Hooker sent word to General Sedgwick 'cross the river. Told him to throw his whole force over to the southside and drive Early from his works. Told him to capture Fredericksburg and everythin' in it and to pursue us vigorously. He assured Sedgwick that we was in desperate retreat tryin' to save our wagon trains and that Sickles was amongst us. Painted himself a rosy picture didn't he!"

"Ah reckon it could be said that Hooker didn't pay 'nuff 'tention to the folks that kept showin' up at the Chancellor house all the day long. Some was couriers, but there was quite a few regimental and brigade commanders. They'd spotted our column...a bunch of 'em did...and they was frantic to warn Hooker. None of 'em got in to see him. His staff people assured each one of them that Howard's flank was secure and that what they was seein' was actually a retreat. When that fella Sickles pitched into us at Catherine Furnace he took himself some prisoners. Ah talked to a few of 'em after they was exchanged later in the war. One of 'em told me how a Yankee soldier was braggin' 'bout how they was gonna bag every Mother's son of us befo' they turned away. 'Course our boys wouldn't take that kind of talk without sayin' somethin' back. Some of 'em told the Federals they was gonna catch hell befo' dark. Another one laughed at the Bluecoats, said how they thought they'd done such a big thing out there at the Furnace, but told 'em to wait and see what was gonna happen when Jackson got around on their flank! Hooker never heard any of this. He remained convinced we was on the run. Like Ah said a few minutes back, he couldn't have been mo' wrong if he tried!"

Having been talking non-stop for several minutes Ivory paused to scan the faces around him illuminated to various degrees by the pale glow of the fire. There was silence for several moments while he assured himself that he had the undivided attention of every person present. Satisfied that every eye was focused on his direction he resumed his discourse, which was rapidly approaching its climax. "4:30 it was and by that time of the afternoon it was considerable warm. Hooker's orders

to Sedgwick was on their way to the other side of the
Rappahannock. Most of our boys was in position on either side of
the Turnpike waitin' fo' the order to charge, but that order seemed
a long time comin' cause we was waitin on those last two brigades
what had to fight the rear guard action.

"Now ah want y'all to picture this," he said as he held both
hands up as though he were some sort of preacher offering a
benediction. "We was deployed in the thickest part of the
Wilderness...long lines of infantry, a mile in that direction," he
stretched his left arm out and pointed, "another mile that way,"
he repeated the motion to the right. "They was vines and sharp
brambles everywhere you looked. The boys was hot and tired, all
the day long they'd been on the march, and they was sho' nuff
feelin' it. Flies and gnats was everywhere, buzzin' 'round our faces,
crawlin' into people's eyes and such. There was bees too, some of
them yella-jackets wasn't really happy 'bout us bein' there and they
made a bit of a nuisance of themselves but we held our own against
'em, and no one made noise. Most of us was starvin'. No one had
eaten since breakfast 'cause there was never the time. Ah'll tell'
you true, some of the boys was so weak they could scarcely stand!
Ah ain't lyin'! They couldn't even hold their hands steady...they
was tremblin' like y'all might if you was shiverin' in the cold. Ah
did what ah could fo' these boys. Ah had me some biscuits in mah
wagon left over from breakfast...a few dozen not much mo' than
that. They'd long since gone stale but they was still edible. And ah
grabbed me a wooden bucket and some ladles, filled the bucket
with water and started makin' mah way along the first line of troops
handin' out biscuits and water till ah had no mo' to give."

"I had one of those biscuits," the voice came from a sixty
year-old man well back in the crowd. He had long, thin, stringy,
whitish-gray hair which nearly reached his shoulders. Little could

be seen of his face as he was too far back for the light of the fire to be of much help. "Still remember it" he continued eagerly, though he was not one who was much used to speaking in front of a crowd. "I was some kinda scared, I gotta admit. Starvin' just like Ivory said. He come by me with the biscuits and water and I sho' did help myself. Ivory says they was stale. Reckon so but they sho' didn't seem that way to me. I honestly didn't think I was gonna live through that fight and I was thinkin' that ol' biscuit was gonna be the last thing I'd have to eat in this life. Figured them pearly gates was gonna be my next stop. Every bite of that biscuit tasted every bit as good as the beef we had for supper this evenin'. Ivory," he raised his voice a little to make sure the old black man could hear him, "when you got to me that afternoon and handed me the biscuit and filled my cup with water I was convinced you had to be an angel from God Himself."

Feeling a little self-conscious at the praise coming in his direction Ivory stammered his reply, "Why thank you, suh. Ah just did what ah could fo' you boys. Did mah duty same as you was doin' yours."

"Still the same," returned the old soldier, "I ain't never forgotten it and I never will."

Ivory smiled and nodded at the veteran then quickly resumed the story of Chancellorsville. "You boys remember who was waitin' fo' us over there with Howard?"

"Germans," came the reply from one of the older soldiers.

"Lots of 'em," concurred another.

"Sho'nuff!" nodded Ivory, "A whole bunch of Howard's corps was Germans."

"If memory serves me," General Longstreet spoke for the first time in quite awhile, "Something like one in five Union soldiers

was foreign mostly Irish or German. The United States did the
same thing Great Britain did during the American Revolution. They
hired mercenaries to go kill their former countrymen." There was
just a hint of disgust in Longstreet's voice as he relayed this information.

"That's right," concurred Ivory, "and a whole bunch of
these Germans was under Howard's command at
Chancellorsville, and a good number of them wasn't too
thrilled about their corps commander that's fo' sho'!" As fo'
this man, Howard, he was convinced same as Hooker that we
was on the run. His people spotted us and they kept sendin' him
warnin's but he just told 'em not to worry; said everythin' was fine,
that what they was seein' was just a screen to cover our retreat.
He got one message from a Major a li'l' bit befo' three; told him we
was massin' in front and begged him to make some sort of disposition to receive us when we charged. The thing is, in Howard's mind
anyhow, that disposition had already been made. He had two guns,
that's all, just two, sittin' side by side on the pike facin' west.
Stonewall done spotted 'em when he rode off with Fitz Lee. Along
with the guns he put two regiments out there, maybe nine hundred
men in all. That's the preparation which he assured Hooker was
enough to blunt any attack from the west."

"A slight miscalculation on his part," quipped Seth
Reilly with a chuckle.

"Ever so slight," grinned Ivory. "Ah'll tell y'all why he
was so confident 'bout his flank. Remember where we were?
The Wilderness. And Stonewall's boys was standin' right there in
the thick of it. General Howard was convinced that no one could
penetrate all that undergrowth. He figured it was sorta like a wall
protectin' him from any threat. He thought the Orange Turnpike
offered the only avenue for attackers to use and he figured two guns

GRAY VISIONS

with two regiments of them Germans would be enough to plug that avenue good and proper. Didn't turn out that way.

"Five o'clock rolled around," he held up a hand with all five fingers extended, "those last two brigades of A. P. Hill was tryin' to catch up to the rest of us. There was scarcely two hours of daylight left to us and patience was runnin' thin. Across the way, the Yankees had started up their cook fires so as to get supper goin'. Our forward lines was maybe a thousand yards away from theirs and the smoke from their fires drifted our way. Whatever it was they was cookin', it sho' smelled good, 'specially to folks like us what hadn't seen the first morsel of food since sun-up. Our boys was hankerin' to get at 'em ah'm tellin' ya true!

"Come 5:15 and still no sign of them last two brigades but Stonewall...well Stonewall just couldn't wait a minute mo'. He was standin' next to General Rodes out there by the first line of infantry and he asked Rodes if he was ready. Rodes replied that he was and Stonewall just said it was time to go forward. Rodes gave his boys the order and away we went! Bugles was ringin' out up and down the line, but the Federals didn't react. They musta thought those bugles belonged to their own cavalry. Our boys started through the woods as fast as they could move, but it wasn't all that quick cause the growth was so thick. Thorns and brambles tore at their uniforms every step of the way so that some of the boys was awful close to bein naked by the time they cleared the woods.

"Now tell me somethin,'" he sat back upright and crossed his arms over his chest, "suppose you was a deer or turkey or some such, and you was hangin 'round in those woods munchin' on leaves, mindin' your own business, just as happy as you could be. All of a sudden you look up and comin' toward ya is thousands of men all of 'em carryin guns. Now just what do ya think ya might do?"

"Run like hell," replied Jefferson a little too quickly. Then looking sheepishly at his father he said, "Sorry, didn't mean to curse."

"No problem," smiled Levi. "I think I'd have answered the same way."

"And he's right too!" exclaimed Ivory. "That's just what they did! There was dozens of 'em! Deer, turkey, rabbits! Anythin' that couldn't climb a tree was runnin' in front of us like a herd of cattle! These animals was the first hint the Yankees had that somethin' wasn't quite the way it oughta be! When they saw all them animals boltin' out of the woods like the devil himself was nibblin' at their tails they thought it was funny. They was gatherin' 'round, callin' their buddies, pointin' at all that game and laughin like they was spectators at a carnival side-show or some such. Then all of a sudden-like they ain't lookin' at the animals no mo' and all those smiles on their faces vanished. Why you say? 'Cause they got their first glimpse of our boys that's why. Long lines of us appeared from the woods stretchin' as far as anybody could see in either direction with nothin' but open ground in front of us. A lot of our troops was half-naked cause of all them thorns and briars and that just made them look all the mo' fierce. Panic set in at the first sight of Jackson's boys. Ah'm tellin' ya true!

"Then came the yell!" Ivory shook his head and one could almost see his fleshy jowls quivering beneath his fleecy white beard. "And oh what a terrible yell it was! Y'all know which yell ah'm talkin' 'bout, don't ya? That ol' Rebel yell, Yessuh! The Yankees called it hellish, but Stonewall looked at it through different eyes. He once said it was the sweetest music he ever heard, and ah'll tell ya what, he must've had himself one happy set of ears that afternoon."

"You know it Ivory!" a middle-aged veteran called out

from the crowd.

"Tell em! Tell em!" echoed another within that crowd at least a dozen loosed rebel yells which triggered chills up and down the spines of their comrades in Ivory's audience. Ivory himself just sat there smiling, relishing "the sweetest music" as the last echoes of those rebel yells faded in the night. The expression on his face seemed that of a man who had been taken twenty years back in time and was thoroughly enjoying the journey. After the last yell died away he returned abruptly to the present and fixed his warm gaze on the youngsters who couldn't tear their eyes from him. "Where was I?" he asked.

"They started the charge against Howards flank," replied David.

"So they did," the old black man nodded and paused but a moment or two longer to gather his thoughts. Aside from the night sounds reverberating through the surrounding woods there was silence. No one spoke. All eyes were on the former slave from South Carolina. "Once clear of the woods our boys could break into a run at last and you'd best believe that's just what they did. Some of the Yankees tried to make a stand but they had no chance. Rodes swept 'em aside and bore straight down on the Union flank. As for the Yankees...well...they just ran and ah'm tellin' ya true, they ran every bit as fast as all them deer and rabbits they was laughin' at only minutes befo'! Within fifteen minutes the rout was on! Those two Yankee guns Ah told y'all 'bout earlier fell into southern hands, straight away and our boys turned 'em on the Yankees! All them Yankee soldiers in the trenches behind their breastworks facin' south suddenly looked up to see their comrades runnin' pellmell fo' safety behind them. These men knew they couldn't make a stand so they abandoned everythin' and joined the rout, swellin' its numbers considerable with every passin' minute!

The ground was littered with knapsacks and muskets. Most of the straps on the knapsacks had been cut with knives, that's how desperate the Yankees was to shed any extra weight that might slow 'em down while they was runnin'. Ah figure it took maybe twenty or thirty minutes for Jackson to reduce Howard's corps to a mob of panic-stricken fugitives. Howard himself did all he could to stem the rout but his Germans paid him no mind. The po' man only had one arm. He snatched up one stand of regimental colors someone had dropped and clutched it to his body with the stump of his lost arm. That left him one hand with which to control his horse, and believe me, that horse wasn't too keen on the idea of jumpin' into the middle of the battle. Howard kept shoutin' to his men to stand and form, stand and form, but it didn't do the first bit of good! They ran past him like he wasn't even there!"

"Where was Stonewall?" demanded a youngster of perhaps ten years.

"Stonewall?" Ivory repeated the lad's question. "Why right in the middle of it all, where else? Ah was up there pretty close to it mahself, carryin' water and ammo, helpin' with the wounded...that sort of thing. Stonewall was ridin' from one end of the line to the other, urgin' his officers to push ahead, to press the Federals with no let-up. He rode right past me a couple of times. Once while ah was helpin' a man with a leg wound, ah heard one of his officers yell out that the Yankees was runnin' too fast for us, that we couldn't keep up with 'em, but Stonewall would hear none of that! He looked right at that man and said, `they never run too fast for me suh. Press them. Press them!'" Here he paused to catch his breath and sip from a mug of water which Miles had passed his way.

"We were comin' in on Hazel Grove 'bout that time and the sun was just 'bout gone. Lemme give you an idea how thorough was the stampede of Howard's corp, though we didn't really get to see what ah'm tellin' ya 'bout till after the battle. On the far side of Hazel Grove was a marsh some fifty yards across. That's where we found a whole bunch of Howard's cattle, his mules, ambulances, artillery, wagons and horses, all of them hopelessly stuck in the mud. It wasn't possible to look at all that and not realize what a panic had taken hold of them Federals, ah'm tellin' ya true!

"Now ah suppose y'all might be wonderin' what Mr. F. J. Hooker was doin' all this time. Well, fo' the first hour he didn't do much a'tall. That's cause he didn't know anythin' was wrong. Where Jackson struck Howard was maybe three miles from the Chancellor house. Hooker was relaxin' on the veranda enjoyin' the afternoon with some of his staff folks. The roar of our battle barely reached their ears. Ah 'magine it was the denseness of the Wilderness what cushioned the noise. What they did hear they managed to misinterpret. They thought the racket was comin' from Catherine Furnace. They was jokin' 'bout all the havoc Sickles must of been raisin' with our wagon trains. Just befo' the sun set one of his officers stepped off the porch and looked out toward the west. Lemme think on this a second...one of the prisoners ah talked to after the battle told me 'bout it...oh, yeah, I got it! He looked out that way and saw what was left of Howard's corp runnin' toward him on the Pike. They was shoulder to shoulder on that road and fear filled their eyes. That fella said, `My God! Here they come!' That was a least an hour after we launched our attack and that was the first hint Hooker got that his army was fallin' apart.

"But we gotta give credit where it's due, don't we? Hooker didn't go into shock or nothin' like that. He reacted quick like a cat. One of Sickles divisions had been pulled into reserve right there by the Chancellor House. Hooker threw 'em right into it.

He kept shoutin', `Receive them on your bayonets! Receive them on your bayonets!' The thing is," he started to chuckle and shook his head, "the thing is, Sickles's boys wasn't too sure who they should receive on their bayonets. Their bluecoated comrades on the road or our boys nibblin' at their heels! As fo' Hooker he didn't wait 'round to explain it to 'em. Up on to that snow white horse he jumped and away he galloped, straight into the battle itself!"

Here he paused again and this time the expression on his face changed notably. "Like ah said," he continued in a decidedly more somber tone, "the sun had disappeared and darkness was comin' on. Stonewall Jackson was elated. His triumph was 'bout as lopsided as anyone could ask fo', but he knew it would all be in vain if we couldn't drive 'em all the way to the river, like we did here on the North Anna. He didn't think there was too much standin' between us and Chancellorsville, and he figured that would be our next objective after resistance collapsed near Dowdall's Tavern, maybe a mile from the Chancellor house. The biggest problem wasn't the Yankees, it was daylight, cause there wasn't any. But the moon was fast on the rise and Stonewall figured moonlight was bettern' no light at all. Rodes' division was pretty well exhausted by this time and runnin' low on ammo. So was Colston. In fact, those two divisions had mo' or less merged into one big mob of men. It was time fo' these two to stop and sort out their respective regiments. But A. P. Hill's men had yet to see any real action. All fo' of his brigades was up by now. They was rested and their ammo pouches was full. Jackson ordered 'em to the front. He figured we had no choice but to keep the attack goin' well into the night, cause if Hooker was able to regain his balance he could still turn the tables on us, and Jackson was still a ways off from linkin' back up with Marse Robert. He couldn't let this thing stall with our two wings still divided like they was. Aside from the Chancellor house Stonewall had two things in mind. First, he wanted to drive well into Hooker's rear to keep him off balance and cut him off from U.S. Ford. That way he'd be trapped on our side of the Rappahannock. The second thing he had in mind was to link back up with General Lee so we could all tear into the Federals together. A. P. Hill was the only one left capable of keepin' up the pressure on the Yankees. Stonewall found him and spelled out what he wanted him to do. Ah was unloadin' powder from a munitions wagon close by while they was talkin'. Stonewall...well now ah reckon he was the very picture of excitement as he talked with General Hill. You could sense the urgency he was feelin'! You could see it in his face and his gestures. Ah couldn't hear everythin' they was sayin', but ah heard the last thing Stonewall said to him 'cause he raised his voice considerable. He said, `Press them! Cut them off from the United States Ford, Hill! Press them!'" Then they parted company.

"This is where Stonewall did somethin' he shouldn't have done. He decided to ride out ahead on his own along with some of his staff to scout the area General Hill was ordered to attack. They moved out beyond our pickets and rode on for another two hundred yards or so. They found a secondary road and followed it through the woods to the left of the turnpike. They could hear the sound of men swingin' axes up ahead and figured the Yankees was buildin' mo' breastworks. One of his officers asked Stonewall if he didn't think this was the wrong place fo' him to be, but Stonewall shrugged him off. He insisted the danger was over and the enemy was routed. He told a courier to go back and let A. P. Hill know he should press right ahead. Meanwhile, he snuck even closer to the Union lines till the sound of them Yankee axes was ringin' in his ears and their pickets spotted him and took a couple of potshots in his direction. That's when he figured it might be a good idea to get hisself back to our lines. Comin' back he came across A. P. Hill and his staff ridin' out to examine the ground they was ordered to take. Since Jackson had already looked it over there weren't no need fo' anybody else to go out there, so both parties started back toward our lines together.

"This is how the problem started. Since A. P. Hill was on hand that meant his men were up. They had already replaced the boys who was in the lines when Stonewall left to ride out and scout the lay of the land. What ah'm tryin' to say is that the men in the lines who had seen Stonewall ride out there were gone. A North Carolina regiment took their place and those boys just didn't know that their own commander was out there in front of the lines. Now ah got to tell you folks somethin' fo' ah go any further. It's important so's y'all can understand how and why this all happened. Just after sundown a regiment of Yankee cavalry, ah think they mighta been from Pennsylvania, got orders to leave their position near Hazel Grove and move off to join Howard at Wilderness Church. They didn't know Howard had been attacked or that his men were completely routed. They was comin' up through the woods real casual-like in a column of twos. They didn't realize we had penetrated so far into their lines. Anyhow, just as they was comin' up on the turnpike their commander spots our boys on the road and orders his own boys to draw their sabers and charge. They had to fight their way through Hill's division to escape and that's exactly what they did, 'cept a bunch of 'em didn't make it. The point ah'm tryin' to make is this: The boys on the receivin' end of those Yankee sabers was North Carolina boys, the same boys what was movin' into position along the turnpike right where Jackson was comin' back into our lines. It was gettin' darker by the minute and nobody could see real good. These North Carolina boys was real nervous 'bout horsemen comin' out of the darkness and ah reckon they had good cause."

Ivory took a long deep breath as he prepared to continue and the expression on his face was such that sadness seemed to burst from every pore. "Back came Stonewall and General Hill along with their parties. Must've been twenty riders maybe mo. In the dark twenty horses movin' fast can sound like a hundred or better, ain't that so? Our fo'ward pickets heard em' comin', and they thought it was another bunch of Yankee cavalry so they opened fire -- just one volley mind ya. They didn't hit nobody with that volley and General Hill cried out to 'em to cease fire! So did one of Stonewall's officers and he shouted out that they was firin' into their own men. Sad to say the regimental commander didn't believe what he was hearin'. He figured it to be a Yankee trick sho'nuff. He wanted to know who gave the order to cease fire. Said what they heard was a lie and ordered his boys to pour it into 'em. They did just like they was told, and this time they didn't miss. Two staff officers was killed straightaway. One was named Boswell. He was a Captain ah think. The other man was a signal sergeant but ah swear ah can't remember his name."

"Cunliffe," cried one of the veterans in the crowd. "Sergeant Cunliffe. He was one of my best friends. We grew up together."

"Cunliffe," repeated Ivory. "And the two of them wasn't all, fourteen of the horses was killed. And Stonewall..." he paused to search for the right words, "the most tellin' blow of them all..." every eye was on him as his voice wavered ever so slightly..."the boys shot Stonewall Jackson. Lawd knows they didn't mean to but that's what happened. When the first shots rang out they spooked Little Sorrel, Stonewall's horse what he captured way back at Harpers Ferry. Little Sorrel reared back and took off back toward the Yankees. Stonewall got him under control and turned him 'round. He was comin' back toward us but he angled off the road to the edge of the woods. He had the reins in his left hand and had his right hand up in front of his face like this," he raised his right hand the same way Jackson had done. "He was tryin' to protect his face from all them low-lyin' branches 'n such. That's when the second volley was fired on 'em. Stonewall got hit three times. One went through his left hand and wrist," Ivory held up his left hand and pointed to the places that were struck on Stonewall Jackson's left hand. "Another one shattered the bone in his upper left arm" he grabbed his own left arm up around the biceps. "The third one hit him in the right hand and lodged there," he hesitated once again, his voice choked with emotion. "Little Sorrel done panicked again," he said. "Ah reckon y'all can understand why. He bolted and started back toward the Yankees a second time. Stonewall's left arm was broken and just hung there by his side so he grabbed the reins with his right hand, but it was bleedin' pretty bad and the blood made the reins slippery. Branches from the trees knocked his kepi off and scratched his face pretty bad, but he finally got the horse back under control and turned around. He was comin' back into our lines but Little Sorrel didn't show no signs of slowin' down and it didn't 'pear like Stonewall could handle him. One of the other survivors whose horse had been killed by the second volley grabbed hold of Little Sorrel's bridle and stopped him. Another man came over and braced the General in his saddle. They could see how stunned he was but they couldn't tell how badly he'd been hurt. He was starin' straight ahead but then he look down at the officer who held Little Sorrel's bridle. `Wild fire, that, sir,' he said, `Wild fire.' All around wounded men and animals was groanin' and cryin' in pain. Now and then a pistol shot would ring out as they put down the wounded horses. One of Stonewall's officers asked him how he felt and he replied, `You had better take me down. My arm is broken'. He was already so weak he couldn't pull his own feet out of the stirrups. They helped him out of the saddle and carried him to a tree where they laid him down on the ground. The artery in his left arm had been severed. One man tried to stop the bleedin' and the other took off to find a surgeon. As fo' Little Sorrel, he took off too, back toward the Yankee lines fo' the third time. This time no one stopped him. Stonewall was mutterin' to himself like he couldn't believe what had happened to him. `My own men,' he stammered, `My own men.'"

Ivory fell silent and reached for the glass of water which Miles held out to him. For three or four minutes he said nothing but simply stared out into the night. No one spoke. An occasional whippoorwill could be heard and of course the endless drone of the cicadas. Aside from these silence prevailed. Somber expressions marked the faces of the men and boys in that assemblage. Some couldn't take their eyes from Ivory. Others joined the old black man in staring out into the night. Still others stared blankly at the fire seemingly transfixed by the dancing flames.

"Ivory," Miles Turner spoke the name softly. "You can't leave these folks hangin'".

"Reckon not," came the reply.

Another minute or two lapsed.

"Ivory?" Again from Miles.

"Hmmm? Oh'...Ah'm sorry. Reckon ah was driftin'. It's all comin' to mah mind, Miles. Ah can see it all, every detail of it...just like ah can see all those stars up there. Didn't think ah could remember it all but it's just flowin' in like a ragin' river. Seems like that was one of the worse nights of mah life. Just seems like everythin' went sour for a spell. Lot's of confusion everywhere you looked. The Yankees took good advantage of this time to thwart any ideas Jackson had 'bout continuing the attack in the dark. One of their cavalry commanders, ah think it was General Pleasonton, had managed to gather twenty-two guns up on the ridge at Hazel Grove where he could fire right down into the woods where Hill's boys were gettin' ready to jump off. They double-shotted them guns with canister and opened up on us straight away. Another thirty-four guns over near Fairview was doin' the same from a different angle. What a mess it was! You older boys out there remember what canister was like...wicked stuff! Men was fallin' everywhere. Those that wasn't hurt was huggin the ground and prayin' to the Lawd! It was like a storm of lead and steel shreddin' the bark off the trees and the flesh from our bones; and it was through that storm we had to evacuate Stonewall Jackson.

"The officer who ran for the surgeon managed to find him and bring him up. That ol' doctor knew there wasn't much that could be done out there in the woods with a battle still ragin'. He ordered the General taken to the rear. We put together a litter and ah'm proud to say ah was one of the fo' what tried to carry him out of there. But we didn't get far. Shells was burstin' everywhere around us. The air was full of splinters from the trees and all that canister. One of the men helpin' with the litter was cut down, but as he fell one of A. P. Hill's staff officers grabbed hold of the litter and steadied it so's Stonewall wouldn't fall out. Ah think it was Major Leigh what did that...Watkins Leigh."

"It was," confirmed Longstreet.

"Thank you," nodded Ivory. "When the man went down all of us took hits. Ah think ah was bleedin' in eight or ten places but they was all flesh wounds, but ah reckon all of us could have said the same. The Yankees were loadin' and firin' as fast as they could and fo' us it was just impossible to move. We set the litter on the

~ 191 ~

ground and took cover behind trees. Stonewall's aid, a captain named James Power Smith held the General down and sheltered his body with his own. What a barrage that was! A. P. Hill was wounded in both legs. Colonel Crutchfield, who was chief of artillery in Jackson's corps lost a leg and the rest of us was just prayin' it would end.

    "A few minutes later the Federals shifted their aim to another section of our line, so we had a chance to try again. Captain Smith helped Stonewall to his feet and propped him up. He got him across the road to the south side but he collapsed there, just too weak to go on cause of all that blood he was losin'. We brought the litter across and hoisted him up on our shoulders a second time but we only took a few steps when another hailstorm of canister swept through the woods. One of mah fellow litter-bearers was killed outright and this time there wasn't nobody to catch hold of it. Stonewall fell hard to the ground and landed on that broken left arm. He cried out in pain and ah'm tellin' ya true, it was the only time ah heard him cry out that night. We knew we'd never make it back like that and that an ambulance was the only hope out of those woods alive. Wagons was mah line of work in those days and ah knew just where to find one. Ah took off to find it and ah got back in maybe ten minutes or so. We loaded Stonewall on board and ah took off as fast as ah could drive those mules, considerin' it was dark and all. We got him back to an aid station near Wilderness Tavern. Dr. McGuire was there...Hunter McGuire, Stonewall's medical director. Ah was standin' by while the doctor examined him and ah heard him remark 'bout how rigid Stonewall's face was and that he was bitin' his lips so hard you could see the impression of his teeth through the lips themselves. The General must've been in terrible pain. Dr. McGuire knew that arm would have to come off and he ordered that Stonewall be made ready for surgery. They administered chloroform and ah can remember what Stonewall was sayin' as they put him under just like it was yesterday. `What an infinite blessin',' he said and then he kept repeatin' that word...blessin'...blessin'...till he was out. Off came the arm. Dr. McGuire was as skilled a surgeon as anybody could ask fo' and he worked quick and clean. When he was done Stonewall had a two-inch stump where his left arm used to be. Ah remember a woman bein there, can't rightly remember her name, after all this time, but ah remember how she took that mangled arm of Stonewall's and wrapped it in cloth. Seems to me she took that arm and buried it herself."

Once again there was silence but it didn't last particularly long as Ivory was eager to draw from the flood of memories washing through his mind. "The General came to maybe a half hour later and he started to talk to us. Said he would remember the most delightful music while he was out, but he figured it must've been the singin' of the bone-saw. We was all doin' our best to make him comfortable when in comes a staff officer with bad news. Ah already told ya how A. P. Hill took shell fragments in both legs. His wounds were bad enough that he had to take himself out of the battle. He was the rankin' divisional commander so he was next to take command when Stonewall went down, and now he had to pass command on to the next in line but that would've been General Rodes except this was his first time in charge of a division and Hill didn't think he was quite ready for a corps so he sent a message to ol' Jeb Stuart and asked him to take command. Stuart was in charge sho'nuff but he really had no idea what Jackson had been plannin' so he sent this officer fo' instructions.

"Now Stonewall was still awful weak but when he heard that message it kinda revived him some. Just fo' a minute ah saw that fire come back to his eyes but it faded real fast. He was just too spent to be plannin' out any battle. He just stammered that he didn't know what to do, he just couldn't tell. He rolled his head a little and looked at that officer and told him this, `Say to General Stuart he must do what he thinks best.' Ol' Jeb...he set about to do just that.

"It was late that night when Marse Robert got word of all this. Ah understand he couldn't even bear to hear the details of Stonewall bein' wounded and even asked the courier to stop talkin' 'bout it. He remarked 'bout how dear a victory it was that would deprive our army of the services of Stonewall Jackson even fo' a short time. Said something 'bout Stonewall losin' his left arm but that he had lost his right. That'll give y'all an idea how much Stonewall Jackson meant to Robert E. Lee. Yet even in the midst of bad news Marse Robert knew what Jackson had in mind befo' he was shot. He knew how vital it was to keep Hooker off balance or Jackson's efforts would've been fo' nothin'. He wrote a note to Stuart tellin' him how necessary it was to push the Federals with the utmost vigor so they'd have no time to rally. Instructed him to drive the enemy from Chancellorsville itself which would allow the two wings of our army to reunite.

"Now ah got to ask y'all what you want me to do. This all started cause these boys here wanted me to tell 'em 'bout Stonewall Jackson and what happened to him. Ah could finish that or ah could finish tellin' Chancellorsville."

"Couldn't you do both?" pressed Jefferson.

"Ah suppose," a weary smile crept across Ivory's face.

"Could you finish the battle first?" asked David, "then tell us how Stonewall died?"

"Ah could do that," he replied with a nod. "Let's get back into it. Ah've mentioned General Alexander to ya befo'. He was the chief of artillery fo' General Longstreet here and he was chosen by Jackson to be part of the flankin' movement. When Crutchfield went down someone had to be picked to lead the artillery and that someone was Alexander. Stuart made the choice and he told Alexander to be ready to attack the enemy at daybreak everywhere along the line. Ah've had many a conversation with General Alexander over the years and ah thinks ah can recall most of what he told me. Ol' Jeb could tell him nothin' 'bout the enemy position or 'bout the roads we'd be usin'. It was up to Alexander to scout all this out fo' himself and that's what he spent the next six hours doin', from 9:00 p.m. til about 3:00 a.m. He took one courier with him and started to explore the region between our lines. The night was clear and calm with a big ol' full moon watchin' over the whole affair. He moved from the enemy's extreme right all the way to his left. He explored all the places we could use roads to move our guns and sometimes he got so close to the Federals he could hear their axes and picks so he knew their line was gettin' stronger by the hour. Sometimes he'd get too close and their pickets would fire on him and force him to dive fo' cover. Once a whole brigade opened up with one tremendous volley, but he managed to get behind a tree real quick like and all they did was waste their lead. What he was lookin' fo' in particular was a way to get at those Federal guns up to Hazel Grove. Worked on it all night but he only found one open approach. Turns out that's all he needed. He called it a "vista." It was a clearing 'bout two hundred yards long and maybe a hundred feet across and it offered a view of part of the enemy position at the Grove, and believe me, that ridge was the key to the new Yankee line, so Alexander decided to place a battery there. He also put two four-gun batteries on the Plank Road one in front of the other. The guns in the rear would be firin' over the heads of those in front, so they was restricted to firin' solid shot. He knew there probably wasn't much of a chance for effective aimin' but he planned to make a whole lot of noise hopin' to demoralize the enemy and encourage our boys. Later on he found two more positions fo' guns includin' a little conical hill which was cleared up on top. They wouldn't have a clear view of the ridge on Hazel Grove cause of all the trees, but they had both the distance and direction to take it under fire.

"After he finished scoutin' he came back inside our lines to find the guns and crews he planned to send out. It was 'bout three o'clock in the mornin' and he told me how eerie it was to move through our lines in the middle of the night. Our boys had fallen asleep in the line of battle with their guns in their hands. Fatigue had taken its toll, so had the excitement of chasin' the Yankees across two or three miles of landscape. He told me it looked like ours was an army of dead men lyin' where they fell 'neath the light of the moon. Made him think of how many of 'em would be dead fo' the next day was out.

"Lemme tell y'all somethin', we was in one hell of a pickle that night. The army was still divided in two, and with our combined numbers we was still facin' three times our number. Even though the flank attack had been a great victory Hooker was still very much intact. When the sun came up we'd be lookin' a critical situation square in the face. The way Alexander put it nothin' but a combination of desperate fightin' and some ol' fashion good luck could save us. When day dawned our boys were ready for the fightin' part of it, and the Good Lawd blessed us with some decent luck to boot!"

He paused and scratched behind his right ear as he sorted through his thoughts. "Mornin' was fast comin' and the brass on both sides looked at Hazel Grove as the key to whatever was goin' to happen that day. Mr. F. J. Hooker had already adjusted his defenses with that in mind and ol' Jeb...well...ol' Jeb knew exactly what we had to do when the sun came up. Our assault on the Grove was ordered to begin right at dawn and this turned out to be one of the few times in the war that one of our attacks began right on schedule, and ah mean right to the minute! We didn't cook no breakfast fo' anyone. There was kind of a mutual understandin' that the boys were gonna make do with whatever rations they may have stashed in their haversacks. Just as soon as that ol' sun peeked over the trees to the east we was on the move! Infantry moved forward first and kept on till they made contact with the Yankees, who was dug in pretty solid in their trenches protected by log breastworks. As soon as contact was made the air seemed to explode with musketry...both sides slammin' each other as fast as they could reload! Then all them guns General Alexander had positioned durin' the night opened up with a roar, with Yankee guns answerin' each barrage with one of their own. Smoke was everywhere! It filled our lungs, burned our eyes and made it real hard to see the enemy, or fo' them to see us! General Alexander told me a few stories after it was all over. He said his wife and baby could hear the noise of the battle that mo'nin' all the way to Mt. Carmel, where they was stayin'. His little girl weren't but eighteen months old ya' understand and wasn't prone to say a whole lot. On that mornin' she put together the longest sentence of her young life. Now lemme see, how did it go?" He ran his fingers through his beard as he struggled to remember what General Alexander had told him so long ago. "Oh yeah, ah recall it now!" he exclaimed. "She said, `Hear my pappy shoot Yankee...Boo!' She sho' nuff did!"

He took a deep breath and the fire seemed to dance in his eyes as he immersed himself in the telling of this battle. "He told me some other stories as well," explained the aging black man. "He kept movin' from battery to battery to give whatever assistance he

GRAY VISIONS

could. At one point just befo' he came out on the Plank Road a
Yankee shell came within a hair of takin' his head clean off! Did
y'all know you can actually see a cannonball comin' at ya? It ain't
easy mind ya. Your eye's got to be almost in the shell's exact line of
flight, but it is possible. Alexander saw that shell comin' right at
him, said it passed within two inches of his ear! Ah'm tellin' y'all
true! Same as he told me.

    "He told me somethin' else from that same mornin'. Right
'bout the time he came up behind the two guns we had on the Plank
Road one of our boys come out of the woods with two Yankee
prisoners. He's lookin' right sharp, don't ya know! Got his musket
at right-shoulder shift, and a prisoner on either side as they come up
the road itself. All of a sudden a percussion shell from one of the
Federal guns came flyin' through and tore off his left leg right at the
knee befo' it hit the road and exploded. That soldier dropped his
musket and fell backwards but he caught himself with his hands
behind him. Then he holds up the bloody stump of his leg, kinda
points it at one of the Yankee prisoners and shouts at the both of
them! `Pick me up!' he yells.  `Why in hell don't you pick me up!'
Course them Yankees was plenty shook by now, what with shells
explodin' all over the place and all. They ducked fo' cover behind
the trees. Just then one of our powder monkeys come runnin' up
bringin' ammo. He was just a little boy mind ya, but he could
screech with the best of 'em! He laughed at those two prisoners
crouchin' terrified in the bushes and yelled at 'em, wanted to know
why in the hell they was runnin' from their own shells!" He started
to chuckle and shook his head as though he found it hard to believe
his own story, though every detail of it he had on good authority
from E. P. Alexander himself, a man not particularly prone to wild
exaggerations.

    "Seems like ah drifted off on a tangent or somethin'." he

grinned as he scratched the top of his bald head, "Where was ah?"

"Stuart's attack the mornin' after Stonewall went down," reminder Turner.

"Sho' nuff," nodded Ivory. "Anyhow it seemed like we couldn't get the Yankees to budge for the longest time. Both sides just kept slammin' away at each other fo' nigh on two hours or better but then our boys on the right flank broke through and drove the Federals off of Hazel Grove Ridge. Remember what ah said 'bout the ridge now, hear? It was good ground...nice high ground capable of dominatin' everythin' around it. It would be the key to that battle, ah'm tellin ya true!

"Stuart was close by when our boys carried the ridge and he knew just what to do. He told General Alexander to get thirty guns up on that ridge pronto! Alexander was ready. He had all thirty guns standin' by ready to go. Away they went! Horses pullin' guns and caissons up that hill faster'n a hill full of ants'll swarm all over a pile of sugar! From that ridge our gunners could see most of the open ground that surrounded Chancellorsville. They could even see the Chancellor house 'bout two thousand yards in the distance. Even after we took Hazel Grove the Yankees continued to cling to their position along the Plank Road. They was dug in strong there with maybe twenty-five guns backin' 'em up. We couldn't force 'em out from the front, but once our guns was up on the ridge the tide began to shift. We caught 'em in a crossfire, sho' did! Alexander had another thirty guns blazin' away from up around the turnpike where Howard's headquarters had been the day befo'. Southeast of there twenty-fo' mo' guns was hammerin' the Federals from the Plank Road. Eighty-four guns was rainin' lead on those folks from three different angles. I 'magine from their point of view this was a nightmare and nothin' short of it!

"We finally winged 'em," he said after a quick pause for a

deep breath of air, "and it went somethin' like this. When our boys took Hazel Grove they overran the tail end of a column of Yankee infantry. It was Sickles boys they hit, the same ones who had pitched into our wagon trains at Catherine Furnace. They panicked just like them German fellahs the day befo', and that panic infected the men of Slocum's corps and Couch's too! That's what broke their will to resist! The battle was won then and there! Them Yankees started runnin' like jackrabbits the whole lot of 'em! Ol' Jeb was right there when they broke. General Alexander said he was in fine spirits, that he was singin' `Ol' Joe Hooker, would you come out of the Wilderness.' The two of them came out of the woods just as a Virginia brigade swept the left side of the Federal line. They had two guns with 'em and put those cannons straight to work, sho'nuff! Ol' Jeb rode back to fetch more guns and Alexander...he took off to bring those thirty pieces off of Hazel Grove! Ah'm tellin' ya' true, the whole Yankee army was runnin' like a herd of cattle spooked by thunder!

"It got worse for the Bluecoats and it happened real fast. By the time Alexander got his artillery set up on the open plain of Chancellorsville most of the fugitives we'd routed were clustered around the Chancellor house. Alexander's guns tore 'em up and ah ain't exaggeratin' in the least! Thousands of 'em was concentrated around that house along with all their wagons and caissons, horses and mules. We turned that place into a slaughter-house and didn't give 'em a second of peace to regroup."

Ivory reached for a freshly-filled cup of hot coffee, took two quick sips, wiped his mouth with the sleeve of his left forearm and quickly resumed the story. "Right 'bout here the good Lawd blessed us with a stroke of luck," he explained. "Mr. F. J. Hooker was standin' on the veranda of the Chancellor house leanin' against one of the pillars. They was usin' the place as

a field hospital by then and there was wounded men lyin' everywhere. One of our shells hit the column and split it down the length.
One of the bricks this column was built on shot up and hit Hooker
square in the stomach, hit him so hard it knocked him cold. His
staff people were standin' close by and they snatched him off the
porch real quick-like, and carried him on out into the yard. They
laid him down on a blanket and forced a little brandy down his
throat. Meanwhile the house itself is taking hit after hit and flames
were shootin' skyward from the roof and several windows. From
where we were standin' it was one spectacular sight, ah'm tellin ya
true!

"Hooker wasn't out fo' too long and when he revived
he stood up, but he was standin' on shaky legs fo' sho'! He
started stumblin' 'round callin' for his horse and ah reckon fo' him it
was a good thing he did, 'cause a few seconds later one of our
cannonballs landed right on that blanket he'd been layin' on and
blew it all to smithereens! General Alexander thinks this is another
reason we won the battle. Here's why. That brick what hit Hooker
in the stomach knocked the wind out of him. When he got back up
he really wasn't right...y'all know what ah'm sayin? It's like he
was all of a sudden disconnected from what was goin' on around
him...not really fit to continue as commander. His lieutenants was all
screamin' fo' reinforcements and Lawd knows he had plenty at his
disposal, but not a man did he send! Mr. F. J. Hooker had nearly
six corps of infantry on hand, but he never used mo'n' half of
'em...the rest never saw action all the day long! Now if Hooker
had been killed or wounded real bad then he would've been
replaced...ah think General Couch was next in line to take over, but
he didn't. No one did. Hooker was dazed fo' hours and durin'
those hours we trounced the Army of the Potomac...sho' did!"

"Couch was no match for Marse Robert," said someone in

the crowd.

"Ah'll agree with that," nodded Ivory, "and neither was Mr. F. J. Hooker. Couch actually thought fo' a minute he'd be takin' over. When Hooker got up on his horse he rode all the way back to Meade's position inside his secondary line of defense. They laid him down on a cot inside a tent and he sent fo' General Couch. When he got there Hooker actually told him that he was placin' him in command of the army, but in almost the same breath he gave him explicit instructions on how and where to withdraw it, so he really wasn't turnin' over nothin'.

"Now ah got to tell y'all...Hooker's idea of a proper withdrawal didn't quite match what was happenin' out on the field. It was mayhem out there, ah'll tell ya true! Three corps of Yankees was on the run and runnin' fast, and ah guarantee we was close on their heels! They had one division, Hancock's ah think, tryin' to conduct a rearguard, but they couldn't stand in one place fo' mo' than a minute or two or we'd have cut em off and gobbled 'em up!" Ivory sat back with a hand on either knee looking immensely satisfied.

"That's when we finally got the two wings of our army back together," he explained, "right there at the Chancellor house which was still burnin' like a torch. Ah was there mahself...bringin' an ambulance up to evacuate wounded. Y'all know how it is sometimes...when a certain point of time or an image just kind of freezes itself in yo' mind? That's how it was fo' me that day at the Chancellor house. Seems like every detail stayed with me like it just happened yesterday. What a moment it was! Ah'm tellin' it true! The guns was still roarin' everywhere 'round us! Jackson's boys linkin' up with those of Anderson and Mclaws in the open field around that house. They was cheerin' one another and huggin' each other like long lost brothers! You could feel the heat of it

twenty...thirty yards off. Dead and wounded Yankees was layin'
everywhere; a bunch of 'em was officers that was pulled out of that
house and laid on the ground befo' the flames got to 'em. Ah
'member seein' General Alexander there in the yard. He was
standin' next to a big ol' dog what got killed in the fightin'. It was a
Newfoundland ah think. It was a real big dog with black
fur...looked like a small bear layin' there on the ground, sho' did.
Then Marse Robert rode up on that dapple gray of his. Lawd,
what a moment that was! We cheered him like we never done
befo'! A wild cheer it was...comin' out of thousands of throats!
You boys what was there, you remember how it was don't ya?
This was the kind of thing most generals can only dream about.
Wasn't just a victory...it was triumph...total triumph. The enemy
was fleein' from us like jackrabbits and there we stood next to their
former headquarters! There was just a flood of emotion pourin' out
of us right then, ah'm tellin' ya true! The men who weren't hurt
stopped fightin' fo' those few seconds and cheered like wild men,
wavin' their caps in the air, shoutin' till they went hoarse! You could
see what the smoke from the battle was doin' to 'em cause most of
their faces was every bit as black as mine! Yessuh! Even the
wounded got into it. Tears come to mah eyes while ah watched
these wounded boys strugglin' to sit up so they could cheer and
salute their commander! Some was too weak to even do that. Ah
'member seein' one man lyin' prone on his back. Didn't even have
the strength to roll over on his side, but he could lift one hand in the
air and make a fist. Looked like he was tryin' to cheer too, but his
voice was too weak to be heard. It was almost like we was lookin'
at Marse Robert like he was some sort of god or somethin'. So
long as ah live ah ain't never gonna fo'get those few moments in the
yard by the Chancellor house." He nodded his head as if to affirm
his own words, but then the expression of joy so visible in his eyes

over the last several minutes evaporated and his dark face took on a look which could only be described as deadly serious.

"Just then a courier showed up," he said in a soft voice many had to strain to hear. "He come from Stonewall and his message told Marse Robert 'bout the amputation of Stonewall's arm, and that because of how badly he'd been wounded, General Jackson would have to give up command of his corps. Ah was helpin' to load wounded into the ambulance but ah could see Marse Robert's face and ah could read the grief on his face. Ah watched him dictate an answer to Stonewall, and ah'm sho' y'all know 'bout what he said, how he would have preferred to have been the one wounded 'stead of Stonewall.

"Even so, grief was a luxury none of us could afford to indulge in. There was still a battle to be fought. Marse Robert wanted Hooker driven all the way to the Rappahannock where we could trap him and maybe force his surrender. Problem was we was all too disorganized right then to be pressin' anybody anywhere. Befo' our boys could advance we had to reorganize and that would take a little bit of time. General Lee issued the orders to get this process started, then he sent off a message to Richmond to let the folks down there know 'bout our victory. Seemed like fo'tune was smilin' on us from every quarter, but a couple of hours later word came to us from Fredericksburg what changed the whole complexion of the battle.

"If ah 'member right it was nigh on three o'clock in the afternoon when a courier came ridin' in from Fredericksburg on a horse he 'bout rode to death. The news he had wasn't at all pleasant, ah can tell y'all that fo' a fact. Some of the boys we left up to Fredericksburg was overrun. Ah'll tell y'all mo' 'bout that in a minute, but the main point is this; the Yankees broke through and they was headin' west on the Plank Road which means they was in our rear and comin' on strong! At that moment any plans General Lee had 'bout hammerin' Hooker back to the river had to be put aside. Instead we had to deal with the possibility of bein' squeezed by the two halves of the Army of the Potomac.

"Marse Robert moved fast. He had to! All of a sudden triumph turned into desperation! But ah'll tell you what, the man ain't been born yet who can improvise better'n Robert E. Lee, and improvise he did...not that he had a whole lot of choice in the matter! He postponed the attack on Hooker and ordered General Colston's division to move on up the Ely's Ford Road till he made contact with Hooker. He was to be there to keep Hooker in check, that's all...not to get into any serious engagement. Then he ordered General Mclaws to head east on the Plank Road till he ran into the Federals. His job was to slow 'em down till General Lee figured out what to do next. Now let me tell y'all how all this came to be.

"Ah'm sho' y'all remember ah've told ya how Hooker kept sendin' orders to Sedgwick to attack our boys at Fredericksburg and turn on Chancellorsville. Well now it seems General Sedgwick finally got around to doin' like he was told. The night befo', while Stonewall was gettin his arm sawed off, Sedgwick pulled most of his troops away from General Early's front and massed them in front of Maryes' Heights by the town itself. He added another division under General Gibbon, includin' them boys what called themselves the Iron Brigade. Gibbon had been positioned up at Falmouth, just a short march from Fredericksburg on the north side of the river. This gave Sedgwick close to thirty thousand men to make his punch with; more than a corps of Federals against Early's division and Barksdale's brigade. The bulk of this force was concentrated against General Barksdale, so basically we're talkin' bout a full corps of Yankees, or close to it, against one solitary brigade of our boys.

   "Dawn came and with it came the charge. The Federals threw pontoons across the river and crossed real quick-like. Sedgwick feigned left, and again on the right; and then, just as Stuart was leadin' the attack against Hooker he hit Barksdale right in the middle of his line, and a thin line it was, forced even thinner by Sedgwick's feints against either end. Those Mississippi boys was holdin' ground that twice their number was needed to hold. Up came the Yankees just chargin' all in a rush! Barksdale's boys opened up on em, and they was backed up by four batteries of the Washington Artillery, sixteen guns in all! They tore up that first charge, and ah mean they bloodied 'em up bad! Up they came a second time, but this charge fared no better than the first. Then the Yankees called fo' a truce. They sent a man with a white flag up to our line. Supposedly he was there to talk 'bout gettin' their wounded off the field, but while he was up there he could easily see how thinly held that line was. He went back to his own lines and told his officers what he saw. Then they geared up fo' one mo' all out rush. This one was led by a regiment from Wisconsin. Their colonel gave 'em a little talk just befo' they charged. He told 'em they had to advance at a double-quick pace as soon as they got the order to move forward. They were not to fire their guns, nor were they to stop fo' any reason till they got the order to halt. He waited fo' them to digest those words fo' a second or two then he told 'em they'd never get that order.

   "Off they went," he continued after drawing a deep breath, "them boys from Wisconsin followed by nine other regiments...ten of 'em in all, and each one close to full strength. They charged fo' the stone wall near the base of Maryes Heights and behind that wall was two under-strength regiments of Mississippians. Our boys was overrun, but ah'm tellin' ya true, they fought to the last! Over the wall came the Federals and both sides was fightin' with bayonets. They took the wall and then the sunken road behind it. Up the Heights they stormed straight fo' the guns! Those gunners in the Washington Artillery kept pourin' it into 'em until Bluecoats was swarmin' all over the gunpits and they was fightin' hand to hand! All the guns from Parker's battery were captured along with their crews. The Washington Artillery lost all of their guns too, and so many men that they could never again man more than eight cannons at a time. Only a handful of our gunners escaped. Later on one of our reservists asked a survivor where his guns were. He was hot, ah'll tell ya that much. He said that the guns oughta be damned, and that he figured by now our Southern Confederacy ought to be satisfied that Barksdale's Brigade and the Washington Artillery couldn't whip the whole damned Yankee army! I guess a lot of folks was thinkin' they could after the way they mauled Burnside's boys in the Battle of Fredericksburg. Those three assaults against General Barksdale cost the Yankees fifteen hundred men and cost the Federals some valuable time. After the final attack the Yankees was so busy congratulatin' themselves and celebratin' that they lost all sense of cohesion. They didn't know that Hooker had already been driven from Chancellorsville.

"So there things stood. Our Fredericksburg line was broken. General Early and his men were forced to retreat southeast to cover our supply lines at Guinea Station. General Barksdale with his survivors moved off to the west to link up with the rest of the army. Sedgwick didn't pursue General Early. His orders from Hooker were quite clear. Once he broke through he was to turn right and head fo' Chancellorsville to trap Lee between himself and Hooker. Ah think it was 'bout 11:30 in the mo'nin' when Sedgwick got still another order from Hooker to turn on Lee and attack at once. His boys was still celebratin' up on top of Maryes Heights. It wasn't till 2:00 in the afternoon that he got his troops reorganized and on the march, leavin' one division behind to keep General Early at bay." He paused a moment, scratchin' his beard while searching his memory to be sure he was recalling all those details correctly.

"Through all of this General Lee stayed as cool as a cucumber," he continued, "seemed like his feathers wouldn't ruffle no matter what crisis he had to deal with. There was one officer who came up to Marse Robert all a flutter. There was desperation written all over this man's face and his hands was just-a-flyin' everywhere while he tried to describe what happened on Maryes' Heights. He was tryin' to convince the General that we were in great danger, but Marse Robert cut him short with a single gesture, and then calmly told him we'd be dealin' with Mr. Sedgwick later.

"As fo' General Sedgwick, he didn't get too far and it didn't take too God-awful- much to stop him. The Federals only covered a mile from Maryes Heights when they spotted some of our boys deployed along the crest of a ridge which crossed the road. It was Cadmus Wilcox with one brigade of Alabama boys. Fo' three days they'd been guardin' Banks Ford well to the rear of our boys in Chancellorsville. When General Wilcox heard what happened at Mayres' Heights he moved immediately to place himself between Sedgwick's corps and General Lee. He played a little poker game with Sedgwick and it worked just like he hoped it would. He spread his brigade out on that ridge and made them appear like a skirmish line...a big one...which in turn gave the impression that mo' troops was in position behind the crest of the ridge out of sight of the Federals. Now General Mclaws was on the way, just like ah told ya earlier, and he had General Alexander with him, along with a bunch of guns. Problem was, they hadn't arrived and ol' Wilcox was facin' a whole Yankee corps by his lonesome. Ol' Wilcox...he musta had his best poker face on that day 'cause Sedgwick fell fo' the bluff and deployed fo' battle. Wilcox gave ground slowly at first, but two of Sedgwick's divisions was chewin' away at his single brigade and as they realized he was out there alone they began to step up the pressure. But he did what he knew he had to do...which was to slow the Yankees down. It took 'em three hours to reach Salem Church, which was no mo' than fo' miles from where they started. They drove our boys past the church and thought they was gonna have their way, and then they saw Mclaws in a heavy line of battle with Alexander's guns backin' him up all along its length. They stopped the Federals cold then drove 'em back! They recaptured the church but then the Yankees stiffened and the two sides dug in. Sedgwick didn't figure he could push Mclaws aside with the little bit of daylight remainin' so he went into camp fo' the night. Just like that, the threat from Fredericksburg evaporated. When the next day dawned Marse Robert would become the hunter. Sedgwick would be his prey.

Here he paused and yawned loudly as he covered his mouth with his right hand. He rose slowly to a standing position and stretched his body with both hands pressed firmly against the small of his back. "Gettin' tired," he sighed and indeed he had good reason. The hour had grown late and to Ivory it seemed as if he'd been talking for days. "Don't y'all worry none though," he said, "reckon ah got me 'nuff voice left to finish this story." He accepted yet another mug of coffee offered this time by Armelin Linscombe and took several sips, nodding his thanks to the Cajun. Remaining on his feet he resumed the telling of Chancellorsville's final stages.

"Durin' the night, General Lee learned that Early was makin' his way 'round through the woods to help Mclaws against Sedgwick. He sent Jubal a message to do just that and said that he believed the two of them could demolish Sedgwick's corps. Dawn came and the first thing we learned was how strongly Hooker had fortified his position north of Chancellorsville. His line was shaped kinda like a bow, with either end anchored against the Rappahannock. He still had 'bout eighty thousand men, but they were pretty well bottled up inside their entrenchments, and they sho' didn't show no signs of comin' out. Marse Robert figured it would be safe to leave Stuart with Jackskon's corps to keep an eye on Hooker while he took General Anderson's division and turned east to deal with Sedgwick on roughly equal terms. On that mo'nin' Stuart had maybe twenty-five thousand men to keep eighty thousand in check. Turns out, that's all he needed cause Mr. F. J. Hooker had long since lost whatever nerve he had when he first arrived at Chancellorsville.

"Now y'all listen careful, hear? Cause these troop dispositions ah'm tellin' ya 'bout get kinda complicated. It was Monday, the 4th of May, long 'bout noon when Marse Robert reached Salem Church. General Anderson's division had yet to arrive. By this time General Sedgwick's rearguard under Gibbon had abandoned Mayres' Heights and had gone back into the town of Fredericksburg itself. So Barksdale and the men he had left reoccupied those Heights. Early's division was in position a little south and to the east of Sedgwick. Mclaws faced him from the west and Anderson was supposed to swing down and come up at Sedgwick from the south. Our total numbers up there was maybe twenty-two thousand and that's 'bout all Sedgwick had to work with as well.

"Keep somethin' else in mind," he urged as he held up one finger to draw the attention of his audience, which truthfully was in no need of being drawn as most of those present were hanging on his every word. "Hooker crossed the river and marched toward Chancellorsville on the 28th of April. Now it was the 4th of May.

For six straight days our boys had been marchin' and fightin' and most of the time they was doin' it on empty stomachs. Everybody was just 'bout plum wore out by the time we got ready to deal with Sedgwick. That's my way of explainin' that things wasn't goin' quite the way they was planned. General Alexander told me this was the first time he ever saw General Lee lose his temper. There was three things the General was mad about. The first thing was time. A lot was bein' uselessly wasted 'cause people weren't where they was supposed to be. Then he was angry 'bout the fact that nobody had bothered to scout the enemy position, so we didn't know exactly where Sedgwick's line was or which direction it ran in, and it seemed to him that it ought to be somebody's duty to know. Finally he was irate that it now fell on his shoulders to find out all this information personally, which meant even mo' time would be lost befo' anybody could advance a single step!

"To General Alexander it seemed like the best way to find the enemy would be to advance on him till we made contact, but Marse Robert was in such a foul temper by that time that Alexander figured it would be wiser to keep his mouth shut, and that's just what he did.

"General Lee rode off to find the enemy, in particular his left flank, but in the meantime Mclaws, Early and Anderson all seemed to have trouble gettin' themselves ready. Ah reckon the General was hopin' to find Sedgwick's left flank in the air but it wasn't. It was anchored on the river just like his right. The result of all this was a wasted day just what Marse Robert feared most. It wasn't till 6:00 o'clock in the evenin' that the attack finally got started. The idea was fo all three of our divisions to hit Sedgwick from different directions but those plans went by the board. General Early hit the enemy left and with savage fightin' he drove the Federals off their line. Sad to say things didn't go so well with the other two divisions. Mclaws got himself all tangled up in the woods and never really came in contact with the enemy. General Anderson's troops got all turned around and some of 'em ended up shootin' at each other. It just didn't pan out at all like the General had hoped. The sun set and a fog rolled in which just made it that much worse, but Marse Robert was determined not to let Sedgwick get away without a fight. Fo' the first time in the war he ordered a night attack. General Alexander had his guns firin' on Banks Ford to block their retreat and the infantry tried to move forward but it was just impossible, so he finally gave up and called it off. By mornin', Sedgwick was gone. They threw pontoon bridges 'cross the river and got everybody over befo' the sun came up. Gibbon did the same thing over at Fredericksburg so on the mornin' of the 5th they was all back on the north bank of the Rappahannock.

"Now it remained to deal with Hooker and his eighty-thousand. Marse Robert let Anderson and Mclaws rest a spell then put 'em on the road fo' Chancellorsville and ordered Alexander to pile up a bunch of guns on Hooker's left flank. What the General didn't know was that Hooker had no desire to continue the battle. He held himself a council of war with his corps commanders durin' the night while Sedgwick was escapin' and asked 'em to vote whether to go or stay. Three said to stay and fight, two said retreat. Hooker overruled the vote and decided it was time to leave.

"All day long on the 5th they retreated on pontoon bridges. Around midday or so it started to rain and ah mean to tell you it was pourin' buckets out of that sky. The rain put a little suspense into Hooker's withdrawal 'cause the Rappahannock done rose six feet by midnight which threatened to wash away his two bridges. The Federals ended up usin' the pieces of one bridge to keep the other one solid and they kept crossin' all through the night. By mid-mornin' of the sixth they was gone...all of em. They was south of that river fo' one week, and they sho'nuff crawled back with their tails between their legs! The Battle of Chancellorsville was over." Ivory paused to let these words sink in and resumed his seat atop the crates, "but Marse Robert...he just wasn't all that pleased how it ended. His temper was already short 'cause Sedgwick got away, then when he got back to Chancellorsville and found out Hooker was gone...well...that ol' temper of his come bubblin' up again. It was a brigadier what brought him the news, and ah was sho' nuff glad ah wasn't in that man's boots! Marse Robert scolded the po' man. He just fussed up a storm! He said, `You allow those people to get away! I tell you what to do, but you won't do it! Go after them, and damage them all you can!' 'Course there wasn't no mo' damage any of us could do, 'cause the Yankees was plum gone.

"Hooker lost more than seventeen thousand men, and we lost close to thirteen," he continued. "Hooker was whipped. Everybody knew it includin' him. Up North those folks was in a state of shock when the news broke. What was it that fella Greeley said in his newspaper?" He glanced directly at Longstreet, "Do you remember General?"

"Are you referring to Horace Greeley?"

"Yessuh...that's him,"

"If memory serves me," replied Longstreet, "he bemoaned the fact that 130,000 magnificent soldiers had been cut to pieces by fewer than 60,000 half-starved ragamuffins."

"That's what he said all right," nodded Ivory with a grin. "What he didn't say but shoulda said was that the half-starved ragamuffins were the ones who should have been called magnificent soldiers!"

GRAY VISIONS

"Amen, Ivory!" cried one of the veterans there gathered.

"You told it true!" called out another.

There were several other spontaneous accolades from the crowd, each of which drew a nod and a weary smile from the black storyteller who by now was very nearly exhausted.

"Ivory?" The voice belonged to a young boy perhaps twelve years of age. "Can you tell us 'bout Stonewall now?"

An expression both of warmth and sadness could be seen in Ivory's eyes as he gazed at the youngster. "Sho' will," he replied, "and then ah reckon ah'm done for the evenin'. After Gettysburg when we had to retreat out of Pennsylvania and got back here to Virginia, ah was able to speak with some of the folks what was tendin' to Stonewall in his last days, so Ah think Ah can tell y'all pretty true how we lost him fo'ever.

"At first we was all pretty optimistic 'bout Stonewall's gettin' well and comin' back to us," he explained. "The reports comin' from his surgeon, Dr. McGuire, sounded good to us. They said that Stonewall was in excellent spirits when he woke up after the amputation. Stonewall himself said he was wounded but not depressed, that everythin' happened accordin' to the will of God, and that he would wait to see what the Lawd had in sto' fo' him. You folks who knew Stonewall Jackson understand how pious a man he was. He wouldn't even take credit fo' the victories he won. Always he'd say the thanks was owed to God. On that day right after his arm was sawed off he got a message from Marse Robert which praised him fo' the skill and energy he'd displayed durin' our flankin' movement. Do y'all know what he said? He said that General Lee was very kind, but the praise should have been given to God. That was the only time in the war that he had somethin' contrary to say 'bout Robert E. Lee.

"When Sedgwick crossed the river at Fredericksburg and

threatened our rear, Stonewall had to be moved real quick so he wouldn't end up a prisoner. They put him in an ambulance and moved off south, then they cut southeast and rode through Spotsylvania Court House on down to Guinea Station. That's a bit of irony now that ah think 'bout it. Guinea Station is where he met his wife and baby daughter befo' Hooker decided to give us a go. The trip was maybe twenty-five miles altogether and all along the way people was gatherin' by the roadside to pay their respects as he passed. Stonewall Jackson was a man loved by many and not just us soldiers. All them folks along the road wanted to show their love of the man with gifts from their farms: buttermilk, fried chicken, biscuits and things of the like. Ah heard Stonewall was deeply touched by all this affection and it helped keep his spirits up as the ambulance moved farther away from the battle and the rumble of the guns faded from their ears. One of his staff officers was in the ambulance with him and asked him what he thought of Hooker's plan to defeat our army. Stonewall had some praise fo' ol' Hooker, said it was an excellent plan, but that Hooker blundered badly by sendin' away his cavalry. Said it was that mistake which allowed us to move into his rear without his even knowin' it. Stonewall was right pleased by that march of ours, said it was the most successful moment of his life, but he wanted that staff officer to understand God's role in that success." He paused to swat at a moth that had darted over the campfire and began flittering about his head.

"By dark they had reached Guinea Station and the General was given a room at an estate belongin' to the Chandler family. He woke up the next day...Tuesday, ah think it was...feelin' pretty good. The wounds weren't painin' him much and he just relaxed all day long, and all through the next. He talked quite a bit, mostly 'bout religion 'n such. Y'all remember how he used to be whenever there was leisure time. He was doin' so good, Dr. McGuire figured he'd have a complete and quick recovery, even talked 'bout his comin' back to duty sooner than anybody thought. Ah can only reckon it wasn't meant to be. The change hit him late Wednesday night and on into the next mo'nin'. When Dr. McGuire woke up and went in to check on Stonewall he found a restless man tryin' to cope with some serious pain, but it wasn't the wounds botherin' him. Dr. McGuire looked him over and said pneumonia was settin' in and...well...y'all know how deadly that can be. Dr. McGuire was a good man...a fine doctor. He did all we knew how to do in those days. They cupped Stonewall and gave him mercury along with antimony and opium. They gave him morphine so he wouldn't feel the pain so much, but all them drugs just robbed him of that sharp mind of his. He just started driftin' in and out of sleep and a gloom began to creep through that house. Everyone there was startin' to realize we was losin' him, but most of 'em didn't want to believe it was happenin. Prayers was bein' said, lots of 'em but like ah said befo', it just wasn't meant to be.

"They told me Mrs. Jackson arrived at the Chandler house 'round noon on Thursday. She had been tryin' to come north since she got word of his bein' wounded, but it wasn't safe fo' her to travel with all that Yankee cavalry roamin' about. They said she was shocked when she first saw him. The arm that used to hold her close was gone and to her the remainin' stump was a hideous sight. Even his face scared her 'cause his cheeks was all flushed and his breathin'...well, she could tell right away somethin' was wrong. Seemed like the drugs was puttin' him into a different world 'cause when he woke up he acted like he didn't even know who she was." His listeners detected a slight break in Ivory's voice just then as the aging black veteran stopped speakin for a moment. Was it due to the strain of having told so long a story? Perhaps, but as the old man gazed skyward for a moment another possibility presented itself. The pale glow of the fire revealed tears glistening in his eyes. More than twenty years had passed since Stonewall's death, but Ivory Lee Davis still felt the pain of the Jackson family within his own heart. Blinking back the tears Ivory resumed eye contact with those gathered around him and resumed the tale of Stonewall Jackson.

"After awhile all them drugs wore off a bit and he woke up with his mind clear," he said, "that's when he recognized her and he also saw the fear in her eyes. He told her not to wear a long face, said that in a sickroom he loved to see cheerfulness and brightness. A little while later he lapsed into sleep again and when he woke back up he found her sittin' right by his side. He called her his darlin' and told her how very much she was loved, said that she was one of the most precious little wives in the world.

"Later that night he seemed like he might be shakin' off that pneumonia, and when he spoke it was the Stonewall Jackson all of us knew. Dr. McGuire came over to him when it was time fo' mo' of them drugs and asked the General if he'd take his dosage. Stonewall gave him that look that don't allow much of an argument and told him to do his duty, and when the doctor seemed unsure 'bout it he repeated those same words: do your duty. As the night wore on, however, he started to get delirious and his mind was back on the battle. He called out fo' Major Pendleton who was the adjutant on his staff. He was askin' the major to send scouts ahead to determine if there was higher ground, back of Chancellorsville. He was almost shoutin' and said he had to find out if there was high ground between Chancellorsville and the river. He kept callin' fo' Pendleton, tellin' him to take charge of the columns...to push us even harder so we'd put mo' speed into our legs.

"Friday came and the General seemed to get worse by the hour. The same was true Saturday. Dr. McGuire began to fear the worst and sent word to Richmond and to Marse Robert that he didn't think Stonewall would pull through. Like Ah said befo' no one wanted to believe it. General Lee said he didn't think the Lawd would take Stonewall when we needed him so much. One of the newspapers over to Richmond said Stonewall was born fo' a purpose, and that he sho'ly wouldn't leave us befo' that purpose was fulfilled. Ah think Stonewall himself might of believed a little of what that paper was sayin'. Some time on Friday he said that he wasn't 'fraid to die and he'd sho'ly abide by the Lawd's will but he figured the Father still had somethin' fo' him to do in this life. You could see what was on his mind by the song he asked 'em to sing. It was somethin' taken from the fifty-first psalm. Some of you boys out there might remember it. The words asked the Lawd to show pity and forgive, and to let a repentin' rebel live."

"I remember that one," said an old man out in the crowd.

"Me too," echoed another.

"Saturday night was a bad one fo' Stonewall and all those around him," continued Ivory. "He was delirious and couldn't get much sleep. All night long he kept callin' out for A. P. Hill and Wells Hawks, his commissary officer. Most of the time nobody could understand what he was sayin'.

"Sunday mornin' Dr. McGuire told Mrs. Jackson what he knew to be the truth, that her husband would be gone 'fo the day was out. She knelt beside his bed and even though he wasn't conscious she kept tellin' him he'd soon be in heaven. When he woke up she asked him if he'd be willin' to yield himself to God's will even if it meant he'd die that day. He said he preferred it that way. She looked at him and told him befo' the day was over he'd be with the blessed Savior in all his glory. His eyes met hers and he said his would be the infinite gain. Then he dozed

off again, long 'bout noon he woke up again and she told him a
second time he'd be gone 'fo the sun went down. `Oh no,' he said
to her, `you are frightened, my child. Death is not so near. I may
yet get well'. That's all she could take. She'd been so strong
through the whole ordeal but now she just broke down and cried
like a baby, sobbin' that the doctor had told her he'd not make it
through the day. Stonewall didn't seem to believe her at first and
called for Dr. McGuire. `Doctor.' he said, `Anne informs me that
you have told her I am to die today. Is it so?' When the doctor
told him it was, Stonewall kind of retreated into himself fo' a little
while, like maybe he was makin' his peace with the Lawd, then he
spoke up again. `Very good, very good,' he says, `It is all right. It
is the Lord's day, my wish is fulfilled. I have always desired to die
on Sunday.'

"Come 1:30 the doctor told Stonewall he had maybe two
hours left...no mo'. `Very good,' says Stonewall, `it's all right,' but
everyone could see the change comin' over him. His voice was
weak and his breath was comin' hard 'cause that pneumonia was
fast fillin' his lungs. Dr. McGuire tried to get him to sip on some
brandy, thinkin' that would help him hold on, but Stonewall
wouldn't hear of it, he said it would do no good and only delay his
departure. He told the doctor he wanted to preserve his mind to
the last, if that was at all possible. Not long after that he got delirious again. He'd been prayin', then he was back in battle given'
orders left and right. The end came just a few minutes after three in
the afternoon. Stonewall cried out to A. P. Hill, `Order A. P. Hill to
prepare fo' action!' he said. `Pass the infantry to the front! Tell
Major Hawks...and then he stopped. He never finished whatever it
was he wanted to say. The expression on his face changed to one
of peace and serenity. It's like he knew his last instant in this life
was upon him, and that knowledge became a source of immense

relief. That's the feelin' those 'round him got as he was speakin' his last words 'cause his whole tone changed and his face was calm like the surface of a pond when there ain't no breeze. `Let us cross over the river,' he said, `and rest under the shade of the trees.' Those were his last words," explained Ivory, "and then he crossed over."

Ivory sat back and crossed his burly arms over his chest. He tried to turn his face so people wouldn't see the single tear which dropped from his right eye and rolled down his cheek only to disappear into the fleecy white curls of his beard.

The one-time teamster/cook need not have worried about the evidence of his own emotion. No few tears formed and fell from the eyes of those present as the last echoes of the telling of Chancellorsville faded in the night air. No one stirred. Every man and boy seemed lost within his own visions of days gone by, of past deeds enshrined in glory by the blood of patriots, of great men, especially one called Stonewall. The night was suddenly still as if even the cicadas thought it appropriate to observe silence in respect to that fallen leader. Ivory had told the story with the meticulous care one might devote to the weaving of a delicate tapestry, and in so doing had crafted a vivid picture in the minds of those who listened. In the mind of young David Covington that picture did not fade with the tale's end. If anything the opposite was true. He saw within his mind the image of Anne Jackson suddenly a widow, standing by the body of her beloved husband, her face buried in her hands, her shoulders shaking softly as she wept silently, grief stricken like so many other wives and mothers across the land. "Ivory?" David's voice was the first to pierce the silence.

Ivory turned back to face the boy. "Yes, son?"

"I think Stonewall's been watchin' us up there since you started talkin', and I believe he's smilin'."

"Ah hope so," Ivory managed a smile of his own. "Ah sho' do."

Several minutes of silence passed as the hundreds of men and boys there present retreated into their own thoughts. Finally one man well back in the throng rose to his feet and cleared his throat. "Ain't got much of a voice," he announced calmly, "but I got me a song to sing, and I want to dedicate it to the memories of Stonewall Jackson and Robert E. Lee. All you boys out here ... you're my brothers. I hope you'll join in my song." With a voice far more deep and clear than anyone anticipated, the aged veteran began to sing, " I wish I was in the Land of cotton, old times there are not forgotton."

One by one those assembled, old and young, black and white, began rising to their feet. "In Dixie Land where I was born, early on one frosty mornin'!"

At last they were all standing, all of them bareheaded, holding their hats over their hearts. Chills rippled up and down the back of young David Covington as he watched the men of his father's generation standing together, arms on one another's shoulders, joining one another in song. Above them all could be heard the compelling voice of Ivory Lee Davis , "Look away, look away. Look away, Dixie Land."

GRAY VISIONS

~Chapter Four~
1898

William C. Oates, President of the Confederate States of America, put down the report he had been reading at his desk and loosed a weary sigh. With his one hand he removed his spectacles and tried to rub the fatigue from his eyes. "Too many sleepless nights," he grumbled as he pushed himself away from the desk and rose slowly to his feet. Leaving the report to wait he shuffled slowly to a window which offered a southern exposure. Parting the curtains he let his eyes gaze down to the James River. It was a wintery scene which greeted him that January afternoon. An unusually fierce storm had dumped over a foot of snow on Richmond two days prior and the temperature hadn't climbed over thirty degrees since. Dreary, gray skies hovered over central Virginia with the promise of more frosty precipitation in the not-so-distant future.

Leaving the window and its vision of winter, he stepped to his favorite easy chair just paces from the fireplace where crackling tongues of flame licked hungrily at a stack of oak and hickory logs. He eased himself into the chair and sighed as his body was comfortably embraced by its cushions. A smile crept across his face as the warmth from the fire chased the chills from his aging body. As sometimes happened, he thought he felt a twinge of pain shooting up his right arm and was so convinced by the sensation that he actually reacted with his left hand to rub the pain away, pausing and shaking his head with a chuckle, thinking how strange his actions might appear if another person had been in the room watching. Had he continued reaching his left hand would have clutched nothing but an empty sleeve. His right arm was gone, lost in the summer of 1864 only months before the war for Southern independence ended. Over the past three decades he had experienced the same sensation on countless occasions. It always seemed so real! Sometimes he could actually feel his right fist open and close or the bicep muscle flexing. But always it was an illusion... a mirage born of his longing to reclaim the lost limb.

Still enjoying the heat emanating from the fire he let his mind slip back in time to the summer of 1864. He recalled the series of events which led to the amputation of his right arm. General R.E. Lee, ever the crafty one and most dangerous with his back against a wall, had risen from his sickbed and sprung the trap he set for Grant along the North Anna River at Ox Ford. The Confederate victory there was sudden and overwhelming, reversing the tide of war in one swift stroke. Grant would soon capitulate to the determined Lee and with the Army of the Potomac no longer on the chessboard, Lee was quick to seize the federal Capital and its astonished president. It was during this final action, the battle for Washington city, in which then Colonel Oates sustained the wound which cost him his right arm. The long weeks of his recovery proved to be a memorable time as they saw the coming of peace, the abolition of slavery - a move he heartily supported - and the emergence of the Confederate States of America as an independent nation.

A veteran of more than two dozen battles, Colonel Oates returned to his native Alabama after the war and shifted his attention from the military to the political arena. Soon he was serving his home state in the congress in Richmond, building on this service to launch a successful bid for the office of Governor, a position which ultimately landed him in the Confederate White House as the twentieth century drew nigh.

Now this thing in Cuba. He turned his eyes from the fire and stared at the opposite wall of his office. "No point in bogging down in memories," he muttered softly to himself as he returned his attention to the report he'd left on his desk. More than thirty years had passed since the war's end, time enough for the old wounds to heal and for the bitterness to fade. The people of the United States and those of the Confederate States had begrudgingly learned to accept one another, though most of the latter still found if difficult to place any trust in the intentions of their northern neighbors. If not warm, relations between the two peoples had at least been peaceful. The long border between them had long since been demilitarized along the lines of Canada's with the United States. Though commerce and the movement of people back and forth across the border were slow to resume, time had done much to facilitate both. During the 1870's, both countries cast their eyes Westward, but in this regard the United States, with its superior military and its industrial base, had a decided advantage. Oklahoma was the only bright spot for the Confederacy. The people of this territory opted to align themselves with the South an even now were preparing for statehood. It was widely hoped among the leaders of the Confederacy that New Mexico and Arizona would soon follow Oklahoma's lead, but this was not to be. Though the people of these territories expressed a desire to afilliate with the Confederate States, the federal government of the United States moved swiftly to insure the organization of these territories as future states within the Union. Only the Apaches stood in the way of this design, and they would ultimately yield to the relentless pressure of the United States cavalry. With the twentieth century close at hand the geographic boundaries of the Confederacy were fixed as if in stone. In terms of territory, there was little remaining for the two countries to compete over. Except Cuba.

One of the last Spanish possessions in the New World, Cuba was to find itself the object of covetous eyes in both the United and Confederate States. Despite the blatant attention coming from North America, Spain did not appear to be the least bit inclined to part with the last vestiges of her Western Empire. However, the people of Cuba had other plans for their own future. Independence was their goal, and to this end many of them had risen in revolt. The result was turmoil for the island colony. If the Spanish and Cubans had been the only parties involved President Oates would scarcely have taken notice, but this was not the case. The United States had begun to rattle its sabers again and war clouds were building on the horizon. The possibility of the United States engaging in hostilities a mere ninety miles from the shores of the Confederacy raised serious security concerns which left Oates no choice but to quickly become an

expert on Cuban affairs. Hence the report on his desk. He
donned his reading glasses and with a heavy sigh he began to
study the document for the umpteenth time.

Most of the basic information was common knowledge
among many North Americans and required but a perusal. The
population of Cuba was approaching two million. The economy
was primarily agrarian with two crops, tobacco and sugar, gener-
ating most of the island's income. At one time Cuba had been
actively involved in the slave trade and largely dependent on
slave labor. All of that had changed as slavery had been abol-
ished in Cuba just as it had in the United and Confederate States.
However, the demise of the slave-labor system did not translate
into freedom for the common people of Cuba, and many had seen
no salvation for their hopes without armed rebellion.

1868 saw the birth of the "Insurrectos" or freedom
fighters. The were led initially by two men. One of them,
Maximo Gomez, had been a professional soldier and was well
acquainted with war. The other, a close friend of Gomez, was
named Antonio Maceo. He was the descendant of slaves and to
the people he was known as the "Bronze Titan". From both
countries in America came help in the form of supplies and
volunteers. In Cuba the struggle for independence had begun.

None of this was new to President Oates, nor was the
information the report contained about the *Virginius*. The incident occurred back in '73. A ship by the name *Virginius* set sail
from New York City heavily laden with guns and munitions
destined for the Cuban rebels. The ship never reached its destination. She was captured by the Spanish and her crew were declared to be pirates. They were summarily shot by their captors,
an atrocity which generated so much anger in the United States
that Spain felt it necessary to quickly issue a formal apology to
the government in Washington. From the perspective of the
Cuban rebels this turned out to be a public opinion coup more
valuable than all of the guns captured on the ill-fated ship.

Oates decided to skip several pages and was soon studying the events of the Spring of '95. The two leaders mentioned
earlier were joined by a third, one Jose Marti, a one-time poet

who had founded the Cuban Revolutionary Party and its newspaper, Patria. This time it was war on a much larger scale. 54,000 Insurrectos armed with machetes, rifles and cannons took on 240,000 Spanish soldiers. Marti was one of the early casualties and his death left Gomez in charge. Realizing the futility of engaging the Spanish in conventional warfare, Gomez chose to follow a different route. The rebels resorted to guerrilla warfare, bedeviling the Spanish with their deadly, hit and run tactics. Knowing how much the Spanish depended on Cuba's wealth for their own prosperity Gomez made this wealth a target. Suddenly the island's sugar plantations were going up in smoke. Anyone who chose to work for the Spanish found himself a target of the rebels.

By 1896, the Spanish were desperate. They were losing their grip on the island colony and knew drastic measures would have to be taken. To this end a new, military governor was appointed and charged with the responsibility of crushing the rebels. His name was Valeriano Weyler, and he took office in February of that year. He was to become the most hated figure in Cuban history.

"So he admires General Sherman," Oates muttered to himself as he scanned the particulars on Weyler. "I shouldn't wonder."

If William Sherman was his teacher, then Weyler was also an excellent pupil, even to the point of exceeding the ruthlessness often displayed by the former. He divided the island along a North-South line completely clearing a swath of earth two hundred yards wide and sealing off both sides with barbed wire, giving Weyler the dubious distinction of being the first to use this wire as a weapon in war, and ample use he made of it. It was during this phase that Maceo, the "Bronze Titan", was killed leaving only Gomez to keep the fires of independence burning.

As if the answer to scorched earth tactics of the rebels, Weyler responded in kind. He started the reconcentration system, a strategy which involved removing tens of thousands of peasants and farmers from their homes and literally herding them into camps. Before it was all over many of these people would die of starvation and disease. Weyler's soldiers went about their work with a vengeful enthusiasm. To deny food to the rebels they burned off the crops, slaughtered the livestock and poisoned wells. Vast regions of the island were thoroughly depopulated and by war's end, over 400,000 Cubans were to meet their deaths.

Before his own death, Jose Marti had established an organization in the United States for the purpose of swaying public opinion. Here he found an ally in the person of Joseph Pulitzer, the publisher of the *New York World.* Since his newspaper made a practice of sensationalizing the news some folks described it as a comic strip in color, but this particular approach to the reporting of the news was quite effective. Pulitzer sold lots of papers and became known as the "Yellow Kid." Other publishers seeing his obvious financial success were quick to copy his idea and thus was born the Yellow Press in the United States, and it is here that William Randolph Hearst enters the picture. His paper, the *New York Journal*, was the main rival of Pulitzer's *New York World.* On a daily basis the two papers tried to outdo one another with one-sided articles on the situation in Cuba and the "Butcher Weyler."

"Hearst," muttered President Oates with more than a hint of disgust in his voice, "Warmonger."

This description could hardly be called an exaggeration. Hearst had written that newspapers controlled the United States. It was the papers which declared wars and caused Congress to pass laws. He wanted war with Spain and made no secret of it. Oates lifted his eyes from the report and thought about that for a moment. Then he remembered. It had only been a few months since Hearst had dispatched his artist, Frederic Remington, to Cuba with these instructions: "You furnish the pictures, and I'll furnish the war." Several weeks later he printed a story about three Cuban women who were stripped of their clothes and searched by Spanish authorities on board an American Ship. The headline atop the story, in huge, bold letters, asked this question, "Does our flag shield women?" One million copies of this paper were sold. It was the largest run in journalistic history, and calls for war echoed across the United States.

Anytime the United States considered war, the people of the Confederacy had no choice but to pay attention. Moreover, this new phenomenon called the Yellow Press was not confined to the United States. Atlanta, Richmond, Memphis and New Orleans all had newspapers which mirrored the sensationalism so prevalent in the stories printed by Pulitzer and Hearst. Barraged by stories of Spanish cruelty and barbarism, Southerners echoed the outrage of their Northern counterparts. Whatever his own opinions of the Yellow Press, President Oates was not in a position where he could easily ignore the popular sentiment against Spain.

The sentiment in both the United and Confederate States was producing more than public outcry. Volunteers from both countries streamed toward Cuba to help the rebels, including a contingent of the Texas Rangers. It was a matter of common knowledge that the head of artillery for the rebels was an American, a fellow who went by the name of Frederick Funston.

Under the leadership of President Cleveland, the United States remained officialy neutral and resisted the public's loud clamoring for war, much to the relief of President Oates. The advent of the McKinley administration in the United States saw no change in this policy. President McKinley was a Union veteran who hated war. He declared that he had seen the dead piled up, particularly at Sharpsburg, and that he had no desire to ever see another war. However, even he could not remain silent in the face of the daily news barrage coming from Cuba. September of 1897 saw him giving a stern warning to Spain, telling them of drastic action in the future if the war and atrocities in Cuba continued. This move on McKinley's part immediately drew the attention of the Confederate government, leading ultimately to the report now in the hands of William Oates.

As for Spain, the information contained in that report described a virtual basket case. The Spanish once boasted of the largest empire in the history of the world, but precious little remained of it. They now controlled only Cuba, Puerto Rico, and the Philippines. The last thing they wanted was a war with either the United States or the Confederacy. Accordingly, the Spanish government instituted a number of concessions designed to mollify the Cubans and to stem the tide of public opinion which had risen against them in North America. For starters, the odious General Weyler was removed from office. The reconcentration policy which had been Weyler's brainchild was terminated. For the first time Cubans were brought into the government and allowed to have a share in how their island was ruled.

If Spain thought these measures might actually resolve the situation, she was quickly disappointed. To Gomez, the rebel commander, the concessions didn't go far enough. Nothing shy of full independence would suffice, and he urged his people to continue the struggle. The decisions by the Spanish government were not greeted with any enthusiasm on the part of its loyalists on the island of Cuba. If anything, the opposite was true. Believing that Madrid had given up too much, Spaniards took to the streets in protest. With the dawn of 1898, these demonstrations quickly degenerated into full-scale riots. Foreign owned shops in Havanna were looted. Rumors of all sorts began to circulate, and in some of these scenarios the prospect of Americans being murdered was soon raised.

Given this possibility, President McKinley of the United States could hardly afford to sit on his hands despite his personal feelings about war. Therefore he dispatched the battleship, *Maine*, to Havana harbor, hoping this act would send a clear message to the Spanish. American people and property in Cuba had to be protected. If the Spanish would not do this, the United States was prepared to take on that responsibility.

The report in the hands of President Oates followed the dispatch of the *Maine* by no more than ten days, and it contained nothing regarding the ship that the chief executive of the confederacy didn't already know about. Knowledge of the ship's mission, however, did little to dispel the uneasy feeling growing within his gut. He recalled the comment made by one of Ohio's senators following the departure of the *Maine*. He compared McKinley's choice to waving a match in an oil well just for fun. In some ways Oates had to agree with the man. McKinley's

decision was fraught with danger. The prospect of war in the
backyard of the Confederacy loomed as it never had before, and
Oates saw little about this possibility which could be described as
fun. Without thinking he reached with his remaining arm to
grasp the empty sleeve which once would have housed his right
arm. "War," he muttered, "Hearst and Pulitzer treat it like some
sort of game. McKinley speaks of the dead he's seen piled up at
Sharpsburg. I've seen them too, and I've seen the piles of arms
and legs outside the surgeons' tents. One of those limbs was
mine!" Then realizing he was talking aloud to no one but himself, he blushed slightly, wondering what the servants on the
other side of the doors must be thinking. "They'll think I've
taken leave of my senses," he whispered.

Having finished the report, President Oates began pacing
back and forth across his office, pausing once at a window to see
if the weather had changed. It was snowing again, but it didn't
seem to be anything more serious than flurries. He doubted if it
would add much to the stuff already on the ground, and after a
moment or two he turned away, his mind drawn once more to this
affair in Cuba.

William Oates could scarcely be described as a pacifist.
He had fought long and hard during the War for Independence
and had seen more than his share of carnage. Regarding Cuba his
feelings were ambivalent. He shared the loathing most Americans felt toward the Spanish government and its odious policies
toward Cuba, and he wanted to see a change. Was war inevitable?
To this question he had no answer. Only time would tell. Should
war come he knew he'd have the enthusiastic backing of the
Southern people. About this he was not troubled, nor did he feel
any particular concerns about fighting with Spain. He knew that
Spain was long since finished as a world power and would
probably capitulate quickly if hostilities were to commence. It
wasn't neceearily the prospect of fighting which was causing him
so many sleepless nights, although no chief executive could take
such a decision lightly. It was his concerns over the motives of
the United States which kept him awake night after night. What
were they up to ? Having fought the United States government

for all those years he knew better than to believe this whole thing was about freedom for Cubans, nor could it simply be described as a convenient means by which William Randolph Hearst and company could sell newspapers. Something else was afoot, something which in all likelihood could never be found in any position paper from the department of state. Oates pulled his watch from his vest pocket, opened it, and glanced quickly at the time before snapping it shut and dropping it back into the pocket. "If she's punctual she should be here any minute," he thought.

Another ten minutes passed however before he heard the anticipated knock upon the door. "Come in!" he called. The door opened and in stepped one of the servants.

"Good afternoon, Mr. President," he said.

"And a good day to you, James," returned Oates, "What can I do for you?"

"You have a visitor, Mr. President ... a young woman. She came through the servants' entrance and insists she's here to see you."

"Ah, yes, I've been waiting for her arrival. Please show her in. Oh, and James ... I'll want no other interruptions while we're talking."

"I understand, sir," nodded James, who turned stiffly and left the room. Moments later the door opened again, and Sarah Ann Covington stepped into the president's office. She wore a dark green hooded cloak which clasped at her neck. Rapidly melting snowflakes were readily visible where the cloak wrapped around her shoulders as well as on the hood. Once inside she closed the door behind her and reached up to push the hood back from her head, revealing her lovely chestnut hair enveloped within a simple snood which rested along the back of her neck.

"Good afternoon, Mr. President," she bowed her head slightly in greeting.

"Hello, Sarah," replied Oates, "This is obviously not a healthy day to be out and about. I do appreciate you're making the effort to keep this appointment. Have you had an opportunity to go home yet?"

"Yes, sir. I visited with my family for two days and rode

the train into Richmond yesterday."

"How is your father?"

"Not well, Mr. President. It's the old hip-wound he received during the war. The bone seems to be degenerating. He's in pain much of the time and the doctors say he may soon have to be in a wheelchair."

"I'm sorry to hear that," Oates looked away from her, making a conscious effort to resist reaching for the empty sleeve on his right side. "There are still quite a lot of us who find it difficult to forget the old wounds," he sighed.

"It's not so much the pain which troubles him," she said," he's been used to that for years. It's the prospect of not being able to work the farm which gnaws at his spirit. In truth, sir, I'm afraid he may die if he has to live in one of those chairs."

To this Oates could find no reply. He shifted his eyes again to study the woman who stood before him. She was in her early thirties and arguably in the prime of her life. Standing several inches taller than five feet, she could best be described as a lovely full-figured woman. Her skin was virtually flawless, though her cheeks were a bit red due to the frigid conditions outdoors. Her eyes seemed a mixture of green and blue, sometimes one more than the other depending on the quantity and angle of the light. Most often they were serious eyes, but now and then the light-hearted merriment of a child could be detected dancing in her pupils. She hadn't forgotten how to take joy in life.

"May I take your cloak, Madam?" James had followed her into the office.

"Yes, please," she nodded and smiled at the president's butler as she reached up with both hands to release the clasp at her throat. Slipping the cloak from her supple round shoulders she handed it to him. "Thank you," she said softly.

"You're welcome, Miss," James bowed stiffly at the waist. "May I offer you coffee or tea and some cakes?"

"I would love a cup of hot tea," she replied.

"I'll return shortly," he nodded and left the room, cloak in hand.

GRAY VISIONS

President Oates waited until he had gone and the door closed firmly behind him before posing the next question. "Were you able to come here without being followed?"

"Yes, sir," she affirmed, "I walked an irregular route and checked frequently. No one was watching."

"Good," he sighed, "Having you come here on such short notice entails a risk, I know that. Believe me, I would never willingly compromise your safety, but the situation in Cuba seems to be coming to a head. I must know what you've learned."

"You needn't fret so much, Mr. President. My position in New York is quite secure."

"It's been ten months since I asked you to undertake this mission."

"Time enough to learn a great deal," she said.

"You say your position is secure, what position are we talking about?"

"You mean what identity am I living under?"

"That and the circumstances of your new life."

"Very well," she smiled. "I've kept my own identity. It suits my story better than an alias would."

"Exactly what story is that?"

"Why, Mr. President," she teased, "I'm just a simple girl from Virginia yearning for the faster pace and excitement of a big northern city!"

Oates couldn't help but smile at the impish simple-minded facial expression with which she emphasized her point.

Just as quickly she became serious again. "I've had no problems being accepted, Mr. President. I've managed to fit right in."

"Good," he nodded, "What about this trip? Did it require much explanation on your part?"

"Just a brief visit home to see my ailing father and touch base with old friends. I don't believe my leaving aroused any suspicion."

"Splendid," Oates seemed pleased with what he'd heard thus far. "After James brings your tea you can tell me what you've learned."

"As you wish," she agreed.

Moments later James did return bearing a handsome silver tray with a kettle of tea, the appropriate condiments and a tray of cakes. With efficiency born of experience he set up a small table near the woodstove and poured two cups. The president's cup he fixed first then he turned to Sarah Covington. "Would you like sugar, M'am?"

"Please," she smiled, "Two spoons."

"Cream?"

"A dash or two."

James quickly finished and turned to the President. "Will there be anything else, sir?"

"No thank you, James," said Oates, who understood that his previously expressed wishes would be followed, and that they would not be disturbed for the duration of the meeting.

"Very well, Mr. President." The butler made his exit from the room securing the door behind him.

"You've been gone for some time," said the President once they were alone. I've had no word from you."

"I didn't think it wise to attempt any communication," she replied, "To do so would have risked compromising my..." she paused a moment, "My situation."

"I understand," he returned, "Yet I find myself consumed by curiosity. I must know what you have learned and on top of that I would like to know how you came about your information."

"Is it that important? Your second question, I mean. Must you know how I'm doing my job?"

"Yes," he replied a bit emphatically, "How else can I be assured that what I'm hearing is accurate?"

She said nothing to this at first. Taking a seat close to the woodstove she held her hands over it to warm them before turning her attention to the tea and cakes. "This is very good," she said after taking two brief sips.

"It's a special blend we've started importing from India," said he, "I've become rather fond of it. And you, young lady, are avoiding my question."

"I'm not so young anymore."

"To someone as old as I, you are a young woman, and a lovely woman at that. Still the same, my question stands. How have you learned the things you're going to tell me?"

She hesitated several moments more as she sipped her tea and stared at the stove. "This must be held in the strictest confidence," she said in a voice so soft it sounded much like a whisper, "My father must never know. I think it would kill him to know."

"My dear Sarah," there was understanding in the President's smile, "how many spies would I have left if I were to go blabbering their secrets to any who would listen? I would never dream of betraying your confidence, but can you appreciate my need to be absolutely sure of the information I receive? I cannot base decisions which will impact the entire country on intelligence which cannot be verified."

"I understand your position," she nodded and took a deep breath, but chose not to look him in the eye as she said, "I have become a..." she paused a moment, searching for the least offensive word, "companion," she breathed, "a companion to a man of substantial means... a wealthy gentlemen who holds a rather lofty position in New York society."

"May I inquire as to his name?"

"I would prefer you didn't. On this matter I must ask you to trust me. He is not a politician, but he is a man of no little importance in the affairs of the United States. The people with whom he associates... they are the ones making the decisions."

"The power behind the power."

"You could describe them as such."

"If you cannot tell me the name of this gentleman, could you at least tell me the names of some of his associates?"

"Are you familiar with the name John D. Rockefeller?"

"Who isn't?" He answered her question with a rhetorical one of his own.

"J.P. Morgan?"

"A rather powerful man, that one."

"I've been present at very private social gatherings with

these men along with some of their proteges... politicians like Theodore Roosevelt and military men as well."

"What are they planning?"

"There will be war."

"With Spain?'

"Yes... as soon as they can establish a pretext."

"Hearst and Pulitzer have been working on that for some time."

"I've met both of them."

"The fact that war is on the horizon is fairly easy to deduce. The services of a spy with your abilities are hardly necessary to ascertain that much. I'm interested in knowing the reasons for it, because it's within those reasons that I'll be able to determine any threat to our own security."

"I understand that, Mr. President. If memory serves me I recall hearing those same words when you explained this mission to me."

"So I did," smiled Oates. "And to that end, what have you learned?"

"A great deal, I think."

"Then talk to me, young lady. I'm of a mind to hear it."

"It's not about freedom for Cubans, Mr. President, it's about empire. The United States is about to launch itself on a quest for empire."

"Not surprising," he nodded, "I had a feeling that business with the Hawaiian Islands was a prelude to such a quest."

"You were right. With the frontier disappearing, the United States will simply continue with its manifest destiny across the Pacific. Are you familiar with a United States naval officer by the name of Mahan? Alfred T. Mahan?"

"I've heard the name."

"I've had some interesting conversations with him over the last several months. He's been quite active in his efforts to have the United States build a substantial navy, one capable of extending the power of the United States to every corner of the globe. His arguments are often quite persuasive. He says the need for such a navy justifies the taking of an empire, and that having such an empire will in turn justify the need for an even bigger navy."

"One feeds the other."

"More or less," she nodded, "What do you know of Josiah Strong?"

"Not much. Isn't he some sort of missionary or something?"

"Exactly," she replied, "I found him to be rather dedicated to a single idea."

"That being?"

"The supremacy of the Anglo-Saxon race."

"There are no few adherents of such a notion these days."

"I know this, but his version comes with his own peculiar twist. He envisions Anglo-Saxons spreading out over the world to conquer all. When I met him we discussed the future of the world while sipping french wine. His vision of the future is interesting to say the least."

"Please enlighten me," said Oates.

"Of course, Mr. President," she nodded. "He speaks much of the closing of the frontier, of the fact that there are no more new worlds. He refers to the rapid conquest of the unoccupied arable lands on the planet. Once these have been taken he says the world will enter upon a new stage of history. He calls it the final competition of the races, and it's for this, he says, that the Anglo-Saxon race is being schooled. He particularly sees North Americans, more so those of the United States rather than we Southerners, moving down through Mexico, Central America, and South America... also Africa and all the important islands of the Pacific. He sees the immediate future as a competition of the races in which only the fittest will survive."

"An interesting concept," mused Oates, "But not exactly novel. I've read a number of Henry Cabot Lodge's public statements concerning the foreign policy of the United States. The sentiment you've just outlined is heavily represented in his words as well. In any event, it's hard to look around the world and not see those ideas at work first hand. Have not the Europeans done a thorough job of dividing Africa among themselves? Do you know of an Asian people not under the domination of the Europeans?"

"I'm sure there must be some."

"If so they hide themselves well. Tell me, in this war they're planning with Spain, what is it they want? You've already explained the purpose is to acquire empire, but what places do they covet? Cuba? Puerto Rico?"

"Actually neither," she lifted her cup and sipped the tea.

"Neither? Every newspaper in both of our countries has been howling about the atrocities in Cuba for the last couple of years! How can Cuba not be in their plans?"

"Oh, it's in their plans," she placed the cup and saucer back on the table, "But possessing Cuba is viewed more or less as a bonus when compared to their true goals."

"Explain," he said calmly.

"It is the Philippines they desire."

"Philippines?" The expression on the president's face registered his surprise. "The Philippines?" he repeated himself. "My dear lady, I consider myself to be a learned man, but I must confess ignorance as to the Philippines. If you asked me to pinpoint their location on a map I'm afraid I'd end up quite embarrassed."

"Have you a map of the world?"

"Are you trying to embarrass me?"

"No, Mr. President. I'll point them out for you and let me note the only reason I am able to do so is that they were pointed out to me at a social engagement several weeks ago. I believe it was Senator Lodge who enhanced my education in this regard."

"Lodge, eh?" Oates cupped his chin for a moment to reflect on this. "Would you step over here, please?" He moved to his desk, opened a side-drawer and withdrew a world map which he unfolded across the top of the desk. "It's old," he explained, "But I believe it's fairly accurate."

She stood beside him, studied the map for a moment or two and then pointed out the location of the Philippine Islands.

"That's a long way off," mused the president.

GRAY VISIONS

"I know."

"I'm not sure I understand their value. What resources do they have?"

"They are not coveted for their resources, Mr. President. The ruling clique of the United States desires them for their strategic value."

"Which is?"

"Their location. I believe I've already mentioned Captain Mahan to you. He and Theodore Roosevelt offered me a simple formula to explain all of this. They say he who controls the Philippines controls the Pacific Ocean, and he who controls the Pacific will rule the world."

To this Oates had no reply. As he absorbed her words, he continued to stare at the archipelego known as the Philippines. The more he studied the more he concurred with the explanation he'd just heard, but he found little comfort in this knowledge. Instead, an ominous feeling began creeping through his gut.

"This war that's coming," he spoke softly, "It will only set the stage for another. As I study this map I see a number of ominous possibilities in the future. Japan is a rapidly industrial-izing nation. Everything I've read about them suggests they envision themselves as a world power in the not-so-distant future. Do you think they will quietly acquiece while the United States dominates the Pacific?"

"Mr. President," she smiled, "You asked me to gather information. This I have done. Now you're asking me to predict the future. I don't think it would be wise for me to venture predictions."

"I'm sorry." The president shook his head with a chuckle. "I didn't mean to pose the question to you. It was meant for that oligarchy up in New York."

"I understand." The smile did not leave her face.

Oates continued studying the map for several minutes obviously lost in his thoughts.

"Mr. President?"

"Hmm? Yes?" He glanced up.

"I've delivered my report, sir, and I really must be going."

"Yes... Yes, of course... back to New York, I assume, to resume your mission?"

"Yes, sir, I'm to catch a train this evening for Arlington. I'll take a carriage across the river into Washington and from there I'll travel by train to New York City."

"Can you find a way to get word to me if anything major develops?"

"I'll try, Mr. President. Before I leave, however, may I ask a question?"

"Certainly, assuming it's within my power to answer it."

"When war comes what will we do? The Confederacy I mean. Will we take part?"

"I don't honestly know to be honest with you. Speaking as a soldier I'd say yes, and the sooner the better. Personally, I'd like to lead a brigade or two myself and have a go at those Spaniards. 'Course I'm an old man... don't know how much good I could do. However I can't make these types of decisions based on my personal feelings. Ultimately Congress will make that decision. We'll have to figure out how this whole scenario will impact the Confederacy. That will be the basis for our decision. I can tell you one thing, however, if we choose war the people of the South will back us all the way. The prevalent mood in the country right now is vehemently anti-Spanish. I don't see how we can just stand to the side and watch if the United States goes to war in Cuba. We can't ignore what happens in Cuba. It's simply too close to our own shores."

"Then you'd better start your preparations, Mr. President. There will be war."

* * * * * * * * * * * * * * * * * * * *

January gave way to February, and many was the night the midnight oil burned in the government offices in Richmond. President Oates met regularly with his cabinet, his closest advisors, and the leaders of the Confederate Congress. Each new day seemed to bring a new development in Cuba, and the government of the Confederacy was doing its level best to stay on top of the situation as it unfolded. Using the information relayed by Sarah Covington, President Oates was able to acquaint his government with the true motives of the United States regarding Spain. Everyone knew a time was coming when a decision would have to be made. The consensus which emerged from these late night meetings was essentially this: if and when war came, the Confederate states must follow a course with their own best interests in mind. The idea of Cuba becoming a territory of the United States, or even a base for that country, was anathema to a healthy future for the South. This would have to be prevented, even if it meant going to war alongside the United States against Spain.

In early February the Spanish ambassador to the United States, Dupuy de Lome, wrote a letter to a friend in which he described William McKinley as a "hack politician" and a weak, foolish man who only wanted people to like him. A Spy for the Cuban rebels was able to get his hands on this letter, photograph it and send a copy to Randolph Hearst. The headline in the next day's paper read, "Worst Insult to the United States in History!" This revelation led to de Lome's subsequent resignation and departure. As the middle of February approached, tension between the United States and Spain soared to frightening levels.

On the night of February 15, 1898, President Oates, exhausted by the endless schedule of meetings within this atmosphere of crisis, retired to bed early and was sound asleep by 10:00 p.m. Had his dreams been of a peaceful nature perhaps he would have been blessed with a sound sleep, but this was not the case. Instead, he tossed and turned through a fitful reliving of the fighting at Little Roundtop during the Battle of Gettysburg. So it is not surprising that he came awake so quickly when an aid knocked urgently on his door well before dawn.

"Mr. President!" The strain in the young man's voice was readily discernable. "Mr. President!"

"All right! All right! I hear you!" Oates sat up in his bed not feeling the least bit rested, his mind drumming up the old negative feelings he had held for General Peter Longstreet because of Gettysburg.

"Mr. President!" the voice on the other side of that door seemed most persistent.

"I'm coming, damnit!" growled Oates as he swung his feet over the side of the bed and put on his slippers. Rising to his feet he grabbed a robe and put it on over his bedclothes. Stepping quickly to his door he pulled it open and with an angry expression on his face he confronted the source of the voice which brought him to his feet. The only light in the hall came from a small oil lamp on a table several feet away. Lacking his eyeglasses, Oates could barely recognize his own aid in the dim light. "What time is it?" he demanded.

"About half-past four," came the reply.

"I hope you have a good reason to wake me at this hour."

"We've just received a wire from Havanna, sir. It's marked extremely urgent. I thought it best not to wait till morning."

"A wire? Let's have it." He took the telegram and turned back into his room. "Confounded glasses," he grumbled, "Can't remember where I put them! Will you light a lamp for me? Lord only knows why Congress hasn't seen fit to install those new electric lights in this blasted house! We'll soon be in the twentieth century, and the President of these Confederate States has to find matches to light a lousy, little lamp before he can read a message of utmost importance! Can you explain that to me?"

"I'll see to the lamp, Mr. President," the aid moved quickly passed Oates and within moments there were two lamps burning brightly. "Your glasses, Mr. President." He handed Oates his missing spectacles.

"Thank you," sighed Oates. He stuffed the telegram into a pocket of the robe, took hold of his spectacles, put them on and retrieved the message from Havanna. With his one hand he opened the telegram and quietly read its contents. At once the color drained from his face and he reread the message a second and a third time to be sure his aged eyes were not playing tricks on him.

Alarmed by the sudden change in his president's composure, the young assistant moved quickly to his side. "Are you all right?"

"Dear God," murmered Oates.

"Sir? Should I send for your physician?"

"No... no, that won't be necessary." Oates stepped gingerly to the plush leather chair next to his reading table and sat down.

"Mr. President?"

"Hmm?"

"The wire, sir, what word does it bring?"

"Perhaps the outbreak of war, I'm afraid."

"Sir?"

"Do you recall the federal battleship sent by McKinley to Havanna for the purpose of showing their flag?"

"Yes, sir... that would be the _Maine_."

"She's been blown up. She lies now at the bottom of the harbor. Loss of life is said to be heavy."

"I see." The young assistant's stomach did little flips as contrary emotions swept over him. He felt queasy about the prospect of war, but at the same time a strange kind of excitement coursed through his veins.

That very morning the headline in the _New York Journal_ read, "Remember the _Maine_! To Hell with Spain!" War fever raged across the United States and could readily be detected in the Confederate States as well. Yet this long anticipated conflict did not get started right away. The mysterious circumstances of the explosion on the _Maine_ demanded investigation before blame could be properly assigned. Rear Admiral Sampson of the United States conducted an inquiry in which he found that the Captain of the _Maine_, Sigsbee by name, while attending a bull fight in Havanna received a warning which simply said "Look out for your ship". Sampson sent divers down to the sunken ship to take photographs. Hundreds of pictures were taken, some of which revealed that the ship's armor plates were bent inward, an indication that a mine of some sort had exploded just outside the ship's forward powder magazine. Sampson's report contained no evidence as to who may have been responsible for sabotage.

The Spanish conducted an inquiry of their own. Not

surprisingly they came to decidedly different conclusions. They argued that the explosion was internal, though they could not pinpoint the cause. Part of their conclusion was based on what the eyewitnesses did not see. There was no geyser of water, which would have been the case had a mine been the source of the explosion. Nor was there any sort of shock wave or hordes of dead fish floating to the surface, all of which would have been present in the case of an external explosion. The Spanish also pointed to their efforts in rescuing survivors from the _Maine_, and they noted that they had nothing to gain and everything to lose by sinking the battleship.

The Cuban rebels had much to gain in this situation especially if blame for the incident could be laid at the feet of the Spanish. However, no one seriously believed that the rebels had either the skill or the resources to do this kind of thing.

These were among the issues hotly debated during an emergency cabinet meeting held in Richmond nearly three weeks after the _Maine_ settled on the bottom of Havanna Harbor. Who was responsible for the sinking of that federal battleship? Was it the Spanish? The Rebels? Or were there other possibilities? Thomas Clayton, Secretary of the Confederate Navy offered a third explanation to his president and fellow cabinet members. It seems the design of the ship itself may have contributed to the demise of the _Maine_. The ship's coal bunkers were built around the powder magazine. Smoldering coal could well have heated the wall which separated fuel from gunpowder, causing a huge spontaneous combustion which destroyed the ship.

"You mean it may have simply been an accident?" demanded Oates as he leaned over the table and glared at his naval secretary.

"I'm afraid so, Mr. President."

"Great!" groaned Oates as he sat back in his chair, "We may soon be at war, and the immediate cause could turn out to be something very different than any of us imagined. How do we explain that to the people?"

"I don't think we'll have to," noted Jeremy Higgins, the Confederate Secretary of War. "Right now public opinion in both the North and the South fairly screams for war. People up in Washington are wrapping themselves with the stars an stripes, standing on the floors of the federal congress demanding war. I find it interesting that the members of that congress are responding by singing not only the Battle Hymn of the Republic but Dixie as well."

"It's their way of inviting us to join them in their war," noted Oates.

"If so the message is not falling on deaf ears, Mr. President. Our own people are chomping at the bit for a go at the Spaniards."

"I know. Truth be told I wouldn't mind a swing at 'em myself, but for now I think we should wait and see what the United States is going to do."

This wait did not turn out to be interminable. The Yellow Press in the North and the South worked tirelessly to keep the war atmosphere at a fever pitch. President McKinley of the United States was openly branded a coward, sarcastically referred to as "Wobbly Willie." Teddy Roosevelt called his president "a white-livered cur" and said that he "has no more backbone than a chocolate eclair."

McKinley himself agonized over his decision, and it is said he eventually broke down and cried like a child. On the eleventh of April, his indecicion gave way, and he asked the congress of the United States to give him the authority to end the troubles in Cuba. On the nineteenth of April, Congress responded by unilaterally declaring Cuba to be independent, much to the chagrin of Spain and to the delight of the Cuban Rebels. This resolution included a demand that Spain vacate Cuba at once, a demand which the Spanish felt they had no choice but to ignore. On the 25th of April, the Congress of the United States issued a formal declaration of war. To the delight of the empire builders in New York, the conflict was underway.

On the 26th of April, the Confederate Congress met in special session to determine the course of action the South would follow. A formal declaration of war was debated but put aside.

The government of the Confederate States conscious of its responsibility to safeguard the best interests of the nation, made a slightly different decision. Wary of any situation which might entangle the Confederacy too closely with the Union, yet conscious of the public's obvious desire to fight Spain, the Congress passed a resolution authorizing President Oates to use Confederate forces, both on land and sea to assist the United States in the liberation of Cuba. Beyond Cuba, the Confederacy had no intention of becoming further involved. Inherent in the resolution was a message directed toward the government of the United States: Southern cooperation in this endeavor would come with a price, though the nature of that price was left deliberately vague.

Wild outbursts of patriotism exploded across the North American continent as news of the declaration of war spread far and wide. The Spaniards were contemptuously referred to as "Garlics" and hundreds of thousands of men, North and South, flocked to recruiting offices so that they might have an opportunity to show this new enemy a thing or two. President McKinley had called for 125,000 volunteers, perhaps never dreaming that his recruiters would have over a million from which to choose. President Oates of the Confederacy asked for a mere 50,000 volunteers, a request which was met with over 400,000 applications. The impact of Joseph Pulitzer and Randolph Hearst could easily be seen in the long lines at every recruiting station. The unit which received the most attention, however, was called the first volunteer cavalry, a Federal unit made up of a strange mixture of elites from the Northeast and cowboy types from out west. Their Lieutenant Colonel was none otheer than Teddy Roosevelt, and in time they would be known as the "Rough Riders".

Roosevelt's true contribution to the war actually had nothing to do with Cuba. On the 25th of February, well before war was declared, Roosevelt acting in his capacity as Naval Secretary, dispatched Commodore George Dewey to the South Pacific with orders to attack the Spanish in the Philippines as soon as war was declared. Dewey himself was a veteran of the

GRAY VISIONS

War for Southern Independence and was eager to make a name for himself. His brilliant victory at Cavita in Manila Harbor was the best indication of how slim were Spain's chances against the United States. The entire Spanish fleet was destroyed. Dewey lost but one man, and this death was attributed to a heart attack. Dewey became an overnight hero in the United States and was the object of much adoration among the people of the Confederacy as well. The United States had launched its quest for empire as the Confederacy watched with wary eyes.

* * * * * * * * * * * * * * * * * * *

The bullet from a mauser richocheted loudly off a rock sending the men of the First Virginia Cavalry scurrying for cover. Jefferson Henry and David Covington found safety behind a fallen log well to the side of the narrow hilly trail they had been following toward Las Guasimas. The Virginians, along with Roosevelt's Rough Riders, had just taken the left fork of a trail while two other Federal regiments had gone to the right. They had known the Spanish lay ahead of them someplace. They just didn't know where... that is until the ambush was sprung. Even as the fighting started they still couldn't pinpoint the exact location of their antagonists. The Spaniards were using a new German rifle, the mauser, which employed smokeless powder. Lying prone behind the log the two boys hugged the ground and prayed fervently as bullets slammed into wood and flesh all around them. Thus was the introduction of these young Virginians to the world of war.

Two months had passed since the declaration of war, and a tumultuous time it was. Both the United States and the Confederacy were finding out how ill-prepared they were to fight a ground war overseas. Hundreds of thousands of volunteers in both countries had been rejected for military service, and those who were mustered in were hastily assembled into units and launched into primitive training facilities. Both countries fielded all-black regiments, but the Confederacy also raised a number of integrated regiments such as the First Virginia Cavalry. General William R. Shafler, a rather large man at 300 pounds, commanded the force from the United States, while an aging veteran from the War for Southern Independence, Joseph Wheeler, formerly of the Army of Tennessee, led the Confederated forces. As June neared, the men of both armies were chomping at the bit, eager to come to grips with the much-despised Spaniards.

At this point some serious logistical difficulties were encountered. How were all these men, their equipment and their animals going to be transported to Cuba? In terms of warships the federal navy was impressive. Moreover it was designed to project the newfound power of the United States to every corner of the globe. The Confederate Navy, by contrast was pitifully small, its size coinciding with its limited mission, the protection of Southern coasts. However, warships were not particularly suitable for moving large numbers of men and material, and transports were in short supply.

After much haggling between Richmond and Washington, it was agreed to use Tampa, Florida as the jump-off point for the invasion. This was not an easy decision for the Confederate government to make for it meant allowing large numbers of Federal soldiers to traverse the Confederacy by rail enroute to Tampa. The decision also entailed allowing warships of the United States into Southern coastal waters for the first time in more than thirty years.

Tampa itself was normally a quiet peaceful town situated on a magnigicent bay. Overnight it was transformed into a veritable boom-town as civilian merchants rushed to take advantage of the circumstances. A vast array of goods appeared in abundance including everything from bibles and other religious materials to the services offered by those in the world's oldest profession, such services to be found frequently in the bars and restaurants of Tampa. By mid-June when the troops were ordered to their transports handsome profits were being recorded by almost anyone with something to sell.

Putting all these men to sea turned out to be something of a nightmare. A motley collection of ships had been assembled in

GRAY VISIONS

Tampa Bay but their numbers were insufficient for the task at hand. Moreover, there seemed to be no rhyme or reason regarding which units were to be assigned to which ships. Frustrated by this chaos and blatantly eager to fight Spaniards, Teddy Roosevelt simply commandeered a ship which had been assigned to another unit. Quickly hustling his Rough Riders aboard he was soon steaming toward Cuba.

On its sixth day at sea the invasion fleet dropped anchor off the southern coast of Cuba not far from Santiago. A meeting was arranged on shore between the American commanders and a Cuban rebel commander by the name of Garcia. The Cuban suggested a tiny village called Daiquiri as a possible landing spot. There were certain advantages to this spot in that it was only sixteen miles east of Santiago, thus allowing the Americans to come quickly to grips with the main Spanish force on the island. There were disadvantages as well, centering primarily on the lack of facilities with which to make a smooth landing. Aside from one old beat-up pier there was nothing.

The news of the impending landing was greeted with joy by thousands of soldiers who had been crammed like sardines into the holds of the transport ships for six days. They had endured conditions which were dismal at best. Their drinking water smelled like a stagnant frog pond and tasted worse. Beneath the decks the air they breathed was damp and reeked of human sweat and urine. Knowing they were about to land was cause for celebration, and no one celebrated more than Teddy Roosevelt. He was seen by many of the troops as he waved his hat in the air, grinning like a madman, stomping his feet... basically doing his own version of an Indian war dance.

The landing itself was virtually unopposed, but high seas and the lack of facilities combined to make it an adventurous affair. Timing was a crucial element for each soldier as he climbed down ropes along the side of his ship and then had to make a leap into one of the waiting longboats bucking in the waves. The arrival of all these men at the lone pier presented yet another challenge as the structure was built some fifteen feet above the water. Again timing was crucial. Soldiers had to wait until waves raised their boats close to the level of the pier then make the jump. Mistiming one's jump could be fatal as these men were heavily weighted with their own equipment. Two black cavalrymen of the United States army missed their jumps and drowned.

As for the animals they at least did not have to worry about timing their jumps, nor of becoming seasick and vomiting all over their comrades. The horses and mules were simply pushed overboard in the hope they'd find their way to shore. Unfortunately, many of these animals panicked over the sudden change of circumstances and swam out to sea until they were overcome by exhaustion and drowned. Others could not withstand the swift current and were subsequently crushed against the rocks. Despite these setbacks, however, the vast majority of the men and the animals reached shore safely and began to turn their attention toward the heavily wooded hills and the Spaniards concealed therein.

The city of Santiago was the ultimate goal of the Americans, and the road to Santiago led through a gap in the hills which was called Las Guasimas, a narrow defile held by the Spanish. Thus, on the 24th of June, 1898, the men of the United States along with those of the Confederacy began their march inland.

Another bullet shaved bark from the top of the log showering Covington and Henry with splinters. "Ow!" cried David as he slapped his hand against his neck just behind his right ear.

"You hit?" Jefferson cast him a worried glance.

"Nah, it's these damn red ants! Another one bit me! It stings somethin' awful!" Lying there in the dirt with mauser bullets whistling overhead, with the smell of dried vomit emanating from his trousers -- courtesy of a comrade in the longboat -- and with his neck smarting from a series of insect bites, David suddenly found himself questioning his decision to join the army. "Jeff?" he turned his head to face his black companion.

"Uh-huh?'"

"I reckon I'm 'bout as scared as a man can be."

"Me, too."

GRAY VISIONS

"I miss Molly and the kids," he added in a reference to the family he left behind.

"Been thinkin' 'bout my folks a lot too."

"You think it was like this for our fathers when they went to war?"

"Most likely, 'cept neither one of them was married. They was a lot younger than us when they went to fight the Yankees."

Just then they heard Teddy Roosevelt's voice booming out over all the noise, directing his sharpshooters to take aim at the Spanish position which had finally been spotted some hundred yards to the front. At last the Americans could return fire with the hope of maybe hitting something. At once the Rough Riders and their Southern compatriots opened up on the Spaniards with devastating effect. For Jefferson and David it was the first time they had fired their weapons in anger.

Before long, small squads of Americans from both armies had overlapped both Spanish flanks and made their position untenable. The soldiers of Spain were unaccustomed to foes who displayed the brash recklessness these Americans exhibited. They soon broke and fled in disorder in the direction of Santiago. Flushed with victory the two American forces followed close on their heels.

Among the high command in both the Confederate and Federal armies a sense of urgency had developed, one which had little to do wih their armed opposition. It was late in June, and the yellow fever season was merely weeks away. Everyone saw Santiago as the key to bringing the war to a swift conclusion, but the city would have to be taken quickly lest the fever become another weapon in the Spanish arsenal. Moreover, General Shafter was not holding up well in the intense tropical heat. He was spending most of his time supine on his cot and had become more of a liability than an asset, creating something of a vacuum at the top of the federal chain of command. Although the Confederate army under Joe Wheeler was independent of the federals, it had come to Cuba as an auxilliary, to augment the efforts of the United States, not to deliver the main blow. The

Southerners were expected to defer to General Shafter insofar as strategy was concerned. Wheeler spent many a moment fuming while Shafter reclined on his cot.

Having taken Las Guasimos the troops from North America quickly found themselves facing the defences of Santiago itself. At first glance the Spanish presented a formidable front. Arranged along the crest of San Juan Ridge their defences were anchored on the left by El Caney, a position dominated by an ancient Spanish fort said to date back to the days of Cortes. Kettle Hill dominated the middle of the Spanish defensive position and San Juan Hill was the extreme right of their line. It was also the last high point before the city itself.

Shafter's plan was to attack El Caney first with 5,400 men, figuring the thousand or so Spanish defenders would be overwhelmed by sheer weight of numbers. He anticipated no more than an hour to carry out this part of the plan after which ten thousand Federal and Confederate infantry would storm San Juan Hill, thus insuring the fall of Santiago.

There were several drawbacks to his ideas, however, most notably the lack of artillery. All of the heavy guns were still on board the ships. Only a handful of light artillery pieces would be available for the assault. Another factor working against the Americans was the single trail leading from the gap at Las Guasimos to the ridge of San Juan. Spanish riflemen positioned on San Juan Hill could easily keep that trail under fire at a heavy cost to the Americans. One alternative was for the troops to fan out and hack new paths through the jungle-like brush but this was every bit as dangerous. Regardless of the obstacles, the attack on El Caney would move forward as scheduled.

As they waited for the coming of dawn, the troops sweltered through another hot, steamy, Cuban night. David and Jefferson were with their regiment of Virginians on the American left. They would not be among the forces slated to be thrown against El Caney. "Ouch! Damnit!" Jefferson sat up suddenly, one hand reaching for the small land crab which had just latched on to his ear. He yanked the crab away, curshed it inside his fist and hurled it as far as he could in the direction of the enemy.

"Ants and crabs all over this place!" he complained loudly, "How do people live here?"

"Reckon they don't often sleep on the ground," replied David as his eyes swept the immediate area looking for more crabs.

"Little bastard drew blood!" snarled the black man as he ran his fingers over his ear.

"There's no way I'm gonna be able to sleep tonight," said David. "Maybe I oughta try writin' a letter home."

"Don't you be lightin' no candle or lamp," cautioned his companion. "Them Garlics got snipers out there, and they been shootin' straighter than anybody thought they would."

"I've noticed that," admitted David as he reluctantly shoved his writing materials back into a shirt pocket. "You know what I wish?"

"What's that?"

"Wish this mess was over and done with and we were headin' home."

"Me too. Maybe it'll be over after tomorrow."

"You think we're gonna live through this? We gotta charge straight up that hill out there. A lot of us ain't gona make it."

"Let's just hope we're among the lucky ones," sighed Jefferson, "Ain't much else we can do 'cept maybe pray."

"Been doin' more 'n my share of that lately," grunted Covington.

"Me too."

Tthe operation got underway on schedule. Opposite San Juan Hill, weary Americans from North and South lifted their sleepy eyes toward the ridgecrest and the waiting Spanish rifle-men. Well to their right the sounds of battle filled the air well before the arrival of the new day. Shafter's forces were moving toward El Caney. The battle there began with a barrage from four light cannons whose effect was negligible at best. Fortunately for the Americans a way was found to circumvent the face of the hill, thus shielding the attackers from the main Spanish force arrayed along the crest of San Juan Ridge. Swinging well to the right, the Americans were able to concentrate on the left flank of the enemy line. To the Spaniards inside the fort at El Caney, however, fighting from one wall was just as easy as fighting from another. El Caney would prove one hard nut to crack.

Watching these soldiers as they filed into position to storm the fort was a lone figure on horseback dressed in a black business suit. It was William Randolph Hearst come to see the war he had so proudly created with his newspaper. Men from New York who recognized him began to cry out, "Hi, there Willie!" This greeting was soon echoing through the length of the advancing column. Hearst waved to them and wished them luck, referring to them as "my boys". What were his private thoughts as he watched these young fellows marching off to be killed or maimed in "his war"? Did he have misgivings? No answer exists for these questions because Hearst held his tongue aside from greeting the men and wishing them well.

The artillery barrage, such as it was, did not last particularly long. There was a definite limit to the damage four pieces could do to the Spanish fortifications. As the echoes of the last cannon blasts faded away on the early morning breeze, the federal commanders gave the orders which launched the first charge against El Caney. Young men from North and South rose to their feet, leapt from their trenches, and began to race for El Caney's walls.

This was the moment the defenders of the fort had been waiting for. Spanish riflemen stood to their posts and delivered vicious volleys into the ranks of the charging Americans with devastating effect. The first charge was broken up with heavy losses, and those who were not hit scampered quickly back to the relative safety of their trenches. A second charge was ordered and was repulsed in similiar fashion as was a third. After an hour of hard fighting the Americans were no closer to capturing the fort than they were before the day began. Giving up, however, was not an option. The two sides began slugging it out from long range as small groups of Americans crept forward a few paces at a time, a battle which would continue until the afternoon had all but passed.

    Not long after the initial assault was launched against El Caney the men of Virginia alongside of Roosevelt's Rough Riders began moving into position to storm San Juan Hill, the extreme right of the Spanish line. The enemy riflemen took them under fire immediately. As bullets from the mauser rifles used by the Spaniards screeched past their ears, David, Jefferson and their comrades dove into the tall grass, taking advantage of the limited cover it could offer. At the same, time the handful of small caliber artillery pieces available to the Americans opened fire on the enemy, but their effect was minimal.

    "I don't understand that Yankee General Shafter," complained David.

    "What's that?" asked Jefferson as he hugged the ground with bullets flying overhead.

    "Those puny guns ain't gonna do us no good! Even if they was bigger they wouldn't help! You remember what our fathers told us 'bout Gettysburg? The artillery barrage which preceeded Pickett's charge was largely ineffective because of the elevation difference. Our side was firing from the base of Cemetery Ridge toward the crest. Most of our shells passed over the main Yankee line. Same thing's happenin' here."

    "Shafter's got no control over that."

    "Maybe so, but he's got those big ol' Yankee battleships sittin' out there in the water. Those guns could reach that ridge up there and probably drive every one of them Garlics off. We wouldn't even have to charge that hill. We could just wait down here till it was over then mosey on up and make ourselves at home."

    "Wishful thinkin', old friend." Jefferson started to laugh but a Spanish bullet whistled by uncomfortably close to his head causing him to hug the ground like an infant would nuzzle his mother's breast.

    "So how come he ain't usin' the guns on those ships?" demanded David.

    "How in the hell am I supposed to Know?" growled the son of Levi Henry.

"Whatever his reasons, I can tell you one thing," said a white man as he spit out a mouthful of grass and dirt and brushed several fire-ants from his neck, "A lot of boys are gonna die today who really shouldn't be dyin'."

"Probably, let's just hope we're not among 'em."

Orders from officers brought them all to their feet and sent them moving swiftly along side their Northern counterparts down the trail from Las Guasimos toward the Spanish held ridge. All along the way they were taking casualties from the Spanish who were dug in at the crest of the ridge. As they approached the broad meadow which sloped up toward San Juan Ridge, they left their narrow foot path and sought shelter in the waist high grass.

High above their heads a Federal signal corps balloon floated lazily in the air as it was being towed toward the enemy by two men on the ground. Unfortunately, the balloon made an excellent marker by which the Spanish artillery could focus on the men massed beneath, causing quite a number of needless casualties. Southerners and Northerners alike cursed the balloon and cheered lustily when shell fragments ripped it open and sent it crashing to earth. The two officers who had been riding in its basket survived the fall with minor injuries and were able to report that the source of the Americans' misery was located on San Juan Hill, the far right of the enemy line. From that vantage point, the Spanish sharpshooters were able to lay down a highly effective fire on the Americans. At this point, San Juan Hill became the key to whole battle.

Privates Henry and Covington lay prone in the grass having survived the deadly passage along the Las Guasimos trail. "Did you see that dead Yankee lieutenant back there on the trail?" asked Jefferson, "The ants was already eatin' off his eyeballs!"

"Yeah, I saw him. Had a hard time gettin' around that damn major standin' next to his body bawlin' like an infant. Kept hollerin' for his men to cover the body, and they kept tellin' him to do it himself. It's a wonder all them Garlics missed him standin' there like he was."

Bullets from the Spanish line continued to rain down on

the Americans, mowing the grass like a scythe, tearing through flesh and bone with no sign of a let-up.

"What do we do now?" someone cried.

In truth no one knew what to do. Companies and regiments from both American armies were pinned down in the grass at the base of San Juan Ridge. The officers were all waiting for orders to launch the grand charge, but no orders were coming. General Wheeler of the Confederate army was obligated to defer to General Shafter of the federal army. Shafter himself would not leave his cot well to the rear of the fighting, and he was largely clueless as to the progress of the battle he was supposed to be directing. Meanwhile the casualties continued to mount.

In the final analysis, it was a combination of technology and grit which carried the day for the Americans. The former made its presence felt in the form of new weapons, three of them to be exact. They were Gatling guns, nicknamed "coffee grinders" by the foot soldiers. Rather than a trigger they were operated with a hand crank and were capable of firing up to nine hundred rounds a minute. Three of them went into action, peppering the Spanish trenches with a deluge of lead, forcing the enemy to keep their heads low and their mausers quiet. The tide of the battle was clearly turning, but still no orders came.

Their patience largely exhausted, the troops themselves began taking the whole affair into their own hands. It was a Federal officer who set the example, a lieutenant by the name of Jules Ord, the son of General Ord, a Union hero during the War for Southern Independence. He rose to his feet, ripped the shirt off his back, threw it to the side and boldly cried that he was ready for anything. With a pistol in one hand and a bayonet in the other he exhorted his men to follow him up the hill. "Come on!" he cried, "Come on, you men! We can't stay here! Follow me!"

Off he ran toward San Juan Hill joined by perhaps fifty of his federal comrades. Ord reached the hill first, but the reward for his courage was a Spanish bullet which killed him instantly. Dead though he was, his courage inspired all those around him, Federal and Confederate alike. As if on cue, the ordinary foot soldiers in both American armies began rising to their feet, charging toward San Juan Hill, pausing only to fire their rifles from time to time. Bugles began to sing out as the men echoed the war cries of their sergeants. "Get the Garlics!" they shouted, "Charge!"

Up the hill surged the men in blue and those in gray. Jefferson, David and their fellow Virginians were nearing the crest when a lethal volley from the Spanish trenches cut down thirteen of them, five of them killed. A painful grimace could be seen on Jefferson's face as he grasped at the flesh wound on his right thigh.

"You okay?" demanded David after firing three quick shots at the enemy.

"I'll manage," replied the black man through tightly clenched teeth. "Bullet just tore off some meat passin' though."

"You got a hell of a way of puttin' things!" shouted David over the barking of the guns. "Can you get back on your feet?"

"Most likely, you ready?"

"Let's do it! Make for that barbed wire!"

Up to their feet they rose again, stumbling and limping through the tall grass until they reached the barbed wire fences the Spanish had put on the hill to impede their charge. Using their rifles they smashed away two of the posts on which the wire had been strung. Leaping over the flattened wire, the men in gray and those in blue continued their steady surge toward the crest of the hill and the waiting Spanish. One witness to this charge described it as a miracle of self-sacrifice and a triumph of bull-dog courage. He described himself as being breathless with wonder as he watched this drama unfold.

Just to the right of San Juan Hill, Theodore Roosevelt's Rough Riders faced the enemy at Kettle Hill. Roosevelt himself was mounted but seemed impervious to harm. Many a bullet raced by perilously close to him but never was he hit. Seeing the charge against San Juan Hill on his left, Roosevelt knew it was time to take Kettle Hill as well. The order to charge was given and off they went, the Rough Riders along with the black troopers of the ninth and tenth U.S. Cavalry. The only one on horseback,

GRAY VISIONS

Roosevelt galloped up the slope ahead of the rest. Dismounting at a barbed wire fence he encountered a Spanish officer and killed him with one shot from a pistol which had been salvaged from the wreck of the _Maine_. Behind him came his troopers who broke through the barbed wire and stormed the enemy trenches just as their compatriots were doing on San Juan Hill. There in the trenches a brief but fierce fight ensued which culminated in an overwhelming American victory. The surviving Spaniards fled and the triumphant Americans from North and South held the ridge overlooking the city of Santiago.

Jefferson sat on the floor of the Spanish trench with his back to an earthen wall while David cleaned the flesh wound on the black man's thigh and applied a bandage. Nearly thirty minutes had passed since the last shot had been fired, and the Americans were busy consolidating their newly won position and caring for the nearly 1200 wounded. Bodies of Spanish and American soldiers lay all around the two Virginians, and it was hard to move anywhere without encountering a pool of blood.

For most of those present this was their first exposure to death on so large a scale. For some the experience was a glorious thrill, but most were subdued by the bloody sights which greeted their eyes with every turn of their heads. David and Jefferson numbered among the latter and were somewhat taken aback by the appearance of Teddy Roosevelt, fresh from his victory at Kettle Hill, as he rode along the Spanish trench line. He reined his mount to a halt ten or fifteen yards from the Virginians and bent low pointing at one of the enemy bodies.

"Look at those damn Spanish dead!" he urged. "I shot one myself, by God! Look at 'em! This is what it is to be a man!"

He resumed his upright position in the saddle, let his eyes sweep once more across the dead and wounded of both sides in the trench, then raised those same eyes to gaze out toward the city of Santiago. "Our next target, gentlemen," he declared, lifting one hand to point toward the city, "and we'll take it before too much longer". With that he tapped his spurs into the flanks of his mount and continued down the trench line.

"So that's the Teddy Roosevelt we've been hearin' so much about," said David.

"Sho' seems like he's enjoyin' this," returned Private Henry.

"Does at that," sighed Covington. "I'm beginin' to feel less a man fo' not sharin' his glee. You remember the stories our fathers told us 'bout their first action?"

"Groveton," nodded Henry, "The openin' fight at Second Manassas. Your old man heaved up his guts when it was over. Mine too, if my memory serves me... least that's what he felt like doin'."

"That's 'bout how I'm feelin' right now. I wish to hell we was home, old friend. I can tell ya that for a fact."

"Me too," agreed the black man, gazing north toward Virginia, a place which seemed a world away.

There was little time for any of the American soldiers to be homesick. Too much work had to be done. The walking wounded were sent back to the primitive field hospitals which had been set up in tents well behind the line. The more seriously wounded were placed in ambulance wagons pulled by mules. For many of them the bumping, grinding trip toward the surgeon's tents proved to be a grueling form of torture. No few of them begged to be put out by the side of the road so they could at least die peacefully.

Those who had not been wounded went to work strengthening the earthworks against any Spanish counter-attack, a threat which never really materialized. The American field commanders were also unsure as to their next move. Between themselves and Santiago lay more than two miles of interlocking Spanish trenches made all the stronger by a maze of barbed wire. Taking them by storm would most likely incur substantial losses. The time had come to pause and carefully consider the next move.

Fortunately, no move on the part of American infantry would be necessary - this thanks in part to a decision made by General Ramon Blanco, the Spanish governor of Cuba. When he received word of the American victory at San Juan Hill he knew at once Santiago was doomed. He also knew that his country's fleet in the city's harbor had no chance if it remained in port and only the slightest chance if it attempted to flee. Believing a slight chance to be better than no chance he wired the fleet commander, Admiral Cervera, and instructed him to leave at once.

The morning of July third saw six Spanish ships, four of them cruisers, along with two destroyers, steaming swiftly out of Santiago's harbor in a desperate attempt to reach the open sea. Five battleships of the United States Navy awaited them. No ships of the Confederate Navy were involved, and as it turned out none were needed. The federal juggernauts made short work of the smaller enemy ships. All but one were destroyed with relative ease. The lone survivor was the *Christobal Colon* the most modern and certainly the fastest Spanish Cruiser. She broke into the clear heading west, needing only to outpace the battleship *Oregon* to gain freedom. The Spanish ship was smaller and faster than the *Oregon*, and she had a lead of several miles as an extra advantage. To overcome this advantage would require a superhuman effort on the part of the Federal crew, particularly the men who had the unenviable task of stoking the fires in the ship's boilers. It is said the *Oregon* made eighteen knots during the chase, a record for American battleships, and a speed sufficient to bring that vessel to within range of the fleeing Spaniards. She opened fire, hitting the stern of the *Christobal Colon* with a shell from one of her thirteen inch guns. Another volley proved unnecessary as the Spaniards struck their colors almost immediately after they were hit. Cuba's fate was sealed.

Santiago was now cut off from outside help and subjected to a virtual siege, facing no alternative but to eventually surrender. However the conditions under which the two American armies labored were scarcely better than those of the people trapped inside the city. Food was in short supply and clean water was almost impossible to find. Moreover, the first outbreaks of deadly yellow fever began to appear, a turn of events which struck fear into the bravest of American hearts. This development made an early resolution of the conflict more imperative than ever.

The tenth of July saw the implementation of a truce so the opposing commanders could meet and discuss surrender terms. For the Spanish commander saving honor was a prime consideration. Thus it wasn't until the fifteenth of July that he found terms to his liking. His acceptance of these terms on that day meant that the Spanish garrison in Santiago would be sent home at American expense. Officers were allowed to keep their horses and swords. The weapons of the soldiers would also be shipped back to Spain but not on the same ship as the soldiers themselves. Two days later the surrender took place.

For all practical purposes, the war in Cuba was over. Although substantial numbers of Spanish soldiers remained on the island, they did not pose a significant threat. By July's end the United States, in a unilateral move, invaded Puerto Rico and seized it from the Spanish. By this time the government of Spain had seen all the American military prowess it wanted to see and requested a formal cease-fire so peace talks could get underway.

At about the same time a threat far more lethal to the North Americans than Spanish guns arose. Yellow fever, called "Yellow Jack" by the troops, began to sweep through the ranks of Federals and Confederates alike. By July's end nearly four thousand Federals and over half that number of Southerners were stricken with the fever. Both Shafter and Wheeler sent desperate pleas to their capitals in hopes of having their armies removed quickly from Cuba. Both requests were met with deaf ears. Wheeler was informed by President Oates that the Confederate army must remain in Cuba to forestall any attempt by Washington to claim sole possession of the island, as it obviously intended to do with respect to Puerto Rico.
The men would have to tough it out a little while longer until negotiations could determine Cuba's final status.

The third of August saw a dramatic shift in the status quo. A letter written by Teddy Roosevelt and signed by most of his fellow officers emphasized the critical state of affairs and warned of the very real possibility that the entire force could perish if not swiftly removed from Cuba. The letter was forwarded by Shafter to Washington and quickly had its desired effect. On August 7, the Federal forces took ship for home, specifically Montauk Point on Long Island, New York. For them the danger was over.

The same could not be said for the Confederate troops nor for those Federals who had already contracted the fever. They remained in Cuba. President Oates, knowing the danger to his soldiers, but also aware of the strategic importance of Cuba, intensified his negotiations with President McKinley of the United States. Until the island's future was determined to the satisfaction of the Confederacy, the Southern soldiers would stay in Cuba.

The 20th of August dawned with the promise of another intensely uncomfortable day. David Covington groaned in pain as he awoke. He'd spent most of the night writhing on the cot in a pool of his own sweat. Five days had elapsed since he came down with the fever, and the doctors had done all that could be done. Like thousands of others from both American armies he would either recover on his own or he would die. Many had already died. In fact, their number far exceeded the number of deaths due to combat. "Jefferson..." he groaned, "You there? Jefferson?"

"I'm here, ol' friend," the black man said as he slid his stool close to Covington's cot. "You just rest easy."

"Water... I need water."

"I'll fetch you some."

Henry rose to his feet and stepped to the water pail, limping slightly due to the thigh wound he'd received at San Juan Hill. He dipped a ladle into the bucket and poured its contents into a small tin mug. Returning to Covington's side he resumed his seat on the stool, and with one hand he gently lifted his companion's head from the cot. He placed the mug into the white man's hands but found that he had to help steady it lest the precious liquid spill.

Covington drank greedily then collapsed back on to the cot. "Thank you," he muttered weakly. The water was all too warm and didn't taste particularly good. Still, it did momentarily quench his thirst, though it did nothing to ease the fire which consumed his skin. He tried to compensate for the poor quality of the water by dreaming of the many times he had relished the icy, cold, clean water of the many mountain streams which tumbled out of the Blue Ridge. God, how he ached to be home. "Jefferson?" His voice was barely above a whisper.

"I'm here." There was a definite sadness evident in Private Henry's voice as he studied the yellowish tint on Covington's face. The color seemed more intense than it did the day before.

"I'm not gonna make it, am I?"

"Don't you be talkin' like that!" scolded Henry. "You'll pull through, sho' nuff! Yellow Jack's got to run his course that's all."

"I don't think so."

It was said the negotiations over Cuba's future were going smoothly, but those who suffered with the fever in the tent hospitals of Siboney found scant solace in this news. Thousands languished in the fierce tropical heat wondering if each day would be their last on this earth. Most of the soldiers who had volunteered to remain in Cuba to help the sick were black men, and most of these were Southern. Before it was all over, Yellow Fever would take a considerable toll among these men as well.

Had the government of the United States not had specific designs on Spain's possessions in the Pacific, particularly the Philippines, the negotiations over Cuba would have posed a far greater challenge to the Confederate President. The United States, however, was facing the possibility of continued warfare in those islands, not with the Spanish, who knew they were beaten, but with the Filipinos themselves, who mistakenly thought the arrival of the United States would mean liberation and freedom. Accordingly, as September dawned, McKinley decided to acquiesce to the Confederate government and leave Cuba's ultimate disposition to the South. One condition did he attatch to this agreement. The United States was dreaming of a canal across the Central American isthmus. The best location had yet to be determined, but sooner or later the dream would become reality. If the United States was to forego any claims to Cuba,

GRAY VISIONS

then the Confederate States would have to agree to guarantee the
security of the eastern entrance to the canal, when and if it was
built. This was a condition Oates and the Confederate congress
readily agreed to, a step which ushered in a new era in North-
South relations, signalling the closest rapport between the countries since the War for Southern Independence. Cuba's future was
now determined. The island would be sovereign, its independence guaranteed by the Confederate States of America. In return
Cuba agreed to lease Guantanamo Bay to the Confederacy for
one-hundred years. Here, the Confederate Navy would base a
substantial portion of its Caribbean fleet, putting it in a position
to check any threat to the Central American canal, when and if it
was built. The ink had scarcely dried on this new agreement
when President Oates dispatched an order to General Wheeler:
Bring the boys home!

On the morning of the fifth of September, Private
Jefferson Henry made his morning visit to the hospital tent and
sat quietly on the stool next to Covington's cot. "Dave," he
spoke, "are you awake?"

It seemed to require a substantial effort for the stricken
white soldier just to turn his head and open his eyes; eyes which
appeared glassy and dazed. "Too hot to sleep," he whispered.

"Did you hear the news?" There was no change in
Covington's expression. "We're goin' home, Dave!" Henry's
face broke out into a wide grin. "Goin' home," he repeated with
immense satisfaction. "Oates and McKinley made some kind of
agreement. They done signed it and everything. Word is we'll be
pullin' out in two days, three at the outside."

"Don't think I'm gonna be goin' home," Covington raised
his voice a little, but the effort had a noticable effect on his
strength. "Don't think I'll make it another day."

"Come on now," Henry did his best to keep a positive
tone, "You made it this far. Don't you be givin' up now! Just a
few more days ol' friend.. just a few more, then you and me will
be back in Virginia. Fall's comin'. That means the nights'll be
cool. No more of this tropic stuff! We'll be back on our farms!"

Summoning all of his strength, Covington lifted his hand and reached out to rest it on the black man's forearm. "You got to promise me somethin', Jeff."

"You name it."

"Molly... my kids... you'll look after em'?"

Private Henry looked at his friend with eyes full of sadness and took a long deep breath to keep his emotions under control. "Well now, David," he sighed, "Seems like we Henrys and you Covingtons been lookin' out for one another for longer than anyone can remember."

"Your grandma raised my Pa."

"So she did," Jefferson nodded. "Now you stop worryin'hear? You'll be goin' home soon, and you'll be takin' care of your family your own self. Now don't say nothin'." Seeing that Covington wanted to argue he raised one hand as a signal for quiet. "I know what you're gonna say, and I'm tellin' you... ya'll got nothin' to worry 'bout. I'll always be there and I'll always watch over 'em for ya. Now you just close them eyes and rest. You got to build your strength up so you can ride that big ol' boat home."

With great effort Covington removed his hand from the black man's arm. "Thank you," he whispered.

"No thanks called for," said Henry as he reached into a bucket of warm water, pulled out a rag, squeezed it with both hands to wring out the excess, and then used it to wipe away the sweat and grime on his comrade's face.

As it turned out, Private Jeffferson Henry would make the voyage home alone. Late that night Private Covington's strength finally gave out and he succumbed to "Yellow Jack". When Henry returned for his morning visit the next day, he found the cot occupied by another patient and he was overcome by grief.

Covington, like the many who died of Yellow Fever was buried outside of Santiago, Cuba. He was one of over 1900 Condeferate soldiers claimed by the fever, an extraordinary number to be sure, but not nearly as devastating as the 5400 Federal troops who never returned home as a result of Cuba's most deadly weapon... a tropical fever. As the ship ferrying the returning Virginians entered the Chesapeake Bay and turned toward Hampton Roads, Jefferson Henry experienced a moment of joy, but it was quickly clouded by the memory of his life-long friend buried on the island of Cuba.

* * * * * * * * * * * * * * * * * ** *

It was a cold, bitter November wind which whipped across the rolling hills of the Covington farm. Dark heavy clouds rolled across the Shenandoah Valley threatening rain for the fourth day running. Though the weather wasn't particularly conducive to being outdoors, its unforgiving gloom seemed appropriate for a funeral. Arrangements for the event had been anything but easy. Wil Covington had taken the news of his son's death quite hard and sank into the pits of despair for a dangerously long period of time. Ultimately he came to accept that David was gone, but he refused to allow his boy to remain buried on a tropical island half a world away. He petitioned the war department in Richmond to have the body exhumed and shipped home to Virginia. His pleas were met with a barrage of bureaucratic obstacles. Those in the government were concerned that even the bodies of the dead were capable of spreading the fever and were loathe to even take the risk. To citizens whose loved ones lay buried in Cuba they offered much by way of sympathy, but precious little in the manner of cooperation. All of this served only to deepen the despair which gripped the elder Covington.

In the end, the situation required a little outside assistance before its resolution could be achieved. Upon hearing of her brother's death in Cuba, Sarah Ann Covington took leave of her friends and companions in New York to return home. Alarmed by the despondency in which she found her parents, she determined to see her father's wish fulfilled. Thus did she make another visit to Richmond, making it a point to call unannounced on the President of the Confederate States. This time there was no talk of espionage or of the grand global visions coming from the imperial powers. This time a simple Southern woman appeared before President Oates to present her entreaty, a request that the president intervene and allow for the return from Cuba of the remains of her fallen brother. Considering the contributions this particular woman continued to make to the security of the Confederacy, Oates was hardly in a position to deny her request, even if he had been of such a mind.

"I'll make the necessary arrangements on one condition," he had said.

"Which is?" she asked, feeling alarmed by some of the possibilities which raced quickly through her mind.

"When you have the funeral, I would like to attend. I'd like the opportunity to pay my respects, and to offer my condolences to your parents... particularly to your father."

"Mr. President, we, of course, would be honored by your presence, but I can't help but wonder if that same presence might arouse suspicions which might compromise my work in the North."

"I don't think my being there will jeopardize your position," he returned, "The press will pay scant attention to the affair, and will doubtless note this as another of the dozens of such funerals I've attended since the liberation of Cuba. Trust me, my dear lady Covington, I would never dream of risking the loss of your services, not in a thousand years."

"Then please join us, sir, and know how welcome you will be among my family."

True to his word, President Oates set the official wheels in motion so that Private David Covington would find his final resting place in the Shenendoah Valley of Virginia.

Despite the foul frigid weather, David's funeral was quite well-attended. Both the Covingons and Henrys were there of course, but in addition there were scores of people from nearby farms and villages. No few came from Staunton and Waynesboro as well. All of them shared the Covington's grief, but at the same time a fierce pride burned within their breasts... pride in the heroism of a fallen neighbor. The arrival of their president by carriage, just as the ceremony was getting underway served only to fuel that same pride.

GRAY VISIONS

Wil Covington sat in his wheelchair listening intently to the eulogy coming from Preacher Matheson. The pain in his hip challenged him to the limit of his endurance, but the casual observer would not have been able to judge this by the stoic expression on the crippled man's face. Emily stood just behind him with her gloved hands upon his shoulders, from time to time adjusting the collar of his overcoat to make sure he did not catch a chill.

Himself painfully aware of the cold, Preacher Matheson kept the graveside service as brief as he could without doing a disservice to the soldier awaiting burial. Upon the conclusion of the last prayer, seven older men, all of them veterans who had fought with Wil and Levi during the War for Southern Independence, presented themselves wearing winter uniforms of the Army of Northern Virginia. Raising their rifles to the dreary sky they fired in unison three times to salute the fallen son of a man who had partaken in their struggle against the United States oh so long ago.

As the echoes of the final volley drifted away on the winter wind, Private Jefferson Henry and another soldier stepped to the casket and carefully lifted their nation's flag, folding it meticulously into a small triangle. It was Henry who turned to present the flag to Wil and Emily Covington, but instead he found himself standing face to face with President William Oates. Cradling the folded flag in his left arm he quickly drew himself to attention and saluted smartly with his right hand, drawing a similiar salute from his Commander-in-Chief.

"It would be my honor to present the flag," said the President.

"Of course, suh," Private Henry passed the flag to his president at once.

Oates took the banner and stuffed it under the stump of his severed limb so he could shake hands with the soldier with his lone hand. "God bless you," he said softly, then turned to face Wil and Emily Covington. He felt he knew both of them intimately though they had never met. Sarah Covington always spoke of her family when she delivered her reports, and Oates had learned much over the years, about both the Covingtons and the Henrys. Of course he could say nothing of this and proceeded to feign complete ignorance as he stepped close to the wheelchair.

Wil Covington sat as straight as his hip would allow and saluted the president.

"No, please," said Oates, "It is I who should be saluting you. Was he your oldest son?"

"He was," nodded Wil.

"Nothing I can say will ease the pain of your loss," said Oates. "I can only tell you how proud and grateful I am... the country is... to have men such as your son. I can only promise that I'll do all within my power to make sure his death was not in vain. I believe in my heart that the Confederacy is more secure now than it was prior to this affair in Cuba. Your son did his part to cement that security."

"Thank you, Mr. President," sighed Wil, as he shivered against the cold. "Having you here is an unexpected surprise and an honor, both for ourselves and David."

For several moments the two men regarded one another in silence. Both were veterans from the war for Southern Independence. Both had been physically maimed but had overcome their wounds, one to become a successful Virginia farmer, the other to become President of the country they had helped to create. Each held a deep respect for the other, the source of which was no doubt the shared experiences nearly four decades old.

Oates took another step and placed the flag on Wil Covington's lap. He then stepped to one side so the grieving parents, David's widow and his children could watch as the coffin was lowered into the ground.

Most of those assembled began to disperse at this point, boarding their wagons, carriages or buggies for the cold ride home. The Covingtons and Henrys and those closest to them, started toward the main house where sumptuous fare and hot drinks awaited them. Wil had a difficult time getting his wheelchair to move - the earth having grown soft beneath the rain of the last several days. Fortunately several pairs of hands were available, and the elder Covington soon found himself lifted, chair and all, then carried to the house.

Later, having warmed themselves and partaken of the immense quantity of food and drink, Wil Covington, Levi Henry and several aging veterans monopolized President Oates - much to his delight - and passed the time telling old war stories, reliving Second Manassas, South Mountain, Sharpsburg, Fredericksburg, Gettysburg and the North Anna.

As the evening drew to a close and the President of the Confederate States prepared to depart, Wil Covington glanced up from his chair once more. "Mr. President," he said, "This world of ours has become a dangerous place."

"Has it not always been so?" came the reply.

"More dangerous now than ever," continued Wil. "Powerful forces are at work on the other side of the Atlantic."

"And north of the Potomac," added Oates.

"The Empire builders are bound to collide."

"Sooner or later," mused Oates.

"I don't want to lose any more of my sons, suh. I want no more orphaned grandchildren... no more widowed daughters-in-law."

These words weighed heavily on the heart of William Oates. He had no desire to attend a procession of funerals for the young men of the South. "I understand," he returned in a somber tone, "I wish I could say more... I wish I could do more, but right now that's all I can say."

"It's enough," observed Wil before bidding his president a good night.

~Chapter Five~
A World at War

Lamar Jenkins, President of the Confederate States of America, was entirely lost in his thoughts as his automobile made its way slowly through the busy streets of downtown Richmond enroute to the White House of the Confederacy. Pedestrians on the sidewalk peered curiously at his vehicle as it passed, some of them pausing to shout out a curse or two at the noisy machine. His driver, Charles, braked slowly to a stop and turned left on to Broad street. "Not far now," he thought as he gazed out at the people on the sidewalks. Suddenly the car screeched to a frantic stop, slamming its only passenger into the backside of the front seat. A carriage with a two-horse team had pulled out of a side street directly in the path of the car. Charles had refrained from using the horn, not wanting to spook those horses anymore than they already were -- which was considerable.

"Get that gawl-durned machine off of these streets!" shouted the owner of the carriage, altogether unaware of the identity of the object of his tirade. Doubtless he would have yelled even if he had known it was Jenkins in the car. Why should he not? His favorite brace of horses were rearing high on their rear legs, screaming their lungs out, their manes flying wildly, their eyes crazed with fear.

"Those confounded automobiles have no place in the city. Why were those things even invented?" groaned the gentleman as he slumped back in his seat, fervently praying that his driver would soon get the animals back under control.

GRAY VISIONS

"Progress does come with a price," muttered Jenkins as he felt his nose to make sure it was still where it was supposed to be.

"Are you all right, Mr. President?" Charles turned to him with a worried expression in his eyes.

"My nose feels a little out of joint, otherwise I'm fine, save for my dignity, of course."

"If you don't mind my saying so, suh, I still think we should use the presidential carriage when travelling around town like this."

"Your suggestion is duly noted, Charles," smiled the president, "but allow me to point out we're living in the twentieth century... fifteen years into it to be exact. A whole new world is dawning, and I wager it'll belong to vehicles like this, not the carriages of yesteryear."

"That may be suh, but knowin' that still don't make it any easier gettin' through these streets."

"I have complete confidence in you, Charles, and I'm truly not in that big of a hurry."

The driver of the carriage finally got his animals back under control and moved them quickly out of the path of the president's automobile. Over on the corner a young newspaper boy was shouting about the latest news from the war in Europe, news which caught the president's ear until Charles applied the throttle and the noise of the engine drowned the boy's loudest cry.

"No matter," said Jenkins to no one but himself "whatever it was, I'll know about it soon enough."

Once inside the White House he was met immediately by Sullivan Jones, his butler and secretary, the Confederate Congress steadfastly refused to authorize funds for both positions, leaving the twin responsibilities in Sullivan's capable hands.

"Your two o'clock appointment has been waiting for a quarter hour, Mr. President." he said as he deftly relieved Jenkins of his top hat, cloak, and cane.

"Two o'clock? I'm afraid it completely slipped my mind."

"I thought as much."

"Now, now, Sullivan. I've just been loudly chastised by half of Richmond as a result of my choice of transportation. I don't need to be scolded by you as well."

"I wasn't scolding, sir."

"Your voice says otherwise."

"Be that as it may, Mr. President, what should I say to the man who is waiting?"

"Please explain to him that I've only just arrived. Convey my sincerest apologies, but ask if he would mind waiting a few more minutes. I just need time to freshen up a bit and get myself back into sorts, as it were."

"How many minutes?"

"Ten, not a minute more. I promise."

"Very good, sir. I will pass that word."

Alone in his study, Jenkins poured himself a glass of burgundy, a particularly flavorable vintage of which he was rather fond. As he sipped the wine, he began to wonder if he was indeed the right man for this job. Perhaps, at 67, he had grown too old for this game of politics. War was raging mercilessly throughout Europe. No one in the Confederacy was at all eager to become involved in it. Was he up to the challenge?

"I've seen war," he muttered as he took another sip.

Indeed he had. At the age of sixteen, with a Union army entrenched in Chattanooga, Tennessee, He bid his family farewell and left his home in Macon, Georgia, to become an infantry

man in the Army of Tennessee. He found himself on Missionary Ridge when Bragg's army was routed in disgrace. He
served under Joe Johnston until he was wounded at Kennesaw
Mountain. Lying prone on a stretcher he had seen the burning
of Atlanta, and wept as he witnessed his world falling apart.

Fortunately, only part of his world was put to the torch.
In Virginia, Lee had crushed Grant on the North Anna river,
and then, at Lee's urging, Jefferson Davis replaced General
Johnston with General Longstreet, himself a Georgian.
Longstreet promptly stopped Sherman in his tracks. Thus did
things stand until the two sides negotiated a peace resulting in
an independent Confederacy and the abolition of slavery.
Recovered from his wounds, Lamar Jenkins was mustered out
of the service, his heart full of pride and hope for the future.
Did he ever dream he would one day be the president of these
Confederate states? Never, but here he was, and with his job
came the awesome responsibility of guiding his young country
through the most perilous times the world had ever seen.

"Self-doubt won't do at all," he muttered as he set the
empty glass on a table. Yet he couldn't dismiss the feeling of
being both old and tired.

"Mr. President," Sullivan Jones knocked twice before
opening the door and sticking his head in, "your ten minutes
are up."

"So they are," nodded Jenkins. As he tried to smooth out
the wrinkles in his clothing, his mind raced to recall who he was
about to meet. Was it the woman from the secret service? No, that
was later, the four o'clock appointment. Who then? Ah, yes! It
was a negro he was meeting ... somebody from that organization
which was making such a fuss these days.

"Show him in, Sullivan."

The door opened wide, and in stepped a tall, well-dressed black man with broad, muscular shoulders. Sullivan quickly closed the door, leaving the two men to themselves. The black man, who appeared to be in his late thirties, perhaps early forties, walked resolutely over to the chief executive of the Confederacy and presented himself.

"Good afternoon, Mr. President," he said in a deep voice, "my name is Albert Davis." He offered his hand to Jenkins. That hand was taken by the president's own, and given a hearty shake. Davis was impressed that a man of such an age would have so strong a grip.

"A pleasure to meet you." smiled Jenkins.

"The pleasure's mine, suh."

"May I offer you a glass of wine?"

"No, Mr. President. I've come here on behalf of the National Association for the Advancement of Colored People."

"I'm familiar with your organization, Mr. Davis," said Jenkins. "If I'm correct, it was founded by W.E.B. Dubois."

"Exactly." nodded the black man. "The leaders of our group asked me to come here today. I have with me a list of concerns and ... perhaps it would be best to term them as suggestions."

"As opposed to demands?"

"It is not confrontation we seek, suh, but by the same token we'll not shrink from one, if we feel we're being ignored."

"I see," sighed Jenkins. "Something tells me this could be a long afternoon. Shall we sit down?"

"Of course." nodded Davis.

As they walked to his desk, Jenkins made it a point to apologize for being late. "I could offer an excuse," he said "trying to get one of those new automobiles through these streets poses more of a problem than I imagined."

"I understand, suh. I didn't mind waiting."

"Well, young man, I'd be lying if I tried to say that was the reason. The truth is I'm an old man, and my mind just isn't as sharp as it once was. My secretary informed me of the appointment. I just plain forgot."

"That happens to the best of us, Mr. President. You needn't apologize."

By this time they had arranged themselves in chairs on either side of the president's desk. "A glass of water? asked Jenkins.

"Please."

Jenkins poured a glass for each of them from a pitcher which Sullivan kept on the desk. "I suppose we should start with those concerns you spoke of earlier."

"Very well. We're worried about the disparity in the quality of edu ..."

"One moment, please."

"Suh?"

"Let's hold off on that for a moment. I think I'd like you to tell me about yourself first. I kind of like knowing 'bout the folks I speak with. Gives me a better feel for whatever we might be discussing."

"You want to know about me?"

"Exactly. You told me your name, but that's only a name. I want to know who you are."

Albert sat straight in his chair and seemed to thrust his chest forward a bit as he announced proudly, "I am the son of a Confederate Veteran."

"Are you now? I'm a veteran myself -- Army of Tennessee."

"My father was a teamster and a cook with the Army of Northern Virginia. He served under Robert E. Lee. He was a slave in those days, didn't even have himself a last name `till the war was over, and you folks agreed to end slavery."

"I was sixteen years old in those days." offered Jenkins. "My family didn't own no slaves. We were what folks called Po' White Trash."

"And now you're our president."

"Elected fair and square, I might add. I was lucky enough not to get killed during the war, and I got myself into a school when it was over. Made all the difference in the world -- schoolin' I mean."

"I wouldn't argue with that. Goin' to school has meant everything to me. Made my Papa right proud befo' he passed on. I might add that school is part of the reason I've come to see you today."

"And I'm sure we'll be discussing it before too much longer. Meantime, tell me a little about this organization you're with."

"The NAACP?"

"Exactly. I know a little abut it, but I confess not enough to hold up one end of an intelligent conversation."

"Perhaps that little admission on your part can go a long way toward explaining why the NAACP was put together in the first place."

A twinge of guilt found its way into the President's gut, but he gave no indication of this or any other emotion as he gestured for Albert Davis to continue.

"Do you have any idea what it's like being black, Mr. President?"

"I suppose you know the answer to that question. Unless I was black myself there's no way I could ever know."

"Sometimes it's like bein' invisible. It's like you're there, but not really there ... like maybe folks who are lookin' at you are pretendin' you don't even exist."

Jenkins nodded but made no reply. Race relations had not been a high priority in his campaign to become president. Economic issues and that damn mess over in Europe dominated every debate. This whole race thing was on a back-burner. Come to think of it, that's the way it had been for quite some time. Maybe that's what Davis meant when he referred to the reasons for the founding of the NAACP.

"This new century has brought on a whole new world, but to black folks it doesn't seem like much has changed, and we're finding that to be a source of immense frustration. So we've taken to noticing ourselves, if you know what I mean. Among blacks in the Confederacy a new awareness is taking hold, a consciousness and pride about who we are and where we're from. That's why movements like 'Back to Africa' have been so popular."

"Marcus Garvey," said Jenkins.

"You pay more attention than you let on."

"Sometimes, but don't let me interrupt you. You've manage to pique my curiosity."

"Very well. You've already said you cannot know what it is like to be black. Let's try a different image. What about power? Can you imagine what it would be like to be utterly powerless? To have no control over your own life? Your own decisions? To know that no matter what you do or think, there is someone else who claims always to know what is best for you?"

"Rather like a child's relationship with his parent," mused Jenkins. "To be honest with you, I can still remember having those feelings when I was only a boy."

"Now you're beginning to understand what it is like for us."

Jenkins held the black man's gaze but said nothing.

"Let me try another approach." said Davis. "Our war for independence against the Federals is frequently referred to as the second American revolution. Is this not so?"

"It is indeed."

"Do you remember the reasons for it, Mr. President? Not our war against the North, I'm talking about the revolution against Britain."

"You know, Mr. Davis, I could easily consider you to be an impudent person. Here sits a black man in the office of the President of the Confederate States of America, challenging that same president to remember history lessons from his youth. You are a bold one, I'll give you that."

"I was asked to come here for a reason."

"No doubt!"

A nervous flutter drifted through Davis's stomach, but he held his ground and pressed Jenkins again. "Do you, Mr. President?"

"Of course, I do! The British were taxing the colonists, but the colonists themselves had no say in the Parliament. That was not acceptable to most of the Americans of that time."

"But the British claimed they were represented in Parliament by virtue of the fact that they were British citizens."

"Virtual representation ... I remember the argument. You seem to have done your homework."

"Like I said earlier, Mr. President, a good education

makes all the difference in the world."

"Apparently. Now tell me what you're gettin' at."
Jenkins said this knowing full well where the argument was headed.

"The black citizens of this Confederacy have the same concerns as the white Americans of the 1770's."

"Touche'," smiled the President, "and I can't even offer the virtual representation argument in response."

"We have no voice, Mr. President. We pay taxes like every other citizen, but we have no say about those taxes. We cannot vote, so we have no influence over the legislative bodies that make laws and policies affecting us. Look at every level of government within this country and you see that we're excluded. Town, county, state ... it makes no difference. It's like we're invisible, unless of course, we happen to step outside the law. Then we become visible to everybody. In any event, this is a major reason for the founding of the NAACP. We feel we have a right to participate in the political process just the same as the white folks."

"You do make a compelling case, Mr. Davis, but I don't know if I can be of any help. I don't know that the white population is ready for the kinds of changes you're proposing."

"Haven't we earned the right to vote? During the war against the Yankees, the vast majority of our people were loyal to the South. Many served in the Army and Navy.".

"I know all of that," Jenkins gestured impatiently with one hand.

"My father was wounded at Second Manassas, risking his life to bring up ammunition to the white soldiers dug in on the deep cut".

"I was wounded too, doing my part in a failed bid to save Atlanta from Sherman. A lot of men were wounded, Mr. Davis.

And a whole bunch killed."

"But the white men run the government and the blacks have no place in it."

"Is it any different in the United States? How many black men can vote or hold office in that country."

"We don't live in the United States, Mr. President."

"Fair enough, but you can't say we've just forgotten you completely. The Freedman's bill went a long way toward insuring the financial independence of your people. You know this as well as I. And the government helped establish a whole system of schools for blacks ... all the way up to colleges and universities. You, yourself, have taken full advantage of the opportunities thus provided."

"That was almost fifty years ago, Mr. President. Most of those schools have fallen into a state of disrepair, and there never seems to be enough funds in anybody's budget for the maintenance of black schools."

"Stop right there." gestured the president. An expression of alarm appeared briefly on the face of the black man, and he wondered if he was about to get the presidential boot. Seeing the worried look in the other man's eyes, Jenkins moved quickly to ease his fears. "No," he said as if reading Davis's mind, "I'm not kicking you out. Though our time for this meeting does grow short, and I have another one immediately upon your departure. I stopped you because you've told me enough, and I'm starting to understand the plight you've described to me."

"I hope so, Mr. President," returned Davis with a sigh of genuine relief, "because frustration is building among my people, even more so since the war to liberate Cuba. That anger and resentment does not bode well for the relations between our races.

We've earned equality, Mr. President. It's time we had it."

"Then be still and listen to your president for a minute or two. I appreciate the danger generated by anger and resentment, but I may not be the best person to talk to. This is a Confederation, not a Federal system like the United States. I cannot rule by decree. I cannot snap my fingers or wave a magic wand and make these problems disappear. You and your association will have more success by approaching the individual state legislatures. That's where the power lies in a confederacy, Mr. Davis. Change can be made to happen one state at a time, if you are both persistent and patient. I can't stress the patient part of that equation enough."

"We've been patient a long time, Mr. President."

"I know you have, but long held beliefs don't easily die. My gut feeling tells me you'll have what you seek, but it probably will take another generation ... maybe two. Patience will be the key to your success, Mark my words. Now, there's one area that I may be able to help you, and that revolves around the budgetary issues you touched upon a few minutes ago. I'm not without influence with the congress. I think I can shake some money loose and earmark it specifically for the renovation of black schools."

"That would certainly be a positive first step, Mr. President."

"If I can do it, do you think it will have a positive impact on colored people?"

"It couldn't hurt, but can you deliver? Congress has the last word on how the money is spent."

"Which is as it should be, but like I said, I have allies there, and I'm confident I can impress upon them that this is no trivial matter."

"Suffice it to say, Mr. President, the NAACP will be anxiously awaiting the results of your efforts."

"Of that I have no doubt. Now, suppose we put business aside. I still have a few minutes before my next appointment. Tell me some more about your father. To have reared a son like yourself he must have been a fine man. What unit was he with durin' the war?"

"The Stonewall Brigade."

"Stonewall's boys? Now there's some of the finest soldiers ever to walk God's green earth! Tell me more."

For the next half hour they swapped tales, those of Davis having come from his father while President Jenkins was dipping into the memories of his own youth. At last, with a glance at his pocket watch, the president realized they had gone well into his four o'clock appointment, a meeting he knew he could ill afford to neglect.

"Well, Mr. Davis," he said, "it seems we talk too much. I'm afraid I must bid you a rather abrupt farewell. There's someone out in the waiting room and I've kept her out there too long ... as I did with you as well. I'm just not very good with time and schedules ... that sort of thing. Everything seems to be at such a fast pace these days."

"I understand, Mr. President." Davis reached for his hat and briefcase then rose to leave. "It's been a very pleasant, and I hope productive, afternoon."

"Let me walk you out."

Just as they reached the door there came a knock, and Sullivan's voice came from the other side, "Mr. President? Your evening appointment has arrived."

Jenkins opened the door to see his butler, and behind him a pleasant looking middle-aged woman, "Mr. Davis was just leaving," he announced.

Albert Davis looked past Sullivan to appraise the woman who was about to meet with the president. Their eyes met and for some reason he felt as if he already knew her, or at least he should. The expression in her eyes seemed to indicate a similar feeling on her part.

As Sullivan deftly stood to one side, Jenkins addressed himself to the woman: "You must be Sarah Covington."

"A pleasure to meet you, Mr. President," she offered her hand which he took within his own.

"This is Albert Davis," the president nodded in the direction of the black man. "He's just been here pleading a case for the Negroes. It seems they want the right to vote. No doubt you're here to make the same argument for women."

Sensing the President's ploy, she immediately did her part. "The day is coming, Mr. President. You men cannot keep us disenfranchised forever. I do hope you'll hear me out."

"That seems to be what fate has in store for me today." Again he gestured toward Davis. "His father was a veteran from the Army of Northern Virginia -- Stonewall Brigade at that."

"Really? My father was in the same army. In fact, he knew several men from the Stonewall Brigade."

"The President did say your name was Covington, right?"

"He did indeed," smiled Sarah.

"My father spoke often of a soldier of the same name ... Wil, that's it. Wil Covington."

"That was my father," her smile broadened. "and your father must be Ivory."

"He was indeed," grinned Davis.

"My Lord," she offered. "I feel as if I've known your father all my life. My father spoke of him constantly."

"Likewise." returned Davis. "What is it they say? It's a small world."

"So it is." she nodded. "We have an address for you in South Carolina -- Charleston, I think. Are you still there?"

"No, I've moved here to Richmond. I'm with the NAACP."

"I see," she smiled.

Both of them realized at that point that the White House was perhaps not the best place to hold a first generation reunion of old friends.

"Please excuse me," Davis bowed his head slightly "I've already taken enough of your time." As he shook her hand and moved past her, he offered these parting words, "Good luck with our dear president. He's not an easy man to bargain with." With a parting nod in Jenkin's direction, he released Sarah's hand and followed Sullivan toward the door. After they had disappeared from sight, President Jenkins shifted his gaze to study the woman. And for a woman in her late forties, she was rather lovely. Her dress, shawl, and parasol were of the latest and most fashionable designs, certainly giving her the appearance of a woman of means. Her hair was obviously long, but she wore it piled high on her head beneath one of the latest Parisian hats -- he found it remarkable that the French could continue producing stylish clothing in the midst of so desperate a war. Much of her hair had gone to gray, but the change in color did nothing to detract from her beauty. "You must be a woman of sharp wit, Madam," he said, "to so quickly detect and support my ruse."

"Mine is a dangerous business, Mr. President." she

returned. "My wit has become a most valuable weapon."

"No doubt exceeded only by your charm."

"You flatter me, Mr. President."

"Although I've never met you," he said, "I feel that I already know you. Among the recent occupants of this home you've built a rather strong reputation." He reached for her hand. "Lamar Jenkins," he introduced himself.

"Sarah Covington," she allowed him to lightly brush her hand with his lips.

"Will you join me in my study?" he asked. "I believe there are matters we must discuss."

"Certainly." she moved gracefully past him through the open door to his office.

Entering behind her, he closed and locked the door. "Please be seated," he gestured toward a plush couch near the meddle of the room. As she moved toward the couch, he continued. "Each of my predecessors have spoken of you in the most glowing terms."

"I hope my service to our country will continue to merit praise."

He seated himself in a chair opposite the sofa. "I understand you enjoy hot tea," he said, "may I offer you a cup? I can assure our selection has only improved since last you were here."

"Perhaps later." she smiled. "Your butler prepared a cup for me while I was waiting, and it was delightful."

"Please do not think ill of me for bringing this up," he continued, "but I was told that you have a ... shall we say close relationship ... with a powerful man in New York society. Is this still the case?"

"It is."

"And your relationship with this gentleman allows you to learn much of the intentions behind the policies of the United States government?"

"It does indeed."

"This is why I felt it necessary to request a visit by you. This war in Europe show no signs of ending anytime soon, even though those people are killing one another at a rather alarming rate. In public, President Wilson speaks glowingly of neutrality, but my gut instincts tell me he has other intentions. Am I wrong?"

"I don't think so."

"Interesting." he mused, cupping his chin with one hand, leaning forward slightly. "Wilson is not a man I trust. I don't understand how a native Virginian could leave his own country and go on to become the president of her greatest nemesis."

"He was only a child when his family moved to the United States. He had no control over that decision."

"Be that as it may, he grew up here didn't he? Did he return to his native land? And now he leads the same government which did its level best to destroy us."

"That was a long time ago, Mr. President. We've been at peace with the United States for decades."

"And I plan to keep us at peace. I want no war with the United States, nor any with the Germans. In truth, it's the latter I fear most. The Northern press seems bound and determined to create a war mentality in North America and I refuse to buy into it. If either of us end up participating in that war I feel the long-term consequences could be disastrous. George Washington's farewell speech, way back when, was right on the mark. It's a mistake to meddle in the affairs of foreign nations...an absolute mistake."

"Nevertheless, Mr. President, the people with the strongest influence over the United States government want war. They certainly have the power to make sure it happens."

"Not if I can help it."

"Can the Confederacy stay out of it if the United States enters the war against Germany?"

"I don't know. I suppose it could well depend on how effective their propaganda campaign is."

"Thus far it's quite effective. Is it not?"

"Regrettably so, but that comes as no surprise. There is but one telegraph link between North America and Europe, and it links London to New York. The Germans can't hope to compete with that. Only the English side of the story will be told."

"As I said earlier, Mr. President, the people behind all of this have the power to get their way."

"Then I must know about these people and their designs."

"They are the people who engineered President Wilson's election. It was the creation of the Federal Reserve they sought first and in this regard they succeeded most admirably."

"Did they ever!" snorted Jenkins, sitting up against the back of the chair. "I wonder if the citizens of the United States realize that the creation of the Federal Reserve was in effect a revolution."

"In truth, Mr. President, I'm not at all sure I understand what you mean."

"The Constitution of the United States, as ours, places control of the money supply in the hands of the people's representatives - the Congress. This central bank they've created up there effectively removes control of the money from the people and gives it to the bankers. Mark my words, they'll regret the day that law passed."

"What you're saying reminds me of something I heard President Wilson say at a gathering not long ago. I don't remember his exact words, but the gist of it went something like this: if ordinary people want something of their government, they may find that they are received by their representatives and politely heard, but rarely will the government pay true attention to their desires. By contrast, when the captains of industry snap their fingers, the government follows their lead as if it had no other purpose."

"Hamilton's people," muttered the president.

"Sir?"

"Just a reference to the earliest days of the United States. You'll no doubt recall from your own study of history that Thomas Jefferson and Alexander Hamilton were bitter rivals. In Hamilton's mind it was the bankers, merchants, and manufacturers who should control the government. In other words, the captains of industry."

"They control the government of the United States, Mr. President."

"Which is the primary reason we chose to seek independence back in '61," he returned.

"They are making fortunes on this war, and they plan to make a lot more."

"Of that I have no doubt. Do their plans include us?"

"Most assuredly. The Confederacy figures quite prominently in their designs. They'll not be happy until both of our countries have declared war on the Germans. The conversations I've been privy to indicate a particular desire to get us involved. They intend to play up the prowess of the Southern fighting man to lure our people, but the real thing they want us for is cannon fodder. They'd prefer to see Southerners doing most of the fighting."

"And dying."

"Absolutely."

"And I suppose if we were to lose the flower of our youth in the old world's war, our friends in the United States wouldn't dream of taking advantage of our weakened condition".

"They've discussed possibilities. I get the feeling they might jump on us like vultures on their prey."

"Goodbye to the Confederate States of America."

"A prospect which they relish, but may I point something out to you, sir?"

"By all means."

"If we stay out of the war all of their plotting will have gone for naught. Everything they desire is based on our joining them in a declaration of war on Germany, just as we joined them in the war against Spain."

"We didn't declare war on Spain. We simply helped the Federals liberate Cuba from the Spanish."

"They want much more this time."

"Tell me something. At this point in time Germany has done nothing to provoke war either with us or the United States. How do they plan on changing that?"

"Do you know who Edwin House is?"

"Of course. He's the fellow who styles himself Colonel, even though he's never seen a day of service in the military. What I don't understand is his connection to Wilson. He holds no official position in Wilson's administration, yet he seems to speak for the president. How is that?"

"I've frequently heard President Wilson refer to him as an alter ego. Apparently, they are of like minds on a wide variety of issues. He functions rather like an unofficial emissary for the president."

"All right," nodded Jenkins. "What has he to do with the topic of our discussion?"

"Not long ago he returned from England. Do you know of Winston Churchill?"

"First Lord of the British Admiralty? Yes, of course I do. I hear from him quite often. He wants us in the war, and makes no bones about it."

"House met with him while in Britain. They had a conversation the nature of which I learned at a party only two weeks prior to my making this trip."

"By all means fill me in, dear lady; there's surely no need to hold me in suspense."

"Of course," she nodded and the expression on her face grew most serious. "Mr. Churchill asked Colonel House what the reaction in the United States would be if the Germans were to torpedo and sink a passenger liner, particularly if there were Americans on board."

"I see," the expression on the President's face changed noticeably as he leaned forward to hear more. "And what did our friend, House, have to say to this?"

"That an incident of this sort would provoke so deep a rage that the United States would quickly enter the war on the side of Britain and France."

"A rage sure to be fueled by the Northern press," he observed as he sat back once more. "Of that I have no doubt."

"The _Lusitania_ is soon to sail for England, Mr. President."

"Is she? According to my information she carried Canadian

troops and munitions on her last voyage across. Will she again?"

"Not that I know of, but there's talk of weapons and ammunition...a great deal of it."

"If the Germans learn of that they will surely attempt to stop that ship from reaching its destination."

"Exactly."

"I have other people gathering information in the North," he said as he tapped his fingers on the arms of his chair. "I'll get word to them and make sure the situation is monitored as it develops."

"J. P. Morgan has invested much in the allied cause, Mr. President, and he is a very powerful man. most of the money used to pay for the munitions the *Lusitania* will be carrying was borrowed from his bank, and his is not the only financial institution investing in the war. I can tell you quite plainly he does not want to lose his money. He has a great deal riding on an allied victory."

"So he does," mused Jenkins softly. "Well, my lady," he sighed, "it matters not to me what Morgan does with his money, or what happens to it. My responsibility is this Confederacy and its citizens. It appears once again your country owes you a debt of gratitude. What you told me will help a great deal as we formulate our policy regarding the war."

"If you intend to keep us neutral, Mr. President, you may have an ally in the Wilson administration."

"And who might that be?"

"Secretary of State Bryan ....William Jennings Bryan."

"You're right," nodded Jenkins, "I'm familiar with his thoughts on all this. He's dead set against any American involvement. My doubts about him center on how long he can resist this power behind the throne."

"Unfortunately, Mr. President, I can shed no light on that question. I know him to be sincere, but I don't know whether he's up to the likes of J. P. Morgan and John Rockefeller."

"Time will tell, Madam. You've learned much and done all that can be expected of you plus more. May I renew my offer for a cup of tea?"

"I think I'd like that, Mr. President, if you'll join me.."

*   *   *   *   *   *   *   *   *   *   *

The rapping of Sullivan's knuckles upon the bedroom door woke President Jenkins rather abruptly. "Mr. President!" he called. "Mr. President, are you awake?"

"I am now." growled Jenkins. A quick glance through the window told him it was still dark. Why would Sullivan wake him up at this hour?

"Mr. President," Sullivan knocked lightly on the door again, "I'm afraid I have news of a most distressing nature. It's most urgent, sir ... most urgent."

"All right! All right!" barked Jenkins. "I'll be right there!" He swung his legs over the bed, located his slippers and put them on. Rising to his feet, he adjusted his nightshirt and walked slowly to the door, feeling his age every step of the way. He opened the door to find his butler with a frightfully worried expression on his face. "All right, my dear Sullivan," he said gruffly, "what news forces you to wake up an old man at this ungodly hour?"

Sullivan simply handed him a folded telegraph message. "This wire just arrived from our embassy in Washington," he announced, his expression unchanged. "It appears the

GRAY VISIONS

Germans have sunk the _Lusitania_."

A twinge of fear worked its way quickly up the president's spine as he took the telegram, unfolded it, and began to read. "Heavy loss of life," he muttered moments later. "Quite a few Americans among the dead."

"Will we go to war, sir?"

"Not if I can help it. Will you put on water for tea? I need some time to ponder this development. See if you can get the cooks to put together an early breakfast, will you? Cancel all my appointments for today. Wait until a decent hour, then call the Secretary of State and the Secretary of War. I will want to brief the two of them before we meet with the entire Cabinet."

"Very well, sir." Sullivan bowed stiffly at the waist then turned away.

President Jenkins walked slowly to his desk and sat with a weary sigh as he read the message over a second time. "Well, Mr. Churchill," he said to no one but himself, "you may end up getting your wish."

The weeks following the sinking of the _Lusitania_ by a German submarine were filled with frenzy. The Northern press denounced the act as barbarous and savage, and numerous calls for war were raised across the United States. The Southern press was just as vehement in its condemnation of Germany, but less enthusiastic about demanding war. In response, Germany, no doubt alarmed by the prospect of war with the USA and CSA, pledged to scale back and restrict the use of its submarines. In protest against the tilt of the United States government toward war, President Wilson's Secretary of State, William Jennings Bryan, resigned his post and left the government, depriving the anti-war element of a most eloquent voice.

Spring passed into Summer, and Summer on to Autumn. Still the war raged unchecked with neither side able to gain a decisive advantage, although millions of lives had already been squandered. In October, the Germans presented the British with yet another opportunity to exploit their propaganda advantage. This time the situation revolved around the fate of one individual rather than a ship full of passengers.

The incident involved and English nurse, Edith Cavell by name, a fifty year old woman who worked in a clinic which cared for wounded British and French soldiers inside the German military zone within Belgium. Inspired no doubt by love of her own country, Edith Cavell began to assist her patients in escaping the Germans. Her clinic became a bona fide underground railroad through which Cavell smuggled allied prisoners out of Belgium into neutral Holland, where they easily found their way back to England or France. When the Germans finally caught on to the operation they shut it down and charged Edith Cavell with espionage. At her trial she admitted to everything in rather candid detail, despite being aware of the penalty which her actions carried. She was found guilty and sentenced to death by firing squad. To those who toiled in the British propaganda mills, this was the best possible outcome ... a ready-made coup. Americans were fed a steady diet of stories about the lovely, young English nurse, guilty only of helping to save lives, an angel of mercy, a modern day Joan of Arc, butchered by the hands of the cruel, unfeeling Germans. War fever on the western side of the Atlantic was growing by leaps and bounds.

By early 1916, the pressure for war was growing almost too strong to resist. Northern newspapers frequently featured headlines exhorting the Southern people to join the United

States in a sacred quest against the savage Huns. Against this backdrop, President Jenkins had his Department of State send recall notices to the ambassadors to the United States, Britain, Germany, France, and Russia. When the last of them arrived in Richmond an emergency meeting was called at the White House of the Confederacy. Present at this conference were the aforesaid ambassadors, President Jenkins, his entire Cabinet, and several of the more powerful leaders within the Congress of the Confederacy.

In the brief history of the Confederate States of America such a meeting was unprecedented, but was certainly justified within the context of the time. Not since the most desperate days during the War for Independence had the Confederate government been faced with so daunting a crisis. The impression conveyed by official and unofficial sources within the Federal government was that the United States was ready to take the plunge and was waiting only for word that the Confederacy would join in a declaration of war against Germany. The most powerful men in the North eagerly awaited the conclusion of the Richmond Conference, anticipation a much hoped for decision by the Southerners to join their Northern brethren in a war against the "Teutonic Plague".

It was early afternoon by the time the last of the participants had arrived and were seated around the long rectangular table in the formal dining room of the Richmond White House. For the refreshment of those present the table had been set with a variety of finger foods, cheeses, and an assortment of breads and pastries, as well as fresh fruits recently arrived from Florida. Numerous pitchers with fresh water were arrayed about the table and servants were close by with hot tea or coffee.

"Gentlemen," President Jenkins, who had been seated at

the head of the table, rose to his feet and addressed those assembled. "Might we come to order, please?" A hush fell over the room as he uttered those words and all eyes were trained in his direction. "I have just read a copy of a diplomatic note soon to be sent by the government of the United States to Imperial Germany, protesting the sinking of the French vessel, *Sussex*. The Wilson administration is chomping at the bit to get into this war, but they don't seem too keen about doing it without us. You can rest assured of one thing: there's a lot of folks up North watchin' what we do here, and they're hopin' we opt for war."

"Maybe we should." said an aging senator from Alabama. "Didn't Britain and France stand by us when we broke away from the Federals?"

"Yes and no." said Jenkins in reply. "They did help us with supplies and loans, but they did so largely for their own profit. They sold war material to both sides of that fight, and withheld the one thing which would have helped us the most, diplomatic recognition."

"Mr. President, may I speak?" One of Virginia's senators rose to his feet, a man in his late forties.

"Senator Covington," Jenkins nodded toward the Virginian, "please do."

"Thank you, suh. My gut instincts tell me it's a mistake for us to get into this ... a serious mistake. No one here can accuse my family of shirking its duty, suh. My father suffered a cripplin' wound durin' the War for Independence. It drained his strength over the years and took his life in 1912. His oldest son, my brother, died of Yellow Fever back in '98 when we helped liberate Cuba. We Covingtons are not afraid to step forward when our country calls, but we are firm in our belief that the country should call only when threatened. This war does not concern us. The Europeans are killing one another because of their desire to best one another in the business of building empires. Mr. President, this Confederacy is not in the business of empire, and I see no reason to send our sons to die for somebody else's ill-begotten possessions. I believe we should heed the words of a famous Virginian who warned the American people as he was leaving the presidency of an infant United States, to avoid entanglements with foreign nations. The words of George Washington made sense at the end of the eighteenth century. They make even more sense today. We've been neutral since this war started. We should so remain." Covington, holding the eyes of his President, stood a moment or two longer, before resuming his seat.

"Thank you, Senator." said Jenkins calmly.

"Mr. President," Philip Harding, a congressman from eastern North Carolina rose. "Historically the Confederate States have had close relations with Britain and France. I don't see how we can turn our backs on them in their hour of need."

""In the 1790's the United States had strong ties and certainly a debt of honor to France," replied the President, " but our forefathers did not allow this obligation to draw us into the war then brewing between Britain and France. Perhaps Senator Covington has a point."

"What of Belgium?" This question came from a member of the Cabinet, the Postmaster General to be precise. Was not Germany's violation of Belgian neutrality a gross violation of international law?"

"It was, but what justification can be made for the frequent intervention by the United States in the affairs of Latin

Americans? How many times has Wilson sent troops into countries with whom he is not at war? Haiti? Mexico? Nicaragua?"

"A good point, sir," volunteered the Treasury Secretary.

"Mr. President, may I speak?? The ambassador to Germany raised his hand.

"Ambassador Reilly," Jenkins indicated his approval of the request with a hand gesture.

A heavyset man in his early sixties rose to his feet, his hand moving automatically to grasp the lapels of his open coat. "For those of you who don't know me, I am William Reilly, ambassador of these Confederate States to Imperial Germany. Like the Covingtons, my family has always stood to the colors when called. In fact, it was Senator Covington's father who saved my father's life at Second Manassas. My father ended up with a saber scar down the length of his face. Bore that scar all through his life, he did, right to his grave. My younger brother saw service in Cuba, and I thank the Lord he came home safe and sound. War is not something we should eagerly embrace, gentlemen. Especially this war." He paused and ran the fingers of one hand through the thick, wavy, white hair atop his head.

"I have been living in Germany since 1913," he continued after taking a moment to gather his thoughts. "The Germans are a determined people, you can believe that, but they are not the barbaric savages the press makes them out to be. War with either the United or the Confederate States is something they are judiciously trying to avoid."

"What about those submarine attacks that kill innocent neutrals?" demanded a Mississippi senator.

"The allies are using ships like the *Lusitania* to transport troops and munitions. They've armed these ships and pay handsome rewards for every submarine sunk by one of these types of vessels. Let me ask you this, if we had submarines available to us back in the 1860's, would we not have been within our rights to use them to blockade Northern ports just as their surface ships were doing to ours?"

"Yet they consistently violate international norms for the conduct of war."

"Submarines were not designed with those rules in mind."

"Neither are mines," interjected Covington.

"How's that?" demanded the President.

"I'm merely noting that the underwater contact mines used by the British to facilitate their blockade of the North Sea are just as pernicious as submarines and just about as effective. A mine cannot fire warning shots. It cannot board and search a vessel, nor can it make arrangements for innocent passengers and survivors. It simply explodes upon contact with a ship. The Allies are just as culpable as the central powers when it comes to ignoring rules for the conduct of warfare."

"Exactly my point," nodded Reilly, whose hands had resumed their position on his lapels. "Many of the ideas Americans hold about Germany are the result of the most elaborate and advanced propaganda campaign in the history of the human race. The British have done a brilliant job of using the only telegraph link to North America to their maximum advantage. Remember what you were reading back in `14? I'm talking about the stories of German soldiers tossing Belgian babies into the air and catching them on their bayonets. Nothing of the sort ever happened, but this is typical of the propaganda which abounds in the northern press and in far too many of our own newspapers.

"The *Lusitania* is another case in point. German intelligence found out the ship would be carrying weapons and ammunition in her holds along with a normal booking of passengers. When people were boarding the ship, German agents were present at the ramps handing out flyers to the passengers, telling them of Germany's knowledge of the munitions and the intent of the German government to stop that ship from reaching its destination. The British officers on board ridiculed those charges and assured their passengers that all was well, that their journey would be safe and uneventful. Tell me something," he continued, "how long did it take for the *Lusitania* to sink?"

"Something like eighteen minutes, " volunteered someone at the table.

"Eighteen minutes," repeated Reilly. "One torpedo sank the largest passenger ship in the British Registry in eighteen minutes. Do any of you seriously think that's possible? Do we have a torpedo capable of doing that? All of you know the answer to that question."

"So what's your theory, Ambassador?"

"I think it hit one of the holds where ammunition was stored. The resulting explosion was huge. That's why the ship sank so fast. Now, I ask you, who are the true culprits?"

"What about that young nurse the Germans executed?" demanded the Secretary of Navy, a Texan from Beaumont.

"Young nurse?" Ambassador Reilly appeared puzzled for just a moment. "Are you referring to the Cavell woman?"

"Edith Cavell," nodded the Texan. "The newspapers were full of stories about her after the Germans arrested her. She was a lovely young woman."

"Well, you're wrong on that point," countered Reilly.

GRAY VISIONS

"I've seen some of the stories you're referring to, and the pictures which accompanied them. Neither were particularly accurate. I had the good fortune of meeting Miss Cavell before she was executed, and I found her to be a most impressive woman, though not at all young, and not all that striking in appearance. She was at least fifty years old and more of a grandmother type than the young maiden in distress she's been made out to be. Are you all familiar with the charges against her in court? She knew the risks when she started smuggling prisoners out of Belgium, and she was quite willing to accept the consequences. She was a British patriot, motivated by love of her country. She was a person worthy of our esteem to be sure, but do any of us want to send our sons and grandsons to die because she chose to risk her life for Britain?"

As the ambassador finished speaking, his remarks were followed by several minutes of murmuring and discussion among those gathered around the table until President Jenkins rose to his feet and requested quiet. "Thank you," he acknowledged as the talking ceased. "I'm gettin' too damn old to have to be raisin' my voice over the din the likes of you boys can make. In any event, we've heard from a number of you, and I think it's my turn to say my piece. I'm tellin' each of you right now where I stand on all this. I'm dead set against our bein' involved, period. When I look to the other side of the Atlantic, I don't see good guys and bad guys tearin' each other up. There are no good guys and bad guys over there. The major powers in Europe -- the colonial powers I'm talkin' about -- were all chompin' at the bit for this war to start since the turn of the century. The war is the result of their insatiable greed, the race for more imperial control, not to mention those foolhardy secret alliances. It's a mess we don't need to be a part of. The Europeans made this particular bed, now they've got to lie in it." He paused here and sipped from a glass of water.

"The Wilson administration is aching to get the United States into the war, Mr. President," observed the Secretary of State, Sterling Beaudraux, "and as you noted earlier, they want us to go along with them. How will you be able to resist? Especially if the press gets the people all riled up like it did in `98?"

"I know it won't be easy," admitted the president. "There's a lot of northern money ridin' on the outcome of that war, but our duty lies here first and foremost, not in Europe. I don't suppose any of you paid close attention to the casualty reports which are coming out of that battle over on the Somme. Trust me, they're astronomical. The British may lose a half-million men! A half-million! That's just one battle, mind you, one murderous battle! And for what? Has any real estate changed hands? Precious little. All those English and German boys are dyin' for nothin', and I won't send Southern boys to do the same. I don't care what Woodrow Wilson says any more than I care about J.P. Morgan's money."

"Back in '98, President Oates didn't give a fig for the imperial ambitions of the United States, yet we still ended up in the war over Cuba. Staying out won't be as easy as you imagine."

"Cuba was different." argued Jenkins. "For one thing, we had a vested interest in the outcome, and could not allow Federal domination, and occupation of that island. Admittedly, the United States led and we followed like faithful puppies, but this time it wil be different."

"Mr. President," the Texan spoke again. "You keep saying this will be different. How?"

GRAY VISIONS

"Because we're going to use our heads!" barked Jenkins, a trifle impatiently. "Tell me this, do any of you trust Wilson or his administration, or the United States itself?" Not a hand was raised.

"My feelings exactly." nodded Jenkins with a satisfied grunt. "Now imagine this. Suppose we go along with the Federals and jump into this war. Let's say we raise an army of a half-million men, maybe twice that. What happens to us if we send all those boys and our best generals to fight Germans, and they end up like all those English boys dyin' along the Somme. Who will defend our frontiers if the folks up North decide to get even for 1864? If our best soldiers are on the other side of the Atlantic, how long do you think we'd last if the Union decides to conquer us? That scenario could come to pass even if our boys were to whip the Germans and suffer no casualties in the process."

"How so?"

"Could we transport 500,000 men and all their supplies and weapons to Europe?"

"Whose ships would take our boys to Europe?"

"Yankee ships." several men offered this reply at about the same time.

"Exactly," huffed Jenkins "and what if those same Yankees decide not to use their ships to bring our boys back? Do you see what I'm tryin' to say here?" The murmuring which followed this question affirmed the understanding of his audience, much to the satisfaction of Lamar Jenkins.

After gesturing for quiet one more time, he offered his closing words. "As you can all see by their presence, I recently recalled all of our ambassadors from the warring nations. Now, I'm sending them back to their posts. They'll each carry the same message: that these Confederate States will remain neutral. We will not enter the war, but we are willing to mediate a solution if any of them wish to avail themselves of the opportunity."

"In any event, I think we've done enough business for one day. Let's talk no more of it. Dinner's on the way, and it's on me. You boys eat hearty, hear?"

* * * * * * * * * * *

President Jenkins had done much to project confidence and determination to his cabinet and the Congressional leadership, but this appearance belied his true feelings. As the United States edged close to war with the Central powers his apprehension grew. How could he withstand the pressure he knew was coming? Nightly he prayed for the inner strength to resist the pleading and cajoling of the Wilson administration, but he continued to be plagued by self doubt. Ironically, it was the German government which ultimately provided a viable way out for the Confederacy, though such could hardly be described as their intention.

The first call came from Secretary Beaudraux at half-past nine in the morning. To Jenkins his voice seemed a trifle agitated, but the Secretary wasn't particularly candid as to why. He said only that a note had just arrived form a European government and that it would be prudent to discuss it before the day was out. Might he call sometime in the afternoon? Perhaps three o'clock? Jenkins replied in the affirmative and turned his attention back to breakfast.

By eleven o'clock that same morning all hell began to break loose. Telegrams started piling up. The telephone seemed to be forever ringing...something about a story being carried in the morning papers throughout the United States...a treacherous note from the German government, not just one, but two. War was now inevitable. Then Beaudraux was standing at the door to the president's study, looking a lot more agitated than he had sounded earlier on the telephone. Behind him stood Peter Dinena, the ambassador from the United States. "Mr. President," stammered Beaudraux, "I'm afraid we must speak earlier than planned. May we come in?"

"Of course," gestured Jenkins. "I'll have Sullivan prepare something hot to drink."

"That won't be necessary," growled Dinena in a voice which fairly oozed venom.

"For you maybe," Jenkins fixed a cold stare on the American ambassador. "I'd like something, and I'm quite sure Secretary Beaudraux will join me."

"This is not a social call, President Jenkins," Dinena held to his sinister tone, yet he remained behind Beaudraux. "Let's dispense with all this Southern hospitality nonsense and get to business."

"Ambassador Dinena," Jenkins made a determined effort to control the level of hostility rising in his own voice, "may I remind you that you are not posted in Nicaragua? You are not here as Pro-consul, but as ambassador. Whatever the problem which brought you here, this attitude of yours can hardly be described as helpful."

"I'll be the judge of that."

"So you think," thought Jenkins as he invited the two men in and turned to the butler standing close at hand. "Sullivan, would you brew a pot of tea for the Secretary and myself?"

"Of course, sir."

"I think Earl Grey would be nice."

"As you wish, Mr. President."

Joining the others, Jenkins seated himself in his favorite easy chair, glancing first at Beaudraux then at Dinena. "Well," he said, "suppose one of you fill me in on what all this ruckus is about."

"It's about this note," said Beaudraux, reaching into his vest pocket and handing a folded piece of paper to the president. "This is the reason I called this morning."

"That and the one they sent to the Mexicans." snapped Dinena, his voice having lost neither its hostility nor its arrogance.

"Mexico, eh?" Jenkins learned back in his chair, adjusted his reading glasses and unfolded the note. It had been delivered by the German ambassador and had been written by Alfred Zimmerman, Foreign Minister in the Imperial German Government. Essentially, it assumed the inevitability of war with the United States, and suggested the possibility of an alliance with the Confederate States, promising German support if the Southerners were to declare war on their neighbors to the North. "Mexico got one of these too?" he asked as he finished the note, refolded it and handed it back to Beaudraux.

"Apparently with the same offer," came the reply.

"Germany must be desperate."

"They're grasping at straws!" snapped Dinena. "Only this time they've gone too far! They need to be spanked and put in their place. President Wilson intends to seek a declaration of war, and he expects the Confederacy to join us."

"I'm well aware of President Wilson's expectations Ambassador, but I'm afraid this Confederacy does not exist to please the United States."

"Are you trying to say you're not joining us in this

crusade?" Dinena jumped to his feet, rage rising in his voice as his face turned scarlet. "How dare you! How can you sit by idly while the civilized world teeters on the brink of extinction!"

"Ambassador," Beaudraux looked up with genuine alarm in his eyes, "this is highly irregular! I think a little self-control on your part might be in order. Perhaps you should resume your seat."

"I can't believe what I'm hearing!" Dinena shook his head in disgust.

"Sit down, Ambassador," there was ice in Jenkin's voice as he issued this command, "or I shall have Sullivan escort you out." For several tense moments the two men glared angrily at one another until Dinena finally sat back down and took a deep breath to calm himself. "That's better," said Jenkins. "I would prefer to continue this discussion as members of the civilized world you just made reference to," continued the Southern President. "If that proves to be impossible, I'll simply terminate this meeting." Again his eyes locked onto those eyes carefully. The man's anger was painfully obvious. In truth, it seemed to burst from his pupils, as did the arrogance which surfaced every time he had official dealings with the Confederate government. But for an instant Jenkins thought he detected another emotion lurking within those baby blues. Was it fear? Dinena certainly reacted quickly when Jenkins revealed his own reluctance to engage in the European war.

That was it! As much as the Northerner wanted to hide it, he was afraid of something. His display of emotion was a mistake, and he well knew it, but what was it he feared? Suddenly Jenkins knew the answer to the riddle, and at once he experienced an overwhelming sensation of relief, though he maintained the same icy expression which was coming from Dinena.

For months the Southern President had been dreading this day, the day when he could no longer avoid the inevitable, the day when the Federals would announce their intention to go to war and expect the Confederacy to fall into line, just as she had in 1898. In the mind of Lamar Jenkins, this day had as much appeal as a trip to the dentist, because in declining the invitation to go to war, he would be forced to admit to the fears he held about the possibility of renewed Northern aggression. An admission of this sort would only be seen as a sign of weakness, which in turn might provoke a hostile move by the United States. So he had lived in dread waiting for this day, all the while hoping it would never come.

Until that moment when Dinena's eyes betrayed him, it had never occurred to Jenkins that the United States might have the same fears. The diplomatic note from the German foreign Minister, which somehow found its way into the custody of the United Government, had presented the Southern President with a trump card. The Federals had no desire to leave their own underbelly weakened by sending a huge army overseas unless the armed strength of the Confederacy vacated North America as well. The Wilson administration feared the possibility of a Southern attack. Perhaps more crucial to Wilson's policies, this fear, whether it was mild or strong, stood in the way of everything Wilson desired relating both to the war and the post-war period. All of Wilson's designs hinged on Southern cooperation in the war itself. Suddenly feeling ten years younger, as though a monumental weight had been lifted from his shoulders, Jenkins moved to play the trump card which had fallen so unexpectedly into his hand. "Ambassador," he said, letting go of the ice in his voice, assuming an air which could almost be described as indifferent, "You may inform President Wilson that it is the official policy of the government of this Confederacy that this madness must stop. We do not intend to be drawn into it, although I must say I find this note from Zimmerman to be ... shall we say interesting?"

The fear in Dinena's eyes was becoming more apparent. He had been entrusted with the mission of securing Southern cooperation, and had nothing to show for his efforts. "What will be your answer to the Germans?" he demanded hotly.

"My answer is of no concern to you."

"It most certainly is!" Once again Dinena's control over his emotions slipped. He started to rise, but stayed himself, his hands gripping the arms of his chair so tightly, he thought his knuckles might burst.

"I'm afraid I have to disagree, Ambassador. Whether you accept it, or like it, or not, my government ... my country ... is not an appendage of the United States, nor one of its colonial possessions." Jenkins was now finding it much easier to be calm in the face of Dinena's anger.

"Now, sir, I must inform you that your participation in this meeting has come to an end. You may inform your president of my response to his solicitation. You may also advise him of the need to choose another ambassador. I'll not suffer your insolence a moment longer, nor your presence on Southern soil. Consider yourself Persona Non Grata. You have twenty-four hours to leave this country. Sullivan will show you to the door. I bid you good-day, sir."

Dinena rose in a huff, straightened his coat, and walked briskly to the door, paused there for a moment, turning to glare once more at Jenkins. "You'll regret this," he said in a still defiant tone.   Then he was gone, with only the sound of his shoes on the floor to indicate his progress toward the main entrance of the President's home.

"My, my," sighed Secretary Beaudraux, who had remained silent through most of the exchange. He crossed his hands over his chest and began twiddling his thumbs. "There goes a dangerously frustrated man."

"Rather him than either of us," returned Jenkins.

"How do you think Wilson will respond?"

"I don't plan on giving him an opportunity. I think its time someone made a move to bring this whole affair to a close. I assume you are familiar with Wilson's ideas about the future."

"I am indeed, sir. He speaks fondly of the idea of peace without victory, and longs for the creation of some sort of international association to prevent war. He refers to it as a League of Nations."

"Then I think the best way to defang people like Dinena would be to see Wilson's desires fulfilled."

"How? Wilson has more than his share of enemies in the United States. His detractors think him too much of an idealist."

"Which he may well be, but this is too good an opportunity to let pass. The fear we have about Northern aggression is mirrored in Washington. I saw it in that ambassador's eyes. It surfaced in every move he made ... every word he spoke. Simply by refusing to go along we have stopped the United States from going to war."

"Temporarily, sir, only temporarily. The warhawks will find a way."

"If they are given time. Let's not give it to them. I want you to prepare a series of messages to all the warring parties. Tell them the Confederate States are sponsoring a peace conference. It can be held here in Richmond or in a neutral European country ... the Netherlands for instance. Contact their ambassador and see if they'd be willing to host it. Advise all the belligerents that we wil be happy to serve as a mediator to end this thing. As an aside, tell the Germans we're keeping our options open. Tell `em we'd prefer not to get involved at all, but if there's a chance of us ending up in this ... well ... tell `em we like the map of Europe prior to 1914. Tell `em whatever you can to keep them a little off balance. I don't want them to see this as an opportunity to go all out and take the whole damn continent."

"I understand, Mr. President. I guess it's time for me to sharpen my diplomatic skills, but I think I'm up to it."

"I have the utmost confidence in you, my friend. If anybody can pull this off, you can."

"I hope you're right." Beaudraux rose from his chair, finished the cup of tea he'd been sipping, and looked directly at his President. "Now for the challenge of a lifetime," he said with a grim smile and started for the door.

"Sterling," called Jenkins just as Beaudraux was reaching the door.

"Sir?"

"This note Zimmerman sent to us and the Germans ... at first I thought it an act of desperation. I mean, after all ... Mexico? Do the Germans think the United States trembles at the thought of war with Mexico? The thought is almost laughable. But he sent the same note to us. Again this could be seen as a desperate move, but now I'm beginning to wonder. Maybe it was a stroke of genius. He's playing us one off the other. It's a move which may have been calculated to keep us both on the sidelines."

"Could be," nodded Beaudraux. "In any event, if our plans come to fruition, I'll soon be talking with Zimmerman face to face. I'll try to find out what he was up to."

"You do that," nodded Jenkins with a smile.

* * * * * * * * * * *

Surprisingly, it was Germany which agreed first to the idea of a peace conference. The British, seeing that the United States was not following through with a declaration of war also agreed, and with the two foremost powers agreeing to sit at the same table, all the warring nations soon signed on. The Netherlands agreed to host the conference in Hague. A cease fire in place was arranged, and for the first time in three years the guns fell silent all across Europe. All eyes turned toward Holland, anxiously awaiting the outcome of the conference.

Bringing the war to a close proved to be a more difficult challenge than the leaders of the Confederacy, or anybody else for that matter, anticipated. The issues which divided the Western European powers were far less a challenge than those in the East, particularly the Balkans. Fully two months expired before a series of agreements could be hammered out, but in the end perseverance on the part of the various negotiating teams proved to be the key ingredient in the success of the conference. Having already witnessed the horrid deaths of millions of men, no one wanted to see the war resume.

The key details of the settlement were more or less these: Germany agreed to pull back to its pre-1914 borders and to pay a small indemnity to Belgium for having violated that nation's neutrality. Britain agreed to withdraw all of her troops from the continent. The Treaty of Brest-Litovsk, between Germany and Russia, was left untouched, primarily because no one was sure what Russia's future would be. The only thing which seemed certain was upheaval. Austria granted independence to her Balkan provinces, including Serbia, and each of these provinces became independent nations. The Colonial empires of the major powers were left intact, but at the same time it was recognized that all of the colonial peoples around the world fiercely desired independence, and that such an outcome was more or less inevitable. To facilitate the transitions as they took place, and to settle differences between countries as they arose, a League of Nations was established, not so much as a governing body, but as an international association with peace as its foremost priority. As part of the treaty it was agreed that no single nation or government was to blame for the war. Mutual responsibility was accepted by all the combatants. Britain, Germany, and France all agreed to reduce the size of their armed forces by one-half. Both Germany and France agreed not to concentrate sizable forces within thirty miles of each other's borders. There were other provisions of course, too many to recount actually, but these formed the nucleus of a series of treaties which brought the war in Europe, the Great War as some called it, to a close. Peace had come to Planet Earth. No American, Federal or Confederate, would have to shed his blood on European soil.

Epilogue

In a German military hospital in Munich, Bavaria, a young corporal form Austria lay in bed recovering from injuries sustained during a mustard gas attack. He was just dozing off to sleep in the early afternoon when he heard the sound of a single crutch being used on the wooden floor. "Adolph!" He recognized the voice of a comrade, Dieter Muller, who was recovering from a leg wound. "Adolph! Don't go to sleep yet! I have wonderful news!"

Adolph turned his head in the direction of that voice. "Is that you, Dieter?"

"Of course it is! Are you awake?"

"I am now. I heard you say something about wonderful news. I've some good news of my own. The doctors say my blindness is only temporary. They say in a few weeks I should have full use of my eyes again."

"Marvelous! I know how relieved you must be."

"When I can see again, then I'll be relieved. What is this wonderful news you mentioned?"

"You're not going to believe it!"

"Tell me, and let me be the judge of that."

"The war is over!" Dieter's face was beaming, though his friend could not ascertain this by sight.

"Over? Are you serious?"

"Would I joke about something like that? The peace conference that convened shortly after we were wounded has concluded its work. Treaties have been signed. The war is over."

"Treaties?" Adolph turned his bandaged eyes toward his friend.

"I have the newspaper right here. I'll read you what it says." Reading slowly he covered the major tenets of the various agreements which had brought the war to an end. When he finished he looked over at this blind companion. "Well," he quizzed, "What do you think?"

Several moments elapsed before Adolph replied. "I'm not sure what to think. It's not victory, but it certainly isn't defeat either." He paused to reflect another moment or two. "It seems to be an honorable peace ... it appears to leave our future intact." He crossed his arms over his chest and turned his eyes toward the window so the sun might warm his face. "If what you've read to me is true, we'll all be able to return to our lives ... and hold our heads up as well. I think it is a peace we can live with."

"So do I," sighed his friend. "God be thanked."

thus concludes *Gray Visions*, bringing my *Alternative History Trilogy* to Journey's end.

Deo Vindice
RWR